The Right Of Way
— Complete

by

Gilbert Parker

Double 9
BOOKS

The right of way — complete
by Gilbert Parker

Copyright © 2024

All Rights reserved.

ISBN: 978-93-64288-90-3

Published by

DOUBLE 9 BOOKS

2/13-B, Ansari Road
Daryaganj, New Delhi – 110002
info@double9books.com
www.double9books.com
Tel. 011-40042856

This book is under public domain

ABOUT THE AUTHOR

Gilbert Parker (1862-1932) was a renowned Canadian novelist and politician, known for his vivid storytelling and rich depictions of early Canadian life. Born in Camden East, Ontario, Parker's upbringing in a rural environment deeply influenced his literary work, often reflecting the landscapes and cultural dynamics of Canada. Parker's literary career began with contributions to various periodicals, but he soon transitioned to writing novels that captured the essence of Canadian and British life. His works often combined elements of romance, adventure, and historical fiction, earning him a significant readership. Some of his notable novels include "The Seats of the Mighty," which is set during the British conquest of Quebec, and "The Right of Way," which explores themes of redemption and identity in the Canadian wilderness. His writing style was characterized by detailed descriptions, strong character development, and an ability to weave historical facts with engaging narratives. Parker's novels were well-received both in Canada and abroad, cementing his reputation as a distinguished author of his time. Parker's contributions to literature and politics were widely recognized. He was knighted in 1902, becoming Sir Gilbert Parker, in recognition of his literary achievements and his service to the British Empire. Despite his success in England, Parker maintained a strong connection to his Canadian roots, and his works continued to celebrate the country's history and culture.

Gilbert Parker's legacy endures through his novels, which remain significant for their historical insights and narrative craftsmanship. His ability to blend historical events with compelling storytelling has left a lasting impact on Canadian literature, making him a celebrated figure in the annals of literary history.

was full of people, and not the people whom I had expected to see. The Governor seized my hand, and Grahame Hallward sprang forward and grasped the other.

"Lord Gascoyne, your innocence has been established beyond question. The real culprit has confessed."

It sounded like a speech out of a melodrama. Luckily, I retained my self-possession sufficiently to say something expressive of my thanks to Providence. I think it met the occasion.

Who the real culprit could be I failed to understand.

"I have given instructions," said the Governor, "for you to be taken to a comfortable room till the actual order for your release arrives."

Then I recollected my manuscript on the table. No one had seen it but myself, but if it were noticed it would be awkward.

It was a terrible moment. I expected the Governor as I picked it up to say: "Anything written in a prison becomes the property of the Crown," but I was allowed to walk off with it.

Escorted by a congratulatory group, I was taken to a room which was quite luxurious. Grahame Hallward and myself breakfasted together.

Then he told me all about it.

"You remember the governess at Hammerton Castle?" he asked.

I nodded.

"Well, it is very sad for Lady Gascoyne, but it appears that Lord Gascoyne had made love to her, that she was about to become a mother, and that she poisoned his tea that evening as she had already poisoned the wine. The servants remember now that she had been in the dining-room. She intended at the time to kill herself as well, but she had not the courage. Last night, however, she did so, having written to your wife and to the Home Secretary, your lawyer, and others, so as to make sure of the news arriving in time."

I looked at him, striving to hide the sheer horror which I felt for the first time in my life.

I was not surprised at the sacrifice, for it was the sort of gigantic thing that a nature like Esther's would have conceived and carried out. Nevertheless, the news filled me with a profound gloom.

It was better, however, to be sitting there finishing my coffee and smoking a cigarette than meandering out on to the unknown.

"Sibella has been awfully ill, Israel."

"Did people think me guilty?" I asked.

He avoided my question, and said:

"The revulsion of feeling has been tremendous. Everybody will be delighted."

And so it turned out. People had not at all liked the idea of a real, live lord becoming an unreal, dead lord by such means. The Home Secretary sent the order for my release the same afternoon. The dead Lord Gascoyne became a monster of iniquity, and I was congratulated by everyone on the *dénouement*.

But to this day, there is a sadness in my wife's manner, and although she tries to hide a shuddering aversion for me when we are alone, it shows itself unexpectedly in trifles. In some way she has grasped the truth. Indeed, she must have done, for there can be no other explanation of her conduct. We have two children, and perhaps there is something pathetic in the amount of moral training she gives them. I am sure there is no need for Hammerton to turn out other than well. I have done the work. He has only to reap the benefit and the reward. The second boy is a gentle little creature, Oriental in his nature, and most devoted to his father, as they both are, but the second boy especially so.

Sibella is still—Sibella.

CONTENTS

INTRODUCTION

In a book called 'The House of Harper', published in this year, 1912, there are two letters of mine, concerning 'The Right of Way', written to Henry M. Alden, editor of Harper's Magazine. To my mind those letters should never have been published. They were purely personal. They were intended for one man's eyes only, and he was not merely an editor but a beloved and admired personal friend. Only to him and to W. E. Henley, as editors, could I ever have emptied out my heart and brain; and, as may be seen by these two letters, one written from London and the other from a place near Southampton, I uncovered all my feelings, my hopes and my ambitions concerning The Right of Way. Had I been asked permission to publish them I should not have granted it. I may wear my heart upon my sleeve for my friend, but not for the universe.

The most scathing thing ever said in literature was said by Robert Buchanan on Dante Gabriel Rossetti's verses—"He has wheeled his nuptial bed into the street." Looking at these letters I have a great shrinking, for they were meant only for the eyes of an aged man for whom I cared enough to let him see behind the curtain. But since they have been printed, and without a "by your leave," I will use one or two passages in them to show in what mood, under what pressure of impulse, under what mental and, maybe, spiritual hypnotism it was written. I first planned it as a story of twenty-five thousand words, even as 'Valmond' was planned as a story of five thousand words, and 'A Ladder of Swords' as a story of twenty thousand words; but I had not written three chapters before I saw what the destiny of the tale was to be. I had gone to Quebec to start the thing in the atmosphere where Charley Steele belonged, and there it was borne in upon me that it must be a three-decker novel, not a novelette. I telegraphed to Harper & Brothers to ask them whether it would suit them just as well if I made it into a long novel. They telegraphed their assent at once; so I went on. At that time Mr. F. N. Doubleday was a sort of director of Harper's firm. To him I had told the tale in a railway train, and he had carried me off at once to Henry M.

Alden, to whom I also told it, with the result that Harper's Magazine was wide open to it, and there in Quebec, soon after my interview with Mr. Alden and Mr. Doubleday, the book was begun.

The first of the letters published in The House of Harper, however, was apparently written immediately after my return to London when the novel was well on its way. Evidently the first paragraph of the letter was an apology for having suddenly announced the development of the book from a long short story to a long novel; for I used these words:

"Yet if you really take an interest in the working of the human mind in its relation to the vicissitudes of life, you will appreciate what I am going to tell you, and will recognise that there is only stability in evolution which the vulgar call chance.... Now, sir, perpend. Charley Steele is going to be a novel of one hundred thousand words or one hundred and twenty thousand—a real bang-up heartful of a novel."

Then there follows the confidence of a friend to a friend. As I look at the words I am not sorry that I wrote them. They were a part of me. They were the inveterate truth, but I would not willingly have uncovered my inner self to any except the man to whom the words were written. But here is what I wrote:

"I am a bit of a fool over this book. It catches me at every tender corner of my nature. It has aroused all the old ardent dreams of youth and springtime puissance. I cannot lay it down, and I cannot shorten it, for story, character, soul and reflection, imagination, observation are dragging me along after them.... This novel will make me or break me—prove me human and an artist, or an affected literary bore. If you want it you must take the risk. But, my dear Alden, you will be investing in a man's heart—which may be a fortune or a folly. Why, I ought to have seen—and far back in my brain I did see—that the character of Charley Steele was a type, an idiosyncrasy of modern life, a resultant of forces all round us, and that he would demand space in which to live and tell his story to the world.... And behold with what joy I follow him, not only lovingly but sternly and severely, noting him down as he really is, condoning naught, forgiving naught, but above all else, understanding him—his wilful mystification of the world, his shameless disdain of it, but the old law of interrogation, of sad yet eager inquiry and wonder and 'non possumus' with him to the end."

This letter was evidently written in December, 1899, and the other went to Mr. Alden on the 7th August, 1900; therefore, eight or nine months later. The work had gone well. Week after week, month after month it had unfolded itself with an almost unpardonable ease. Evidently, the very ease with which the book was written troubled me, because I find that in this letter of the 7th August, 1900, to Mr. Alden, I used these words:

"A kind of terror has seized me, and instead of sending a dozen more chapters to you as I proposed to do, I am setting to to break this love story anew under the stones of my most exacting criticism and troubled regard. I go to bury myself at a solitary little seaside place" (it was Mablethorpe in Lincolnshire), "there to live alone with Rosalie and Charley, and if I do not know them hereafter, never ask me to write for 'Harper's' again.... This book has been written out of something vital in me—I do not mean the religious part of it, I mean the humanity that becomes one's own and part of one's self, by observation, experience, and understanding got from dead years."

Anyhow that shows the spirit in which the book was written, and there must have been something in it that rang true, because not only did it have an enormous sale and therefore a multitude of readers, but I received hundreds of letters from people who in one way or another were deeply interested in the story.

The majority of them were inquisitive letters. A great many of them said that the writer had shared in controversy as to what the relations of Charley and Rosalie were, and asked me to set for ever queries and controversies at rest by declaring either that the relations of these two were what, in the way of life's stern conventions, they ought not to be, or that Rosalie passed unscathed through the fire. I had foreseen all this, though I could not have foreseen the passionately intense interest which my readers would take in the life-story of these unhappy yet happy people. I had, however, only one reply. It was that all I had meant to say concerning Charley and Rosalie had been said in the book, to the last word. All I had meant not to say would not be said after the book was written. I asked them to take exactly the same view of Charley and Rosalie as they would in real life regarding two human beings with whom they were acquainted, and concerning whom, to their minds, there was sufficient evidence, or not sufficient evidence, to come to a conclusion as to what their relations were. I added that, as in real life we used our judgment upon such things with a reasonable amount of accuracy, I asked them to apply that judgment to Charley Steele and Rosalie Evanturel. They and their story were there for eyes to see and read, and when I had ended my manuscript in the year 1900 I had said the last word I ever meant to say as to their history. The controversy therefore continues, for the book still makes its appeal to an ever increasing congregation of new readers.

But another kind of letter came to me—the letter of some man who had just such a struggle as Charley Steele, or whose father or brother or friend had had such a struggle. Letters came from clergymen who had preached concerning the book; from men who told me in brief their own life problems and tragedies. These letters I prize; most of them had the real thing in them, the human truth.

That the book drew wide attention to the Dominion of Canada, particularly to French Canada, and crystallised something of the life of that dear Province, was a deep pleasure to me; and I was glad that I had been able to culminate my efforts to portray the life of the French-Canadian as I saw it, by a book which arrested the attention of so comprehensive a public.

I have seen many statements as to the original of Charley Steele, but I have never seen a story which was true. Many people have told me that they had seen the original of Charley Steele in an American lawyer. They knew he was the original, because he himself had said so. The gentleman was mistaken; I have never seen him. As with the purple cow, I never hope to see him. Whoever he is or whatever he is, the original Charley was an abler and a more striking man. I knew him as a boy, and he died while I was yet a boy, taking with him, save in the memory of a few, a rare and wonderful, if not wholly lovable personality. For over twenty years I had carried him in my mind, wondering whether, and when, I should-make use of him. Again and again I was tempted, but was never convinced that his time had come; yet through all the years he was gaining strength, securing possession of my mind, and gathering to him, magnet-like, the thousand observations which my experience sent in his direction. In my mind his life-story ended with his death at the Cote Dorion. For years and years I saw his ending there. Yet it all seemed to me so futile, despite the wonder of his personality, that I could make nothing of him, and though always fascinated by his character I was held back from exploiting it, because of the hopelessness of it all. It led nowhere. It was the 'quid refert' of the philosopher, and I could not bring myself to get any further than an interrogation mark at the end of a life which was all scepticism, mind and matter, and nothing more.

There came a day, however, when that all ended, when the doors were flung wide to a new conception of the man, and of what he might have become. I was going to America, and I paid an angry and reluctant visit to my London tailor thirty-six hours before I was to start. A suit of clothes had been sent home which, after an effective trying-on, was a monstrosity. I went straight to my tailor, put on the clothes and bade him look at them. He was a great tailor-he saw exactly what I saw, and what I saw was bad; and when a tailor will do that, you may be quite sure he is a good and a great man. He said the clothes were as bad as they could be, but he added: "You shall have them before you sail, and they shall be exactly as you want them. I'll have the foreman down." He rang a bell. Presently the door swung open and in stepped a man with an eyeglass in his eye. There, with a look at once reflective and penetrating, with a figure at once slovenly and alert, was a caricature of Charley Steele as I had known him, and of all his characteristics. There was such a resemblance as an ugly child in a family may have to his handsome brother. It was Charley Steele with a twist—gone to seed. Looking at him in blank amazement, I burst out: "Good heavens, so you didn't die, Charley Steele! You became a tailor!"

All at once the whole new landscape of my story as it eventually became, spread out before me. I was justified in waiting all the years. My discontent with the futile end of the tale as I originally knew it and saw it was justified. Charley Steele, brilliant, enigmatic and epigrammatic, did not die at the Cote Dorion, but lived in that far valley by Dalgrothe Mountain, and became a tailor! So far as I am concerned he became much more. He was the beginning of a new epoch in my literary life. I had got into subtler methods, reached more intimate understandings, had come to a place where analysis of character had shaken itself free—but certainly not quite free— from a natural yet rather dangerous eloquence.

As a play The Right of Way, skilfully and sympathetically dramatised by Mr. Eugene Presbery, has had a career extending over several years, and still continues to make its appearance.

> "They had lived and loved, and walked and worked in their own way, and the world went by them. Between them and it a great gulf was fixed: and they met its every catastrophe with the Quid Refert? of the philosophers."

> "I want to talk with some old lover's ghost, Who lived before the god of love was born."

> "There are, it may be, so many kinds of voices in the world, and none of them is without signification."

CHAPTER I
THE WAY TO THE VERDICT

"Not guilty, your Honour!"

A hundred atmospheres had seemed pressing down on the fretted people in the crowded court-room. As the discordant treble of the huge foreman of the jury squeaked over the mass of gaping humanity, which had twitched at skirts, drawn purposeless hands across prickling faces, and kept nervous legs at a gallop, the smothering weights of elastic air lifted suddenly, a great suspiration of relief swept through the place like a breeze, and in a far corner of the gallery a woman laughed outright.

The judge looked up reprovingly at the gallery; the clerk of the court angrily called "Silence!" towards the offending corner, and seven or eight hundred eyes raced between three centres of interest—the judge, the prisoner, and the prisoner's counsel. Perhaps more people looked at the prisoner's counsel than at the prisoner, certainly far more than looked at the judge.

Never was a verdict more unexpected. If a poll had been taken of the judgment of the population twenty-four hours before, a great majority would have been found believing that there was no escape for the prisoner, who was accused of murdering a wealthy timber merchant. The minority would have based their belief that the prisoner had a chance of escape, not on his possible innocence, not on insufficient evidence, but on a curious faith in the prisoner's lawyer. This minority would not have been composed of the friends of the lawyer alone, but of outside spectators, who, because Charley Steele had never lost a criminal case, attached to him a certain incapacity for bad luck; and of very young men, who looked upon him as the perfect pattern of the person good to see and hard to understand.

During the first two days of the trial the case had gone wholly against the prisoner, who had given his name as Joseph Nadeau. Witnesses had heard him quarrelling with the murdered man, and the next day the body of the victim had been found by the roadside. The prisoner was a stranger in the lumber-camp where the deed was done, and while there had been morose and lived apart; no one knew him; and he refused to tell even his lawyer whence he came, or what his origin, or to bring witnesses from his home to speak for his character.

One by one the points had been made against him—with no perceptible effect upon Charley Steele, who seemed the one cool, undisturbed person in the courtroom.

Indifferent as he seemed, seldom speaking to the prisoner, often looking out of the windows to the cool green trees far over on the hill, absorbed and unbusinesslike, yet judge and jury came to see, before the second day was done, that he had let no essential thing pass, that the questions he asked had either a pregnant aptness, opened up new avenues of deliberation, or were touched with mystery—seemed to have a longer reach than the moment or the hour.

Before the end of this second day, however, more attention was upon him than upon the prisoner, and nine-tenths of the people in the court-room could have told how many fine linen handkerchiefs he used during the afternoon, how many times he adjusted his monocle to look at the judge meditatively. Probably no man, for eight hours a day, ever exasperated and tried a judge, jury, and public, as did this man of twenty-nine years of age, who had been known at college as Beauty Steele, and who was still so spoken of familiarly; or was called as familiarly, Charley Steele, by people who never had attempted to be familiar with him.

The second day of the trial had ended gloomily for the prisoner. The coil of evidence had drawn so close that extrication seemed impossible. That the evidence was circumstantial, that no sign of the crime was upon the prisoner, that he was found sleeping quietly in his bed when he was arrested, that he had not been seen to commit the deed, did not weigh in the minds of the general public. The man's guilt was freely believed; not even the few who clung to the opinion that Charley Steele would yet get him off thought that he was innocent. There seemed no flaw in the evidence, once granted its circumstantiality.

During the last two hours of the sitting the prisoner had looked at his counsel in despair, for he seemed perfunctorily conducting the case: was occupied in sketching upon the blotting-pad before him, looking out of the window, or turning his head occasionally towards a corner where sat a half-dozen well-dressed ladies, and more particularly towards one lady who watched him in a puzzled way—more than once with a look of disappointment. Only at the very close of the sitting did he appear to rouse himself. Then, for a brief ten minutes, he cross-examined a friend of the murdered merchant in a fashion which startled the court-room, for he suddenly brought out the fact that the dead man had once struck a woman in the face in the open street. This fact, sharply stated by the prisoner's counsel, with no explanation and no comment, seemed uselessly intrusive and malicious. His ironical smile merely irritated all concerned. The thin, clean-shaven face of the prisoner grew more pinched and downcast, and he turned almost pleadingly towards the judge. The judge pulled his long side-whiskers nervously, and looked over his glasses in severe annoyance, then hastily adjourned the sitting and left the bench, while the prisoner saw with dismay his lawyer leave the court-room with not even a glance towards him.

On the morning of the third day Charley Steele's face, for the first time, wore an expression which, by a stretch of imagination, might be called anxious. He also took out his monocle frequently, rubbed it with his handkerchief, and screwed it in again, staring straight before him much of the time. But twice he spoke to the prisoner in a low voice, and was hurriedly answered in French as crude as his own was perfect. When he spoke, which was at rare intervals, his voice was without feeling, concise, insistent, unappealing. It was as though the business before him was wholly alien to him, as though he were held there against his will, but would go on with his task bitterly to the bitter end.

The court adjourned for an hour at noon. During this time Charley refused to see any one, but sat alone in his office with a few biscuits and an ominous bottle before him, till the time came for him to go back to the court-house. Arrived there he entered by a side door, and was not seen until the court opened once more.

For two hours and a half the crown attorney mercilessly made out his case against the prisoner. When he sat down, people glanced meaningly at each other, as though the last word had been said, then looked at the prisoner, as at one already condemned.

Yet Charley Steele was to reply. He was not now the same man that had conducted the case during the past two days and a half. Some great change had passed over him. There was no longer abstraction, indifference, or apparent boredom, or disdain, or distant stare. He was human, intimate and eager, yet concentrated and impelling: he was quietly, unnoticeably drunk.

He assured the prisoner with a glance of the eye, with a word scarce above a whisper, as he slowly rose to make his speech for the defence.

His first words caused a new feeling in the courtroom. He was a new presence; the personality had a changed significance. At first the public, the jury, and the judge were curiously attracted, surprised into a fresh interest. The voice had an insinuating quality, but it also had a measured force, a subterranean insistence, a winning tactfulness. Withal, a logical simplicity governed his argument. The flaneur, the poseur—if such he was—no longer appeared. He came close to the jurymen, leaned his hands upon the back of a chair—as it were, shut out the public, even the judge, from his circle of interest—and talked in a conversational tone. An air of confidence passed from him to the amazed yet easily captivated jury; the distance between them, so gaping during the last two days, closed suddenly up. The tension of the past estrangement, relaxing all at once, surprised the jury into an almost eager friendliness, as on a long voyage a sensitive traveller finds in some exciting accident a natural introduction to an exclusive fellow-passenger, whom he discovers as human as he had thought him offensively distant.

Charley began by congratulating the crown attorney on his statement of the case. He called it masterly; he said that in its presentations it was irrefutable; as a precis of evidence purely circumstantial it was—useful and interesting. But, speech-making aside, and ability—and rhetoric—aside, and even personal conviction aside, the case should stand or fall by its total, not its comparative, soundness. Since the evidence was purely circumstantial, there must be no flaw in its cable of assumption, it must be logically inviolate within itself. Starting with assumption only, there must be no straying possibilities, no loose ends of certainty, no invading alternatives. Was this so in the case of the man before them? They were faced by a curious situation. So far as the trial was concerned, the prisoner himself was the only person who could tell them who he was, what was his past, and, if he committed the crime, what was—the motive of it: out of what spirit—of revenge, or hatred—the dead man had been sent to his account. Probably in the whole history of crime there never was a more peculiar case. Even himself the prisoner's counsel was dealing with one whose life was hid from him previous to the day the murdered man was discovered by the roadside. The prisoner had not sought to prove an alibi; he had done no more than formally plead not guilty. There was no material for defence save that offered by the prosecution. He had undertaken the defence of the prisoner because it was his duty as a lawyer to see that the law justified itself; that it satisfied every demand of proof to the last atom of certainty; that it met the final possibility of doubt with evidence perfect and inviolate if circumstantial, and uncontradictory if eye-witness, if tell-tale incident, were to furnish basis of proof.

Judge, jury, and public riveted their eyes upon Charley Steele. He had now drawn a little farther away from the jury-box; his eye took in the judge as well; once or twice he turned, as if appealingly and confidently, to the people in the room. It was terribly hot, the air was sickeningly close, every one seemed oppressed—every one save a lady sitting not a score of feet from where the counsel for the prisoner stood. This lady's face was not one that could flush easily; it belonged to a temperament as even as her person was symmetrically beautiful. As Charley talked, her eyes were fixed steadily, wonderingly upon him. There was a question in her gaze, which never in the course of the speech was quite absorbed by the admiration—the intense admiration—she was feeling for him. Once as he turned with a concentrated earnestness in her direction his eyes met hers. The message he flashed her was sub-conscious, for his mind never wavered an instant from the cause in hand, but it said to her:

"When this is over, Kathleen, I will come to you." For another quarter of an hour he exposed the fallacy of purely circumstantial evidence; he raised in the minds of his hearers the painful responsibility of the law, the awful tyranny of miscarriage of justice; he condemned prejudice against a prisoner because that prisoner demanded that the law should prove him guilty instead of his proving himself innocent. If a man chose to stand to that, to sternly assume this perilous position, the law had no right to take advantage of it. He turned towards the prisoner and traced his possible history: as the sensitive, intelligent son of godly Catholic parents from some remote parish in French Canada. He drew an imaginary picture of the home from which he might have come, and of the parents and brothers and sisters who would have lived weeks of torture knowing that their son and brother was being tried for his life. It might at first glance seem quixotic, eccentric, but was it unnatural that the prisoner should choose silence as to his origin and home, rather than have his family and friends face the undoubted peril lying before him? Besides, though his past life might have been wholly blameless, it would not be evidence in his favour. It might, indeed, if it had not been blameless, provide some element of unjust suspicion against him, furnish some fancied motive. The prisoner had chosen his path, and events had so far justified him. It must be clear to the minds of judge and jury that there were fatally weak places in the circumstantial evidence offered for the conviction of this man.

There was the fact that no sign of the crime, no drop of blood, no weapon, was found about him or near him, and that he was peacefully sleeping at the moment the constable arrested him.

There was also the fact that no motive for the crime had been shown. It was not enough that he and the dead man had been heard quarrelling. Was there any certainty that it was a quarrel, since no word or sentence of the conversation had been brought into court? Men with quick tempers might quarrel over trivial things, but exasperation did not always end in bodily injury and the taking of life; imprecations were not so uncommon that they could be taken as evidence of wilful murder. The prisoner refused to say what that troubled conversation was about, but who could question his right to take the risk of his silence being misunderstood?

The judge was alternately taking notes and looking fixedly at the prisoner; the jury were in various attitudes of strained attention; the public sat open mouthed; and up in the gallery a woman with white face and clinched hands listened moveless and staring. Charley Steele was holding captive the emotions and the judgments of his hearers. All antipathy had gone; there was a strange eager intimacy between the jurymen and himself. People no longer looked with distant dislike at the prisoner, but began to see innocence in his grim silence, disdain only in his surly defiance.

But Charley Steele had preserved his great stroke for the psychological moment. He suddenly launched upon them the fact, brought out in evidence, that the dead man had struck a woman in the face a year ago; also that he had kept a factory girl in affluence for two years. Here was motive for murder—if motive were to govern them—far greater than might be suggested by excited conversation which listeners who could not hear a word construed into a quarrel—listeners who bore the prisoner at the bar ill-will because he shunned them while in the lumber-camp. If the prisoner was to be hanged for motive untraceable, why should not these two women be hanged for motive traceable!

Here was his chance. He appeared to impeach subtly every intelligence in the room for having had any preconviction about the prisoner's guilt. He compelled the jury to feel that they, with him, had made the discovery of the unsound character of the evidence. The man might be guilty, but their personal guilt, the guilt of the law, would be far greater if they condemned the man on violable evidence. With a last simple appeal, his hands resting on the railing before the seat where the jury sat, his voice low and conversational again, his eyes running down the line of faces of the men who had his client's life in their hands, he said:

"It is not a life only that is at stake, it is not revenge for a life snatched from the busy world by a brutal hand that we should heed to-day, but the awful responsibility of that thing we call the State, which, having the power of life and death without gainsay or hindrance, should prove to the last inch of necessity its right to take a human life. And the right and the reason should bring conviction to every honest human mind. That is all I have to say."

The crown attorney made a perfunctory reply. The judge's charge was brief, and, if anything, a little in favour of the prisoner—very little, a casuist's little; and the jury filed out of the room. They were gone but ten minutes. When they returned, the verdict was given: "Not guilty, your Honour!"

Then it was that a woman laughed in the gallery. Then a whispering voice said across the railing which separated the public from the lawyers: "Charley! Charley!"

Though Charley turned and looked at the lady who spoke, he made no response.

A few minutes later, outside the court, as he walked quickly away, again inscrutable and debonair, the prisoner, Joseph Nadeau, touched him on the arm and said:

"M'sieu', M'sieu', you have saved my life—I thank you, M'sieu'!"

Charley Steele drew his arm away with disgust. "Get out of my sight! You're as guilty as hell!" he said.

CHAPTER II
WHAT CAME OF THE TRIAL

"When this is over, Kathleen, I will come to you." So Charley Steele's eyes had said to a lady in the court room on that last day of the great trial. The lady had left the court-room dazed and exalted. She, with hundreds of others, had had a revelation of Charley Steele; had had also the great emotional experience of seeing a crowd make the 'volte face' with their convictions; looking at a prisoner one moment with eyes of loathing and anticipating his gruesome end, the next moment seeing him as the possible martyr to the machinery of the law. She whose heart was used to beat so evenly had felt it leap and swell with excitement, awaiting the moment when the jury filed back into the court-room. Then it stood still, as a wave might hang for an instant at its crest ere it swept down to beat upon the shore.

With her as with most present, the deepest feeling in the agitated suspense was not so much that the prisoner should go free, as that the prisoner's counsel should win his case. It was as if Charley Steele were on trial instead of the prisoner. He was the imminent figure; it was his fate that was in the balance—such was the antic irony of suggestion. And the truth was, that the fates of both prisoner and counsel had been weighed in the balance that sweltering August day.

The prisoner was forgotten almost as soon as he had left the court-room a free man, but wherever men and women met in Montreal that day, one name was on the lips of all-Charley Steele! In his speech he had done two things: he had thrown down every barrier of reserve—or so it seemed—and had become human and intimate. "I could not have believed it of him," was the remark on every lip. Of his ability there never had been a moment's doubt, but it had ever been an uncomfortable ability, it had tortured foes and made friends anxious. No one had ever seen him show feeling. If it was a mask, he had worn it with a curious consistency: it had been with him as a child, at school, at college, and he had brought it back again to the town where he was born. It had effectually prevented his being popular, but it had made him—with his foppishness and his originality—an object of perpetual interest. Few men had ventured to cross swords with him. He left his fellow-citizens very much alone. He was uniformly if distantly courteous, and he was respected in his own profession for his uncommon powers and for an utter indifference as to whether he had cases in court or not.

Coming from the judge's chambers after the trial he went to his office, receiving as he passed congratulations more effusively offered than, as people presently found, his manner warranted.

For he was again the formal, masked Charley Steele, looking calmly through the interrogative eye-glass. By the time he reached his office, greetings became more subdued. His prestige had increased immensely in a few short hours, but he had no more friends than before. Old relations were soon re-established. The town was proud of his ability as it had always been, irritated by his manner as it had always been, more prophetic of his future than it had ever been, and unconsciously grateful for the fact that he had given them a sensation which would outlast the summer.

All these things concerned him little. Once the business of the court-room was over, a thought which had quietly lain in waiting behind the strenuous occupations of his brain leaped forward to exclude all others.

As he entered his office he was thinking of that girl's face in the court-room, with its flush of added beauty which he and his speech had brought there. "What a perfect loveliness!" he said to himself as he bathed his face and hands, and prepared to go into the street again. "She needed just such a flush to make her supreme Kathleen!" He stood, looking out into the square, out into the green of the trees where the birds twittered. "Faultless—faultless in form and feature. She was so as a child, she is so as a woman." He lighted a cigarette, and blew away little clouds of smoke. "I will do it. I will marry her. She will have me: I saw it in her eye. Fairing doesn't matter. Her uncle will never consent to that, and she doesn't care enough for him. She cares, but she doesn't care enough,.... I will do it."

He turned towards a cupboard into which he had put a certain bottle before he went to the court-room two hours before. He put the key in the lock, then stopped. "No, I think not!" he said. "What I say to her shall not be said forensically. What a discovery I've made! I was dull, blank, all iron and ice; the judge, the jury, the public, even Kathleen, against me; and then that bottle in there—and I saw things like crystal! I had a glow in my brain, I had a tingle in my fingers; and I had success, and"—his face clouded—"He was as guilty as hell!" he added, almost bitterly, as he put the key of the cupboard into his pocket again.

There was a knock at the door, and a youth of about nineteen entered.

"Hello!" he said. "I say, sir, but that speech of yours struck us all where we couldn't say no. Even Kathleen got in a glow over it. Perhaps Captain Fairing didn't, for he's just left her in a huff, and she's looking—you remember those lines in the school-book:

"'A red spot burned upon her cheek,

Streamed her rich tresses down—'"

He laughed gaily. "I've come to ask you up to tea," he added. "The Unclekins is there. When I told him that Kathleen had sent Fairing away with a flea in his ear, he nearly fell off his chair. He lent me twenty dollars on the spot. Are you coming our way?" he continued, suddenly trying to imitate Charley's manner. Charley nodded, and they left the office together and moved away under a long avenue of maples to where, in the shade of a high hill, was the house of the uncle of Kathleen Wantage, with whom she and her brother Billy lived. They walked in silence for some time, and at last Billy said, 'a propos' of nothing:

"Fairing hasn't a red cent."

"You have a perambulating mind, Billy," said Charley, and bowed to a young clergyman approaching them from the opposite direction.

"What does that mean?" remarked Billy, and said "Hello!" to the young clergyman, and did not wait for Charley's answer.

The Rev. John Brown was by no means a conventional parson. He was smoking a cigarette, and two dogs followed at his heels. He was certainly not a fogy. He had more than a little admiration for Charley Steele, but he found it difficult to preach when Charley was in the congregation. He was always aware of a subterranean and half-pitying criticism going on in the barrister's mind. John Brown knew that he could never match his intelligence against Charley's, in spite of the theological course at Durham, so he undertook to scotch the snake by kindness. He thought that he might be able to do this, because Charley, who was known to be frankly agnostical, came to his church more or less regularly.

The Rev. John Brown was not indifferent to what men thought of him. He had a reputation for being "independent," but his chief independence consisted in dressing a little like a layman, posing as the athletic parson of the new school, consorting with ministers of the dissenting denominations when it was sufficiently effective, and being a "good fellow" with men easily bored by church and churchmen. He preached theatrical sermons to societies and benevolent associations. He wanted to be thought well of on all hands, and he was shrewd enough to know that if he trimmed between ritualism on one hand and evangelicism on the other, he was on a safe road. He might perforate old dogmatical prejudices with a good deal of freedom so long as he did not begin bringing "millinery" into the service of the church. He invested his own personal habits with the millinery. He looked a picturesque figure with his blond moustache, a little silk-lined brown cloak thrown carelessly over his shoulder, a gold-headed cane, and a brisk jacket half ecclesiastical, half military.

He had interested Charley Steele, also he had amused him, and sometimes he had surprised him into a sort of admiration; for Brown had a temperament capable of little inspirations—such a literary inspiration as might come to a second-rate actor—and Charley never belittled any man's ability, but seized upon every sign of knowledge with the appreciation of the epicure.

John Brown raised his hat to Charley, then held out a hand. "Masterly-masterly!" he said. "Permit my congratulations. It was the one thing to do. You couldn't have saved him by making him an object of pity, by appealing to our sympathies."

"What do you take to be the secret, then?" asked Charley, with a look half abstracted, half quizzical. "Terror—sheer terror. You startled the conscience. You made defects in the circumstantial evidence, the imminent problems of our own salvation. You put us all on trial. We were under the lash of fear. If we parsons could only do that from the pulpit!"

"We will discuss that on our shooting-trip next week. Duck-shooting gives plenty of time for theological asides. You are coming, eh?"

John Brown scarcely noticed the sarcasm, he was so delighted at the suggestion that he was to be included in the annual duck-shoot of the Seven, as the little yearly party of Charley and his friends to Lake Aubergine was called. He had angled for this invitation for two years.

"I must not keep you," Charley said, and dismissed him with a bow. "The sheep will stray, and the shepherd must use his crook."

Brown smiled at the badinage, and went on his way rejoicing in the fact that he was to share the amusements of the Seven at Lake Aubergine—the

Lake of the Mad Apple. To get hold of these seven men of repute and position, to be admitted into this good presence!—He had a pious exaltation, but whether it was because he might gather into the fold erratic and agnostical sheep like Charley Steele, or because it pleased his social ambitions, he had occasion to answer in the future. He gaily prepared to go to the Lake of the Mad Apple, where he was fated to eat of the tree of knowledge.

Charley Steele and Billy Wantage walked on slowly to the house under the hill.

"He's the right sort," said Billy. "He's a sport. I can stand that kind. Did you ever hear him sing? No? Well, he can sing a comic song fit to make you die. I can sing a bit myself, but to hear him sing 'The Man Who Couldn't Get Warm' is a show in itself. He can play the banjo too, and the guitar—but he's best on the banjo. It's worth a dollar to listen to his Epha-haam—that's Ephraim, you know—Ephahaam Come Home,' and 'I Found Y' in de Honeysuckle Paitch.'"

"He preaches, too!" said Charley drily.

They had reached the door of the house under the hill, and Billy had no time for further remark. He ran into the drawing-room, announcing Charley with the words: "I say, Kathleen, I've brought the man that made the judge sit up."

Billy suddenly stopped, however, for there sat the judge who had tried the case, calmly munching a piece of toast. The judge did not allow himself the luxury of embarrassment, but bowed to Charley with a smile, which he presently turned on Kathleen, who came as near being disconcerted as she had ever been in her life.

Kathleen had passed through a good deal to look so unflurried. She had been on trial in the court-room as well as the prisoner. Important things had been at stake with her. She and Charley Steele had known each other since they were children. To her, even in childhood, he had been a dominant figure. He had judicially and admiringly told her she was beautiful—when he was twelve and she five. But he had said it without any of those glances which usually accompanied the same sentiments in the mouths of other lads. He had never made boy-love to her, and she had thrilled at the praise of less splendid people than Charley Steele. He had always piqued her, he was so superior to the ordinary enchantments of youth, beauty, and fine linen.

As he came and went, growing older and more characteristic, more and more "Beauty Steele," accompanied by legends of wild deeds and days at college, by tales of his fopperies and the fashions he had set, she herself had grown, as he had termed it, more "decorative." He had told her so, not in the least patronisingly, but as a simple fact in which no sentiment lurked. He thought her the most beautiful thing he had ever seen, but he had never regarded her save as a creation for the perfect pleasure of the eye; he thought her the concrete glory of sensuous purity, no more capable of sentiment than himself. He had said again and again, as he grew older and left college and began the business of life after two years in Europe, that sentiment would spoil her, would scatter the charm of her perfect beauty; it would vitalise her too much, and her nature would lose its proportion; she would be decentralised! She had been piqued at his indifference to sentiment; she could not easily be content without worship, though she felt none. This pique had grown until Captain Tom Fairing crossed her path.

Fairing was the antithesis of Charley Steele. Handsome, poor, enthusiastic, and none too able, he was simple and straightforward, and might be depended on till the end of the chapter. And the end of it was, that in so far as she had ever felt real sentiment for anybody, she felt it for Tom Fairing of the Royal Fusileers. It was not love she felt in the old, in the big, in the noble sense, but it had behind it selection and instinct and natural gravitation.

Fairing declared his love. She would give him no answer. For as soon as she was presented with the issue, the destiny, she began to look round her anxiously. The first person to fill the perspective was Charley Steele. As her mind dwelt on him, her uncle gave forth his judgment, that she should never have a penny if she married Tom Fairing. This only irritated her, it did not influence her. But there was Charley. He was a figure, was already noted in his profession because of a few masterly successes in criminal cases, and if he was not popular, he was distinguished, and the world would talk about him to the end. He was handsome, and he was well-to-do-he had a big unoccupied house on the hill among the maples. How many people had said, What a couple they would make-Charley Steele and Kathleen Wantage!

So, as Fairing presented an issue to her, she concentrated her thoughts as she had never done before on the man whom the world set apart for her, in a way the world has.

As she looked and looked, Charley began to look also. He had not been enamoured of the sordid things of the world; he had been merely curious. He thought vice was ugly; he had imagination and a sense of form. Kathleen was beautiful. Sentiment had, so he thought, never seriously disturbed her; he did not think it ever would. It had not affected him. He did not understand it. He had been born non-intime. He had had acquaintances, but never friendships, and never loves or love. But he had a fine sense of the fitting and the proportionate, and he worshipped beauty in so far as he could worship anything. The homage was cerebral, intellectual, temperamental, not of the heart. As he looked out upon the world half pityingly, half ironically, he was struck with wonder at the disproportion which was engendered by "having heart," as it was called. He did not find it necessary.

Now that he had begun to think of marriage, who so suitable as Kathleen? He knew of Fairing's adoration, but he took it as a matter of course that she had nothing to give of the same sort in return. Her beauty was still serene and unimpaired. He would not spoil it by the tortures of emotion. He would try to make Kathleen's heart beat in harmony with his own; it should not thunder out of time. He had made up his mind that he would marry her.

For Kathleen, with the great trial, the beginning of the end had come. Charley's power over her was subtle, finely sensuous, and, in deciding, there were no mere heart-impulses working for Charley. Instinct and impulse were working in another direction. She had not committed her mind to either man, though her heart, to a point, was committed to Fairing.

On the day of the trial, however, she fell wholly under that influence which had swayed judge, jury, and public. To her the verdict of the jury was not in favour of the prisoner at the bar—she did not think of him. It was in favour of Charley Steele.

And so, indifferent as to who heard, over the heads of the people in front of her, to the accused's counsel inside the railings, she had called, softly: "Charley! Charley!"

Now, in the house under the hill, they were face to face, and the end was at hand: the end of something and the beginning of something.

There was a few moments of casual conversation, in which Billy talked as much as anybody, and then Kathleen said:

"What do you suppose was the man's motive for committing the murder?"

Charley looked at Kathleen steadily, curiously, through his monocle. It was a singular compliment she paid him. Her remark took no heed of the verdict of the jury. He turned inquiringly towards the judge, who, though slightly shocked by the question, recovered himself quickly.

"What do you think it was, sir?" Charley asked quietly.

"A woman—and revenge, perhaps," answered the judge, with a matter-of-course air.

A few moments afterwards the judge was carried off by Kathleen's uncle to see some rare old books; Billy, his work being done, vanished; and Kathleen and Charley were left alone.

"You did not answer me in the court-room," Kathleen said. "I called to you."

"I wanted to hear you say them here," he rejoined. "Say what?" she asked, a little puzzled by the tone of his voice.

"Your congratulations," he answered.

She held out a hand to him. "I offer them now. It was wonderful. You were inspired. I did not think you could ever let yourself go."

He held her hand firmly. "I promise not to do it again," he said whimsically.

"Why not?"

"Have I not your congratulations?" His hand drew her slightly towards him; she rose to her feet.

"That is no reason," she answered, confused, yet feeling that there was a double meaning in his words.

"I could not allow you to be so vain," he said. "We must be companionable. Henceforth I shall congratulate myself—Kathleen."

There was no mistaking now. "Oh, what is it you are going to say to me?" she asked, yet not disengaging her hand.

"I said it all in the court-room," he rejoined; "and you heard."

"You want me to marry you—Charley?" she asked frankly.

"If you think there is no just impediment," he answered, with a smile.

She drew her hand away, and for a moment there was a struggle in her mind—or heart. He knew of what she was thinking, and he did not consider it of serious consequence. Romance was a trivial thing, and women were prone to become absorbed in trivialities. When the woman had no brains, she might break her life upon a trifle. But Kathleen had an even mind, a serene temperament. Her nerves were daily cooled in a bath of nature's perfect health. She had never had an hour's illness in her life.

"There is no just or unjust impediment, Kathleen," he added presently, and took her hand again.

She looked him in the eyes clearly. "You really think so?" she asked.

"I know so," he answered. "We shall be two perfect panels in one picture of life."

CHAPTER III
AFTER FIVE YEARS

"You have forgotten me?"

Charley Steele's glance was serenely non-committal as he answered drily:

"I cannot remember doing so."

The other man's eyelids drew down with a look of anger, then the humour of the impertinence worked upon him, and he gave a nervous little laugh and said: "I am John Brown."

"Then I'm sure my memory is not at fault," remarked Charley, with an outstretched hand. "My dear Brown! Still preaching little sermons?"

"Do I look it?" There was a curious glitter in John Brown's eyes. "I'm not preaching little sermons, and you know it well enough." He laughed, but it was a hard sort of mirth. "Perhaps you forgot to remember that, though," he sneeringly added. "It was the work of your hands."

"That's why I should remember to forget it—I am the child of modesty." Charley touched the corners of his mouth with his tongue, as though his lips were dry, and his eyes wandered to a saloon a little farther down the street.

"Modesty is your curse," rejoined Brown mockingly.

"Once when you preached at me you said that beauty was my curse." Charley laughed a curt, distant little laugh which was no more the spontaneous humour lying for ever behind his thoughts than his eye-glass was the real sight of his eyes, though since childhood this laugh and his eye-glass were as natural to all expression of himself as John Brown's outward and showy frankness did not come from the real John Brown.

John Brown looked him up and down quickly, then fastened his eyes on the ruddy cheeks of his old friend. "Do they call you Beauty now as they used to?" he asked, rather insolently.

"No. They only say, 'There goes Charley Steele!'" The tongue again touched the corners of the mouth, and the eyes wandered to the doorway down the street, over which was written in French: "Jean Jolicoeur, Licensed to sell wine, beer, and other spirituous and fermented liquors."

Just then an archdeacon of the cathedral passed them, bowed gravely to Charley, glanced at John Brown, turned colour slightly, and then with a cold stare passed on too quickly for dignity.

"I'm thinking of Bunyan," said the aforetime friend of Charley Steele. "I'll paraphrase him and say: 'There, but for beauty and a monocle, walks John Brown.'"

Under the bitter sarcasm of the man, who, five years ago, had gone down at last beneath his agnostic raillery, Charley's blue eye did not waver, not a nerve stirred in his face, as he replied: "Who knows!"

"That was what you always said—who knows! That did for John Brown."

Charley seemed not to hear the remark. "What are you doing now?" he asked, looking steadily at the face whence had gone all the warmth of manhood, all that courage of life which keeps men young. The lean parchment visage had the hunted look of the incorrigible failure, had written on it self-indulgence, cunning, and uncertainty.

"Nothing much," John Brown replied.

"What last?"

"Floated an arsenic-mine on Lake Superior."

"Failed?"

"More or less. There are hopes yet. I've kept the wolf from the door."

"What are you going to do?"

"Don't know—nothing, perhaps; I've not the courage I had."

"I'd have thought you might find arsenic a good thing," said Charley, holding out a silver cigarette-case, his eyes turning slowly from the startled, gloomy face of the man before him, to the cool darkness beyond the open doorway of that saloon on the other side of the street.

John Brown shivered—there was something so cold-blooded in the suggestion that he might have found arsenic a good thing. The metallic glare of Charley's eye-glass seemed to give an added cruelty to the words. Charley's monocle was the token of what was behind his blue eye-one ceaseless interrogation. It was that everlasting questioning, the ceaseless who knows! which had in the end unsettled John Brown's mind, and driven him at last from the church and the possible gaiters of a dean into the rough business of life, where he had been a failure. Yet as Brown looked at Charley the old fascination came on him with a rush. His hand suddenly caught Charley's as he took a cigarette, and he said: "Perhaps I'll find arsenic a good thing yet."

For reply Charley laid a hand on his arm-turned him towards the shade of the houses opposite. Without a word they crossed the street, entered the saloon, and passed to a little back room, Charley giving an unsympathetic stare to some men at the bar who seemed inclined to speak to him.

As the two passed into the small back room with the frosted door, one of the strangers said to the other: "What does he come here for, if he's too proud to speak! What's a saloon for! I'd like to smash that eye-glass for him!"

"He's going down-hill fast," said the other. "He drinks steady—steady."

"Tiens—tiens!" interposed Jean Jolicoeur, the landlord. "It is not harm to him. He drink all day, an' he walk a crack like a bee-line."

"He's got the handsomest wife in this city. If I was him, I'd think more of myself," answered the Englishman.

"How you think more—hein? You not come down more to my saloon?"

"No, I wouldn't come to your saloon, and I wouldn't go to Theophile Charlemagne's shebang at the Cote Dorion."

"You not like Charlemagne's hotel?" said a huge black-bearded pilot, standing beside the landlord. "Oh, I like Charlemagne's hotel, and I like to talk to Suzon Charlemagne, but I'm not married, Rouge Gosselin—"

"If he go to Charlemagne's hotel, and talk some more too mooch to dat Suzon Charlemagne, he will lose dat glass out of his eye," interrupted Rouge Gosselin.

"Who say he been at dat place?" said Jean Jolicoeur. "He bin dere four times las' month, and dat Suzon Charlemagne talk'bout him ever since. When dat Narcisse Bovin and Jacques Gravel come down de river, he better keep away from dat Cote Dorion," sputtered Rouge Gosselin. "Dat's a long story short, all de same for you—bagosh!"

Rouge Gosselin flung off his glass of white whiskey, and threw after it a glass of cold water.

"Tiens! you know not M'sieu' Charley Steele," said Jean Jolicoeur, and turned on his heel, nodding his head sagely.

CHAPTER IV
CHARLEY MAKES A DISCOVERY

A hot day a month later Charley Steele sat in his office staring before him into space, and negligently smoking a cigarette. Outside there was a slow clacking of wheels, and a newsboy was crying "La Patrie! La Patrie! All about the War in France! All about the massacree!" Bells—wedding-bells—were ringing also, and the jubilant sounds, like the call of the newsboy, were out of accord with the slumberous feeling of the afternoon. Charley Steele turned his head slowly towards the window. The branches of a maple-tree half crossed it, and the leaves moved softly in the shadow they made. His eye went past the tree and swam into the tremulous white heat of the square, and beyond to where in the church-tower the bells were ringing-to the church doors, from which gaily dressed folk were issuing to the carriages, or thronged the pavement, waiting for the bride and groom to come forth into a new-created world—for them.

Charley looked through his monocle at the crowd reflectively, his head held a little to one side in a questioning sort of way, on his lips the ghost of a smile—not a reassuring smile. Presently he leaned forward slightly and the monocle dropped from his eye. He fumbled for it, raised it, blew on it, rubbed it with his handkerchief, and screwed it carefully into his eye again, his rather bushy brow gathering over it strongly, his look sharpened to more active thought. He stared straight across the square at a figure in heliotrope, whose face was turned to a man in scarlet uniform taller than herself two glowing figures towards whom many other eyes than his own were directed, some curiously, some disdain fully, some sadly. But Charley did not see the faces of those who looked on; he only saw two people—one in heliotrope, one in scarlet.

Presently his white firm hand went up and ran through his hair nervously, his comely figure settled down in the chair, his tongue touched the corners of his red lips, and his eyes withdrew from the woman in heliotrope and the man in scarlet, and loitered among the leaves of the tree at the window. The softness of the green, the cool health of the foliage, changed the look of his eye from something cold and curious to something companionable, and scarcely above a whisper two words came from his lips:

"Kathleen! Kathleen!"

By the mere sound of the voice it would have been hard to tell what the words meant, for it had an inquiring cadence and yet a kind of distant doubt, a vague anxiety. The face conveyed nothing—it was smooth, fresh, and immobile. The only point where the mind and meaning of the man worked according to the law of his life was at the eye, where the monocle was caught now as in a vise. Behind this glass there was a troubled depth which belied the self-indulgent mouth, the egotism speaking loudly in the red tie, the jewelled finger, the ostentatiously simple yet sumptuous clothes.

At last he drew in a sharp, sibilant breath, clicked his tongue—a sound of devil-may-care and hopelessness at once—and turned to a little cupboard behind him. The chair squeaked on the floor as he turned, and he frowned, shivered a little, and kicked it irritably with his heel.

From the cupboard he took a bottle of liqueur, and, pouring out a small glassful, drank it off eagerly. As he put the bottle away, he said again, in an abstracted fashion, "Kathleen!"

Then, seating himself at the table, as if with an effort towards energy, he rang a bell. A clerk entered. "Ask Mr. Wantage to come for a moment," he said. "Mr. Wantage has gone to the church—to the wedding," was the reply.

"Oh, very well. He will be in again this afternoon?"

"Sure to, sir."

"Just so. That will do."

The clerk retired, and Charley, rising, unlocked a drawer, and taking out some books and papers, laid them on the table. Intently, carefully, he began to examine them, referring at the same time to a letter which had lain open at his hand while he had been sitting there. For a quarter of an hour he studied the books and papers, then, all at once, his fingers fastened on a point and stayed. Again he read the letter lying beside him. A flush crimsoned his face to his hair—a singular flush of shame, of embarrassment, of guilt—a guilt not his own. His breath caught in his throat.

"Billy!" he gasped. "Billy, by God!"

CHAPTER V
THE WOMAN IN HELIOTROPE

The flush was still on Charley's face when the door opened slowly, and a lady dressed in heliotrope silk entered, and came forward. Without a word Charley rose, and, taking a step towards her, offered a chair; at the same time noticing her heightened colour, and a certain rigid carriage not in keeping with her lithe and graceful figure. There was no mistaking the quiver of her upper lip—a short lip which did not hide a wonderfully pretty set of teeth.

With a wave of the hand she declined the seat. Glancing at the books and papers lying on the table, she flashed an inquiry at his flushed face, and, misreading the cause, with slow, quiet point, in which bitterness or contempt showed, she said meaningly:

"What a slave you are!"

"Behold the white man work!" he said good-naturedly, the flush passing slowly from his face. With apparent negligence he pushed the letter and the books and papers a little to one side, but really to place them beyond the range of her angry eyes. She shrugged her shoulders at his action.

"For 'the fatherless children and widows, and all that are desolate and oppressed?'" she said, not concealing her malice, for at the wedding she had just left all her married life had rushed before her in a swift panorama, and the man in scarlet had fixed the shooting pictures in her mind.

Again a flush swept up Charley's face and seemed to blur his sight. His monocle dropped the length of its silken tether, and he caught it and slowly adjusted it again as he replied evenly:

"You always hit the nail on the head, Kathleen." There was a kind of appeal in his voice, a sort of deprecation in his eye, as though he would be friends with her, as though, indeed, there was in his mind some secret pity for her.

Her look at his face was critical and cold. It was plain that she was not prepared for any extra friendliness on his part—there seemed no reason why he should add to his usual courtesy a note of sympathy to the sound of her name on his lips. He had not fastened the door of the cupboard from which he had taken the liqueur, and it had swung open a little, disclosing the bottle and the glass. She saw. Her face took on a look of quiet hardness.

"Why did you not come to the wedding? She was your cousin. People asked where you were. You knew I was going."

"Did you need me?" he asked quietly, and his eyes involuntarily swept to the place where he had seen the heliotrope and scarlet make a glow of colour on the other side of the square. "You were not alone."

She misunderstood him. Her mind had been overwrought, and she caught insinuation in his voice. "You mean Tom Fairing!" Her eyes blazed. "You are quite right—I did not need you. Tom Fairing is a man that all the world trusts save you."

"Kathleen!" The words were almost a cry. "For God's sake! I have never thought of 'trusting' men where you are concerned. I believe in no man"—his voice had a sharp bitterness, though his face was smooth and unemotional—"but I trust you, and believe in you. Yes, upon my soul and honour, Kathleen."

As he spoke she turned quickly and stepped towards the window, an involuntary movement of agitation. He had touched a chord. But even as she reached the window and glanced down to the hot, dusty street, she heard a loud voice below, a reckless, ribald sort of voice, calling to some one to, "Come and have a drink."

"Billy!" she said involuntarily, and looked down, then shrank back quickly. She turned swiftly on her husband. "Your soul and honour, Charley!" she said slowly. "Look at what you've made of Billy! Look at the company he keeps—John Brown, who hasn't even decency enough to keep away from the place he disgraced. Billy is always with him. You ruined John Brown, with your dissipation and your sneers at religion and your-'I-wonder-nows!' Of what use have you been, Charley? Of what use to anyone in the world? You think of nothing but eating, and drinking, and playing the fop."

He glanced down involuntarily, and carefully flicked some cigarette-ash from his waistcoat. The action arrested her speech for a moment, and then, with a little shudder, she continued: "The best they can say of you is, 'There goes Charley Steele!'"

"And the worst?" he asked. He was almost smiling now, for he admired her anger, her scorn. He knew it was deserved, and he had no idea of making any defence. He had said all in that instant's cry, "Kathleen!"—that one awakening feeling of his life so far. She had congealed the word on his lips by her scorn, and now he was his old debonair, dissipated self, with the impertinent monocle in his eye and a jest upon his tongue.

"Do you want to know the worst they say?" she asked, growing pale to the lips. "Go and stand behind the door of Jolicoeur's saloon. Go to any street corner, and listen. Do you think I don't know what they say? Do you think the world doesn't talk about the company you keep? Haven't I seen you going into Jolicoeur's saloon when I was walking on the other side of the street? Do you think that all the world, and I among the rest, are blind? Oh, you fop, you fool, you have ruined my brother, you have ruined my life, and I hate and despise you for a cold-blooded, selfish coward!"

He made a deprecating gesture and stared—a look of most curious inquiry. They had been married for five years, and during that time they had never been anything but persistently courteous to each other. He had never on any occasion seen her face change colour, or her manner show chagrin or emotion. Stately and cold and polite, she had fairly met his ceaseless foppery and preciseness of manner. But people had said of her, "Poor Kathleen Steele!" for her spotless name stood sharply off from his negligence and dissipation. They called her "Poor Kathleen Steele!" in sympathy, though they knew that she had not resisted marriage with the well-to-do Charley Steele, while loving a poor captain in the Royal Fusileers. She preserved social sympathy by a perfect outward decorum, though the man of the scarlet coat remained in the town and haunted the places where she appeared, and though the eyes of the censorious world were watching expectantly. No voice was raised against her. Her cold beauty held the admiration of all women, for she was not eager for men's company, and she kept her poise even with the man in scarlet near her, glacially complacent, beautifully still, disconcertingly emotionless. They did not know that the poise with her was to an extent as much a pose as Charley's manner was to him.

"I hate you and despise you for a cold-blooded, selfish coward!" So that was the way Kathleen felt! Charley's tongue touched his lips quickly, for they were arid, and he slowly said:

"I assure you I have not tried to influence Billy. I have no remembrance of his imitating me in anything. Won't you sit down? It is very fatiguing, this heat."

Charley was entirely himself again. His words concerning Billy Wantage might have been either an impeachment of Billy's character and, by deduction, praise of his own, or it may have been the insufferable egoism of the fop, well used to imitators. The veil between the two, which for one sacred moment had seemed about to lift, was fallen now, leaded and weighted at the bottom.

"I suppose you would say the same about John Brown! It is disconcerting at least to think that we used to sit and listen to Mr. Brown as he waved his arms gracefully in his surplice and preached sentimental sermons. I suppose you will say, what we have heard you say before, that you only asked questions. Was that how you ruined the Rev. John Brown—and Billy?"

Charley was very thirsty, and because of that perhaps, his voice had an unusually dry tone as he replied: "I asked questions of John Brown; I answer them to Billy. It is I that am ruined!"

There was that in his voice she did not understand, for though long used to his paradoxical phrases and his everlasting pose—as it seemed to her and all the world—there now rang through his words a note she had never heard before. For a fleeting instant she was inclined to catch at some hidden meaning, but her grasp of things was uncertain. She had been thrown off her balance, or poise, as Charley had, for an unwonted second, been thrown off his pose, and her thought could not pierce beneath the surface.

"I suppose you will be flippant at Judgment Day," she said with a bitter laugh, for it seemed to her a monstrous thing that they should be such an infinite distance apart.

"Why should one be serious then? There will be no question of an alibi, or evidence for the defence—no cross-examination. A cut-and-dried verdict!"

She ignored his words. "Shall you be at home to dinner?" she rejoined coldly, and her eyes wandered out of the window again to that spot across the square where heliotrope and scarlet had met.

"I fancy not," he answered, his eyes turned away also—towards the cupboard containing the liqueur. "Better ask Billy; and keep him in, and talk to him—I really would like you to talk to him. He admires you so much. I wish—in fact I hope you will ask Billy to come and live with us," he added half abstractedly. He was trying to see his way through a sudden confusion of ideas. Confusion was rare to him, and his senses, feeling the fog, embarrassed by a sudden air of mystery and a cloud of futurity, were creeping to a mind-path of understanding.

"Don't be absurd," she said coldly. "You know I won't ask him, and you don't want him."

"I have always said that decision is the greatest of all qualities—even when the decision is bad. It saves so much worry, and tends to health." Suddenly he turned to the desk and opened a tin box. "Here is further practice for your admirable gift." He opened a paper. "I want you to sign off for this building—leaving it to my absolute disposal." He spread the paper out before her.

She turned pale and her lips tightened. She looked at him squarely in the eyes. "My wedding-gift!" she said. Then she shrugged her shoulders. A moment she hesitated, and in that moment seemed to congeal. "You need it?" she asked distantly.

He inclined his head, his eye never leaving hers. With a swift angry motion she caught the glove from her left hand, and, doubling it back, dragged it off. A smooth round ring came off with it and rolled upon the floor.

Stooping, he picked up the ring, and handed it back to her, saying: "Permit me." It was her wedding-ring. She took it with a curious contracted look and put it on the finger again, then pulled off the other glove quietly. "Of course one uses the pen with the right hand," she said calmly.

"Involuntary act of memory," he rejoined slowly, as she took the pen in her hand. "You had spoken of a wedding, this was a wedding-gift, and— that's right, sign there!"

There was a brief pause, in which she appeared to hesitate, and then she wrote her name in a large firm hand, and, throwing down the pen, caught up her gloves, and began to pull them on viciously.

"Thanks. It is very kind of you," he said. He put the document in the tin box, and took out another, as without a word, but with a grave face in which scorn and trouble were mingled, she now turned towards the door.

"Can you spare a minute longer?" he said, and advanced towards her, holding the new document in his hand. "Fair exchange is no robbery. Please take this. No, not with the right hand; the left is better luck—the better the hand, the better the deed," he added with a whimsical squint and a low laugh, and he placed the paper in her left hand. "Item No. 2 to take the place of item No. 1."

She scrutinised the paper. Wonder filled her face. "Why, this is a deed of the homestead property—worth three times as much!" she said. "Why— why do you do this?"

"Remember that questions ruin people sometimes," he answered, and stepped to the door and turned the handle, as though to show her out. She was agitated and embarrassed now. She felt she had been unjust, and yet she felt that she could not say what ought to be said, if all the rules were right.

"Thank you," she said simply. "Did you think of this when—when you handed me back the ring?"

"I never had an inspiration in my life. I was born with a plan of campaign."

"I suppose I ought to—kiss you!" she said in some little confusion.

"It might be too expensive," he answered, with a curious laugh. Then he added lightly: "This was a fair exchange"—he touched the papers—"but I should like you to bear witness, madam, that I am no robber!" He opened the door. Again there was that curious penetrating note in his voice, and that veiled look. She half hesitated, but in the pause there was a loud voice below and a quick foot on the stairs.

"It's Billy!" she said sharply, and passed out.

CHAPTER VI
THE WIND AND THE SHORN LAMB

A half-hour later Charley Steele sat in his office alone with Billy Wantage, his brother-in-law, a tall, shapely fellow of twenty-four. Billy had been drinking, his face was flushed, and his whole manner was indolently careless and irresponsible. In spite of this, however, his grey eyes were nervously fixed on Charley, and his voice was shaky as he said, in reply to a question as to his finances: "That's my own business, Charley."

Charley took a long swallow from the tumbler of whiskey and soda beside him, and, as he drew some papers towards him, answered quietly: "I must make it mine, Billy, without a doubt."

The tall youth shifted in his chair and essayed to laugh.

"You've never been particular about your own business. Pshaw, what's the use of preaching to me!"

Charley pushed his chair back, and his look had just a touch of surprise, a hint of embarrassment. This youth, then, thought him something of a fool: read him by virtue of his ornamentations, his outer idiosyncrasy! This boy, whose iniquity was under his finger on that table, despised him for his follies, and believed in him less than his wife—two people who had lived closer to him than any others in the world. Before he answered he lifted the glass beside him and drank to the last drop, then slowly set it down and said, with a dangerous smile:

"I have always been particular about other people's finances, and the statement that you haven't isn't preaching, it's an indictment—so it is, Billy."

"An indictment!" Billy bit his finger-nails now, and his voice shook.

"That's what the jury would say, and the judge would do the preaching. You have stolen twenty-five thousand dollars of trust-moneys!"

For a moment there was absolute silence in the room. From outside in the square came the Marche-t'en! of a driver, and the loud cackling laugh of some loafer at the corner. Charley's look imprisoned his brother-in-law, and

Billy's eyes were fixed in a helpless stare on Charley's finger, which held like a nail the record of his infamy.

Billy drew himself back with a jerk of recovery, and said with bravado, but with fear in look and motion: "Don't stare like that. The thing's done, and you can't undo it, and that's all there is about it." Charley had been staring at the youth-staring and not seeing him really, but seeing his wife and watching her lips say again: "You are ruining Billy!" He was not sober, but his mind was alert, his eccentric soul was getting kaleidoscopic glances at strange facts of life as they rushed past his mind into a painful red obscurity.

"Oh yes, it can be undone, and it's not all there is about it!" he answered quietly.

He got up suddenly, went to the door, locked it, put the key in his pocket, and, coming back, sat down again beside the table.

Billy watched him with shrewd, hunted eyes. What did Charley mean to do? To give him in charge? To send him to jail? To shut him out from the world where he had enjoyed himself so much for years and years? Never to go forth free among his fellows! Never to play the gallant with all the pretty girls he knew! Never to have any sports, or games, or tobacco, or good meals, or canoeing in summer, or tobogganing in winter, or moose-hunting, or any sort of philandering!

The thoughts that filled his mind now were not those of regret for his crime, but the fears of the materialist and sentimentalist, who revolted at punishment and all the shame and deprivation it would involve.

"What did you do with the money?" said Charley, after a minute's silence, in which two minds had travelled far.

"I put it into mines."

"What mines?"

"Out on Lake Superior."

"What sort of mines?"

"Arsenic."

Charley's eye-glass dropped, and rattled against the gold button of his white waistcoat.

"In arsenic-mines!" He put the monocle to his eye again. "On whose advice?"

"John Brown's."

"John Brown's!" Charley Steele's ideas were suddenly shaken and scattered by a man's name, as a bolting horse will crumple into confusion a crowd of people. So this was the way his John Brown had come home to roost. He lifted the empty whiskey-glass to his lips and drained air. He was terribly thirsty; he needed something to pull himself together. Five years of dissipation had not robbed him of his splendid native ability, but it had, as it were, broken the continuity of his will and the sequence of his intellect.

"It was not investment?" he asked, his tongue thick and hot in his mouth.

"No. What would have been the good?"

"Of course. Speculation—you bought heavily to sell on an expected rise?"

"Yes."

There was something so even in Charley's manner and tone that Billy misinterpreted it. It seemed hopeful that Charley was going to make the best of a bad job.

"You see," Billy said eagerly, "it seemed dead certain. He showed me the way the thing was being done, the way the company was being floated, how the market in New York was catching hold. It looked splendid. I thought I could use the money for a week or so, then put it back, and have a nice little scoop, at no one's cost. I thought it was a dead-sure thing—and I was hard up, and Kathleen wouldn't lend me any more. If Kathleen had only done the decent thing—"

A sudden flush of anger swept over Charley's face—never before in his life had that face been so sensitive, never even as a child. Something had waked in the odd soul of Beauty Steele.

"Don't be a sweep—leave Kathleen out of it!" he said, in a sharp, querulous voice—a voice unnatural to himself, suggestive of little use, as though he were learning to speak, using strange words stumblingly through a melee of the emotions. It was not the voice of Charley Steele the fop, the poseur, the idlest man in the world.

"What part of the twenty-five thousand went into the arsenic?" he said, after a pause. There was no feeling in the voice now; it was again even and inquiring.

"Nearly all."

"Don't lie. You've been living freely. Tell the truth, or—or I'll know the reason why, Billy."

"About two-thirds-that's the truth. I had debts, and I paid them."

"And you bet on the races?"

"Yes."

"And lost?"

"Yes. See here, Charley; it was the most awful luck—"

"Yes, for the fatherless children and widows, and all that are oppressed!"

Charley's look again went through and beyond the culprit, and he recalled his wife's words and his own reply. A quick contempt and a sort of meditative sarcasm were in the tone. It was curious, too, that he could smile, but the smile did not encourage Billy Wantage now.

"It's all gone, I suppose?" he added.

"All but about a hundred dollars."

"Well, you have had your game; now you must pay for it."

Billy had imagination, and he was melodramatic. He felt danger ahead.

"I'll go and shoot myself!" he said, banging the table with his fist so that the whiskey-tumbler shook.

He was hardly prepared for what followed. Charley's nerves had been irritated; his teeth were on edge. This threat, made in such a cheap, insincere way, was the last thing in the world he could bear to hear. He knew that Billy lied; that if there was one thing Billy would not do, shooting himself was that one thing. His own life was very sweet to Billy Wantage. Charley hated him the more at that moment because he was Kathleen's brother. For if there was one thing he knew of Kathleen, it was that she could not do a mean thing. Cold, unsympathetic she might be, cruel at a pinch perhaps, but dishonourable—never! This weak, cowardly youth was her brother! No one had ever seen such a look on Charley Steele's face as came upon it now—malicious, vindictive. He stooped over Billy in a fury.

"You think I'm a fool and an ass—you ignorant, brainless, lying cub! You make me a thief before all the world by forging my name, and stealing the money for which I am responsible, and then you rate me so low that you think you'll bamboozle me by threats of suicide. You haven't the courage to shoot yourself—drunk or sober. And what do you think would be gained by it? Eh, what do you think would be gained? You can't see that you'd insult your sister as well as—as rob me."

Billy Wantage cowered. This was not the Charley Steele he had known, not like the man he had seen since a child. There was something almost uncouth in this harsh high voice, these gauche words, this raw accent; but it was powerful and vengeful, and it was full of purpose. Billy quivered, yet his adroit senses caught at a straw in the words, "as rob me!" Charley was counting it a robbery of himself, not of the widows and orphans! That gave him a ray of hope. In a paroxysm of fear, joined to emotional excitement, he fell upon his knees, and pleaded for mercy—for the sake of one chance in life, for the family name, for Kathleen's sake, for the sake of everything he had ruthlessly dishonoured. Tears came readily to his eyes, real tears—of excitement; but he could measure, too, the strength of his appeal.

"If you'll stand by me in this, I'll pay you back every cent, Charley," he cried. "I will, upon my soul and honour! You shan't lose a penny, if you'll only see me through. I'll work my fingers off to pay it back till the last hour of my life. I'll be straight till the day I die—so help me God!"

Charley's eyes wandered to the cupboard where the liqueurs were. If he could only decently take a drink! But how could he with this boy kneeling before him? His breath scorched his throat.

"Get up!" he said shortly. "I'll see what I can do—to-morrow. Go away home. Don't go out again to-night. And come here at ten o'clock in the morning."

Billy took up his hat, straightened his tie, carefully brushed the dust from his knees, and, seizing Charley's hand, said: "You're the best fellow in the world, Charley." He went towards the door, dusting his face of emotion as he had dusted his knees. The old selfish, shrewd look was again in his eyes. Charley's gaze followed him gloomily. Billy turned the handle of the door. It was locked.

Charley came forward and unlocked it. As Billy passed through, Charley, looking sharply in his face, said hoarsely: "By Heaven, I believe you're not worth it!" Then he shut the door again and locked it.

He almost ran back and opened the cupboard. Taking out the bottle of liqueur, he filled a glass and drank it off. Three times he did this, then seated himself at the table with a sigh of relief and no emotion in his face.

CHAPTER VII
"PEACE, PEACE, AND THERE IS NO PEACE"'

The sun was setting by the time Charley was ready to leave his office. Never in his life had he stayed so late in "the halls of industry," as he flippantly called his place of business. The few cases he had won so brilliantly since the beginning of his career, he had studied at night in his luxurious bedroom in the white brick house among the maples on the hill. In every case, as at the trial of Joseph Nadeau, the man who murdered the timber-merchant, the first prejudice of judge and jury had given way slowly before the deep-seeing mind, which had as rare a power of analysis as for generalisation, and reduced masses of evidence to phrases; and verdicts had been given against all personal prejudice—to be followed outside the court by the old prejudice, the old look askance at the man called Beauty Steele.

To him it had made no difference at any time. He cared for neither praise nor blame. In his actions a materialist, in his mind he was a watcher of life, a baffled inquirer whose refuge was irony, and whose singular habits had in five years become a personal insult to the standards polite society and Puritan morality had set up. Perhaps the insult had been intended, for irregularities were committed with an insolent disdain for appearances. He did nothing secretly; his page of life was for him who cared to read. He played cards, he talked agnosticism, he went on shooting expeditions which became orgies, he drank openly in saloons, he whose forefathers had been gentlemen of King George, and who sacrificed all in the great American revolution for honour and loyalty—statesmen, writers, politicians, from whom he had direct inheritance, through stirring, strengthening forces, in the building up of laws and civilisation in a new land. Why he chose to be what he was—if he did choose—he alone could answer. His personality had impressed itself upon his world, first by its idiosyncrasies and afterwards by its enigmatical excesses.

What was he thinking of as he laid the papers away in the tin box in a drawer, locked it, and put the key in his pocket? He had found to the smallest detail Billy's iniquity, and he was now ready to shoulder the responsibility, to save the man, who, he knew, was scarce worth the saving. But Kathleen—there was what gave him pause. As he turned to the window and looked out over the square he shuddered. He thought of the exchange of documents he had made with her that day, and he had a sense of satisfaction. This defalcation of Billy's would cripple him, for money had flown these last few years. He had had heavy losses, and he had dug deep into his capital. Down past the square ran a cool avenue of beeches to the water, and he could see his yacht at anchor. On the other side of the water, far down the shore, was a house which had been begun as a summer cottage, and had ended in being a mansion. A few Moorish pillars, brought from Algiers for the decoration of the entrance, had necessitated the raising of the roof, and then all had to be in proportion, and the cottage became like an appanage to a palace. So it had gone, and he had cared so little about it all, and for the consequences. He had this day secured Kathleen from absolute poverty, no matter what happened, and that had its comfort. His eyes wandered among the trees. He could see the yellow feathers of the oriole and catch the note of the whippoorwill, and from the great church near the voices of the choir came over. He could hear the words "Lord, now lettest thou thy servant depart in peace, according to thy word."

Depart in peace—how much peace was there in the world? Who had it? The remembrance of what Kathleen said to him at the door—"I suppose I ought to kiss you"—came to him, was like a refrain in his ears.

"Peace is the penalty of silence and inaction," he said to himself meditatively. "Where there is action there is no peace. If the brain and body fatten, then there is peace. Kathleen and I have lived at peace, I suppose. I never said a word to her that mightn't be put down in large type and pasted on my tombstone, and she never said a word to me—till to-day—that wasn't like a water-colour picture. Not till to-day, in a moment's strife and trouble, did I ever get near her. And we've lived in peace. Peace? Where is the right kind of peace? Over there is old Sainton. He married a rich woman, he has had the platter of plenty before him always, he wears ribbons and such like baubles given by the Queen, but his son had to flee the country. There's Herring. He doesn't sleep because his daughter is going to marry an Italian count. There's Latouche. His place in the cabinet is begotten in corruption, in the hotbed of faction war. There's Kenealy. His wife has led him a dance of deep damnation. There's the lot of them—every one, not an ounce of peace among them, except with old Casson, who weighs eighteen stone, lives like a pig, grows stuffier in mind and body every day, and drinks half a bottle of whiskey every night. There's no one else—yes, there is!"

He was looking at a small black-robed figure with clean-shaven face, white hair, and shovel-hat, who passed slowly along the wooden walk beneath, with meditative content in his face.

"There's peace," he said with a laugh. "I've known Father Hallon for twenty-five years, and no man ever worked so hard, ever saw more trouble, ever shared other people's bad luck mere than he; ever took the bit in his teeth, when it was a matter of duty, stronger than he; and yet there's peace; he has it; a peace that passes all understanding—mine anyhow. I've never had a minute's real peace. The World, or Nature, or God, or It, whatever the name is, owes me peace. And how is It to give it? Why, by answering my questions. Now it's a curious thing that the only person I ever met who could answer any questions of mine—answer them in the way that satisfies—is Suzon. She works things down to phrases. She has wisdom in the raw, and a real grip on life, and yet all the men she has known have been river-drivers and farmers, and a few men from town who mistook the sort of Suzon she is. Virtuous and straight, she's a born child of Aphrodite too— by nature. She was made for love. A thousand years ago she would have had a thousand loves! And she thinks the world is a magnificent place, and she loves it, and wallows—fairly wallows—in content. Now which is right: Suzon or Father Hallon—Aphrodite or the Nazarene? Which is peace—as the bird and the beast of the field get it—the fallow futile content, or—"

He suddenly stopped, hiccoughed, then hurriedly drawing paper before him, he sat down. For an hour he wrote. It grew darker. He pushed the table nearer the window, and the singing of the choir in the church came in upon him as his pen seemed to etch words into the paper, firm, eccentric, meaning. What he wrote that evening has been preserved, and the yellow sheets lie loosely in a black despatch-box which contains the few records Charley Steele left behind him. What he wrote that night was the note of his mind, the key to all those strange events through which he began to move two hours after the lines were written:

> Over thy face is a veil of white sea-mist,
> Only thine eyes shine like stars; bless or blight me,
> I will hold close to the leash at thy wrist,
> O Aphrodite!

Thou in the East and I here in the West,
Under our newer skies purple and pleasant:
Who shall decide which is better — attest,
Saga or peasant?

Thou with Serapis, Osiris, and Isis,
I with Jehovah, in vapours and shadows;
Thou with the gods' joy-enhancing devices,
Sweet-smelling meadows!

What is there given us? — Food and some raiment,
Toiling to reach to some Patmian haven,
Giving up all for uncertain repayment,
Feeding the raven!

Striving to peer through the infinite azure,
Alternate turning to earthward and falling,
Measuring life with Damastian measure,
Finite, appalling.

What does it matter! They passed who with Homer
Poured out the wine at the feet of their idols:
Passing, what found they? To-come a misnomer,
It and their idols?

Sacristan, acolyte, player, or preacher,
Each to his office, but who holds the key?
Death, only Death — thou, the ultimate teacher
Wilt show it to me.

And when the forts and the barriers fall,
Shall we then find One the true, the almighty,
Wisely to speak with the worst of us all —
Ah, Aphrodite!

Waiting, I turn from the futile, the human,

Gone is the life of me, laughing with youth

Steals to learn all in the face of a woman,

Mendicant Truth!

Rising with a bitter laugh, and murmuring the last lines, he thrust the papers into a drawer, locked it, and going quickly from the room, he went down-stairs. His horse and cart were waiting for him, and he got in.

The groom looked at him inquiringly. "The Cote Dorion!" he said, and they sped away through the night.

CHAPTER VIII
THE COST OF THE ORNAMENT

One, two, three, four, five, six miles. The sharp click of the iron hoofs on the road; the strong rush of the river; the sweet smell of the maple and the pungent balsam; the dank rich odour of the cedar swamp; the cry of the loon from the water; the flaming crane in the fishing-boat; the fisherman, spear in hand, staring into the dark waters tinged with sombre red; the voice of a lonely settler keeping time to the ping of the axe as, lengthening out his day to nightly weariness, he felled a tree; river-drivers' camps spotted along the shore; huge cribs or rafts which had swung down the great stream for scores of miles, the immense oars motionless, the little houses on the timbers blinking with light; and from cheerful raftsmen coming the old familiar song of the rivers:

"*En roulant, ma boule roulant,*

En roulant ma boule!"

Not once had Charley Steele turned his head as the horse sped on. His face was kept straight along the line of the road; he seemed not to see or to hear, to be unresponsive to sound or scene. The monocle at his eye was like a veil to hide the soul, a defence against inquiry, itself the unceasing question, a sort of battery thrown forward, a kind of field-casemate for a lonely besieged spirit.

It was full of suggestion. It might have been the glass behind which showed some mediaeval relic, the body of some ancient Egyptian king whose life had been spent in doing wonders and making signs—the primitive, anthropomorphic being. He might have been a stone man, for any motion that he made. Yet looking at him closely you would have seen discontent in the eye, a kind of glaze of the sardonic over the whole face.

What is the good! the face asked. What is there worth doing? it said. What a limitless futility! it urged, fain to be contradicted too, as the grim melancholy of the figure suggested.

"To be an animal and soak in the world," he thought to himself—"that is natural; and the unnatural is civilisation, and the cheap adventure of the mind into fields of baffling speculation, lighted by the flickering intelligences of dead speculators, whose seats we have bought in the stock-exchange of mortality, and exhaust our lives in paying for. To eat, to drink, to lie fallow, indifferent to what comes after, to roam like the deer, and to fight like the tiger—"

He came to a dead stop in his thinking. "To fight like the tiger!" He turned his head quickly now to where upon a raft some river-drivers were singing:

"And when a man in the fight goes down,

Why, we will carry him home!"

"To fight like the tiger!" Ravage—the struggle to possess from all the world what one wished for one's self, and to do it without mercy and without fear-that was the clear plan in the primitive world, where action was more than speech and dominance than knowledge. Was not civilisation a mistake, and religion the insinuating delusion designed to cover it up; or, if not designed, accepted by the original few who saw that humanity could not turn back, and must even go forward with illusions, lest in mere despair all men died and the world died with them?

His eyes wandered to the raft where the men were singing, and he remembered the threat made: that if he came again to the Cote Dorion he "would get what for!" He remembered the warning of Rouge Gosselin conveyed by Jolicoeur, and a sinister smile crossed over his face. The contradictions of his own thoughts came home to him suddenly, for was it not the case that his physical strength alone, no matter what his skill, would be of small service to him in a dark corner of contest? Primitive ideas could only hold in a primitive world. His real weapon was his brain, that which civilisation had given him in lieu of primitive prowess and the giant's strength.

They had come to a long piece of corduroy-road, and the horse's hoofs struck rumbling hollow sounds from the floor of cedar logs. There was a swamp on one side where fire-flies were flickering, and there flashed into Charley Steele's mind some verses he had once learned at school:

"They made her a grave too cold and damp

For a soul so warm and true—"

It kept repeating itself in his brain in a strange dreary monotone.

"Stop the horse. I'll walk the rest of the way," he said presently to the groom. "You needn't come for me, Finn; I'll walk back as far as the

Marochal Tavern. At twelve sharp I'll be there. Give yourself a drink and some supper"—he put a dollar into the man's hand—"and no white whiskey, mind: a bottle of beer and a leg of mutton, that's the thing." He nodded his head, and by the light of the moon walked away smartly down the corduroy-road through the shadows of the swamp. Finn the groom looked after him.

"Well, if he ain't a queer dick! A reg'lar 'centric—but a reg'lar brick, cutting a wide swathe as he goes. He's a tip-topper; and he's a sort of tough too—a sort of a kind of a tough. Well, it's none of my business. Get up!" he added to the horse, and turning round in the road with difficulty, he drove back a mile to the Tavern Marochal for his beer and mutton—and white whiskey.

Charley stepped on briskly, his shining leather shoes, straw hat, and light cane in no good keeping with his surroundings. He was thinking that he had never been in such a mood for talk with Suzon Charlemagne. Charlemagne's tavern of the Cote Dorion was known over half a province, and its patrons carried news of it half across a continent. Suzon Charlemagne—a girl of the people, a tavern-girl, a friend of sulking, coarse river-drivers! But she had an alert precision of brain, an instinct that clove through wastes of mental underbrush to the tree of knowledge. Her mental sight was as keen and accurate as that which runs along the rifle-barrel of the great hunter with the red deer in view. Suzon Charlemagne no company for Charley Steele? What did it matter! He had entered into other people's lives to-day, had played their games with them and for them, and now he would play his own game, live his own life in his own way through the rest of this day. He thirsted for some sort of combat, for the sharp contrasts of life, for the common and the base; he thirsted even for the white whiskey against which he had warned his groom. He was reckless—not blindly, but wilfully, wildly reckless, caring not at all what fate or penalty might come his way.

"What do I care!" he said to himself. "I shall never squeal at any penalty. I shall never say in the great round-up that I was weak and I fell. I'll take my gruel expecting it, not fearing it—if there is to be any gruel anywhere, or any round-up anywhere!"

A figure suddenly appeared coming round the bend of the road before him. It was Rouge Gosselin. Rouge Gosselin was inclined to speak. Some satanic whim or malicious foppery made Charley stare him blankly in the face. The monocle and the stare stopped the bon soir and the friendly warning on Rouge Gosselin's tongue, and the pilot passed on with a muttered oath.

Gosselin had not gone far, however, before he suddenly stopped and laughed outright, for at the bottom he had great good-nature, in keeping with his "six-foot" height, and his temper was friendly if quick. It seemed so absurd, so audacious, that a man could act like Charley Steele, that he at once became interested in the phenomenon, and followed slowly after Charley, saying as he went: "Tiens, there will be things to watch to-night!"

Before Charley was within five hundred yards of the tavern he could hear the laughter and song coming from the old seigneury which Theophile Charlemagne called now the Cote Dorion Hotel, after the name given to the point on which the house stood. Low and wide-roofed, with dormer windows and a wide stoop in front, and walls three feet thick, behind, on the river side, it hung over the water, its narrow veranda supported by piles, with steps down to the water-side. Seldom was there an hour when boats were not tied to these steps. Summer and winter the tavern was a place of resort. Inside, the low ceiling, the broad rafters, the great fireplace, the well-worn floor, the deep windows, the wooden cross let into the wall, and the varied and picturesque humanity frequenting this great room, gave it an air of romance. Yet there were people who called the tavern a "shebang" — slander as it was against Suzon Charlemagne, which every river-driver and woodsman and habitant who frequented the place would have resented with violence. It was because they thought Charley Steele slandered the girl and the place in his mind, that the river-drivers had sworn they would make it hot for him if he came again. Charley was the last man in the world to undeceive them by words.

When he coolly walked into the great room, where a half-dozen of them were already assembled, drinking white "whiskey-wine," he had no intention of setting himself right. He raised his hat cavalierly to Suzon and shook hands with her.

He took no notice of the men around him. "Brandy, please!" he said. "Why do I drink, do you say?" he added, as Suzon placed the bottle and glass before him.

She was silent for an instant, then she said gravely: "Perhaps because you like it; perhaps because something was left out of you when you were made, and—"

She paused and went no further, for a red-shirted river-driver with brass rings in his ears came close to them, and called gruffly for whiskey. He glowered at Charley, who looked at him indolently, then raised his glass towards Suzon and drank the brandy.

"Pish!" said Red Shirt, and, turning round, joined his comrades. It was clear he wanted a pretext to quarrel.

"Perhaps because you like it; perhaps because something was left out of you when you were made—" Charley smiled pleasantly as Suzon came over to him again. "You've answered the question," he said, "and struck the thing at the centre. Which is it? The difficulty to decide which has divided the world. If it's only a physical craving, it means that we are materialists naturally, and that the soil from which the grape came is the soil that's in us; that it is the body feeding on itself all the time; that like returns to like, and we live a little together, and then mould together for ever and ever, amen. If it isn't a natural craving—like to like—it's a proof of immortality, for it represents the wild wish to forget the world, to be in another medium.

"I am only myself when I am drunk. Liquor makes me human. At other times I'm merely Charley Steele! Now isn't it funny, this sort of talk here?"

"I don't know about that," she answered, "if, as you say, it's natural. This tavern's the only place I have to think in, and what seems to you funny is a sort of ordinary fact to me."

"Right again, ma belle Suzon. Nothing's incongruous. I've never felt so much like singing psalms and hymns and spiritual songs as when I've been drinking. I remember the last time I was squiffy I sang all the way home that old nursery hymn:

"'On the other side of Jordan,

In the sweet fields of Eden,

Where the tree of life is blooming,

There is rest for you.

There is rest for the weary,

There is rest for the weary,

There is rest for the weary,

There is rest for you!'"

"I should have liked to hear you sing it—sure!" said Suzon, laughing.

Charley tossed off a quarter-tumbler of brandy, which, instead of flushing the face, seemed only to deepen the whiteness of the skin, showing up more brightly the spots of colour in the cheeks, that white and red which had made him known as Beauty Steele. With a whimsical humour, behind which was the natural disposition of the man to do what he listed without thinking of the consequences, he suddenly began singing, in a voice shaken a little now by drink, but full of a curious magnetism:

"On the other side of Jordan—"

"Oh, don't; please don't!" said the girl, in fear, for she saw two river-drivers entering the door, one of whom had sworn he would do for Charley Steele if ever he crossed his path.

"Oh, don't—M'sieu' Charley!" she again urged. The "Charley" caught his ear, and the daring in his eye brightened still more. He was ready for any change or chance to-night, was standing on the verge of any adventure, the most reckless soul in Christendom.

"On the other side of Jordan,

In the sweet fields of Eden,

Where the tree of life is blooming,

There is rest for you!"

What more incongruous thing than this flaneur in patent leathers and red tie, this "hell-of-a-fellow with a pane of glass in his eye," as Jake Hough, the horse-doctor, afterwards said, surrounded by red and blue-shirted river-men, woodsmen, loafers, and toughs, singing a sacred song with all the unction of a choir-boy; with a magnetism, too, that did its work in spite of all prejudice? It was as if he were counsel in one of those cases when, the minds and sympathies of judge and jury at first arrayed against him, he had irresistibly cloven his way to their judgment—not stealing away their hearts, but governing, dominating their intelligences. Whenever he had done this he had been drinking hard, was in a mental world created by drink, serene, clear-eyed, in which his brain worked like an invincible machine, perfect and powerful. Was it the case that, as he himself suggested, he was never so natural as when under this influence? That then and only then the real man spoke, that then and only then the primitive soul awakened, that it supplied the thing left out of him at birth?

"There is rest for the weary,

There is rest for the weary,

There is rest for the weary,

There is rest for you!"

One, two verses he sang as the men, at first snorting and scornful, shuffled angrily; then Jake Hough, the English horse-doctor, roared in the refrain:

"There is rest for the weary,

There is rest for you!"

Upon which, carried away, every one of them roared, gurgled, or shouted

"There is rest for the weary,

There is rest for you!"

Rouge Gosselin, who had entered during the singing, now spoke up quickly in French:

"A sermon now, M'sieu'!"

Charley took his monocle out of his eye and put it back again. Now each man present seemed singled out for an attack by this little battery of glass. He did not reply directly to Rouge Gosselin, but standing perfectly still, with one hand resting on the counter at which Suzon stood, he prepared to speak.

Suzon did not attempt to stop him now, but gazed at him in a sort of awe. These men present were Catholics, and held religion in superstitious respect, however far from practising its precepts. Many of them had been profane and blasphemous in their time; may have sworn "sacre bapteme!" one of the worst oaths of their race; but it had been done in the wildness of anger, and they were little likely to endure from Charley Steele any word that sounded like blasphemy. Besides, the world said that he was an infidel, and that was enough for bitter prejudice.

In the pause—very short—before Charley began speaking, Suzon's fingers stole to his on the counter and pressed them quickly. He made no response; he was scarcely aware of it. He was in a kind of dream. In an even, conversational tone, in French at once idiomatic and very simple, he began:

"My dear friends, this is a world where men get tired. If they work they get tired, and if they play they get tired. If they look straight ahead of them they walk straight, but then they get blind by-and-by; if they look round them and get open-eyed, their feet stumble and they fall. It is a world of contradictions. If a man drinks much he loses his head, and if he doesn't drink at all he loses heart. If he asks questions he gets into trouble, and if he doesn't ask them he gets old before his time. Take the hymn we have just sung:

"'On the other side of Jordan,

In the sweet fields of Eden,

Where the tree of life is blooming,

There is rest for you!'

"We all like that, because we get tired, and it isn't always summer, and nothing blooms all the year round. We get up early and we work late, and we sleep hard, and when the weather is good and wages good, and there's plenty in the house, we stay sober and we sadly sing, 'On the other side of Jordan'; but when the weather's heavy and funds scarce, and the pork and molasses and bread come hard, we get drunk, and we sing the comic chanson 'Brigadier, vows avez raison!' We've been singing a sad song to-night when we're feeling happy. We didn't think whether it was sad or not, we only knew it pleased our ears, and we wanted those sweet fields of Eden, and the blooming tree of life, and the rest under the tree. But ask a question or two. Where is the other side of Jordan? Do you go up to it, or down to it? And how do you go? And those sweet fields of Eden, what do they look like, and how many will they hold? Isn't it clear that the things that make us happiest in this world are the things we go for blind?"

He paused. Now a dozen men came a step or two nearer, and crowded close together, looking over each others' shoulders at him with sharp, wondering eyes.

"Isn't that so?" he continued. "Do you realise that no man knows where that Jordan and those fields are, and what the flower of the tree of life looks like? Let us ask a question again. Why is it that the one being in all the world who could tell us anything about it, the one being who had ever seen Jordan or Eden or that tree of life-in fact, the one of all creation who could describe heaven, never told? Isn't it queer? Here he was—that one man-standing just as I am among you, and round him were the men who followed him, all ordinary men, with ordinary curiosity. And he said he had come down from heaven, and for years they were with him, and yet they never asked him what that heaven was like: what it looked like, what it felt like, what sort of life they lived there, what manner of folk were the angels, what was the appearance of God. Why didn't they ask, and why didn't he answer? People must have kept asking that question afterwards, for a man called John answered it. He described, as only an oriental Jew would or could, a place all precious stones and gold and jewels and candles, in oriental language very splendid and auriferous. But why didn't those twelve men ask the One Man who knew, and why didn't the One answer? And why didn't the One tell without being asked?"

He paused again, and now there came a shuffling and a murmuring, a curious rumble, a hard breathing, for Charley had touched with steely finger the tender places in the natures of these Catholics, who, whatever their lives, held fast to the immemorial form, the sacredness of Mother Church. They were ever ready to step into the galley which should bear them all home, with the invisible rowers of God at the oars, down the wild rapids, to the haven of St. Peter. There was savagery in their faces now.

He saw, and he could not refrain from smiling as he stretched out his hand to them again with a little quieting gesture, and continued soothingly:

"But why should we ask? There's a thing called electricity. Well, you know that if you take a slice out of anything, less remains behind. We can take the air out of this room, and scarcely leave any in it.

"We take a drink out of a bottle, and certainly there isn't as much left in it! But the queer thing is that with this electricity you take it away and just as much remains. It goes out from your toe, rushes away to Timbuctoo, and is back in your toe before you can wink. Why? No one knows. What's the good of asking? You can't see it: you can only see what it does. What good would it do us if we knew all about it? There it is, and it's going to revolutionise the world. It's no good asking—no one knows what it is and where it comes from, or what it looks like. It's better to go it blind, because you feel the power, though you can't see where it comes from. You can't tell where the fields of Eden are, but you believe they're somewhere, and that you'll get to them some day. So say your prayers, believe all you can, don't ask questions, and don't try to answer 'em; and remember that Charley Steele preached to you the fear of the Lord at the Cote Dorion, and wound up the service with the fine old hymn:

"'I'll away, I'll away, to the promised land—'"

A whole verse of this camp-meeting hymn he sang in an ominous silence now, for it had crept into their minds that the hymn they had previously sung so loudly was a Protestant hymn, and that this was another Protestant hymn of the rankest sort. When he stopped singing and pushed over his glass for Suzon to fill it, the crowd were noiseless and silent for a moment, for the spell was still on them. They did not recover themselves until they saw him lift his glass to Suzon, his back on them, again insolently oblivious of them all. They could not see his face, but they could see the face of Suzon Charlemagne, and they misunderstood the light in her eye, the flush on her cheek. They set it down to a personal interest in Charley Steele.

Charley had, however, thrown a spell over her in another fashion. In her eye, in her face, was admiration, the sympathy of a strong intelligence, the wonder of a mind in the presence of its master, but they thought they saw passion, love, desire, in her face—in the face of their Suzon, the pride of the river, the flower of the Cote Dorion. Not alone because Charley had blasphemed against religion did they hate him at this moment, but because every heart was scorched with envy and jealousy—the black unreasoning jealousy which the unlettered, the dull, the crude, feels for the lettered, the able and the outwardly refined.

Charley was back again in the unfriendly climate of his natural life. Suzon felt the troubled air round them, saw the dark looks on the faces of the men, and was at once afraid and elated. She loved the glow of excitement, she had a keen sense of danger, but she also felt that in any possible trouble to-night the chances of escape would be small for the man before her.

He pushed out his glass again. She mechanically poured brandy into it.

"You've had more than enough," she said, in a low voice.

"Every man knows his own capacity, Suzon. Love me little, love me long," he added, again raising his glass to her, as the men behind suddenly moved forward upon the bar.

"Don't—for God's sake!" she whispered hastily. "Do go—or there'll be trouble!"

The black face of Theophile Charlemagne was also turned anxiously in Charley's direction as he pushed out glasses for those who called for liquor.

"Oh, do, do go—like a good soul!" Suzon urged. Charley laughed disdainfully. "Like a good soul!" Had it come to this, that Suzon pleaded with him as if he were a foolish, obstreperous child!

"Faithless and unbelieving!" he said to Suzon in English. "Didn't I play my game well a minute ago—eh—eh—eh, Suzon?"

"Oh, yes, yes, M'sieu'," she replied in English; "but now you are differen' and so are they. You must goah, so, you must!"

He laughed again, a queer sardonic sort of laugh, yet he put out his hand and touched the girl's arm lightly with a forefinger. "I am a Quaker born; I never stir till the spirit moves me," he said.

He scented conflict, and his spirits rose at the thought. Some reckless demon of adventure possessed him; some fatalistic courage was upon him. So far as the eye could see, the liquor he had drunk had done no more than darken the blue of his eye, for his hand was steady, his body was well poised, his look was direct; there seemed some strange electric force in leash behind his face, a watchful yet nonchalant energy of spirit, joined to an indolent pose of body. As the girl looked at him something of his unreckoning courage passed into her. Somehow she believed in him, felt that by some wild chance he might again conquer this truculent element now almost surrounding him. She spoke quickly to her step-father. "He won't go. What can we do?"

"You go, and he'll follow," said Theophile, who didn't want a row—a dangerous row-in his house.

"No, he won't," she said; "and I don't believe they'd let him follow me."

There was no time to say more. The crowd were insistent and restless now. They seemed to have a plan of campaign, and they began to carry it out. First one, then another, brushed roughly against Charley. Cool and collected, he refused to accept the insults.

"Pardon," he said, in each case; "I am very awkward."

He smiled all the time; he seemed waiting. The pushing and crowding became worse. "Don't mention it," he said. "You should learn how to carry your liquor in your legs."

Suddenly he changed from apology to attack. He talked at them with a cheerful scorn, a deprecating impertinence, as though they were children; he chided them with patient imprecations. This confused them for a moment and cleared a small space around him. There was no defiance in his aspect, no aggressiveness of manner; he was as quiet as though it were a drawing-room and he a master of monologues. He hurled original epithets at them in well-cadenced French, he called them what he listed, but in language which half-veiled the insults—the more infuriating to his hearers because they did not perfectly understand.

Suddenly a low-set fellow, with brass rings in his ears, pulled off his coat and threw it on the floor. "I'll eat your heart," he said, and rolled up blue sleeves along a hairy arm.

"My child," said Charley, "be careful what you eat. Take up your coat again, and learn that it is only dogs that delight to bark and bite. Our little hands were never made to tear each other's eyes."

The low-set fellow made a rush forward, but Rouge Gosselin held him back. "No, no, Jougon," he said. "I have the oldest grudge."

Jougon struggled with Rouge Gosselin. "Be good, Jougon," said Charley.

As he spoke a heavy tumbler flew from the other side of the room. Charley saw the missile thrown and dodged. It missed his temple, but caught the rim of his straw hat, carrying it off his head, and crashed into a lantern hanging against the wall, putting out the light. The room was only lighted now by another lantern on the other side of the room. Charley stooped, picked up his hat, and put it on his head again coolly.

"Stop that, or I'll clear the bar!" cried Theophile Charlemagne, taking the pistol Suzon slipped into his hand. The sight of the pistol drove the men wild, and more than one snatched at the knife in his belt.

At that instant there pushed forward into the clear space beside Charley Steele the great figure of Jake Hough, the horse-doctor, the strongest man, and the most popular Englishman on the river. He took his stand by Charley, raised his great hand, smote him in the small of his back, and said:

"By the Lord, you have sand, and I'll stand by you!" Under the friendly but heavy stroke the monocle shot from Charley's eye the length of the string. Charley lifted it again, put it up, and staring hard at Jake, coolly said:

"I beg your pardon—but have I ever—been introduced to you?"

What unbelievable indifference to danger, what disdain to friendliness, made Charley act as he did is a matter for speculation. It was throwing away his one chance; it was foppery on the scaffold—an incorrigible affectation or a relentless purpose.

Jake Hough strode forward into the crowd, rage in his eye. "Go to the devil, then, and take care of yourself!" he said roughly.

"Please," said Charley.

They were the last words he uttered that night, for suddenly the other lantern went out, there was a rush and a struggle, a muffled groan, a shrill woman's voice, a scramble and hurrying feet, a noise of a something splashing heavily in the water outside. When the lights were up again the room was empty, save for Theophile Charlemagne, Jake Hough, and Suzon, who lay in a faint on the floor with a nasty bruise on her forehead.

A score of river-drivers were scattering into the country-side, and somewhere in the black river, alive or dead, was Charley Steele.

CHAPTER IX
OLD DEBTS FOR NEW

Jo Portugtais was breaking the law of the river—he was running a little raft down the stream at night, instead of tying up at sundown and camping on the shore, or sitting snugly over cooking-pot by the little wooden caboose on his raft. But defiance of custom and tradition was a habit with Jo Portugais. He had lived in his own way many a year, and he was likely to do so till the end, though he was a young man yet. He had many professions, or rather many gifts, which he practised as it pleased him. He was river-driver, woodsman, hunter, carpenter, guide, as whim or opportunity came to him. On the evening when Charley Steele met with his mishap he was a river-driver—or so it seemed. He had been up nor'west a hundred and fifty miles, and he had come down-stream alone with his raft-which in the usual course should take two men to guide it—through slides, over rapids, and in strong currents. Defying the code of the river, with only one small light at the rear of his raft, he voyaged the swift current towards his home, which, when he arrived opposite the Cote Dorion, was still a hundred miles below. He had watched the lights in the river-drivers' camps, had seen the men beside the fires, and had drifted on, with no temptation to join in the songs floating out over the dark water, to share the contents of the jugs raised to boisterous lips, or to thrust his hand into the greasy cooking-pot for a succulent bone.

He drifted on until he came opposite Charlemagne's tavern. Here the current carried him inshore. He saw the dim light, he saw dark figures in the bar-room, he even got a glimpse of Suzon Charlemagne. He dropped the house behind quickly, but looked back, leaning on the oar and thinking how swift was the rush of the current past the tavern. His eyes were on the tavern door and the light shining through it. Suddenly the light disappeared, and the door vanished into darkness. He heard a scuffle, and then a heavy splash.

"There's trouble there," said Jo Portugais, straining his eyes through the night, for a kind of low roar, dwindling to a loud whispering, and then a noise of hurrying feet, came down the stream, and he could dimly see dark figures running away into the night by different paths.

"Some dirty work, very sure," said Jo Portugais, and his eyes travelled back over the dark water like a lynx's, for the splash was in his ear, and a sort of prescience possessed him. He could not stop his raft. It must go on down the current, or be swerved to the shore, to be fastened.

"God knows, it had an ugly sound," said Jo Portugais, and again strained his eyes and ears. He shifted his position and took another oar, where the raft-lantern might not throw a reflection upon the water. He saw a light shine again through the tavern doorway, then a dark object block the light, and a head thrust forward towards the river as though listening.

At this moment he fancied he saw something in the water nearing him. He stretched his neck. Yes, there was something.

"It's a man. God save us—was it murder?" said Jo Portugais, and shuddered. "Was it murder?"

The body moved more swiftly than the raft. There was a hand thrust up—two hands.

"He's alive!" said Jo Portugais, and, hurriedly pulling round his waist a rope tied to a timber, jumped into the water.

Three minutes later, on the raft, he was examining a wound in the head of an insensible man.

As his hand wandered over the body towards the heart, it touched something that rattled against a button. He picked it up mechanically and held it to the light. It was an eye-glass.

"My God!" said Jo Portugais, and peered into the man's face. "It's him." Then he remembered the last words the man had spoken to him—"Get out of my sight. You're as guilty as hell!" But his heart yearned towards the man nevertheless.

CHAPTER X
THE WAY IN AND THE WAY OUT

In his own world of the parish of Chaudiere Jo Portugais was counted a widely travelled man. He had adventured freely on the great rivers and in the forests, and had journeyed up towards Hudson's Bay farther than any man in seven parishes.

Jo's father and mother had both died in one year—when he was twenty-five. That year had turned him from a clean-shaven cheerful boy into a morose bearded man who looked forty, for it had been marked by his disappearance from Chaudiere and his return at the end of it, to find his mother dead and his father dying broken-hearted. What had driven Jo from home only his father knew; what had happened to him during that year only Jo himself knew, and he told no one, not even his dying father.

A mystery surrounded him, and no one pierced it. He was a figure apart in Chaudiere parish. A dreadful memory that haunted him, carried him out of the village, which clustered round the parish church, into Vadrome Mountain, three miles away, where he lived apart from all his kind. It was here he brought the man with the eye-glass one early dawn, after two nights and two days on the river, pulling him up the long hill in a low cart with his strong faithful dogs, hitching himself with them and toiling upwards through the dark. In his three-roomed hut he laid his charge down upon a pile of bear-skins, and tended him with a strange gentleness, bathing the wound in the head and binding it again and again.

The next morning the sick man opened his eyes heavily. He then began fumbling mechanically on his breast. At last his fingers found his monocle. He feebly put it to his eye, and looked at Jo in a strange, questioning, uncomprehending way.

"I beg—your pardon," he said haltingly, "have I ever—been intro—" Suddenly his eyes closed, a frown gathered on his forehead. After a minute his eyes opened again, and he gazed with painful, pathetic seriousness at Jo. This grew to a kind of childish terror; then slowly, as a shadow passes, the perplexity, anxiety and terror cleared away, and left his forehead calm, his eyes unvexed and peaceful. The monocle dropped, and he did not heed it. At length he said wearily, and with an incredibly simple dependence:

"I am thirsty now."

Jo lifted a wooden bowl to his lips, and he drank, drank, drank to repletion. When he had finished he patted Jo's shoulder.

"I am always thirsty," he said. "I shall be hungry too. I always am."

Jo brought him some milk and bread in a bowl. When the sick man had eaten and drunk the bowlful to the last drop and crumb, he lay back with a sigh of content, but trembling from weakness and the strain, though Jo's hand had been under his head, and he had been fed like a little child.

All day he lay and watched Jo as he worked, as he came and went. Sometimes he put his hand to his head and said to Jo: "It hurts." Then Jo would cool the wound with fresh water from the mountain spring, and he would drag down the bowl to drink from it greedily.

It was as though he could never get enough water to drink. So the first day in the hut at Vadrome Mountain passed without questioning on the part of either Charley Steele or his host.

With good reason. Jo Portugais saw that memory was gone; that the past was blotted out. He had watched that first terrible struggle of memory to reassert itself, as the eyes mechanically looked out upon new and strange surroundings, but it was only the automatic habit of the sight, the fumbling of the blind soul in its cell-fumbling for the latch which it could not find, for the door which would not open. The first day on the raft, as Charley had opened his eyes upon the world again after that awful night at the Cote Dorion, Jo. had seen that same blank uncomprehending look—as it were, the first look of a mind upon the world. This time he saw, and understood what he saw, and spoke as men speak, but with no knowledge or memory behind it—only the involuntary action of muscle and mind repeated from the vanished past.

Charley Steele was as a little child, and having no past, and comprehending in the present only its limited physical needs and motions, he had no hope, no future, no understanding. In three days he was upon his feet, and in four he walked out of doors and followed Jo into the woods, and watched him fell a tree and do a woodsman's work. Indoors he regarded all Jo did with eager interest and a pleased, complacent look, and readily did as he was told. He seldom spoke—not above three or four times a day, and then simply and directly, and only concerning his wants. From first to last he never asked a question, and there was never any inquiry by look or word. A hundred and twenty miles lay between him and his old home, between him and Kathleen and Billy and Jean Jolicoeur's saloon, but between him and his past life the unending miles of eternity intervened. He was removed from it as completely as though he were dead and buried.

A month went by. Sometimes Jo went down to the village below, and then, at first, he locked the door of the house behind him upon Charley. Against this Charley made no motion and said no word, but patiently awaited Jo's return. So it was that, at last, Jo made no attempt to lock the door, but with a nod or a good-bye left him alone. When Charley saw him returning he would go to meet him, and shake hands with him, and say "Good-day," and then would come in with him and help him get supper or do the work of the house.

Since Charley came no one had visited the house, for there were no paths beyond it, and no one came to the Vadrome Mountain, save by chance. But after two months had gone the Cure came. Twice a year the Cure made it a point to visit Jo in the interests of his soul, though the visits came to little, for Jo never went to confession, and seldom to mass. On this occasion the Cure arrived when Jo was out in the woods. He discovered Charley. Charley made no answer to his astonished and friendly greeting, but watched him with a wide-eyed anxiety till the Cure seated himself at the door to await Jo's coming. Presently, as he sat there, Charley, who had studied his face as a child studies the unfamiliar face of a stranger, brought him a bowl of bread and milk and put it in his hands. The Cure smiled and thanked him, and Charley smiled in return and said: "It is very good."

As the Cure ate, Charley watched him with satisfaction, and nodded at him kindly.

When Jo came he lied to the Cure. He said he had found Charley wandering in the woods, with a wound in his head, and had brought him home with him and cared for him. Forty miles away he had found him.

The Cure was perplexed. What was there to do? He believed what Jo said. So far as he knew, Jo had never lied to him before, and he thought he understood Jo's interest in this man with the look of a child and no memory: Jo's life was terribly lonely; he had no one to care for, and no one cared for him; here was what might comfort him! Through this helpless man might come a way to Jo's own good. So he argued with himself.

What to do? Tell the story to the world by writing to the newspaper at Quebec? Jo pooh-poohed this. Wait till the man's memory came back? Would it come back—what chance was there of its ever coming back? Jo said that they ought to wait and see—wait awhile, and then, if his memory did not return, they would try to find his friends, by publishing his story abroad.

Chaudiere was far from anywhere: it knew little of the world, and the world knew naught of it, and this was a large problem for the Cure. Perhaps Jo was right, he thought. The man was being well cared for, and what more could be wished at the moment? The Cure was a simple man, and when Jo urged that if the sick man could get well anywhere in the world it would be at Vadrome Mountain in Chaudiere, the Cure's parochial pride was roused, and he was ready to believe all Jo said. He also saw reason in Jo's request that the village should not be told of the sick man's presence. Before he left, the Cure knelt down and prayed, "for the good of this poor mortal's soul and body."

As he prayed, Charley knelt down also, and kept his eyes-calm unwondering eyes-full fixed on the good M. Loisel, whose grey hair, thin peaceful face, and dark brown eyes made a noble picture of patience and devotion.

When the Cure shook him by the hand, murmuring in good-bye, "God be gracious to thee, my son," Charley nodded in a friendly way. He watched the departing figure till it disappeared over the crest of the hill.

This day marked an epoch in the solitude of the hut on Vadrome Mountain. Jo had an inspiration. He got a second set of carpenter's tools, and straightway began to build a new room to the house. He gave the extra set of tools to Charley with an encouraging word. For the first time since he had been brought here, Charley's face took on a look of interest. In half-an-hour he was at work, smiling and perspiring, and quickly learning the craft. He seldom spoke, but he sometimes laughed a mirthful, natural boy's laugh of good spirits and contentment. From that day his interest in things increased, and before two months went round, while yet it was late autumn, he looked in perfect health. He ate moderately, drank a great deal of water, and slept half the circle of the clock each day. His skin was like silk; the colour of his face was as that of an apple; he was more than ever Beauty Steele. The Cure came two or three times, and Charley spoke to him but never held conversation, and no word concerning the past ever passed his tongue, nor did he have memory of what was said to him from one day to the next. A hundred ways Jo had tried to rouse his memory. But the words Cote Dorion had no meaning to him, and he listened blankly to all names and phrases once so familiar. Yet he spoke French and English in a slow, passive, involuntary way. All was automatic, mechanical.

The weeks again wore on, and autumn became winter, and then at last one day the Cure came, bringing his brother, a great Parisian surgeon lately arrived from France on a short visit. The Cure had told his brother the story, and had been met by a keen, astonished interest in the unknown man on Vadrome Mountain. A slight pressure on the brain from accident had before now produced loss of memory—the great man's professional curiosity was aroused: he saw a nice piece of surgical work ready to his hand; he asked to be taken to Vadrome Mountain.

Now the Cure had lived long out of the world, and was not in touch with the swift-minded action and adventuring intellects of such men as his brother, Marcel Loisel. Was it not tempting Providence, a surgical operation? He was so used to people getting ill and getting well without a doctor—the nearest was twenty miles distant—or getting ill and dying in what seemed a natural and preordained way, that to cut open a man's head and look into his brain, and do this or that to his skull, seemed almost sinful. Was it not better to wait and see if the poor man would not recover in God's appointed time?

In answer to his sensitively eager and diverse questions, Marcel Loisel replied that his dear Cure was merely mediaeval, and that he had sacrificed his mental powers on the altar of a simple faith, which might remove mountains but was of no value in a case like this, where, clearly, surgery was the only providence.

At this the Cure got to his feet, came over, laid his hand on his brother's shoulder, and said, with tears in his eyes:

"Marcel, you shock me. Indeed you shock me!"

Then he twisted a knot in his cassock cords, and added "Come then, Marcel. We will go to him. And may God guide us aright!"

That afternoon the two grey-haired men visited Vadrome Mountain, and there they found Charley at work in the little room that the two men had built. Charley nodded pleasantly when the Cure introduced his brother, but showed no further interest at first. He went on working at the cupboard under his hand. His cap was off and his hair was a little rumpled where the wound had been, for he had a habit of rubbing the place now and then—

an abstracted, sensitive motion—although he seemed to suffer no pain. The surgeon's eyes fastened on the place, and as Charley worked and his brother talked, he studied the man, the scar, the contour of the head. At last he came up to Charley and softly placed his fingers on the scar, feeling the skull. Charley turned quickly.

There was something in the long, piercing look of the surgeon which seemed to come through limitless space to the sleeping and imprisoned memory of Charley's sick mind. A confused, anxious, half-fearful look crept into the wide blue eyes. It was like a troubled ghost, flitting along the boundaries of sight and sense, and leaving a chill and a horrified wonder behind. The surgeon gazed on, and the trouble in Charley's eye passed to his face, stayed an instant. Then he turned away to Jo Portugais. "I am thirsty now," he said, and he touched his lips in the way he was wont to do in those countless ages ago, when, millions upon millions of miles away, people said: "There goes Charley Steele!"

"I am thirsty now," and that touch of the lip with the tongue, were a revelation to the surgeon.

A half-hour later he was walking homeward with the Cure. Jo accompanied them for a distance. As they emerged into the wider road-paths that began half-way down the mountain, the Cure, who had watched his brother's face for a long time in silence, said:

"What is in your mind, Marcel?" The surgeon turned with a half-smile.

"He is happy now. No memory, no conscience, no pain, no responsibility, no trouble—nothing behind or before. Is it good to bring him back?"

The Cure had thought it all over, and he had wholly changed his mind since that first talk with his brother. "To save a mind, Marcel!" he said.

"Then to save a soul?" suggested the surgeon. "Would he thank me?"

"It is our duty to save him."

"Body and mind and soul, eh? And if I look after the body and the mind?"

"His soul is in God's hands, Marcel."

"But will he thank me? How can you tell what sorrows, what troubles, he has had? What struggles, temptations, sins? He has none now, of any sort; not a stain, physical or moral."

"That is not life, Marcel."

"Well, well, you have changed. This morning it was I who would, and you hesitated."

"I see differently now, Marcel."

The surgeon put a hand playfully on his brother's shoulder.

"Did you think, my dear Prosper, that I should hesitate? Am I a sentimentalist? But what will he say?

"We need not think of that, Marcel."

"But yet suppose that with memory come again sin and shame—even crime?"

"We will pray for him."

"But if he isn't a Catholic?"

"One must pray for sinners," said the Curb, after a silence.

This time the surgeon laid a hand on the shoulder of his brother affectionately. "Upon my soul, dear Prosper, you almost persuade me to be reactionary and mediaeval."

The Curb turned half uneasily towards Jo, who was following at a little distance. This seemed hardly the sort of thing for him to hear.

"You had better return now, Jo," he said.

"As you wish, M'sieu'," Jo answered, then looked inquiringly at the surgeon.

"In about five days, Portugais. Have you a steady hand and a quick eye?"

Jo spread out his hands in deprecation, and turned to the Curb, as though for him to answer.

"Jo is something of a physician and surgeon too, Marcel. He has a gift. He has cured many in the parish with his herbs and tinctures, and he has set legs and arms successfully."

The surgeon eyed Jo humorously, but kindly. "He is probably as good a doctor as some of us. Medicine is a gift, surgery is a gift and an art. You shall hear from me, Portugais." He looked again keenly at Jo. "You have not given him 'herbs and tinctures'?"

"Nothing, M'sieu'."

"Very sensible. Good-day, Portugais."

"Good-day, my son," said the priest, and raised his fingers in benediction, as Jo turned and quickly retraced his steps.

"Why did you ask him if he had given the poor man any herbs or tinctures, Marcel?" said the priest.

"Because those quack tinctures have whiskey in them."

"What do you mean?"

"Whiskey in any form would be bad for him," the surgeon answered evasively.

But to himself he kept saying: "The man was a drunkard—he was a drunkard."

CHAPTER XI
THE RAISING OF THE CURTAIN

M. Marcel Loisel did his work with a masterly precision, with the aid of his brother and Portugais. The man under the instruments, not wholly insensible, groaned once or twice. Once or twice, too, his eyes opened with a dumb hunted look, then closed as with an irresistible weariness. When the work was over, and every stain or sign of surgery removed, sleep came down on the bed—a deep and saturating sleep, which seemed to fill the room with peace. For hours the surgeon sat beside the couch, now and again feeling the pulse, wetting the hot lips, touching the forehead with his palm. At last, with a look of satisfaction, he came forward to where Jo and the Cure sat beside the fire.

"It is all right," he said. "Let him sleep as long as he will." He turned again to the bed. "I wish I could stay to see the end of it. Is there no chance, Prosper?" he added to the priest.

"Impossible, Marcel. You must have sleep. You have a seventy-mile drive before you to-morrow, and sixty the next day. You can only reach the port now by starting at daylight to-morrow."

So it was that Marcel Loisel, the great surgeon, was compelled to leave Chaudiere before he knew that the memory of the man who had been under his knife had actually returned to him. He had, however, no doubt in his own mind, and he was confident that there could be no physical harm from the operation. Sleep was the all-important thing. In it lay the strength for the shock of the awakening—if awakening of memory there was to be.

Before he left he stooped over Charley and said musingly: "I wonder what you will wake up to, my friend?" Then he touched the wound with a light caressing finger. "It was well done, well done," he murmured proudly.

A moment afterwards he was hurrying down the hill to the open road, where a cariole awaited the Cure and himself.

For a day and a half Charley slept, and Jo watched him with an affectionate solicitude. Once or twice, becoming anxious, because of the heavy breathing and the motionless sleep, he had forced open the teeth, and poured a little broth between.

Just before dawn on the second morning, worn out and heavy with slumber, Jo lay down by the piled-up fire and dropped into a sleep that wrapped him like a blanket, folding him away into a drenching darkness.

For a time there was a deep silence, troubled only by Jo's deep breathing, which seemed itself like the pulse of the silence. Charley appeared not to be breathing at all. He was lying on his back, seemingly lifeless. Suddenly on the snug silence there was a sharp sound. A tree outside snapped with the frost.

Charley awoke. The body seemed not to awake, for it did not stir, but the eyes opened wide and full, looking straight before them—straight up to the brown smoke-stained rafters, along which were ranged guns and fishing-tackle, axes and bear-traps. Full clear blue eyes, healthy and untired as a child's fresh from an all-night's drowse, they looked and looked. Yet, at first, the body did not stir; only the mind seemed to be awakening, the soul creeping out from slumber into the day. Presently, however, as the eyes gazed, there stole into them a wonder, a trouble, an anxiety. For a moment they strained at the rafters and the crude weapons and implements there, then the body moved, quickly, eagerly, and turned to see the flickering shadows made by the fire and the simple order of the room.

A minute more, and Charley was sitting on the side of his couch, dazed and staring. This hut, this fire, the figure by the hearth in a sound sleep-his hand went to his head: it felt the bandage there!

He remembered now! Last night at the Cote Dorion! Last night he had talked with Suzon Charlemagne at the Cote Dorion; last night he had drunk harder than he had ever drunk in his life, he had defied, chaffed, insulted the river-drivers. The whole scene came back: the faces of Suzon and her father; Suzon's fingers on his for an instant; the glass of brandy beside him; the lanterns on the walls; the hymn he sang; the sermon he preached— he shuddered a little; the rumble of angry noises round him; the tumbler thrown; the crash of the lantern, and only one light left in the place! Then Jake Hough and his heavy hand, the flying monocle, and his disdainful, insulting reply; the sight of the pistol in the hand of Suzon's father; then a rush, a darkness, and his own fierce plunge towards the door, beyond which were the stars and the cool night and the dark river. Curses, hands that battered and tore at him, the doorway reached, and then a blow on the head and—falling, falling, falling, and distant noises growing more distant, and suddenly and sweetly—absolute silence.

Again he shuddered. Why? He remembered that scene in his office yesterday with Kathleen, and the one later with Billy. A sensitive chill swept all over him, making his flesh creep, and a flush sped over his face from chin to brow. To-day he must pick up all these threads again, must make things right for Billy, must replace the money he had stolen, must face Kathleen again he shuddered. Was he at the Cote Dorion still? He looked round him. No, this was not the sort of house to be found at the Cote Dorion. Clearly this was the hut of a hunter. Probably he had been fished out of the river by this woodsman and brought here. He felt his head. The wound was fresh and very sore. He had played for death, with an insulting disdain, yet here he was alive.

Certainly he was not intended to be drowned or knifed—he remembered the knives he saw unsheathed—or kicked or pummelled into the hereafter. It was about ten o'clock when he had had his "accident"—he affected a smile, yet somehow he did not smile easily—it must be now about five, for here was the morning creeping in behind the deer-skin blind at the window.

Strange that he felt none the worse for his mishap, and his tongue was as clean and fresh as if he had been drinking milk last night, and not very doubtful brandy at the Cote Dorion. No fever in his hands, no headache, only the sore skull, so well and tightly bandaged but a wonderful thirst, and an intolerable hunger. He smiled. When had he ever been hungry for breakfast before? Here he was with a fine appetite: it was like coals of fire heaped on his head by Nature for last night's business at the Cote Dorion. How true it was that penalties did not always come with—indiscretions. Yet, all at once, he flushed again to the forehead, for a curious sense of shame flashed through his whole being, and one Charley Steele—the Charley Steele of this morning, an unknown, unadventuring, onlooking Charley Steele—was viewing with abashed eyes the Charley Steele who had ended a doubtful career in the coarse and desperate proceedings of last night. With a nervous confusion he sought refuge in his eye-glass. His fingers fumbled over his waistcoat, but did not find it. The weapon of defence and attack, the symbol of interrogation and incomprehensibility, was gone. Beauty Steele was under the eyes of another self, and neither disdain, nor contempt, nor the passive stare, were available. He got suddenly to his feet, and started forward, as though to find refuge from himself.

The abrupt action sent the blood to his head, and feeling a blindness come over him, he put both hands up to his temples, and sank back on the couch, dizzy and faint.

His motions waked Jo Portugais, who scrambled from the floor, and came towards him.

"M'sieu'," he said, "you must not. You are faint." He dropped his hands supportingly to Charley's shoulders.

Charley nodded, but did not yet look up. His head throbbed sorely. "Water—please!" he said.

In an instant Jo was beside him again, with a bowl of fresh water at his lips. He drank, drank, drank, until the great bowl was drained to the last drop.

"Whew! That was good!" he said, and looked up at Jo with a smile. "Thank you, my friend; I haven't the honour of your acquaintance, but—"

He stopped suddenly and stared at Jo. Inquiry, mystification, were in his look.

"Have I ever seen you before?" he said. "Who knows, M'sieu'!"

Since Jo had stood before Charley in the dock near six years ago he had greatly changed. The marks of smallpox, a heavy beard, grey hair, and solitary life had altered him beyond Charley's recognition.

Jo could hardly speak. His legs were trembling under him, for now he knew that Charley Steele was himself again. He was no longer the simple, quiet man-child of three days ago, and of these months past, but the man who had saved him from hanging, to whom he owed a debt he dare not acknowledge. Jo's brain was in a muddle. Now that the great crisis was over, now that the expected thing had come, and face to face with the cure, he had neither tongue, nor strength, nor wit. His words stuck in his throat where his heart was, and for a minute his eyes had a kind of mist before them.

Meanwhile Charley's eyes were upon him, curious, fixed, abstracted.

"Is this your house?"

"It is, M'sieu'."

"You fished me out of the river by the Cote Dorion?" He still held his head with his hands, for it throbbed so, but his eyes were intent on his companion.

"Yes, M'sieu'."

Charley's hand mechanically fumbled for his monocle. Jo turned quickly to the wall, and taking it by its cord from the nail where it had been for these long months, handed it over. Charley took it and mechanically put it in his eye. "Thank you, my friend," he said. "Have I been conscious at all since you rescued me last night?" he asked.

"In a way, M'sieu'."

"Ah, well, I can't remember, but it was very kind of you—I do thank you very much. Do you think you could find me something to eat? I beg your pardon—it isn't breakfast-time, of course, but I was never so hungry in my life!"

"In a minute, M'sieu'—in one minute. But lie down, you must lie down a little. You got up too quick, and it makes your head throb. You have had nothing to eat."

"Nothing, since yesterday noon, and very little then. I didn't eat anything at the Cote Dorion, I remember." He lay back on the couch and closed his eyes. The throbbing in his head presently stopped, and he felt that if he ate something he could go to sleep again, it was so restful in this place—a whole day's sleep and rest, how good it would be after last night's racketing! Here was primitive and material comfort, the secret of content, if you liked! Here was this poor hunter-fellow, with enough to eat and to drink, earning it every day by every day's labour, and, like Robinson Crusoe no doubt, living in a serene self-sufficiency and an elysian retirement. Probably he had no responsibilities in the world, with no one to say him nay, himself only to consider in all the universe: a divine conception of adequate life. Yet himself, Charley Steele, an idler, a waster, with no purpose in life, with scarcely the necessity to earn his bread-never, at any rate, until lately—was the slave of the civilisation to which he belonged. Was civilisation worth the game?

His hand involuntarily went to his head. It changed the course of his thoughts. He must go back to-day to put Billy's crime right, to replace the trust-moneys Billy had taken by forging his brother-in-law's name. Not a moment must be lost. No doubt he was within driving distance of his office, and, bandaged head or no bandaged head, last night's disgraceful doings notwithstanding, it was his duty to face the wondering eyes—what did he care for wondering eyes? hadn't he been making eyes wonder all his life?—

face the wondering eyes in the little city, and set a crooked business straight. Fool and scoundrel certainly Billy was, but there was Kathleen!

His lips tightened; he had a strange anxious flutter of the heart. When had his heart fluttered like this? When had he ever before considered Kathleen's feelings as to his personal conduct so delicately? Well, since yesterday he did feel it, and a sudden sense of pity sprang up in him— vague, shamefaced pity, which belied the sudden egotistical flourish with which he put his monocle to his eye and tried futilely to smile in the old way.

He had lain with his eyes closed. They opened now, and he saw his host spreading a newspaper as a kind of cloth on a small rough table, and putting some food upon it-bread, meat, and a bowl of soup. It was thoughtful of this man to make his soup overnight-he saw Jo lift it from beside the fire where it had been kept hot. A good fellow-an excellent fellow, this woodsman.

His head did not throb now, and he drew himself up slowly on his elbow-then, after a moment, lifted himself to a sitting posture.

"What is your name, my friend?" he said.

"Jo Portugais, M'sieu'," Jo answered, and brought a candle and put it on the table, then lifted the tin-plate from over the bowl of savoury soup.

Never before had Charley Steele sat down to such a breakfast. A roll and a cup of coffee had been enough, and often too much, for him. Yet now he could not wait to eat the soup with a spoon, but lifted the bowl and took a long draught of it, and set it down with a sigh of content. Then he broke bread into the soup—large pieces of black oat bread—until the bowl was a mass of luscious pulp. This he ate almost ravenously, his eye wandering avidly the while to the small piece of meat beside the bowl. What meat was it? It looked like venison, yet summer was not the time for venison. What did it matter! Jo sat on a bench beside the fire, his face turned towards his guest, dreading the moment when the man he had nursed and cared for, with whom he had eaten and drunk for so long, should know the truth about himself. He could not tell him all there was to tell, he was taking another means of letting him know.

Charley did not speak. Hunger was a new sensation, a delicious thing, too good to be broken by talking. He ate till he had cleared away the last crumbs of bread and meat and drunk the last drop of soup. He looked at the woodsman as though wondering if he would bring more. Jo evidently thought he had had enough, for he did not move. Charley's glance withdrew from Jo, and busied itself with the few crumbs remaining upon the table. He saw a little piece of bread on the floor. He picked it up and ate it with relish, laughing to himself.

"How long will it take us to get to town? Can we do it this morning?"

"Not this morning, M'sieu'," said Jo, in a sort of hoarse whisper.

"How many hours would it take?"

He was gathering the last crumbs of his feast with his hand, and looking casually down at the newspaper spread as a table-cloth.

All at once his hand stopped, his eyes became fixed on a spot in the paper. He gave a hoarse, guttural cry, like an animal in agony. His lips became dry, his hand wiped a blinding mist from his eyes.

Jo watched him with an intense alarm and a horrified curiosity. He felt a base coward for not having told Charley what this paper contained. Never had he seen such a look as this. He felt his beads, and told them over and over again, as Charley Steele, in a dry, croaking sort of whisper, read, in letters that seemed monstrous symbols of fire, a record of himself:

"To-day, by special license from the civil and ecclesiastical courts [the paragraph in the paper began], was married, at St. Theobald's Church, Mrs. Charles Steele, daughter of the late Hon. Julien Wantage, and niece of the late Eustace Wantage, Esq., to Captain Thomas Fairing, of the Royal Fusileers—"

Charley snatched at the top of the paper and read the date "Tenth of February, 18-!" It was August when he was at the Cote Dorion, the 5th August, 18-, and this paper was February 10th, 18-. He read on, in the month-old paper, with every nerve in his body throbbing now: a fierce beating that seemed as if it must burst the heart and the veins:

"—Captain Thomas Fairing, of the Royal Fusileers, whose career in our midst has been marked by an honourable sense of public and private duty. Our fellow-citizens will unite with us in congratulating the bride, whose previous misfortunes have only increased the respect in which she is held. If all remember the obscure death of her first husband (though the body was not found, there has never been a doubt of his death), and the subsequent discovery that he had embezzled trust-moneys to the extent of twenty-five thousand dollars, thereby setting the final seal of shame upon a misspent life, destined for brilliant and powerful uses, all have conspired to forget the association of our beautiful and admired townswoman with his career.

It is painful to refer to these circumstances, but it is only within the past few days that the estate of the misguided man has been wound up, and the money he embezzled restored to its rightful owners; and it is better to make these remarks now than repeat them in the future, only to arouse painful memories in quarters where we should least desire to wound.

"In her new life, blessed by a romantic devotion known and admired by all, Mrs. Fairing and her husband will be followed by the affectionate good wishes of the whole community."

The man on the hearth-stone shrank back at the sight of the still, white face, in which the eyes were like sparks of fire. His impulse had been to go over and offer the hand of sympathy to the stricken man, but his simple mind grasped the fact that no one might, with impunity, invade this awful quiet. Charley was frozen in body, but his brain was awake with the heat of "a burning fiery furnace."

Seven months of unconscious life-seven months of silence—no sight, no seeing, no knowing; seven months of oblivion, in which the world had buried him out of ken in an unknown grave of infamy! Seven months—and Kathleen was married again to the man she had always loved. To the world he himself was a rogue and thief. Billy had remained silent—Billy, whom he had so befriended, had let decent men heap scorn and reproaches on his memory. Here was what the world thought of him—he read the lines over again, his eyes scorching, but his finger steady, as it traced the lines slowly: "the obscure death..." "embezzled trustmoneys..." "the final seal of shame upon a misspent life!"

These were the epitaphs on the tombstone of Charley Steele; dead and buried, out of sight, out of repute, soon to be out of mind and out of memory, save as a warning to others—an old example raked out of the dust-bin of time by the scavengers of morality, to toss at all who trod the paths of dalliance.

What was there to do? Go back? Go back and knock at Kathleen's door, another Enoch Arden, and say: "I have come to my own again?" Return and tell Tom Fairing to go his way and show his face no more? Break up this union, this marriage of love in which these two rejoiced? Summon Kathleen out of her illegal intercourse with the man who had been true to her all these years?

To what end? What had he ever done for her that he might destroy her now? What sort of Spartan tragedy was this, that the woman who had been the victim of circumstances, who had been the slave to a tie he never felt, yet which had been as iron-bound to her, should now be brought out to be mangled body and soul for no fault of her own? What had she done? What had she ever done to give him right to touch so much as a hair of her head?

Go back, and bring Billy to justice, and clear his own name? Go back, and send Kathleen's brother, the forger, to jail? What an achievement in justice! Would not the world have a right to say that the only decent thing he could do was to eliminate himself from the equation? What profit for him in the great summing-up, that he was technically innocent of this one thing, and that to establish his innocence he broke a woman's heart and destroyed a boy's life? To what end! It was the murderer coming back as a ghost to avenge himself for being hanged. Suppose he went back—the death's-head at the feast—what would there be for himself afterwards; for any one for whom he was responsible? Living at that price?

To die and end it all, to disappear from this petty life where he had done so little, and that little ill? To die?

No. There was in him some deep, if obscure, fatalism after all. If he had been meant to die now, why had he not gone to the bottom of the river that yesterday at the Cote Dorion? Why had he been saved by this yokel at the fire, and brought here to lie in oblivion in this mountain hut, wrapped in silence and lost to the world? Why had his brain and senses lain fallow all these months, a vacuous vegetation, an empty consciousness? Was it fate? Did it not seem probable that the Great Machine had, in its automatic movement, tossed him up again on the shores of Time because he had not fallen on the trap-door predestined for his eternal exit?

It was clear to him that death by his own hand was futile, and that if there were trap-doors set for him alone, it were well to wait until he trod upon them and fell through in his appointed hour in the movement of the Great Machine.

What to do—where to live—how to live?

He got slowly to his feet and took a step forward half blindly. The man on the bench stirred. Crossing the room he dropped a hand on the man's shoulder. "Open the blind, my friend."

Jo Portugais got to his feet quickly, eyes averted—he did not dare look into Charley's face—and went over and drew back the deer-skin blind. The clear, crisp sunlight of a frosty morning broke gladly into the room. Charley turned and blew out the candle on the table where he had eaten, then walked feebly to the window. Standing on the crest of the mountain the hut looked down through a clearing, flanked by forest trees.

It was a goodly scene. The green and frosted foliage of the pines and cedars; the flowery tracery of frost hanging like cobwebs everywhere; the poudre sparkle in the air; the hills of silver and emerald sloping down to the valley miles away, where the village clustered about the great old parish church; the smoke from a hundred chimneys, in purple spirals, rising straight up in the windless air; over all peace and a perfect silence.

Charley mechanically fixed his eye-glass and stood with hands resting on the window-sill, looking, looking out upon a new world.

At length he turned.

"Is there anything I can do for you, M'sieu'?" said Jo huskily.

Charley held out his hand and clasped Jo's. "Tell me about all these months," he said.

CHAPTER XII
THE COMING OF ROSALIE

Charley Steele saw himself as he had been through the eyes of another. He saw the work that he had done in the carpentering shed, and had no memory of it. The real Charley Steele had been enveloped in oblivion for seven months. During that time a mild phantom of himself had wandered, as it were in a somnambulistic dream, through the purlieus of life. Open-eyed, but with the soul asleep, all idiosyncrasy laid aside, all acquired impressions and influences vanished, he had been walking in the world with no more complexity of mind than a new-born child, nothing intervening between the sight of the eyes and the original sense.

Now, when the real Charley Steele emerged again, the folds of mind and soul unrolling to the million-voiced creation and touched by the antenna of a various civilisation, the phantom Charley was gone once more into obscurity. The real Charley could remember naught of the other, could feel naught, save, as in the stirring industrious day, one remembers that he has dreamed a strange dream the night before, and cannot recall it, though the overpowering sense of it remains.

He saw the work of his hands, the things he had made with adze and plane, with chisel and hammer, but nothing seemed familiar save the smell of the glue pot, which brought back in a cloudy impression curious unfamiliar feelings. Sights, sounds, motions, passed in a confused way through his mind as the smell of the glue crept through his nostrils; and he struggled hard to remember. But no—seven months of his life were gone for ever. Yet he knew and felt that a vast change had gone over him, had passed through him. While the soul had lain fallow, while the body had been growing back to childlike health again, and Nature had been pouring into his sick senses her healing balm; while the medicaments of peace and sleep and quiet labour had been having their way with him, he had been reorganised, renewed, flushed of the turgid silt of dissipation. For his sins and weaknesses there had been no gall and vinegar to drink.

As Charley stood looking round the workshop, Jo entered, shaking the snow from his moccasined feet. "The Cure, M'sieu' Loisel, has come," he said. Charley turned, and, without a word, followed Jo into the house. There, standing at the window and looking down at the village beneath, was the Cure. As Charley entered, M. Loisel came forward with outstretched hand.

"I am glad to see you well again, Monsieur," he said, and his cool thin hand held Charley's for a moment, as he looked him benignly in the eye.

With a kind of instinct as to the course he must henceforth pursue, Charley replied simply, dropping his eye-glass as he met that clear soluble look of the priest—such a well of simplicity he had never before seen. Only naked eye could meet that naked eye, imperfect though his own sight was.

"It is good of you to feel so, and to come and tell me so," he answered quietly. "I have been a great trouble, I know."

There was none of the old pose in his manner, none of the old cryptic quality in his words.

"We were anxious for your sake—and for the sake of your friends, Monsieur."

Charley evaded the suggestion. "I cannot easily repay your kindness and that of Jo Portugais, my good friend here," he rejoined.

"M'sieu'," replied Jo, his face turned away, and his foot pushing a log on the fire, "you have repaid it."

Charley shook his head. "I am in a conspiracy of kindness," he said. "It is all a mystery to me. For why should one expect such treatment from strangers, when, besides all, one can never make any real return, not even to pay for board and lodging!"

"'I was a stranger and ye took me in,'" said the Cure, smiling by no means sentimentally. "So said the Friend of the World."

Charley looked the Curb steadily in the eyes. He was thinking how simply this man had said these things; as if, indeed, they were part of his life; as though it were usual speech with him, a something that belonged, not an acquired language. There was the old impulse to ask a question, and he put the monocle to his eye, but his lips did not open, and the eye-glass fell again. He had seen familiarity with sacred names and things in the uneducated, in excited revivalists, worked up to a state clairvoyant and conversational with the Creator; but he had never heard an educated man speak as this man did.

At last Charley said: "Your brother—Portugais tells me that your brother, the surgeon, has gone away. I should have liked to thank him—if no more."

"I have written him of your good recovery. He will be glad, I know. But my brother, from one stand-point—a human stand-point—had scruples. These I did not share, but they were strong in him, Monsieur. Marcel asked himself—" He stopped suddenly and looked towards Jo.

Charley saw the look, and said quickly: "Speak plainly. Portugais is my friend."

Jo turned slowly towards him, and a light seemed to come to his eyes—a shining something that resolved itself into a dog-like fondness, an utter obedience, a strange intense gratitude.

"Marcel asked himself," the Cure continued, "whether you would thank him for bringing you back to—to life and memory. I fear he was trying to see what I should say—I fear so. Marcel said, 'Suppose that he should curse me for it? Who knows what he would be brought back to—to what suffering and pain, perhaps?' Marcel said that."

"And you replied, Monsieur le Cure?"

"I replied that Nature required you to answer that question for yourself, and whether bitterly or gladly, it was your duty to take up your life and live it out. Besides, it was not you alone that had to be considered. One does not live alone or die alone in this world. There were your friends to consider."

"And because I had no friends here, you were compelled to think for me!" answered Charley calmly. "Truth is, it was not a question of my friends, for what I was during those seven months, or what I am now, can make no difference to them."

He looked the Cure in the eyes steadily, and as though he would convey his intentions without words. The Curb understood. The habit of listening to the revelations of the human heart had given him something of that clairvoyance which can only be pursued by the primitive mind, unvexed by complexity.

"It is, then, as though you had not come to life again? It is as though you had no past, Monsieur?"

"It is that, Monsieur."

Jo suddenly turned and left the room, for he heard a step on the frosty snow without.

"You will remain here, Monsieur?" said the Cure. "I cannot tell."

The Cure had the bravery of simple souls with a duty to perform. He fastened his eyes on Charley. "Monsieur, is there any reason why you should not stay here? I ask it now, man to man—not as a priest of my people, but as man to man."

Charley did not answer for a moment. He was wondering how he should put his reply. But his look did not waver, and the Cure saw the honesty of the gaze. At length he replied: "If you mean, have I committed any crime which the law may punish?—I answer no, Monsieur. If you mean, have I robbed or killed, or forged—or wronged a woman as men wrong women? No. These, I take it, are the things that matter first. For the rest, you can think of me as badly as you will, or as well, for what I do henceforth is the only thing that really concerns the world, Monsieur le Cure."

The Cure came forward and put out his hand with a kindly gesture. "Monsieur, you have suffered," he said.

"Never, never at all, Monsieur. Never for a moment, until I was dropped down here like a stone from a sling. I had life by the throat; now it has me there—that is all."

"You are not a Catholic, Monsieur?" asked the priest, almost pleadingly, and as though the question had been much on his mind.

"No, Monsieur."

The Cure made no rejoinder. If he was not a Catholic, what matter what he was? If he was not a Catholic, were he Buddhist, pagan, or Protestant, the position for them personally was the same. "I am very sorry," he said gently. "I might have helped you had you been a Catholic."

The eye-glass came like lightning to the eye, and a caustic, questioning phrase was on the tongue, but Charley stopped himself in time. For, apart from all else, this priest had been his friend in calamity, had acted with a charming sensibility. The eye-glass troubled the Cure, and the look on Charley's face troubled him still more, but it passed as Charley said, in a voice as simple as the Cure's own:

"You may still help me as you have already done. I give you my word, too"—strange that he touched his lips with his tongue as he did in the old days when his mind turned to Jean Jolicoeur's saloon—"that I will do nothing to cause regret for your humanity and—and Christian kindness." Again the tongue touched the lips—a wave of the old life had swept over him, the old thirst had rushed upon him. Perhaps it was the force of this feeling which made him add, with a curious energy, "I give you my word, Monsieur le Cure." At that moment the door opened and Jo entered.

"M'sieu'," he said to Charley, "a registered parcel has come for you. It has been brought by the postmaster's daughter. She will give it to no one but yourself."

Charley's face paled, and the Cure's was scarcely less pale. In Charley's mind was the question, Who had discovered his presence here? Was he not, then, to escape? Who should send him parcels through the post?

The Cure was perturbed. Was he, then, to know who this man was—his name and history? Was the story of his life now to be told?

Charley broke the silence. "Tell the girl to come in." Instantly afterwards the postmaster's daughter entered. The look of the girl's face, at once delicate and rosy with health, almost put the question of the letter out of his mind for an instant. Her dark eyes met his as he came forward with outstretched hand.

"This is addressed, as you will see, 'To the Sick Man at the House of Jo Portugais, at Vadrome Mountain.' Are you that person, Monsieur?" she asked.

As she handed the parcel, Charley's eyes scanned her face quickly. How did this habitant girl come by this perfect French accent, this refined manner? He did not know the handwriting on the parcel; he hastily tore it open. Inside were a few dozen small packets. Here also was a sheet of paper. He opened and read it quickly. It said:

Monsieur, I am not sure that you have recovered your memory and your
health, and I am also not sure that in such case you will thank me
for my work. If you think I have done you an injury, pray accept my
profound apologies. Monsieur, you have been a drunkard. If you
would reverse the record now, these powders, taken at opportune
moments, will aid you. Monsieur, with every expression of my good-
will, and the hope that you will convey to me without reserve your
feelings on this delicate matter, I append my address in Paris, and
I have the honour to subscribe myself, with high consideration,
Monsieur, yours faithfully,
MARCEL LOISEL.

The others looked at him with varied feelings as he read. Curiosity, inquiry, expectation, were common to them all, but with each was a different personal feeling. The Cure's has been described. Jo Portugais' mind was asking if this meant that the man who had come into his life must now go out of it; and the girl was asking who was this mysterious man, like none she had ever seen or known.

Without hesitation Charley handed over the letter to the Cure, who took it with surprise, read it with amazement, and handed it back with a flush on his face.

"Thank you," said Charley to the girl. "It is good of you to bring it all this way. May I ask—"

"She is Mademoiselle Rosalie Evanturel," said the Cure smiling.

"I am Charles Mallard," said Charley slowly. "Thank you. I will go now, Monsieur Mallard," the girl said, lifting her eyes to his face. He bowed. As she turned and went towards the door her eyes met his. She blushed.

"Wait, Mademoiselle; I will go back with you," said the Cure kindly. He turned to Charley and held out his hand. "God be with you, Monsieur— Charles," he said. "Come and see me soon." Remembering that his brother had written that the man was a drunkard, his eyes had a look of pity. This was the man's own secret and his. It was a way to the man's heart; he would use it.

As the two went out of the door, the girl looked back. Charley was putting the surgeon's letter into the fire, and did not see her; yet she blushed again.

CHAPTER XIII
HOW CHARLEY WENT ADVENTURING
AND WHAT HE FOUND

A week passed. Charley's life was running in a tiny circle, but his mind was compassing large revolutions. The events of the last few days had cut deep. His life had been turned upside down. All his predispositions had been suddenly brought to check, his habits turned upon the flank and routed, his mental postures flung into confusion. He had to start life again; but it could not be in the way of any previous travel of mind or body. The line of cleavage was sharp and wide, and the only connection with the past was in the long-reaching influence of evil habits, which crept from their coverts, now and again, to mock him as his old self had mocked life—to mock him and to tempt him. Through seven months of healthy life for his body, while brain and will were sleeping, the whole man had made long strides towards recreation. But with the renewal of will and mind the old weaknesses, roused by memory, began to emerge intermittently, as water rises from a spring. There was something terrible in this repetition of sensation—the law of habit answering to the machine-like throbbing of memory, as, a kaleidoscope turning, turning, its pictures pass a certain point at fixed intervals—an automatic recurrence. He found himself at times touching his lips with his tongue, and with this act came the dry throat, the hot eye, the restless hand feeling for a glass that eluded his fingers.

Twice in one week did this fever surge up in him, and it caught him in those moments when, exhausted by the struggle of his mind to adapt itself to the new conditions, his senses were delicately susceptible. Visions of Jolicoeur's saloon came to his mind's eye. With a singular separateness, a new-developed dual sense, he saw himself standing in the summer heat, looking over to the cool dark doorway of the saloon, and he caught again the smell of the fresh-drawn beer. He was conscious of watching himself do this and that, of seeing himself move here and there. He began to look upon Charley Steele as a man he had known—he, Charles Mallard, had known— while he had to suffer for what Charley Steele had done. Then, all at once, as he was thinking and dreaming and seeing, there would seize upon him the old appetite, coincident with the seizure of his brain by the old sense of cynicism at its worst—such a worst as had made him insult Jake Hough when the rough countryman was ready to take his part that wild night at the Cote Dorion.

At such moments life became a conflict—almost a terror—for as yet he had not swung into line with the new order of things. In truth, there was no order of things; for one life was behind him and the new one was not yet decided upon, save that here he would stay—here out of the world, out of the game, far from old associations, cut off, and to be for ever cut off, from all that he had ever known or seen or felt or loved!... Loved! When did he ever love? If love was synonymous with unselfishness, with the desire to give greater than the desire to get, then he had never known love. He realised now that he had given Kathleen only what might be given across a dinner-table—the sensuous tribute of a temperament, passionate without true passion or faith or friendship. Kathleen had known that he gave her nothing worth the having; for in some meagre sense she knew what love was, and had given it meagrely, after her nature, to another man, preserving meanwhile the letter of the law, respecting that bond which he had shamed by his excesses.

Kathleen was now sitting at another man's table—no, probably at his own table—his, Charley Steele's own table in his own house—the house he had given her by deed of gift the day he died. Tom Fairing was sitting where he used to sit, talking across the table—not as he used to talk—looking into Kathleen's face as he had never looked. He was no more to them than a dark memory. "Well, why should I be more?" he asked himself. "I am dead, if not buried. They think me down among the fishes. My game is done; and when she gets older and understands life better, Kathleen will say, 'Poor Charley—he might have been anything!' She'll be sure to say that some day, for habit and memory go round in a circle and pass the same point again and again. For me—they take me by the throat—" He put his hand up as if to free his throat from a grip, his tongue touched his lips, his hands grew restless.

"It comes back on me like a fit of ague, this miserable thirst. If I were within sight of Jolicoeur's saloon, I should be drinking hard this minute. But I'm here, and—" His hand felt his pocket, and he took out the powders the great surgeon had sent him.

"He knew—how did he know that I was a drunkard? Does a man carry in his face the tale he would not tell? Jo says I didn't talk of the past, that I never had delirium, that I never said a word to suggest who I was, or where I came from. Then how did the doctor—man know? I suppose every particular habit carries its own signal, and the expert knows the ciphers." He opened the paper containing the powders, and looked round for water, then paused, folded the paper up, and put it in his pocket again. He went over to the window and looked out. His shoulders set square. "No, no, no, not a speck on my tongue!" he said. "What I can't do of my own will is not worth doing. It's too foolish, to yield to the shadow of an old appetite. I play this game alone—here in Chaudiere."

He looked out and down. The sweet sun of early spring was shining hard, and the snow was beginning to pack, to hang like a blanket on the branches, to lie like a soft coverlet over all the forest and the fields. Far away on the frozen river were saplings stuck up to show where the ice was safe—a long line of poles from shore to shore—and carioles were hurrying across to the village. Being market-day, the place was alive with the cheerful commerce of the habitant. The bell of the parish church was ringing. The sound of it came up distantly and peacefully. Charley drew a long breath, turned away to a pail of water, filled a dipper half full, and drank it off gaspingly. Then he returned to the window with a look of relief.

"That does it," he said. "The horrible thing is gone again—out of my brain and out of my throat."

As he stood there, Jo came up the hill with a bundle in his arms. Charley watched him for a moment, half whimsically, half curiously. Yet he sighed once too as Portugais opened the door and came into the room. "Well done, Jo!" said he. "You have 'em?"

"Yes, M'sieu'. A good suit, and I believe they'll fit. Old Trudel says it's the best suit he's made in a year. I'm afraid he'll not make many more suits, old Trudel.

"He's very bad. When he goes there'll be no tailor—ah, old Trudel will be missed for sure, M'sieu'!"

Jo spread the clothes out on the table—a coat, waistcoat, and trousers of fulled cloth, grey and bulky, and smelling of the loom and the tailor's iron. Charley looked at them interestedly, then glanced at the clothes he had on, the suit that had belonged to him last year—grave-clothes.

He drew himself up as though rousing from a dream. "Come, Jo, clear out, and you shall have your new habitant in a minute," he said. Portugais left the room, and when he came back, Charley was dressed in the suit of grey fulled cloth. It was loose, but comfortable, and save for the refined face—on which a beard was growing now—and the eye-glass, he might easily have passed for a farmer. When he put on the dog-skin fur cap and a small muffler round his neck, it was the costume of the habitant complete.

Yet it was no disguise, for it was part of the life that Charles Mallard, once Charley Steele, should lead henceforth.

He turned to the door and opened it. "Good-bye, Portugais," he said.

Jo was startled. "Where are you going, M'sieu'?"

"To the village."

"What to do, M'sieu'?"

"Who knows?"

"You will come back?" Jo asked anxiously.

"Before sundown, Jo. Good-bye!"

This was the first long walk he had taken since he had become himself again. The sweet, cold air, with a bracing wind in his face, gave peace to the nerves but now strained and fevered in the fight with appetite. His mind cleared, and he drank in the sunny air and the pungent smell of the balsams. His feet light with moccasins, he even ran a distance, enjoying the glow from a fast-beating pulse.

As he came into the high-road, people passed him in carioles and sleighs. Some eyed him curiously. What did he mean to do? What object had he in coming to the village? What did he expect? As he entered the village his pace slackened. He had no destination, no object. He was simply aware that his new life was beginning.

He passed a little house on which was a sign, "Narcisse Dauphin, Notary." It gave him a curious feeling. It was the old life before him. "Charles Mallard, Notary?"—No, that was not for him. Everything that reminded him of the past, that brought him in touch with it, must be set aside. He moved on. Should he go to the Cure? No; one thing at a time, and today he wanted his thoughts for himself. More people passed him, and spoke of him to each other, though there was no coarse curiosity—the habitant has manners.

Presently he passed a low shop with a divided door. The lower half was closed, the upper open, and the winter sun was shining full into the room, where a bright fire burned.

Charley looked up. Over the door was painted, in straggling letters: "Louis Trudel, Tailor." He looked inside. There, on a low table, bent over his work, with a needle in his hand, sat Louis Trudel the tailor. Hearing footsteps, feeling a shadow, he looked up. Charley started at the look of the shrunken, yellow face; for if ever death had set his seal, it was on that haggard parchment. The tailor's yellow eyes ran from Charley's face to his clothes.

"I knew they'd fit," he said, with a snarl. "Drove me hard, too!"

Charley had an inspiration. He opened the halfdoor, and entered.

"Do you want help?" he said, fixing his eyes on the tailor's, steady and persistent.

"What's the good of wanting—I can't get it," was the irritable reply, as he uncrossed his legs.

Charley took the iron out of his hand. "I'll press, if you'll show me how," he said.

"I don't want a fiddling ten-minutes' help like that."

"It isn't fiddling. I'm going to stay, if you think I'll do."

"You are going to stop-every day?" The old man's voice quavered a little.

"Precisely that." Charley wetted a seam with water as he had often seen tailors do. He dropped the hot iron on the seam, and sniffed with satisfaction.

"Who are you?" said the tailor.

"A man who wants work. The Cure knows. It's all right. Shall I stay?"

The tailor nodded, and sat down with a colour in his face.

CHAPTER XIV
ROSALIE, CHARLEY, AND THE MAN THE WIDOW PLOMONDON JILTED

From the moment there came to the post-office the letter addressed to "The Sick Man at the House of Jo Portugais at Vadrome Mountain," Rosalie Evanturel dreamed dreams. Mystery, so fascinating a thing in all the experiences of life, took hold of her. The strange man in the lonely hut on the hill, the bandaged head, the keen, piercing blue eyes, the monocle, like a masked battery of the mind, levelled at her—all appealed to that life she lived apart from the people with whom she had daily commerce. Her world was a world of books and dreams, and simple, practical duties of life. Most books were romance to her, for most were of a life to which she had not been educated. Even one or two purely Protestant books of missionary enterprise, found in a box in her dead mother's room, had had all the charms of poetry and adventure. It was all new, therefore all delightful, even when the Protestant sentiments shocked her as being not merely untrue, but hurting that aesthetic sense never remote from the mind of the devout Catholic.

She had blushed when monsieur had first looked at her, in the hut on Vadrome Mountain, not because there was any soft sentiment about him in her heart—how could there be for a man she had but just seen!—but because her feelings, her imagination, were all at high temperature; because the man compelled attention. The feeling sprang from a deep sensibility, a natural sense, not yet made incredulous by the ironies of life. These had never presented themselves to her in a country, in a parish, where people said of fortune and misfortune, happiness and sorrow, "C'est le bon Dieu!"— always "C'est le bon Dieu!"

In some sense it was a pity that she had brains above the ordinary, that she had had a good education and nice tastes. It was the cultivation of the primitive and idealistic mind, which could not rationalise a sense of romance, of the altruistic, by knowledge of life. As she sat behind the post-office counter she read all sorts of books that came her way. When she learned English so as to read it almost as easily as she read French, her greatest joy was to pore over Shakespeare, with a heart full of wonder, and, very often, eyes full of tears—so near to the eyes of her race. Her imagination inhabited Chaudiere with a different folk, living in homes very unlike these wide, sweeping-roofed structures, with double windows and clean-scrubbed steps, tall doors, and wide, uncovered stoops. Her people— people of bright dreaming—were not quarrelsome, or childish, or merely traditional, like the habitants. They were picturesque and able and simple, doing good things in disguise, succouring distress, yielding their lives without thought for a cause, or a woman, and loving with an undying love.

Charley was of these people—from the first instant she saw him. The Cure, the Avocat, and the Seigneur were also of them, but placidly, unimportantly. "The Sick Man at Jo Portugais' House" came out of a mysterious distance. Something in his eyes said, "I have seen, I have known," told her that when he spoke she would answer freely, that they were kinsfolk in some hidden way. Her nature was open and frank; she lived upon the house-tops, as it were, going in and out of the lives of the people of Chaudiere with neighbourly sympathy and understanding. Yet she knew that she was not of them, and they knew that, poor as she was, in her veins flowed the blood of the old nobility of France. For this the Cure could vouch. Her official position made her the servant of the public, and she did her duty with naturalness.

She had been a figure in the parish ever since the day she returned from the convent at Quebec, and took her dead mother's place in the home and the parish. She had a quick temper, but there was not a cheerless note in her nature, and there was scarce a dog or a horse in the parish but knew her touch, and responded to it. Squirrels ate out of her hand, she had even tamed two partridges, and she kept in her little garden a bear she had brought up from a cub. Her devotion to her crippled father was in keeping with her quick response to every incident of sorrow or joy in the parish—only modified by wilful prejudices scarcely in keeping with her unselfishness.

As Mrs. Flynn, the Seigneur's Irish cook, said of her: "Shure, she's not made all av wan piece, the darlin'! She'll wear like silk, but she's not linen for everybody's washin'." And Mrs. Flynn knew a thing or two, as was conceded by all in Chaudiere. No gossip was Mrs. Flynn, but she knew well what was going on in the parish, and she had strong views upon all subjects, and a special interest in the welfare of two people in Chaudiere. One of these was the Seigneur, who, when her husband died, leaving behind him a name for wit and neighbourliness, and nothing else, proposed that she should come to be his cook. In spite of her protest that what was "fit for Teddy was not fit for a gintleman of quality," the Seigneur had had his way, never repenting of his choice. Mrs. Flynn's cooking was not her only good point. She had the rarest sense and an unfailing spring of good-nature—life bubbled round her. It was she that had suggested the crippled M. Evanturel to the Seigneur when the office of postmaster became vacant, and the Seigneur had acted on her suggestion, henceforth taking greater interest in Rosalie.

It was Mrs. Flynn who gave Rosalie information concerning Charley's arrival at the shop of Louis Trudel the tailor. The morning after Charley came, Mrs. Flynn had called for a waistcoat of the Seigneur, who was expected home from a visit to Quebec. She found Charley standing at a table pressing seams, and her quick eye took him in with knowledge and instinct. She was the one person, save Rosalie, who could always divert old Louis, and this morning she puckered his sour face with amusement by the story of the courtship of the widow Plomondon and Germain Boily the horse-trainer, whose greatest gift was animal-training, and greatest weakness a fondness for widows, temporary and otherwise. Before she left the shop, with the stranger's smile answering to her nod, she had made up her mind that Charley was a tailor by courtesy only. So she told Rosalie a few moments afterwards.

"'Tis a man, darlin', that's seen the wide wurruld. 'Tis himisperes he knows, not parrishes. Fwhat's he doin' here, I dun'no'. Fwhere's he come from, I dun'no'. French or English, I dun'no'. But a gintleman born, I know. 'Tis no tailor, darlin', but tailorin' he'll do as aisy as he'll do a hunderd other things anny day. But how he shlipped in here, an' when he shlipped in here, an' what's he come for, an' how long he's stayin', an' meanin' well, or doin' ill, I dun'no', darlin', I dun' no'."

"I don't think he'll do ill, Mrs. Flynn," said Rosalie, in English.

"An' if ye haven't seen him, how d'ye know?" asked Mrs. Flynn, taking a pinch of snuff.

"I have seen him—but not in the tailor-shop. I saw him at Jo Portugais' a fortnight ago."

"Aisy, aisy, darlin'. At Jo Portugais'—that's a quare place for a stranger. 'Tis not wid Jo's introducshun I'd be comin' to Chaudiere."

"He comes with the Cure's introduction."

"An' how d'ye know that, darlin'?"

"The Curb was at Jo Portugais' with monsieur when I went there."

"You wint there!"

"To take him a letter—the stranger." "What's his name, darlin'?"

"The letter I took him was addressed, 'To the Sick Man at Jo Portugais' House at Vadrome Mountain.'"

"Ah, thin, the Cure knows. 'Tis some rich man come to get well, and plays at bein' tailor. But why didn't the letther come to his name, I wander now? That's what I wander."

Rosalie shook her head, and looked reflectively through the window towards the tailor-shop.

"How manny times have ye seen him?"

"Only once;" answered Rosalie truthfully. She did not, however, tell Mrs. Flynn that she had thrice walked nearly to Vadrome Mountain in the hope of seeing him again; and that she had gone to her favourite resort, the Rest of the Flax-Beaters, lying in the way of the riverpath from Vadrome Mountain, on the chance of his passing. She did not tell Mrs. Flynn that there had scarcely been a waking hour when she had not thought of him.

"What Portugais knows, he'll not be tellin'," said Mrs. Flynn, after a moment. "An' 'tis no business of ours, is it, darlin'? Shure, there's Jo comin' out of the tailor-shop now!"

They both looked out of the window, and saw Jo encounter Filion Lacasse the saddler, and Maximilian Cour the baker. The three stood in the middle of the street for a minute, Jo talking freely. He was usually morose and taciturn, but now he spoke as though eager to unburden his mind— Charley and he had agreed upon what should be said to the people of Chaudiere.

The sight of the confidences among the three was too much for Mrs. Flynn. She opened the door of the post office and called to Jo. "Like three crows shtandin' there!" she said. "Come in—ma'm'selle says come in, and tell your tales here, if they're fit to hear, Jo Portugais. Who are you to say no when ma'm'selle bids!" she added.

Very soon afterwards Jo was inside the post-office, telling his tale with the deliberation of a lesson learned by heart.

"It's all right, as ma'm'selle knows," he said. "The Cure was there when ma'm'selle brought a letter to M'sieu' Mallard. The Cure knows all. M'sieu' come to my house sick-and he stayed there. There is nothing like the pine-trees and the junipers to cure some things. He was with me very quiet some time. The Cure come and come. He knows. When m'sieu' got well, he say, 'I will not go from Chaudiere; I will stay. I am poor, and I will earn my bread here.' At first, when he is getting well, he is carpent'ring. He makes cupboards and picture-frames. The Cure has one of the cupboards in the sacristy; the frames he puts on the Stations of the Cross in the church."

"That's good enough for me!" said Maximilian Cour. "Did he make them for nothing?" asked Filion Lacasse solemnly.

"Not one cent did he ask. What's more, he's working for Louis Trudel for nothing. He come through the village yesterday; he see Louis old and sick on his bench, and he set down and go to work."

"That's good enough for me," said the saddler. "If a man work for the Church for nothing, he is a Christian. If he work for Louis Trudel for nothing, he is a fool—first-class—or a saint. I wouldn't work for Louis Trudel if he give me five dollars a day."

"Tiens! the man that work for Louis Trudel work for the Church, for all old Louis makes goes to the Church in the end—that is his will. The Notary knows," said Maximilian Cour.

"See there, now," interposed Mrs. Flynn, pointing across the street to the tailor-shop. "Look at that grocer-man stickin' in his head; and there's Magloire Cadoret and that pig of a barber, Moise Moisan, starin' through the dure, an'—"

As she spoke, the barber and his companion suddenly turned their faces to the street, and started forward with startled exclamations, the grocer following. They all ran out from the post-office. Not far up the street a crowd was gathering. Rosalie locked the office-door and followed the others quickly.

In front of the Hotel Trois Couronnes a painful thing was happening. Germain Boily, the horse-trainer, fresh from his disappointment with the widow Plomondon, had driven his tamed moose up to the Trois Couronnes, and had drunk enough whiskey to make him ill-tempered. He had then begun to "show off" the animal, but the savage instincts of the moose being roused, he had attacked his master, charging with wide-branching horns, and striking with his feet. Boily was too drunk to fight intelligently. He went down under the hoofs of the enraged animal, as his huge boarhound, always with him, fastened on the moose's throat, dragged him to the ground, and tore gaping wounds in his neck.

It was all the work of a moment. People ran from the doorways and sidewalks, but stayed at a comfortable distance until the moose was dragged down; then they made to approach the insensible man. Before any one could reach him, however, the great hound, with dripping fangs, rushed to his master's body, and, standing over it, showed his teeth savagely. The hotel-keeper approached, but the bristles of the hound stood up, he prepared to attack, and the landlord drew back in haste. Then M. Dauphin, the Notary, who had joined the crowd, held out a hand coaxingly, and with insinuating rhetoric drew a little nearer than the landlord had done; but he retreated precipitously as the hound crouched back for a spring. Some one called for a gun, and Filion Lacasse ran into his shop. The animal had now settled down on his master's body, his bloodshot eyes watching in menace. The one chance seemed to be to shoot him, and there must be no bungling, lest his prostrate master suffer at the same time. The crowd had melted away into the houses, and were now standing at doorways and windows, ready for instant retreat.

Filion Lacasse's gun was now at disposal, but who would fire it? Jo Portugais was an expert shot, and he reached out a hand for the weapon.

As he did so, Rosalie Evanturel cried: "Wait, oh, wait!" Before any one could interfere she moved along the open space to the mad beast, speaking soothingly, and calling his name.

The crowd held their breath. A woman fainted. Some wrung their hands, and Jo Portugais, with blanched face, stood with gun half raised. With assured kindness of voice and manner, Rosalie walked deliberately over to the hound. At first the animal's bristles came up, and he prepared to spring, but murmuring to him, she held out her hand, and presently laid it on his huge head. With a growl of subjection, the dog drew from the body of his master, and licked Rosalie's fingers as she knelt beside Boily and felt his heart. She put her arm round the dog's neck, and said to the crowd, "Some one come—only one—ah, yes, you, Monsieur!" she added, as Charley, who had just arrived on the scene, came forward. "Only you, if you can lift him. Take him to my house."

Her arm still round the dog, she talked to him, as Charley came forward, and, lifting up the body of the little horse-trainer, drew him across his shoulder. The hound at first resented the act, but under Rosalie's touch became quiet, and followed at their heels towards the post-office, licking the wounded man's hands as they hung down. Inside M. Evanturel's house the injured man was laid upon a couch. Charley examined his wounds, and, finding them severe, advised that the Cure be sent for, while he and Jo Portugais set about restoring him to consciousness. Jo had skill of a sort, and his crude medicaments were efficacious.

When the Cure came, the injured man was handed over to his care, and he arranged that in the evening Boily should be removed to his house, to await the arrival of the doctor from the next parish.

This was Charley's public introduction to the people of Chaudiere, and it was his second meeting with Rosalie Evanturel.

The incident brought him into immediate prominence. Before he left the post-office, Filion Lacasse, Maximilian Cour, and Mrs. Flynn had given forth his history, as related by Jo Portugais. The village was agog with excitement.

But attention was not centred on himself, for Rosalie's courage had set the parish talking. When the Notary stood on the steps of the saddler's shop, and with fine rhetoric proposed a vote of admiration for the girl, the cheering could be heard inside the post-office, and it brought Mrs. Flynn outside.

"'Tis for her, the darlin'—for Ma'm'selle Rosalie—they're splittin' their throats!" she said to Charley as he was making his way from the sick man's room to the street door. "Did ye iver see such an eye an' hand? That avil baste that's killed two Injins already—an' all the men o' the place sneakin' behind dures, an' she walkin' up cool as leaf in mornin' dew, an' quietin' the divil's own! Did ye iver see annything like it, sir—you that's seen so much?"

"Madame, it is not touch of hand alone, or voice alone," answered Charley.

"Shure, 'tis somethin' kin in baste an' maid, you're manin' thin?"

"Quite so, Madame."

"Simple like, an' understandin' what Noah understood in that ark av his—for talk to the bastes he must have, explainin' what was for thim to do."

"Like that, Madame."

"Thrue for you, sir, 'tis as you say. There's language more than tongue of man can shpake. But listen, thin, to me"—her voice got lower—"for 'tis not the furst time, a thing like that, the lady she is—granddaughter of a Seigneur, and descinded from nobility in France! 'Tis not the furst time to be doin' brave things. Just a shlip of a girl she was, three years ago, afther her mother died, an' she was back from convint. A woman come to the parish an' was took sick in the house of her brother—from France she was. Small-pox they said at furst. 'Twas no small-pox, but plague, got upon the seas. Alone she was in the house—her brother left her alone, the black-hearted coward. The people wouldn't go near the place. The Cure was away. Alone the woman was—poor soul! Who wint—who wint and cared for her? Who do ye think, sir?"

"Mademoiselle?"

"None other. 'Go tell Mrs. Flynn,' says she, 'to care for my father till I come back,' an' away she wint to the house of plague. A week she stayed, an' no one wint near her. Alone she was with the woman and the plague. 'Lave her be,' said the Cure when he come back; ''tis for the love of God. God is with her—lave her be, and pray for her,' says he. An' he wint himself, but she would not let him in. ''Tis my work,' says she. ''Tis God's work for me to do,' says she. 'An' the woman will live if 'tis God's will,' says she. 'There's an agnus dei on her breast,' says she. 'Go an' pray,' says she. Pray the Cure did, an' pray did we all, but the woman died of the plague. All alone did Rosalie draw her to the grave on a stone-boat down the lane, an' over the hill, an' into the churchyard. An' buried her with her own hands at night, no one knowin' till the mornin', she did. So it was. An' the burial over, she wint back an' burned the house to the ground—sarve the villain right that lave the sick woman alone! An' her own clothes she burned, an' put on the clothes I brought her wid me own hand. An' for that thing she did, the love o' God in her heart, is it for Widdy Flynn or Cure or anny other to forgit? Shure the Cure was for iver broken-hearted, for that he was sick abed for days an' could not go to the house when the woman died, an' say to Rosalie, 'Let me in for her last hour.' But the word of Rosalie—shure 'twas as good as the words of a praste, savin' the Cure prisince wheriver he may be!"

This was the story of Rosalie which Mrs. Flynn told Charley, as he stood at the street door of the post-office. When she had finished, Charley went back into the room where Rosalie sat beside the sick man's couch, the hound at her feet. She came forward, surprised, for he had bade her good-bye but a few minutes before.

"May I sit and watch for an hour longer, Mademoiselle?" he said. "You will have your duties in the post-office."

"Monsieur—it is good of you," she answered.

For two hours Charley watched her going in and out, whispering directions to Mrs. Flynn, doing household duty, bringing warmth in with her, and leaving light behind her.

It was afternoon when he returned to his bench in the tailor-shop, and was received by old Louis Trudel in peevish silence. For an hour they worked in silence, and then the tailor said:

"A brave girl—that. We will work till nine to-night!"

CHAPTER XV
THE MARK IN THE PAPER

Chaudiere was nearing the last of its nine-days' wonder. It had filed past the doorway of the tailor-shop; it had loitered on the other side of the street; it had been measured for more clothes than in three months past—that it might see Charley at work in the shop, cross-legged on a bench, or wielding the goose, his eye glass in his eye. Here was sensation indeed, for though old M. Rossignol, the Seigneur, had an eye-glass, it was held to his eye—a large bone-bound thing with a little gold handle; but no one in Chaudiere had ever worn a glass in his eye like that. Also, no one in Chaudiere had ever looked quite like "M'sieu'"—for so it was that, after the first few days (a real tribute to his importance and sign of the interest he created) Charley came to be called "M'sieu'," and the Mallard was at last entirely dropped.

Presently people came and stood at the tailor's door and talked, or listened to Louis Trudel and M'sieu' talking. And it came to be noised abroad that the stranger talked as well as the Cure and better than the Notary. By-and-by they associated his eye-glass with his talent, so that it seemed, as it were, to be the cause of it. Yet their talk was ever of simple subjects, of everyday life about them, now and then of politics, occasionally of the events of the world filtered to them through vast tracts of country. There was one subject which, however, was barred; perhaps because there was knowledge abroad that M'sieu' was not a Catholic, perhaps because Charley himself adroitly changed the conversation when it veered that way.

Though the parish had not quite made up its mind about him, there were a number of things in his favour. In the first place, the Cure seemed satisfied; secondly, he minded his own business. Also, he was working for Louis Trudel for nothing. These things Jo Portugais diligently impressed on the minds of all who would listen.

From above the frosted part of the windows of the post-office, in the corner where she sorted letters, Rosalie could look over at the tailor's shop at an angle; could sometimes even see M'sieu' standing at the long table with a piece of chalk, a pair of shears, or a measure. She watched the tailor-shop herself, but it annoyed her when she saw any one else do so. She resented—

she was a woman and loved monopoly—all inquiry regarding M'sieu', so frequently addressed to her.

One afternoon, as Charley came out, on his way to the house on Vadrome Mountain, she happened to be outside. He saw her, paused, lifted his fur cap, and crossed the street to her.

"Have you, perhaps, paper, pens, and ink for sale, Mademoiselle?"

"Yes, oh yes; come in, Monsieur Mallard."

"Ah, it is nice of you to remember me," he answered. "I see you every day—often," she answered.

"Of course, we are neighbours," he responded. "The man—the horse-trainer—is quite well again?"

"He has gone home almost well," she answered. She placed pens, paper, and ink before him. "Will these do?"

"Perfectly," he answered mechanically, and laid a few pens and a bottle of ink beside the paper.

"You were very brave that day," he said—they had not talked together since, though seeing each other so often.

"Oh, no; I knew he would make friends with me—the hound."

"Of course," he rejoined.

"We should show animals that we trust them," she said, in some confusion, for being near him made her heart throb painfully.

He did not answer. Presently his eye glanced at the paper again, and was arrested. He ran his fingers over it, and a curious look flashed across his face. He held the paper up to the light quickly, and looked through it. It was thin, half-foreign paper, without lines, and there was a water-mark in it-large, shadowy, filmy—Kathleen.

It was paper made in the mills which had belonged to Kathleen's uncle. This water-mark was made to celebrate their marriage-day. Only for one year had this paper been made, and then the trade in it was stopped. It had gone its ways down the channels of commerce, and here it was in his hand, a reminder, not only of the old life, but, as it were, the parchment for the new. There it was, a piece of plain good paper, ready for pen and ink and his letter to the Cure's brother in Paris—the only letter he would ever write, ever again until he died, so he told himself; but hold it up to the light and there was the name over which his letter must be written—Kathleen, invisible but permanent, obscured, but brought to life by the raising of a hand.

The girl caught the flash of feeling in his face, saw him holding the paper up to the light, and then, with an abstracted air, calmly lay it down.

"That will do, thank you," he said. "Give me the whole packet." She wrapped it up for him without a word, and he laid down a two-dollar note, the last he had in the world.

"How much of this paper have you?" he asked. The girl looked under the counter. "Six packets," she said. "Six, and a few sheets over."

"I will take it all. But keep it for me, for a week, or perhaps a fortnight, will you?" He did not need all this paper to write letters upon, yet he meant to buy all the paper of this sort that the shop contained. But he must get money from Louis Trudel—he would speak about it to-morrow.

"Monsieur does not want me to sell even the loose sheets?"

"No. I like the paper, and I will take it all."

"Very good, Monsieur."

Her heart was beating hard. All this man did had peculiar significance to her. His look seemed to say: "Do not fear. I will tell you things."

She gave him the parcel and the change, and he turned to go. "You read much?" he asked, almost casually, yet deeply interested in the charm and intelligence of her face.

"Why, yes, Monsieur," she answered quickly. "I am always reading."

He did not speak at once. He was wondering whether, in this primitive place, such a mind and nature would be the wiser for reading; whether it were not better to be without a mental aspiration, which might set up false standards.

"What are you reading now?" he asked, with his hand on the door.

"Antony and Cleopatra, also Enoch Arden," she answered, in good English, and without accent.

His head turned quickly towards her, but he did not speak.

"Enoch Arden is terrible," she added eagerly. "Don't you think so, Monsieur?"

"It is very painful," he answered. "Good-night." He opened the door and went out.

She ran to the door and watched him go down the street. For a little she stood thinking, then, turning to the counter, and snatching up a sheet of the paper he had bought, held it up to the light. She gave a cry of amazement.

"Kathleen!" she exclaimed.

She thought of the start he gave when he looked at the water-mark; she thought of the look on his face when he said he would buy all this paper she had.

"Who was Kathleen?" she whispered, as though she was afraid some one would hear. "Who was Kathleen!" she said again resentfully.

CHAPTER XVI
MADAME DAUPHIN HAS A MISSION

One day Charley began to know the gossip of the village about him from a source less friendly than Jo Portugais. The Notary's wife, bringing her boy to be measured for a suit of broadcloth, asked Charley if the things Jo had told about him were true, and if it was also true that he was a Protestant, and perhaps an Englishman. As yet, Charley had been asked no direct questions, for the people of Chaudiere had the consideration of their temperament; but the Notary's wife was half English, and being a figure in the place, she took to herself more privileges than did old Madame Dugal, the Cure's sister.

To her ill-disguised impertinence in English, as bad as her French and as fluent, Charley listened with quiet interest. When she had finished her voluble statement she said, with a simper and a sneer-for, after all, a Notary's wife must keep her position—"And now, what is the truth about it? And are you a Protestant?"

There was a sinister look in old Trudel's eyes as, cross-legged on his table, he listened to Madame Dauphin. He remembered the time, twenty-five years ago, when he had proposed to this babbling woman, and had been rejected with scorn—to his subsequent satisfaction; for there was no visible reason why any one should envy the Notary, in his house or out of it. Already Trudel had a respect for the tongue of M'sieu'. He had not talked much the few days he had been in the shop, but, as the old man had said to Filion Lacasse the saddler, his brain was like a pair of shears—it went clip, clip, clip right through everything. He now hoped that his new apprentice, with the hand of a master-workman, would go clip, clip through madame's inquisitiveness. He was not disappointed, for he heard Charley say:

"One person in the witness-box at a time, Madame. Till Jo Portugais is cross-examined and steps down, I don't see what I can do!"

"But you are a Protestant!" said the woman snappishly. This man was only a tailor, dressed in fulled cloth, and no doubt his past life would not bear inspection; and she was the Notary's wife, and had said to people in the village that she would find out the man's history from himself.

"That is one good reason why I should not go to confession," he replied casually, and turned to a table where he had been cutting a waistcoat—for the first time in his life.

"Do you think I'm going to stand your impertinence? Do you know who I am?"

Charley calmly put up his monocle. He looked at the foolish little woman with so cruel a flash of the eye that she shrank back.

"I should know you anywhere," he said.

"Come, Stephan," she said nervously to her boy, and pulled him towards the door.

On the instant Charley's feeling changed. Was he then going to carry the old life into the new, and rebuke a silly garish woman whose faults were generic more than personal? He hurried forward to the door and courteously opened it for her.

"Permit me, Madame," he said.

She saw that there was nothing ironical in this politeness. She had a sudden apprehension of an unusual quality called "the genteel," for no storekeeper in Chaudiere ever opened or shut a shop-door for anybody. She smiled a vacuous smile; she played "the lady" terribly, as, with a curious conception of dignity, she held her body stiff as a ramrod, and with a prim merci sailed into the street.

This gorgeous exit changed her opinion of the man she had been unable to catechise. Undoubtedly he had snubbed her—that was the word she used in her mind—but his last act had enabled her, in the sight of several habitants and even of Madame Dugal, "to put on airs," as the charming Madame Dugal said afterwards.

Thinking it better to give the impression that she had had a successful interview, she shook her head mysteriously when asked about M'sieu', and murmured, "He is quite the gentleman!" which she thought a socially distinguished remark.

When she had gone, Charley turned to old Louis.

"I don't want to turn your customers away," he said quietly, "but there it is! I don't need to answer questions as a part of the business, do I?"

There was a sour grin on the face of old Trudel. He grunted some inaudible answer, then, after a pause, added: "I'd have been hung for murder, if she'd answered the question I asked her once as I wanted her to."

He opened and shut his shears with a sardonic gesture.

Charley smiled, and went to the window. For a minute he stood watching Madame Dauphin and Rosalie at the post-office door. The memory of his talk with Rosalie was vivid to him at the moment. He was thinking also that he had not a penny in the world to pay for the rest of the paper he had bought. He turned round and put on his coat slowly.

"What are you doing that for?" asked the old man, with a kind of snarl, yet with trepidation.

"I don't think I'll work any more to-day."

"Not work! Smoke of the devil, isn't Sunday enough to play in? You're not put out by that fool wife of Dauphin's?"

"Oh no—not that! I want an understanding about wages."

To Louis the dread crisis had come. He turned a little green, for he was very miserly-for the love of God.

He had scarcely realised what was happening when Charley first sat down on the bench beside him. He had been taken by surprise. Apart from the excitement of the new experience, he had profited by the curiosity of the public, for he had orders enough to keep him busy until summer, and he had had to give out work to two extra women in the parish, though he had never before had more than one working for him. But his ruling passion was strong in him. He always remembered with satisfaction that once when the Cure was absent and he was supposed to be dying, a priest from another parish came, and, the ministrations over, he had made an offering of a gold piece. When the young priest hesitated, his fingers had crept back to the gold piece, closed on it, and drawn it back beneath the coverlet again. He had then peacefully fallen asleep. It was a gracious memory.

"I don't need much, I don't want a great deal," continued Charley when the tailor did not answer, "but I have to pay for my bed and board, and I can't do it on nothing."

"How have you done it so far?" peevishly replied the tailor.

"By working after hours at carpentering up there"—he made a gesture towards Vadrome Mountain. "But I can't go on doing that all the time, or I'll be like you too soon."

"Be like me!" The voice of the tailor rose shrilly.

"Be like me! What's the matter with me?"

"Only that you're in a bad way before your time, and that you mayn't get out of this hole without stepping into another. You work too hard, Monsieur Trudel."

"What do you want—wages?"

Charley inclined his head. "If you think I'm worth them."

The tailor viciously snipped a piece of cloth. "How can I pay you wages, if you stand there doing nothing?" "This is my day for doing nothing," Charley answered pleasantly, for the tailor-man amused him, and the whimsical mental attitude of his past life was being brought to the surface by this odd figure, with big spectacles pushed up on a yellow forehead, and shrunken hands viciously clutching the shears.

"You don't mean to say you're not going to work to-day, and this suit of clothes promised for to-morrow night—for the Manor House too!"

With a piece of chalk Charley idly made heads on brown paper. "After all, why should clothes be the first thing in one's mind—when they are some one else's! It's a beautiful day outside. I've never felt the sun so warm and the air so crisp and sweet—never in all my life."

"Then where have you lived?" snapped out the tailor with a sneer. "You must be a Yankee—they have only what we leave over down there!"—he jerked his head southward. "We don't stop to look at weather here. I suppose you did where you come from?"

Charley smiled in a distant sort of way. "Where I came from, when we weren't paid for our work we always stopped to consider our health—and the weather. I don't want a great deal. I put it to you honestly. Do you want me? If you do, will you give me enough to live on—enough to buy a suit of clothes a year, to pay for food and a room? If I work for you for nothing, I have to live on others for nothing, or kill myself as you're doing."

There was no answer at once, and Charley went on: "I came to you because I saw you wanted help badly. I saw that you were hard-pushed and sick—"

"I wasn't sick," interrupted the tailor with a snarl.

"Well, overworked, which is the same thing in the end. I did the best I could: I gave you my hands—awkward enough they were at first, I know, but—"

"It's a lie. They weren't awkward," churlishly cut in the tailor.

"Well, perhaps they weren't so awkward, but they didn't know quite what to do—"

"You knew as well as if you'd been taught," came back in a growl.

"Well, then, I wasn't awkward, and I had a knack for the work. What was more, I wanted work. I wanted to work at the first thing that appealed to me. I had no particular fancy for tailoring—you get bowlegged in time!"—the old spirit was fighting with the new—"but here you were at work, and there I was idle, and I had been ill, and some one who wasn't responsible for me—a stranger-worked for me and cared for me. Wasn't it natural, when you were playing the devil with yourself, that I should step in and give you a hand? You've been better since—isn't that so?" The tailor did not answer.

"But I can't go on as we are, though I want only enough to keep me going," Charley continued.

"And if I don't give you what you want, you'll leave?"

"No. I'm never going to leave you. I'm going to stay here, for you'll never get another man so cheap; and it suits me to stay—you need some one to look after you."

A curious soft look suddenly flashed into the tailor's eyes.

"Will you take on the business after I'm gone?" he asked at last. "It's along time to look ahead, I know," he added quickly, for not in words would he acknowledge the possibility of the end.

"I should think so," Charley answered, his eyes on the bright sun and the soft snow on the trees beyond the window.

The tailor snatched up a pattern and figured on it for a moment. Then he handed it to Charley. "Will that do?" he asked with anxious, acquisitive look, his yellow eyes blinking hard.

Charley looked at it musingly, then said "Yes, if you give me a room here."

"I meant board and lodging too," said Louis Trudel with an outburst of eager generosity, for, as it was, he had offered about one-half of what Charley was worth to him.

Charley nodded. "Very well, that will do," he said, and took off his coat and went to work. For a long time they worked silently. The tailor was in great good-humour; for the terrible trial was over, and he now had an assistant who would be a better tailor than himself. There would be more profit, more silver nails for the church door, and more masses for his soul.

"The Cure says you are all right.... When will you come here?" he said at last.

"To-morrow night I shall sleep here," answered Charley.

So it was arranged that Charley should come to live in the tailor's house, to sleep in the room which the tailor had provided for a wife twenty-five years before—even for her that was now known as Madame Dauphin.

All morning the tailor chuckled to himself. When they sat down at noon to a piece of venison which Charley had prepared himself—taking the frying-pan out of the hands of Margot Patry, the old servant, and cooking it to a turn—Louis Trudel saw his years lengthen to an indefinite period. He even allowed himself to nervously stand up, bow, shake Charley's hand jerkingly, and say:

"M'sieu', I care not what you are or where you come from, or even if you're a Protestant, perhaps an Englishman. You're a gentleman and a tailor, and old Louis Trudel will not forget you. It shall be as you said this morning—it is no day for work. We will play, and the clothes for the Manor can go to the devil. Smoke of hell-fire, I will go and have a pipe with that, poor wretch the Notary!"

So, a wonderful thing happened. Louis Trudel, on a week-day and a market-day, went to smoke a pipe with Narcisse Dauphin, and to tell him that M. Mallard was going to stay with him for ever, at fine wages. He also announced that he had paid this whole week's wages in advance; but he did not tell what he did not know—that half the money had already been given to old Margot, whose son lay ill at home with a broken leg, and whose children were living on bread and water. Charley had slowly drawn from the woman the story of her life as he sat by the kitchen fire and talked to her, while her master was talking to the Notary.

CHAPTER XVII
THE TAILOR MAKES A MIDNIGHT FORAY

Since the day Charley had brought home the paper bought at the post-office, and water-marked Kathleen, he had, at odd times, written down his thoughts, and promptly torn the paper up again or put it in the fire. In the repression of the new life, in which he must live wholly alone, so far as all past habits of mind were concerned, it was a relief to record his passing reflections, as he had been wont to do when the necessity for it was less. Writing them here was like the bursting of an imprisoned stream; it was relaxing the ceaseless eye of vigilance; freeing an imprisoned personality. This personality was not yet merged into that which must take its place, must express itself in the involuntary acts which tell of a habit of mind and body—no longer the imitative and the histrionic, but the inherent and the real.

On the afternoon of the day that old Louis agreed to give him wages, and went to smoke a pipe with the Notary, Charley scribbled down his thoughts on this matter of personality and habit.

"Who knows," he wrote, "which is the real self? A child comes into the world gin-begotten, with the instinct for liquor in his brain, like the scent of the fox in the nostrils of the hound. And that seems the real. But the same child caught up on the hands of chance is carried into another atmosphere, is cared for by ginhating minds and hearts: habit fastens on him—fair, decent, and temperate habit—and he grows up like the Cure yonder, a brother of Aaron. Which is the real? Is the instinct for the gin killed, or covered? Is the habit of good living mere habit and mere acting, in which the real man never lives his real life, or is it the real life?

"Who knows! Here am I, born with a question in my mouth, with the ever-present 'non possumus' in me. Here am I, to whom life was one poor futility; to whom brain was but animal intelligence abnormally developed; to whom speechless sensibility and intelligence was the only reality; to whom nothing from beyond ever sent a flash of conviction, an intimation, into my soul—not one. To me God always seemed a being of dreams, the creation of a personal need and helplessness, the despairing cry of the victims of futility—And here am I flung like a stone from a sling into this field where men believe in God as a present and tangible being; who reply to all life's agonies and joys and exultations with the words 'C'est le bon Dieu.' And what shall I become? Will habit do its work, and shall I cease to be me? Shall I, in the permanency of habit, become like unto this tailor here, whose life narrows into one sole cause; whose only wish is to have the Church draw the coverlet of forgiveness and safety over him; who has solved all questions in a blind belief or an inherited predisposition—which? This stingy, hard, unhappy man—how should he know what I am denied! Or does he know? Is it all illusion? If there is a God who receives such devotion, to the exclusion of natural demand and spiritual anxieties, why does not this tailor 'let his light so shine before men that they may see his good works, and glorify his Father which is in heaven?' That is it. Therefore, wherefore, tailor-man? Therefore, wherefore, God? Show me a sign from Heaven, tailor-man!"

Seated on his bench in the shop, with his eyes ever and anon raised towards the little post-office opposite, he wrote these words. Afterwards he sat and thought till the shadows deepened, and the tailor came in to supper. Then he took up the pieces of paper, and, going to the fire, which was still lighted of an evening, thrust them inside.

Louis Trudel saw the paper burning, and, glancing down, he noticed that one piece—the last—had slipped to the floor and was lying under the table. He saw the pencil still in Charley's hand. Forthwith his natural suspicion leaped up, and the cunning of the monomaniac was upon him. With all his belief in le bon Dieu and the Church, Louis Trudel trusted no one. One eye was ever open to distrust man, while the other was ever closed with blind belief in Heaven.

As Charley stooped to put wood in the fire, the tailor thrust a foot forward and pushed the piece of paper further under the table.

That night the tailor crept down into the shop, felt for the paper in the dark, found it, and carried it away to his room. All kinds of thoughts had raged through his diseased mind. It was a letter, perhaps, and if a letter, then he would gain some facts about the man's life. But if it was a letter, why did he burn it? It was said that he never received a letter and never sent one, therefore it was little likely to be a letter if not a letter, then what could it be? Perhaps the man was English and a spy of the English government, for was there not disaffection in some of the parishes? Perhaps it was a plan of robbery. To such a state of hallucination did his weakened mind come, that he forgot the kindly feeling he had had for this stranger who had worked for him without pay. Suspicion, the bane of sick old age, was hot on him. He remembered that M'sieu' had put an arm through his when they went upstairs, and that now increased suspicion. Why should the man have been so friendly? To lull him into confidence, perhaps, and then to rob and murder him in his sleep. Thank God, his ready money was well hid, and the rest was safe in the bank far away! He crept back to his room with the paper in his hand. It was the last sheet of what Charley had written, and had been accidentally brushed off on the floor. It was in French, and, holding the candle close, he slowly deciphered the crabbed, characteristic handwriting.

His eyes dilated, his yellow cheeks took on spots of unhealthy red, his hand trembled. Anger seized him, and he mumbled the words over and over again to himself. Twice or thrice, as the paper lay in one hand, he struck it with the clinched fist of the other, muttering and distraught.

"This tailor here.... This stingy, hard, unhappy man.... If there is a God!... Therefore, wherefore, tailor-man?... Therefore, wherefore, God?... Show me a sign from Heaven, tailor-man!"

Hatred of himself, blasphemy, the profane and hellish humour of—of the infidel! A Protestant heretic—he was already damned; a robber—you could put him in jail; a spy—you could shoot him or tar and feather him; a murderer—you could hang him. But an infide—this was a deadly poison, a black danger, a being capable of all crimes. An infidel—"Therefore, wherefore, tailor-man?... Therefore, wherefore, God?... Show me a sign from Heaven, tailor-man!"

The devil laughing—the devil incarnate come to mock a poor tailor, to sow plague through a parish where all were at peace in the bosom of the Church. The tailor had three ruling passions—cupidity, vanity, and religion. Charley had now touched the three, and the whole man was alive. His cupidity had been flattered by the unpaid service of a capable assistant, but now he saw that he was paying the devil a wage. His vanity was overwhelmed by a satanic ridicule. His religion and his God had been assaulted in so shameful a way that no punishment could be great enough for the man of hell. In religion he was a fanatic; he was a demented fanatic now.

He thrust the paper into his pocket, then crept out into the hall and to the door of Charley's bedroom. He put his ear to the door. After a moment he softly raised the latch, and opened the door and listened again. 'M'sieu' was in a deep sleep.

Louis Trudel scarcely knew why he had listened, why he had opened the door and stood looking at the figure in the bed, barely definable in the semi-darkness of the room. If he had meant harm to the helpless man, he had brought no weapon; if he had been curious, there the man was peacefully sleeping!

His sick, morbid imagination was so alive, that he scarcely knew what he did. As he stood there listening, hatred and horror in his heart, a voice said to him: "Thou shalt do no murder." The words kept ringing in his ears. Yet he had not thought of murder. The fancied command itself was his first temptation towards such a deed. He had thought of raising the parish, of condign punishment of many sorts, but not this. As he closed the door softly, killing entered his mind and stayed there. "Thou shalt not" had been the first instigation to "Thou shalt."

It haunted him as he returned to his room, undressed himself, and went to bed. He could not sleep. "Show me a sign from Heaven, tailor-man!" The challenge had been to himself. He must respond to it. The duty lay with him; he must answer this black infidel for the Church, for faith, for God.

The more he thought of it, the more Charley's face came before him, with the monocle shining and hard in the eye. The monocle haunted him. That was the infidel's sign. "Show me a sign from Heaven, tailor-man!" What sign should he show?

Presently he sat up straight in bed. In another minute he was out and dressing. Five minutes later he was on his way to the parish church. When he reached it he took a tool from his pocket and unscrewed a small iron cross from the front door. It was a cross which had been blessed by the Pope, and had been brought to Chaudiere by the beloved mother of the Cure, now dead.

"When I have done with it I will put it back," he said, as he thrust it inside his shirt, and hurried stealthily back to his house. As he got into bed he gave a noiseless, mirthless laugh. All night he lay with his yellow eyes wide open, gazing at the ceiling. He was up at dawn, hovering about the fire in the shop.

CHAPTER XVIII
THE STEALING OF THE CROSS

If Charley had been less engaged with his own thoughts, he would have noticed the curious baleful look in the eyes of the tailor; but he was deeply absorbed in a struggle that had nothing to do with Louis Trudel.

The old fever of thirst and desire was upon him. All morning the door of Jolicoeur's saloon was opening and shutting before his mind's eye, and there was a smell of liquor everywhere. It was in his nostrils when the hot steam rose from the clothes he was pressing, in the thick odour of the fulled cloth, in the melting snow outside the door.

Time and again he felt that he must run out of the shop and away to the little tavern where white whiskey was sold to unwise habitants. But he fought on. Here was the heritage of his past, the lengthening chain of slavery to his old self—was it his real self? Here was what would prevent him from forgetting all that he had been and not been, all the happiness he might have had, all that he had lost—the ceaseless reminder. He was still the victim to a poison which gave not only a struggle of body, but a struggle of soul—if he had a soul.

"If he had a soul!" The phrase kept repeating itself to him even as he fought the fever in his throat, resisting the temptation to take that medicine which the Curb's brother had sent him.

"If he had a soul!" The thinking served as an antidote, for by the ceaseless iteration his mind was lulled into a kind of drowse. Again and again he went to the pail of water that stood on the window-sill, and lifting it to his lips, drank deep and full, to quench the wearing thirst.

"If he had a soul!" He looked at Louis Trudel, silent and morose, the clammy yellow of a great sickness in his face and hands, but his mind only intent on making a waistcoat—and the end of all things very near! The words he had written the night before came to him: "Therefore, wherefore, tailor-man? Therefore, wherefore, God?... Show me a sign from Heaven, tailor-man!" As if in reply to his thoughts there came the sound of singing, and of bells ringing in the parish church.

A procession with banners was coming near. It was a holy day, and Chaudiere was mindful of its duties. The wanderers of the parish had come home for Easter. All who belonged to Chaudiere and worked in the woods or shanties, or lived in big cities far away, were returned—those who could return—to take the holy communion in the parish church. Yesterday the parish had been alive with a pious hilarity. The great church had been crowded beyond the doors, the streets had been full of cheerily dressed habitants. There had, however, come a sudden chill to the seemly rejoicings—the little iron cross blessed by the Pope had been stolen from the door of the church!

The fact had been told to the Cure as he said the Mass, and from the altar steps, before going to the pulpit, he referred to the robbery with poignant feeling; for the relic had belonged to a martyr of the Church, who, two centuries before, had laid down his life for the Master on the coast of Africa.

Louis Trudel had heard the Cure's words, and in his place at the rear of the church he smiled sourly to himself. In due time the little cross should be returned, but it had work to do first. He did not take the holy communion this Easter day, or go to confession as was his wont. Not, however, until a certain day later did the Cure realise this, though for thirty years the tailor had never omitted his Easter-time duties.

The people guessed and guessed, but they knew not on whom to cast suspicion at first. No sane Catholic of Chaudiere could possibly have taken the holy thing. Presently a murmur crept about that M'sieu' might have been the thief. He was not a Catholic, and—who could tell? Who knew where he came from? Who knew what he had been? Perhaps a jail-bird-robber-murderer! Charley, however, stitched on, intent upon his own struggle.

The procession passed the doorway: men bearing banners with sacred texts, acolytes swinging censers, a figure of the Saviour carved in wood borne aloft, the Cure under a silk canopy, and a long line of habitants following with sacred song. People fell upon their knees in the street as the procession passed, and the Cure's face was bent here and there, his hand raised in blessing.

Old Louis got up from his bench, and, putting on a coat over his wool jacket, hastened to the doorway, knelt down, made the sign of the cross, and said a prayer. Then he turned quickly towards Charley, who, looking at the procession, then at the tailor, then back again at the procession, smiled.

Charley was hardly conscious of what he did. His mind had ranged far beyond this scene to the large issues which these symbols represented. Was it one universal self-deception? Was this "religion" the pathetic, the soul-breaking make-believe of mortality? So he smiled—at himself, at his own soul, which seemed alone in this play, the skeleton in armour, the thing that did not belong. His own words written that fateful day before he died at the Cote Dorion came to him:

"Sacristan, acolyte, player, or preacher, Each to his office, but who holds the key? Death, only Death, thou, the ultimate teacher, Wilt show it to me!"

He was suddenly startled from his reverie, through which the procession was moving—a cloud of witnesses. It was the voice of Louis Trudel, sharp and piercing:

"Don't you believe in God and the Son of God?"

"God knows!" answered Charley slowly in reply—an involuntary exclamation of helplessness, an automatic phrase deflected from its first significance to meet a casual need of the mind. Yet it seemed like satire, like a sardonic, even vulgar, humour. So it struck Louis Trudel, who snatched up a hot iron from the fire and rushed forward with a snarl. So astounded was Charley that he did not stir. He was not prepared for the sudden onslaught. He did not put up his hand even, but stared at the tailor, who, within a foot of him, stopped short with the iron poised.

Louis Trudel repented in time. With the cunning of the monomaniac he realised that an attack now might frustrate his great stroke. It would bring the village to his shop door, precipitate the crisis upon the wrong incident.

As it chanced, only one person in Chaudiere saw the act. That was Rosalie Evanturel across the way. She saw the iron raised, and looked for M'sieu' to knock the tailor down; but, instead, she beheld the tailor go back and put the iron on the fire again. She saw also that M'sieu' was speaking, though she could hear no words.

Charley's words were simple enough. "I beg your pardon, Monsieur," he said across the room to old Louis; "I meant no offence at all. I was trying to think it out in a human sort of way. I suppose I wanted a sign from Heaven—wanted too much, no doubt."

The tailor's lips twitched, and his hand convulsively clutched the shears at his side.

"It is no matter now," he answered shortly. "I have had signs from Heaven; perhaps you will have one too!"

"It would be worth while," rejoined Charley musingly. Charley wondered bitterly if he had made an irreparable error in saying those ill-chosen words. This might mean a breach between them, and so make his position in the parish untenable. He had no wish to go elsewhere—where could he go? It mattered little what he was, tinker or tailor. He had now only to work his way back to the mind of the peasant; to be an animal with intelligence; to get close to mother earth, and move down the declivity of life with what natural wisdom were possible. It was his duty to adapt himself to the mind of such as this tailor; to acquire what the tailor and his like had found—an intolerant belief and an inexpensive security, to be got through yielding his nature to the great religious dream. And what perfect tranquillity, what smooth travelling found therein.

Gazing across the street towards the little post-office, he saw Rosalie Evanturel at the window. He fell to thinking about her. Rosalie, on her part, kept wondering what old Louis' violence meant.

Presently she saw a half-dozen men come quickly down the street, and, before they reached the tailorshop, stand in a group talking excitedly. Afterwards one came forward from the others quickly—Filion Lacasse the saddler. He stopped short at the tailor's door. Looking at Charley, he exclaimed roughly:

"If you don't hand out the cross you stole from the church door, we'll tar and feather you, M'sieu'." Charley looked up, surprised. It had never occurred to him that they could associate him with the theft. "I know nothing of the cross," he said quietly. "You're the only heretic in the place. You've done it. Who are you? What are you doing here in Chaudiere?"

"Working at my trade," was Charley's quiet answer. He looked towards Louis Trudel, as though to see how he took this ugly charge.

Old Louis responded at once. "Get away with you, Filion Lacasse," he croaked. "Don't come here with your twaddle. M'sieu' hasn't stole the cross. What does he want with a cross? He's not a Catholic."

"If he didn't steal the cross, why, he didn't," answered the saddler; "but if he did, what'll you say for yourself, Louis? You call yourself a good Catholic—bah!—when you've got a heretic living with you."

"What's that to you?" growled the tailor, and reached out a nervous hand towards the iron. "I served at the altar before you were born. Sacre!

I'll make your grave-clothes yet, and be a good Catholic when you're in the churchyard. Be off with you. Ach," he sharply added, when Filion did not move, "I'll cut your hair for you!" He scrambled off the bench with his shears.

Filion Lacasse disappeared with his friends, and the old man settled back on his bench.

Charley, looking up quietly from his work, said "Thank you, Monsieur."

He did not notice what an evil look was in Louis Trudel's face as it turned towards him, but Rosalie Evanturel, standing outside, saw it; and she stole back to the post-office ill at ease and wondering.

All that day she watched the tailor's shop, and even when the door was shut in the evening, her eyes were fastened on the windows.

CHAPTER XIX
THE SIGN FROM HEAVEN

The agitation and curiosity possessing Rosalie all day held her in the evening when the wooden shutters of the tailor's shop were closed and only a flickering light showed through the cracks. She was restless and uneasy during supper, and gave more than one unmeaning response to the remarks of her crippled father, who, drawn up for supper in his wheel-chair, was more than usually inclined to gossip.

Damase Evanturel's mind was stirred concerning the loss of the iron cross; the threat made by Filion Lacasse and his companions troubled him. The one person beside the Cure, Jo Portugais, and Louis Trudel, to whom M'sieu' talked much, was the postmaster, who sometimes met him of an evening as he was taking the air. More than once he had walked behind the wheel-chair and pushed it some distance, making the little crippled man gossip of village matters.

As the two sat at supper the postmaster was inclined to take a serious view of M'sieu's position. He railed at Filion Lacasse; he called the suspicious habitants clodhoppers, who didn't know any better—which was a tribute to his own superior birth; and at last, carried away by a feverish curiosity, he suggested that Rosalie should go and look through the cracks in the shutters of the tailor-shop and find out what was going on within. This was indignantly rejected by Rosalie, but the more she thought, the more uneasy she became. She ceased to reply to her father's remarks, and he at last relapsed into gloom, and said that he was tired and would go to bed. Thereupon she wheeled him inside his bedroom, bade him good-night, and left him to his moodiness, which, however, was soon absorbed in a deep sleep, for the mind of the little grey postmaster could no more hold trouble or thought than a sieve.

Left alone, Rosalie began to be tortured. What were they doing in the house opposite?

Go and look through the windows? But she had never spied on people in her life! Yet would it be spying? Would it not be pardonable? In the interest of the man who had been attacked in the morning by the tailor, who had been threatened by the saddler, and concerning whom she had seen a signal pass between old Louis and Filion Lacasse, would it not be a humane thing to do? It might be foolish and feminine to be anxious, but did she not mean well, and was it not, therefore, honourable?

The mystery inflamed her imagination. Charley's passiveness when he was assaulted by old Louis and afterwards threatened by the saddler seemed to her indifference to any sort of danger—the courage of the hopeless life, maybe. Instantly her heart overflowed with sympathy. Monsieur was not a Catholic perhaps? Well, so much the more he should be befriended, for he was so much the more alone and helpless. If a man was born a Protestant—or English—he could not help it, and should not be punished in this world for it, since he was sure to be punished in the next.

Her mind became more and more excited. The postoffice had been long since closed, and her father was asleep—she could hear him snoring. It was ten o'clock, and there was still a light in the tailor's shop. Usually the light went out before nine o'clock. She went to the post-office door and looked out. The streets were empty; there was not a light burning anywhere, save in the house of the Notary. Down towards the river a sleigh was making its way over the thin snow of spring, and screeching on the stones. Some late revellers, moving homewards from the Trois Couronnes, were roaring at the top of their voices the habitant chanson, 'Le Petit Roger Bontemps':

"For I am Roger Bontemps,

Gai, gai, gai!

With drink I am full and with joy content,

Gai, gaiment!"

The chanson died away as she stood there, and still the light was burning in the shop opposite. A thought suddenly came to her. She would go over and see if the old housekeeper, Margot Patry, had gone to bed. Here was the solution to the problem, the satisfaction of modesty and propriety.

She crossed the street quickly, hurried round the corner of the house, and was passing the side-window of the shop, when a crack in the shutters caught her eye. She heard something fall on the floor within. Could it be that the tailor and M'sieu' were working at so late an hour? She had an irresistible impulse, and glued her eye to the crack.

But presently she started back with a smothered cry. There by the great fireplace stood Louis Trudel picking up a red-hot cross with a pair of pincers. Grasping the iron firmly just below the arms of the cross, the tailor held it up again. He looked at it with a wild triumph, yet with a malignancy little in keeping with the object he held—the holy relic he had stolen from the door of the parish church. The girl gave a low cry of dismay.

She saw old Louis advance stealthily towards the door of the shop leading into the house. In bewilderment, she stood still an instant, then, with a sudden impulse, she ran to the kitchen-door and tried it softly. It was not locked. She opened it, entered quickly, and found old Margot standing in the middle of the room in her night-dress.

"Oh, Rosalie, Rosalie!" cried the old woman, "something's going to happen. M'sieu' Trudel has been queer all evening. I peeped in the key-hole of the shop just now, and—"

"Yes, yes, I've seen too. Come!" said Rosalie, and going quickly to the door, opened it, and passed through to another room. Here she opened another door, leading into the hall between the shop and the house. Entering the hall, she saw a glimmer of light above. It was the reddish glow of the iron cross held by old Louis. She crept softly up the stone steps. She heard a door open very quietly. She hurried now, and came to the landing. She saw the door of Charley's room open—all the village knew what room he slept in—and the moonlight was streaming in at the window.

She saw the sleeping man on the bed, and the tailor standing over him. Charley was lying with one arm thrown above his head; the other lay over the side of the bed.

As she rushed forward, divining old Louis' purpose, the fiery cross descended, and a voice cried: "'Show me a sign from Heaven, tailor-man!'"

This voice was drowned by that of another, which, gasping with agony out of a deep sleep, as the body sprang upright, cried: "God—oh God!" Rosalie's hand grasped old Louis' arm too late. The tailor sprang back with a horrible laugh, striking her aside, and rushed out to the landing.

"Oh, Monsieur, Monsieur!" cried Rosalie, and, snatching a scarf from her bosom, thrust it in upon the excoriated breast, as Charley, hardly realising what had happened, choked back moans of pain.

"What did he do?" he gasped.

"The iron cross from the church door!" she answered. "A minute, one minute, Monsieur!"

She rushed out upon the landing in time to see the tailor stumble on the stairs and fall head forwards to the bottom, at the feet of Margot Patry.

Rosalie paid no heed to the fallen man. "Oil! flour! Quick!" she cried. "Quick! Quick!" She stepped over the body of the tailor, snatched at Margot's arm, and dragged her into the kitchen. "Quick-oil and flour!"

The old woman showed her where they were, moaning and whining.

"He tried to kill Monsieur," cried Rosalie, "burned him on the breast with the holy cross!"

With oil and flour she hurried back, over the body of the tailor, up the stairs, and into Charley's room. Charley was now out of bed and half dressed, though choking with pain, and preserving consciousness only by a great effort.

"Good Mademoiselle!" he said.

She took the scarf off gently, soaked it in oil and splashed it with flour, and laid it quickly back on the burnt flesh.

Margot came staggering into the room.

"I cannot rouse him. I cannot rouse him. He is dead! He is dead!" she whimpered.

"He—"

Charley swayed forward towards the woman, recovered himself, and said:

"Now not a word of what he did to me, remember. Not one word, or you will go to jail with him. If you keep quiet, I'll say nothing. He didn't know what he was doing." He turned to Rosalie. "Not a word of this, please," he moaned. "Hide the cross."

He moved towards the door. Rosalie saw his purpose, and ran out ahead of him and down the stairs to where the tailor lay prone on his face, one hand still holding the pincers. The little iron cross lay in a dark corner. Stooping, she lifted up the tailor's head, then felt his heart.

"He is not dead," she cried. "Quick, Margot, some water," she added, to the whimpering woman. Margot tottered away, and came again presently with the water.

"I will go for some one to help," Rosalie said, rising to her feet, as she saw Charley come slowly down the staircase, his face white with misery. She ran and took his arm to help him down.

"No, no, dear Mademoiselle," he said; "I shall be all right presently. You must get help to carry him up stairs. Bring the Notary; he and I can carry him up."

"You, Monsieur! You—it would kill you! You are terribly hurt."

"I must help to carry him, else people will be asking questions," he answered painfully. "He is going to die. It must not be known—you understand!" His eyes searched the floor until they found the cross. Rosalie picked it up with the pincers. "It must not be known what he did to me," Charley said to the muttering and weeping old woman. He caught her shoulder with his hand, for she seemed scarcely to heed.

She nodded. "Yes, yes, M'sieu', I will never speak." Rosalie was standing in the door. "Go quickly, Mademoiselle," he said. She disappeared with the iron cross, and flying across the street, thrust it inside the post-office, then ran to the house of the Notary.

CHAPTER XX
THE RETURN OF THE TAILOR

Twenty minutes later the tailor was lying in his bed, breathing, but still unconscious, the Notary, M'sieu', and the doctor of the next parish, who by chance was in Chaudiere, beside him. Charley's face was drawn and haggard with pain, for he had helped to carry old Louis to bed, though every motion of his arms gave him untold agony. In the doorway stood Rosalie and Margot Patry.

"Will he live?" asked the Notary.

The doctor shook his head. "A few hours, perhaps. He fell downstairs?"

Charley nodded. There was silence for some time, as the doctor went on with his ministrations, and the Notary sat drumming his fingers on the little table beside the bed. The two women stole away to the kitchen, where Rosalie again pressed secrecy on Margot. In the interest of the cause she had even threatened Margot with a charge of complicity. She had heard the phrase "accessory before the fact," and she used it now with good effect.

Then she took some fresh flour and oil, and thrust them inside the bedroom door where Charley now sat clinching his hands and fighting down the pain. Careful as ever of his personal appearance, however, he had brushed every speck of flour from his clothes, and buttoned his coat up to the neck.

Nearly an hour passed, and then the Cure appeared. When he entered the sick man's room, Charley followed, and again Rosalie and old Margot came and stood within the doorway.

"Peace be to this house!" said the Cure. He had a few minutes of whispered conversation with the doctor, and then turned to Charley.

"He fell down-stairs, Monsieur? You saw him fall?"

"I was in my room—I heard him fall, Cure."

"Had he been ill during the day?"

"He appeared to be feeble, and he seemed moody."

"More than usual, Monsieur?" The Cure had heard of the incident of the morning when Filion Lacasse accused Charley of stealing the cross.

"Rather more than usual, Monsieur."

The Cure turned towards the door. "You, Mademoiselle Rosalie, how came you to know?"

"I was in the kitchen with Margot, who was not well."

The Cure looked at Margot, who tearfully nodded. "I was ill," she said, "and Rosalie was here with me. She helped M'sieu' and me. Rosalie is a good girl, and kind to me," she whimpered.

The Cure seemed satisfied, and after looking at the sick man for a moment, he came close to Charley. "I am deeply pained at what happened to-day," he said courteously. "I know you have had nothing to do with the beloved little cross."

The Notary tried to draw near and listen, but the Cure's look held him back. The doctor was busy with his patient.

"You are only just, Monsieur," said Charley in response, wishing that these kind eyes were fixed anywhere than on his face.

All at once the Cure laid a hand upon his arm. "You are ill," he said anxiously. "You look very ill indeed. See, Vaudrey," he added to the doctor, "you have another patient here!"

The friendly, oleaginous doctor came over and peered into Charley's face. "Ill-sure enough!" he said. "Look at this sweat!" he pointed to the drops of perspiration on Charley's forehead. "Where do you suffer?"

"Severe pains all through my body," Charley answered simply, for it seemed easier to tell the truth, as near as might be.

"I must look to you," said the doctor. "Go and lie down, and I will come to you."

Charley bowed, but did not move. Just then two things drew the attention of all: the tailor showed returning consciousness, and there was noise of many voices outside the house and the tramping of feet below-stairs.

"Go and tell them no one must come up," said the doctor to the Notary, and the Cure made ready to say the last offices for the dying.

Presently the noise below-stairs diminished, and the priest's voice rose in the office, vibrating and touching. The two women sank to their knees, the doctor followed, his eyes still fixed on the dying man. Presently, however, Charley did the same; for something penetrating and reasonable in the devotion touched him.

All at once Louis Trudel opened his eyes. Staring round with acute excitement, his eyes fell on the Cure, then upon Charley.

"Stop—stop, M'sieu' le Cure!" he cried. "There's other work to do." He gasped and was convulsed, but the pallor of his face was alive with fire from the distempered eyes. He snatched from his breast the paper Charley had neglected to burn. He thrust it into the Curb's hand.

"See—see!" he croaked. "He is an infidel—black infidel—from hell!" His voice rose in a kind of shriek, piercing to every corner of the house. He pointed at Charley with shaking finger.

"He wrote it there—on that paper. He doesn't—believe in God."

His strength failed him, his hand clutched tremblingly at the air. He laughed, a dry, crackling laugh, and his mouth opened twice or thrice to speak, but gasping breaths only came forth. With a last effort, however— as the priest, shocked, stretched out his hand and said: "Have done, have done, Trudel!"—he cried, in a voice that quavered shrilly:

"He asked—tailor-man—sign—from—Heaven. Look-look!" He pointed wildly at Charley. "I—gave him—sign of—"

But that was the end. With a shudder the body collapsed in a formless heap, and the tailor-man was gone to tell of the work he had done for his faith on earth.

CHAPTER XXI
THE CURE HAS AN INSPIRATION

White and malicious faces peered through the doorway. There was an ugly murmur coming up the staircase. Many habitants had heard Louis Trudel's last words, and had passed them on with vehement exaggeration.

Chaudiere had been touched in its most superstitious corner. Protestantism was a sin, but atheism was a crime against humanity. The Protestant might be the victim of a mistake, but the atheist was the deliberate son of darkness, the source of fearful dangers. An atheist in their midst was like a scorpion in a flower-bed—no one could tell when and where he would sting. Rough misdemeanours among them had been many, there had once been a murder in the parish, but the undefined horrors of infidelity were more shameful than crimes the eye could see.

To the minds of these excited people the tailor-man's death was due to the infidel before them. They were ready to do all that might become a Catholic intent to avenge the profaned honour of the Church and the faith. Bodily harm was the natural form for their passion to take.

"Bring him out—let us have him!" they cried with fierce gestures, to which Rosalie Evanturel turned a pained, indignant face.

As the Curb stood with the paper in his hand, his face set and bitter, Rosalie made a step forward. She meant to tell the truth about Louis Trudel, and show how good this man was, who stood charged with an imaginary crime. But she met the warning eye of the man himself, calm and resolute, she saw the suffering in the face, endured with what composure! and she felt instantly that she must obey him, and that—who could tell?—his plan might be the best in the end. She looked at the Cure anxiously. What would he say and do? In the Cure's heart and mind a great struggle was going on. All his inherent prejudice, the hereditary predisposition of centuries, the ingrain hatred of atheism, were alive in him, hardening his mind against the man before him. His first impulse was to let Charley take his fate at the hands of the people of Chaudiere, whatever it might be. But as he looked at the man, as he recalled their first meeting, and remembered the simple, quiet life he had lived among them—charitable, and unselfish—the barriers of creed and habit fell down, and tears unbidden rushed into his eyes.

The Cure had, all at once, the one great inspiration of his life—its one beautiful and supreme imagining. For thus he reasoned swiftly:

Here he was, a priest who had shepherded a flock of the faithful passed on to him by another priest before him, who again had received them from a guardian of the fold—a family of faithful Catholics whose thoughts never strayed into forbidden realms. He had done no more than keep them faithful and prevent them from wandering—counselling, admonishing, baptising, and burying, giving in marriage and blessing, sending them on their last great journey with the cachet of Holy Church upon them. But never once, never in all his life, had he brought a lost soul into the fold. If he died tonight, he could not say to St. Peter, when he arrived at Heaven's gate: "See, I have saved a soul!" Before the Throne he could not say to Him who cried: "Go ye into all the world and preach the gospel to every creature"—he could not say: "Lord, by Thy grace I found this soul in the wilderness, in the dark and the loneliness, having no God to worship, denial and rebellion in his heart; and behold, I took him to my breast, and taught him in Thy name, and led him home to Thy haven, the Church!"

Thus it was that the Cure dreamed a dream. He would set his life to saving this lost soul. He would rescue him from the outer darkness.

His face suffused, he handed the paper in his hand back to the man who had written the words upon it. Then he lifted his hand against the people at the door and the loud murmuring behind them.

"Peace—peace!" he said, as though from the altar. "Leave this room of death, I command you. Go at once to your homes. This man"—he pointed to Charley—"is my friend. Who seeks to harm him, would harm me. Go hence and pray. Pray for yourselves, pray for him, and for me; and pray for the troubled soul of Louis Trudel. Go in peace."

Soon afterwards the house was empty, save for the Cure, Charley, old Margot, and the Notary.

That night Charley sat in the tailor's bedroom, rigid and calm, though racked with pain, and watched the candles flickering beside the dead body. He was thinking of the Cure's last words to the people.

"I wonder—I wonder," he said, and through his eyeglass he stared at the crucifix that threw a shadow on the dead man's face. Morning found him there. As dawn crept in he rose to his feet. "Whither now?" he said, like one in a dream.

CHAPTER XXII
THE WOMAN WHO SAW

Up to the moment of her meeting with Charley, Rosalie Evanturel's life had been governed by habit, which was lightly coloured by temperament. Since the eventful hour on Vadrome Mountain it had become a life of temperament, in which habit was involuntary and mechanical. She did her daily duties with a good heart, but also with a sense superior to the practical action. This grew from day to day, until, in the tragical days wherein she had secretly played a great part, she moved as in a dream, but a dream so formal that no one saw any change taking place in her, or associated her with the events happening across the way.

She had been compelled to answer many questions, for it was known she was in the tailor's house when Louis Trudel fell down-stairs, but what more was there to tell than that she had run for the Notary, and sent word to the Cure, and that she was present when the tailor died, charging M'sieu' with being an infidel? At first she was ill disposed to answer any questions, but she soon felt that attitude would only do harm. For the first time in her life she was face to face with moral problems—the beginning of sorrow, of knowledge, and of life.

In all secrets there is a kind of guilt, however beautiful or joyful they may be, or for what good end they may be set to serve. Secrecy means evasion, and evasion means a problem to the moral mind. To the primitive mind, with its direct yes and no, there is danger of it becoming a tragical problem ere it is realised that truth is various and diverse. Perhaps even with that Mary who hid the matter in her heart—the exquisite tragedy and glory of Christendom—there was a delicate feeling of guilt, the guilt of the hidden though lofty and beautiful thing.

If secrecy was guilt, then Charley and Rosalie were bound together by a bond as strong as death: Rosalie held the key to a series of fateful days and doings.

In ordinary course, they might have known each other for five years and not have come to this sensitive and delicate association. With one great plunge she had sprung into the river of understanding. In the moment that she had thrust her scarf into his scorched breast, in that little upper room, the work of years had been done.

As long as he lived, that mark must remain on M'sieu's breast—the red, smooth scar of a cross! She had seen the sort of shining scar a bad burn makes, and at thought of it she flushed, trembled, and turned her head away, as though some one were watching her. Even in the night she flushed and buried her face in the pillow when the thought flashed through her mind; though when she had soaked the scarf in oil and flour and laid it on the angry wound she had not flushed at all, was determined, quiet, and resourceful.

That incident had made her from a girl into a woman, from a child of the convent into a child of the world. She no longer thought and felt as she had done before. What she did think or feel could not easily have been set down, for her mind was one tremulous confusion of unusual thoughts, her heart was beset by new feelings, her imagination, suddenly finding itself, was trying its wings helplessly. The past was full of wonder and event, the present full of surprises.

There was M'sieu' established already in Louis Trudel's place, having been granted a lease of the house and shop by the Curte, on the part of the parish, to which the property had been left; receiving also a gift of the furniture and of old Margot, who remained where she had been so many years. She could easily see Charley at work—pale and suffering still—for the door was generally open in the sweet April weather, with the birds singing, and the trees bursting into blossom. Her wilful imagination traced the cross upon his breast—it almost seemed as if it were outside upon his clothes, exposed to every eye, a shining thing all fire, not a wound inside, for which old Margot prepared oiled linen now.

The parish was as perturbed as her own mind, for the mystery of the stolen cross had never been cleared up, and a few still believed that M'sieu' had taken it. They were of those who kept hinting at dark things which would yet be worked upon the infidel in the tailor's shop. These were they to whom the Curb's beautiful ambition did not appeal. He had said that if the man were an infidel, then they must pray that he be brought into the fold; but a few were still suspicious, and they said in Rosalie's presence: "Where is the little cross? M'sieu' knows."

He did know. That was the worst of it. The cross was in her possession. Was it not necessary, then, to quiet suspicion for his sake? She had locked the relic away in a cupboard in her bedroom, and she carried the key of it always in her pocket. Every day she went and looked at it, as at some ghostly token. To her it was a symbol, not of supernatural things, but of life in its new reality to her. It was M'sieu', it was herself, it was their secret—she chafed inwardly that Margot should share a part of that secret. If it were only between their two selves—between M'sieu' and herself! If Margot—she paused suddenly, for she was going to say, If Margot would only die! She was not wicked enough to wish that; yet in the past few weeks she had found herself capable of thinking things beyond the bounds of any past experience.

She found a solution at last. She would go to-night secretly and nail the cross again on the church door, and so stop the chatter of evil tongues. The moon set very early now, and as every one in Chaudiere was supposed to be in bed by ten o'clock, the chances of not being seen were in her favour. She received the final impetus to her resolution by a quarrelsome and threatening remark of Jo Portugais to some sharp-tongued gossip in the post-office. She was glad that Jo should defend M'sieu', but she was jealous of his friendship for the tailor. Besides, did there not appear to be a secret between Jo and M'sieu'? Was it not possible that Jo knew where M'sieu' came from, and all about him? Of late Jo had come in and gone out of the shop oftener than in the past, had even brought her bunches of mosses for her flower-pots, the first budding lilacs, and some maple-sugar made from the trees on Vadrome Mountain. She remembered that when she was a girl at school, years ago—ten years ago—Jo Portugais, then scarcely out of his teens, a cheerful, pleasant, quick-tempered lad, had brought her bunches of the mountain-ash berry; that once he had mended the broken runner of her sled; and yet another time had sent her a birch-bark valentine at the convent, where it was confiscated by the Mother Superior. Since those days he had become a dark morose figure, living apart from men, never going to confession, seldom going to Mass, unloving and unlovable.

There was only one other person in the parish more unloved. That was the woman called Paulette Dubois, who lived in the little house at the outer gate of the Manor. Paulette Dubois had a bad name in the parish—so bad that all women shunned her, and few men noticed her. Yet no one could say that at the present time she did not live a careful life, justifying, so far as eye could see, the protection of the Seigneur, M. Rossignol, a man of queer habits and queerer dress, a dabbler in physical science, a devout Catholic, and a constant friend of the Cure. He it was who, when an effort was made to drive Paulette out of the parish, had said that she should not go unless she wished; that, having been born in Chaudiere, she had a right to live there and die there; and if she had sinned there, the parish was in some sense to blame. Though he had no lodge-gates, and though the seigneury was but a great wide low-roofed farmhouse, with an observatory, and a chimney-piece dating from the time of Louis the Fourteenth, the Seigneur gave Paulette Dubois a little hut at his outer gate, which had been there since the great Count Frontenac visited Chaudiere. Probably Rosalie spoke to Paulette Dubois more often than did any one else in the parish, but that was because the woman came for little things at the shop, and asked for letters, and every week sent one—to a man living in Montreal. She sent these letters, but not more than once in six months did she get a reply, and she had not had one in a whole year. Yet every week she asked, and Rosalie found it hard to answer her politely, and sometimes showed it.

So it was that the two disliked each other without good cause, save that they were separated by a chasm as wide as a sea. The one disliked the other because she must recognise her; the other chafed because she could be recognised by Rosalie officially only.

The late afternoon of the day in which Rosalie decided to nail the cross on the church door again, Paulette arrived to ask for letters at the moment that the office wicket was closed, and Rosalie had answered that it was after office hours, and had almost closed the door in her face. As she turned away Jo Portugais came out of the tailor-shop opposite. He saw Paulette, and stood still an instant. She did the same. A strange look passed across the face of each, then they turned and went in opposite directions.

Never in her life had time gone so slowly with Rosalie. She watched the clock. A dozen times she went to the front door and looked out. She tried to read—it was no use; she tried to spin-her fingers trembled; she sorted the letters in the office again, and rearranged every letter and parcel and paper in its little pigeonhole—then did it all over again. She took out again the letter Paulette had dropped in the letter-box; it was addressed in the name of the man at Montreal. She looked at it in a kind of awe, as she had ever done the letters of this woman who was without the pale. They had a sense of mystery, an air of forbidden imagination.

She put the letter back, went to the door again, and looked out. It was now time to go. Drawing a hood over her head, she stepped out into the night. There was a little frost, though spring was well forward, and the smell of the rich earth and the budding trees was sweet to the sense. The moon had just set, but the stars were shining, and here and there patches of snow on the hillside and in the fields added to the light. Yet it was not bright enough to see far, and as Rosalie moved down the street she did not notice a figure at a little distance behind, walking on the new-springing grass by the roadside. All was quiet at the tavern; there was no light in the Notary's house—as a rule, he sat up late, reading; and even the fiddle of Maximilian Cour, the baker, was silent. The Cure's windows were dark, and the church with its white tin spire stood up sentinel-like above the village.

Rosalie had the fateful cross in her hand as she softly opened the gate of the churchyard and approached the great oak doors. Taking a screw-driver and some screws from her pocket, she felt with a finger for the old screw-holes in the door. Then she began her work, looking fearfully round once or twice at first. Presently, however, because the screws were larger than the old ones, it became much harder; the task called forth more strength, and drove all thought of being seen out of her mind for a space. At last, however, she gave the final turn to the handle, and every screw was in its place, its top level and smooth with the iron of the cross. She stopped and looked round again with an uneasy feeling. She could see no one, hear no one, but she began to tremble, and, overcome, she fell on her knees before the door, and, with her fingers on the foot of the little cross, prayed passionately; for herself, for Monsieur.

Suddenly she heard footsteps inside the church. They were coming towards the doorway, nearer and nearer. At first she was so struck with terror that she could not move. Then with a little cry she sprang to her feet, rushed to the gate, threw it open, ran out into the road, ind wildly on towards home. She did not stop for at least three hundred yards. Turning and looking back she saw at the church door a pale round light. With another cry she sped on, and did not pause till she reached the house. Then, bursting in and locking the door, she hurried to her room, undressed quickly, got into bed without saying her prayers, and buried her face in the pillow, shivering and overwrought.

The footsteps she had heard were those of the Cure and Jo Portugais. The Cure had sent for Jo to do some last work upon a little altar, to be used the next day for the first time. The carpenter and the carver in wood who were responsible for the work had fallen victims to white whiskey on the very last day of their task, and had been driven from the church by the Cure, who then sent for Jo. Rosalie had not seen the light at the shrine, as it was on the side of the church farthest from the village.

Their labour finished, the two came towards the front door, the Cure's lantern in his hand. Opening the door, Jo heard the sound of footsteps and saw a figure flying down the road. As the Cure came out abstractedly, he glanced sorrowfully towards the place where the little cross was used to be. He gave a wondering cry, and almost dropped the lantern.

"See, see, Portugais," he said, "our little cross again!" Jo nodded. "So it seems, Monsieur," he said.

At that instant he saw a hood lying on the ground, and as the Cure held up the lantern, peering at the little cross, he hastily picked it up and thrust it inside his coat.

"Strange—very strange!" said the Cure. "It must have been done while we were inside. It was not there when we entered."

"We entered by the vestry door," said Jo.

"Ah, true-true," responded the Cure.

"It comes as it went," said Jo. "You can't account for some things."

The Cure turned and looked at Jo curiously. "Are you then so superstitious, Jo? Nonsense; it is the work of human hands—very human hands," he added sadly.

"There is nothing to show," said the Cure, seeing Jo's glance round.

"As you see, M'sieu' le Cure."

"Well, it is a mystery which time no doubt will clear up. Meanwhile, let us be thankful to God," said the Cure.

They parted, the Cure going through a side-gate into his own garden, Jo passing out of the churchyard-gate through which Rosalie had gone. He looked down the road towards the village.

"Well!" said a voice in his ear. Paulette Dubois stood before him.

"It was you, then," he said, with a glowering look. "What did you want with it?"

"What do you want with the hood in your coat there?" She threw her head back with a spiteful laugh. "Whose do you think it is?" he said quietly.

"You and the schoolmaster made verses about her once."

"It was Rosalie Evanturel?" he asked, with aggravating composure.

"You have the hood-look at it! You saw her running down the road; I saw her come, watched her, and saw her go. She is a thief—pretty Rosalie—thief and postmistress! No doubt she takes letters too."

"The ones you wait for, and that never come—eh?" Her face darkened with rage and hatred. "I will tell the world she's a thief," she sneered.

"Who will believe you?"

"You will." She was hard and fierce, and looked him in the eyes squarely. "You'll give evidence quick enough, if I ask you."

"I wouldn't do anything you asked me to-nothing, if it was to save my life."

"I'll prove her a thief without you. She can't deny it."

"If you try it, I'll—" He stopped, husky and shaking.

"You'll kill me, eh? You killed him, and you didn't hang. Oh no, you wouldn't kill me, Jo," she added quickly, in a changed voice. "You've had enough of that kind of thing. If I'd been you, I'd rather have hung—ah, sure!" She suddenly came close to him. "Do you hate me so bad, Jo?" she said anxiously. "It's eight years—do you hate me so bad as then?"

"You keep your tongue off Rosalie Evanturel," he said, and turned on his heel.

She caught his arm. "We're both bad, Jo. Can't we be friends?" she said eagerly, her voice shaking.

He did not reply.

"Don't drive a woman too hard," she said between her teeth.

"Threats! Pah!" he rejoined. "What do you think I'm made of?"

"I'll find that out," she said, and, turning on her heel, ran down the road towards the Manor House. "What had Rosalie to do with the cross?" Jo said to himself. "This is her hood." He took it out and looked at it. "It's her hood—but what did she want with the cross?"

He hurried on, and as he neared the post-office he saw the figure of a woman in the road. At first he thought it might be Rosalie, but as he came nearer he saw it was not. The woman was muttering and crying. She wandered to and fro bewilderedly. He came up, caught her by the arm, and looked into her face.

It was old Margot Patry.

CHAPTER XXIII
THE WOMAN WHO DID NOT TELL

"Oh, M'sieu', I am afraid."

"Afraid of what, Margot?"

"Of the last moment, M'sieu' le Cure."

"There will be no last moment to your mind—you will not know it when it comes, Margot."

The woman trembled. "I am not sorry to die. But I am afraid; it is so lonely, M'sieu' le Cure."

"God is with us, Margot."

"When we are born we do not know. It is on the shoulders of others. When we die we know, and we have to answer."

"Is the answering so hard, Margot?"

The woman shook her head feebly and sadly, but did not speak.

"You have been a good mother, Margot." She made no sign.

"You have been a good neighbour; you have done unto others as you would be done by."

She scarcely seemed to hear.

"You have been a good servant—doing your duty in season and out of season; honest and just and faithful."

The woman's fingers twitched on the coverlet, and she moved her head restlessly.

The Curb almost smiled, for it seemed as if Margot were finding herself wanting. Yet none in Chaudiere but knew that she had lived a blameless life—faithful, friendly, a loving and devoted mother, whose health had been broken by sleepless attendance at sick-beds by night, while doing her daily work at the house of the late Louis Trudel.

"I will answer for the way you have done your duty, Margot," said the Cure. "You have been a good daughter of the Church."

He paused a minute, and in the pause some one rose from a chair by the window and looked out on the sunset sky. It was Charley. The woman heard, and turned her eyes towards him. "Do you wish him to go?" asked the Cure.

"No, no—oh no, M'sieu'!" she said eagerly. She had asked all day that either Rosalie or M'sieu' should be in the room with her. It would seem as though she were afraid she had not courage enough to keep the secret of the cross without their presence. Charley had yielded to her request, while he shrank from granting it. Yet, as he said to himself, the woman was keeping his secret—his and Rosalie's—and she had some right to make demand.

When the Cure asked the question of old Margot, he turned expectantly, and with a sense of relief. He thought it strange that the Cure should wish him to remain. The Cure, on his part, was well pleased to have him in the influence of a Christian death-bed. A time must come when the last confidences of the dying woman could be given to no ears but his own, but meanwhile it was good that M'sieu' should be there.

"M'sieu' le Cure," said the dying woman, "must I tell all?"

"All what, Margot?"

"All that is sin?"

"There is no must, Margot."

"If you should ask me, M'sieu'—"

She paused, and the man at the window turned and looked curiously at her. He saw the problem in the woman's mind: had she the right to die with the secret of another's crime upon her mind?

"The priest does not ask, Margot: it is you who confess your sins. That is between you and God."

The Cure spoke firmly, for he wanted the man at the window to clearly understand.

"But if there are the sins of others, and you know, and they trouble your soul, M'sieu'?"

"You have nothing to do with the sins of others; it is enough to repent of your own sins. The priest has nothing to do with any sins but those confessed by the sinner to himself. Your own sins are your sole concern to-night, Margot."

The woman's face seemed to clear a little, and her eyes wandered to the man at the window with less anxiety. Charley was wondering whether, after all, she would have the courage to keep her word, whether spiritual terror would surmount the moral attitude of honour. He was also wondering how much right he had to put the strain upon the woman in her desperate hour. "How long did the doctor say I could live?" the woman asked presently.

"Till morning, perhaps, Margot."

"I should like to live till sunrise," she answered, "till after breakfast. Rosalie makes good tea," she added musingly.

The Cure almost smiled. "There is the Living Bread, my daughter."

She nodded. "But I should like to see the sunrise and have Rosalie bring me tea," she persisted.

"Very well, Margot. We will ask God for that."

Her mind flew back again to the old question.

"Is it wrong to keep a secret?" she asked, her face turned away from the man at the window.

"If it is the secret of a sin, and the sin is your own—yes, Margot."

"And if the sin is not your own?"

"If you share the sin, and if the secret means injury to others, and a wrong is being done, and the law can right that wrong, then you must go to the law, not to your priest."

The Cure's look was grave, even anxious, for he saw that the old woman's mind was greatly disturbed. But her face cleared now, and stayed so. "It has all been a mix and a muddle," she answered; "and it hurt my poor head, M'sieu' le Cure, but now I think I under stand. I am not afraid; I will confess."

The Cure had made it clear to her that she could carry to her grave the secret of the little cross and the work it had done, and so keep her word and still not injure her chances of salvation. She was content. She no longer needed the helpful presence of M'sieu' or Rosalie. Charley instinctively felt what was in her mind, and came towards the bed.

"I will tell Mademoiselle Rosalie about the tea," he said to her.

She looked up at him, almost smiling. "Thank you, good M'sieu'," she said.

"I will confess now, M'sieu' le Cure" she continued. Charley left the room.

Towards morning Margot waked out of a brief sleep, and found the Cure and his sister and others about her bed.

"Is it near sunrise?" she whispered.

"It is just sunrise. See; God has been good," answered the Cure, drawing open the blind and letting in the first golden rays.

Rosalie entered the room with a cup of tea, and came towards the bed.

Old Margot looked at the girl, at the tea, and then at the Cure.

"Drink the tea for me, Rosalie," she whispered. Rosalie did as she was asked.

She looked round feebly; her eyes were growing filmy. "I never gave— so much—trouble—before," she managed to say. "I never had—so much— attention.... I can keep—a secret too," she said, setting her lips feebly with pride. "But I—never—had—so much—attention—before; have I—Rosalie?"

Rosalie did not need to answer, for the woman was gone. The crowning interest of her life had come all at the last moment, as it were, and she had gone away almost gladly and with a kind of pride.

Rosalie also had a hidden pride: the secret was now her very own—hers and M'sieu's.

CHAPTER XXIV
THE SEIGNEUR TAKES A HAND IN THE GAME

It was St. Jean Baptiste's day, and French Canada was en fete. Every seigneur, every cure, every doctor, every notary—the chief figures in a parish—and every habitant was bent for a happy holiday, dressed in his best clothes, moved in his best spirits, in the sweet summer weather.

Bells were ringing, flags were flying, every road and lane was filled with caleches and wagons, and every dog that could draw a cart pulled big and little people, the old and the blind and the mendicant, the happy and the sour, to the village, where there were to be sports and speeches, races upon the river, and a review of the militia, arranged by the member of the Legislature for the Chaudiere-half of the county. French soldiers in English red coats and carrying British flags were straggling along the roads to join the battalion at the volunteers' camp three miles from the town, and singing:

"*Brigadier, respondez Pandore—*

Brigadier, vous avez raison."

It was not less incongruous and curious when one group presently broke out into 'God save the Queen', and another into the 'Marseillaise', and another still into 'Malbrouck s'en va t'en guerre'. At last songs and soldiers were absorbed in the battalion at the rendezvous, and the long dusty march to the village gave a disciplined note to the gaiety of the militant habitant.

At high noon Chaudiere was filled to overflowing. There were booths and tents everywhere—all sorts of cheap-jacks vaunted their wares, merry-go-rounds and swings and shooting-galleries filled the usual spaces in the perspective. The Cure, M. Rossignol the Seigneur, and the Notary stood on the church steps viewing the scene and awaiting the approach of the soldier-citizens. The Seigneur and the Cure had ceased listening to the babble of M. Dauphin, who seemed not to know that his audience closed its ears and found refuge in a "Well, well!" or "Think of that!" or an abstracted "You surprise me!"

The Notary talked on with eager gesture and wreathing smile, shaking back his oiled ringlets as though they trespassed on his smooth, somewhat jaundiced cheeks, until it began to dawn upon him that there was no coin of real applause to be got at this mint. Fortune favoured him at the critical juncture, for the tailor walked slowly past them, looking neither to right nor to left, his eyes cast upon the ground, apparently oblivious to all round him. Almost opposite the church door, however, Charley was suddenly stopped by Filion Lacasse, who ran out from a group before the tavern, and, standing in front of him with outstretched hand, said loudly:

"M'sieu', it's all right. What you said done it, sure! I'm a thousand dollars richer to-day. You may be an infidel, but you have a head, and you save me money, and you give away your own, and that's good enough for me,"—he wrung Charley's hand,—"and I don't care who knows it—sacre!"

Charley did not answer him, but calmly withdrew his hand, smiled, raised his hat at the lonely cheer the saddler raised, and passed on, scarce conscious of what had happened. Indeed he was indifferent to it, for he had a matter on his mind this day which bitterly absorbed him.

But the Notary was not indifferent. "Look there, what do you think of that?" he asked querulously. "I am glad to see that Lacasse treats Monsieur well," said the Cure.

"What do you think of that, Monsieur?" repeated the Notary excitedly to the Seigneur.

The Seigneur put his large gold-handled glass to his eye and looked interestedly after Charley for a moment, then answered: "Well, Dauphin, what?"

"He's been giving Filion Lacasse advice about the old legacy business, and Filion's taken it; and he's got a thousand dollars; and now there's all that fuss. And four months ago Filion wanted to tar and feather him for being just what he is to-day—an infidel—an infidel!"

He was going to say something else, but he did not like the look the Cure turned on him, and he broke off short.

"Do you regret that he gave Lacasse good advice?" asked the Cure.

"It's taking bread out of other men's mouths."

"It put bread into Filion's mouth. Did you ever give Lacasse advice? The truth now, Dauphin!" said the Seigneur drily.

"Yes, Monsieur, and sound advice too, within the law-precedent and code and every legal fact behind." The Seigneur was a man of laconic speech. "Tut, tut, Dauphin; precedent and code and legal fact are only good when there's brain behind 'em. The tailor yonder has brains."

"Ah, but what does he know about the law?" answered Dauphin, with acrimonious voice but insinuating manner, for he loved to stand well with the Seigneur.

"Enough for the saddler evidently," sharply rejoined the Seigneur.

Dauphin was fighting for his life, as it were. His back was to the wall. If this man was to be allowed to advise the habitants of Chaudiere on their disputes and "going to law," where would his own prestige be? His vanity had been deeply wounded.

"It's guesswork with him. Let him stick to his trade as I stick to mine. That sort of thing only does harm."

"He puts a thousand dollars into the saddler's pocket: that's a positive good. He may or may not take thereby ten dollars out of your pocket: that's a negative injury. In this case there was no injury, for you had already cost Lacasse—how much had you cost him, Dauphin?" continued the Seigneur, with a half-malicious smile. "I've been out of Chaudiere for near a year; I don't know the record—how much, eh, Dauphin?"

The Notary was too offended to answer. He shook his ringlets back angrily, and a scarlet spot showed on each straw-coloured cheek.

"Twenty dollars is what Lacasse paid our dear Dauphin," said the Cure benignly, "and a very proper charge. Lacasse probably gave Monsieur there quite as much, and Monsieur will give it to the first poor man he meets, or send it to the first sick person of whom he hears."

"My own opinion is, he's playing some game here," said the Notary.

"We all play games," said the Seigneur. "His seems to give him hard work and little luxury. Will you bring him to see me at the Manor, my dear Cure?" he added. "He will not go. I have asked him."

"Then I shall visit him at his tailor-shop," said the Seigneur. "I need a new suit."

"But you always had your clothes made in Quebec, Monsieur," said the Notary, still carping.

"We never had such a tailor," answered the Seigneur.

"We'll hear more of him before we're done with him," obstinately urged the Notary.

"It would give Dauphin the greatest pleasure if our tailor proved to be a murderer or a robber. I suppose you believe that he stole our little cross here," the Cure added, turning to the church door, where his eye lingered lovingly on the relic, hanging on a pillar just inside, whither he had had it removed.

"I'm not sure yet he hadn't something to do with it," was the stubborn response.

"If he did, may it bring him peace at last!" said the Cure piously. "I have set my heart on nailing him to our blessed faith as that cross is fixed to the pillar yonder—'I will fasten him like a nail in a sure place,' says the Book. I take it hard that my friend Dauphin will not help me on the way. Suppose the man were evil, then the Church should try to snatch him like a brand from the burning. But suppose that in his past there was no wrong necessary to be hidden in the present—and this I believe with all my heart; suppose that he was wronged, not wronging: then how much more should the Church strive to win him to the light! Why, man, have you no pride in Holy Church? I am ashamed of you, Dauphin, with your great intelligence, your wide reading. With our knowledge of the world we should be broader."

The Seigneur's eyes were turned away, for there was in them at once humour and a suspicious moisture. Of all men in the world he most admired the Cure, for his utter truth and nobility; but he could not help smiling at his enthusiasm—his dear Cure turned evangelist like any "Methody"!—and at the appeal of the Notary on the ground of knowledge of the world. He was wise enough to count himself an old fogy, a provincial, and "a simon-pure habitant," but of the three he only had any knowledge of life. As men of the world the Cure and the Notary were sad failures, though they stood for much in Chaudiere. Yet this detracted nothing from the fine gentlemanliness of the Cure or the melodramatic courtesy of the Notary.

Amused and touched as the Seigneur had been at the Cure's words, he turned now and said: "Always on the weaker side, Cure; always hoping the best from the worst of us."

"I am only following an example at my door—you taught us all charity and justice," answered M. Loisel, looking meaningly at the Seigneur. There was silence a little while, for all three were thinking of the woman of the hut, at the gate of the Seigneur's manor.

On this topic M. Dauphin was not voluble. His original kindness to the woman had given him many troubled hours at home, for Madame Dauphin had construed his human sympathy into the dark and carnal desires of the heart, and his truthful eloquence had made his case the worse. A miserable sentimentalist, the Notary was likely to be misunderstood for ever, and one or two indiscretions of his extreme youth had been a weapon against him through the long years of a blameless married life.

He heaved a sigh of sympathy with the Cure now. "She has not come back yet?" he said to the Seigneur. "No sign of her. She locked up and stepped out, so my housekeeper says, about the time—"

"The day of old Margot's funeral," interposed the Notary. "She'd had a letter that day, a letter she'd been waiting for, and abroad she went—alas! the flyaway—from bad to worse, I fear—ah me!"

The Seigneur turned sharply on him. "Who told you she had a letter that day, for which she had been waiting?" he said.

"Monsieur Evanturel."

The Seigneur's face became sterner still. "What business had he to know that she received a letter that day?"

"He is postmaster," innocently replied the Notary. "He is the devil!" said the Seigneur tartly. "I beg your pardon, Cure; but it is Evanturel's business not to know what letters go to and fro in that office. He should be blind and dumb, so far as we all are concerned."

"Remember that Evanturel is a cripple," the Cure answered gently. "I am glad, very glad it was not Rosalie."

"Rosalie has more than usual sense for her sex," gruffly but kindly answered the Seigneur, a look of friendliness in his eyes. "I shall talk to her about her father; I can't trust myself to speak to the man."

"Rosalie is down there with Madame Dauphin," said the Notary, pointing. "Shall I ask her to come?"

The Seigneur nodded. He was magistrate and magnate, and he was the guarantor of the post-office, and of Rosalie and her father. His eyes fixed in reverie on Rosalie; he and the Cure passively waited her approach.

She came over, pale and a little anxious, but with a courageous look. She had a vague sense of trouble, and she feared it might be the little cross, that haunting thing of all these months.

When she came near, the Cure greeted her courteously, and then, taking the Notary by the arm, led him away.

The Seigneur and Rosalie being left alone, the girl said: "You wish to speak with me, Monsieur?"

The Seigneur scrutinised her sharply. Though her colour came and went, her look was frank and fearless. She had had many dark hours since that fateful month of April. At night, trying to sleep, she had heard the ghostly footsteps in the church, which had sent her flying homeward. Then, there was the hood. She had waited on and on, fearing word would come that it had been found in the churchyard, and that she had been seen putting the cross back upon the church door. As day after day passed she had come at length to realise that, whatever had happened to the hood, she was not suspected. Yet the whole train of circumstances had a supernatural air, for the Cure and Jo Portugais had not made public their experience on the eventful night; she had been educated in a land of legend and superstition, and a deep impression had been made upon her mind, giving to her other new emotions a touch of pathos, of imagination, and adding character to her face. The old Seigneur stroked his chin as he looked at her. He realised that a change had come upon her, that she had developed in some surprising way.

"What has happened—who has happened, Mademoiselle Rosalie?" he asked. He had suddenly made up his mind about that look in her face—he thought it the woman in her which answers to the call of man, not perhaps any particular man, but man the attractive influence, the complement.

Her eyes dropped, then raised frankly to his. "I don't know," —adding, with a quick humour, for he had been very friendly with her, and joked with her in his dry way all her life; "do you, Monsieur?"

He pulled his nose with a quick gesture habitual to him, and answered slowly and meaningly: "The government's a good husband and pays regular wages, Mademoiselle. I'd stick to government."

"I am not asking for a divorce, Monsieur."

He pulled his nose again delightedly—so many people were pathetically in earnest in Chaudiere—even the Cure's humour was too mediaeval and obvious. He had never before thought Rosalie so separate from them all. All at once he had a new interest in her. His cheek flushed a little, his eye kindled, humour relaxed his lips.

"No other husband would intrude so little," he rejoined.

"True, there's little love lost between us, Monsieur." She felt exhilaration in talking with him, a kind of joy in measuring word against word; yet a year ago she would have done no more than smile respectfully and give a demure reply if the Seigneur had spoken to her like this.

The Seigneur noted the mixed emotions in her face and the delicate alertness of expression. As a man of the world, he was inclined to believe that only one kind of experience can bring such looks to a woman's face. He saw in her the awakening of the deeper interests of life, the tremulous apprehension of nascent emotions and passions which, at some time or other, give beauty and importance to the nature of every human being. It did not occur to him that the tailor—the mysterious figure in the parish—might be responsible. He was observant, but not imaginative; he was moved by what he saw, in a quiet, unexplainable manner.

"The government is the best sort of husband. From the other sort you would get more kisses and less ha'pence," he continued.

"That might be a satisfactory balance-sheet, Monsieur."

"Take care, Mademoiselle Rosalie," he rejoined, half seriously, "that you don't miss the ha'pence before you get the kisses."

She turned pale in very fear. What was he going to say? Was the post-office to be taken from them? She came straight to the point.

"What have I done wrong, Monsieur? I've never kept the mail-stage waiting; I've never left the mailbag unlocked; I've never been late in opening the wicket; I've never been careless, and no one's ever complained of a lost letter."

The Seigneur saw her agitation, and was sorry for her. He came to the point as she had done:

"We will have you made postmistress—you alone, Rosalie Evanturel. I've made up my mind to that. But you'll promise not to get married—eh? Anyhow, there's no one in the parish for you to marry. You're too well-born and you've been too well educated for a habitant's wife—and the Cure or I can't marry you."

He was not taken back to see her flush deeply, and it pleased him to see this much life rising to his own touch, this much revelation to give his mind a new interest. He had come to that age when the mind is surprised to find that the things that once charmed charm less, and the things once hated are less acutely repulsive. He saw her embarrassment. He did not know that this was the first time that she had ever thought of marriage since it ceased to be a dream of girlhood, and, by reason of thinking much on a man, had become a possibility, which, however, she had never confessed to herself. Here she was faced by it now in the broad open day: a plain, hard statement, unrelieved by aught save the humour of the shrewd eyes bent upon her.

She did not answer him at once. "Do you promise not to marry so useless a thing as man, and to remain true to the government?" he continued.

"If I wished to marry a man, I should not let the government stand in my way," she said, in brave confusion.

"But do you wish to marry any man?" he asked abruptly, even petulantly.

"I have not asked myself that question, Monsieur, and — should you ask it, unless —" she said, and paused with as pretty and whimsical a glance of merriment as could well be.

He burst out laughing at the swift turn she had given her reply, and at the double suggestion. Then he suddenly changed. A curious expression filled his eyes. A smile, almost beautiful, came to his lips.

"'Pon my honour," he said, in a low tone, "you have me caught! And I beg to say — I beg to say," he added, with a flush mounting in his own face, a sudden inspiration in his look, "that if you do not think me too old and crabbed and ugly, and can endure me, I shall be profoundly happy if you will marry me, Rosalie."

He stood upright, holding himself very hard, for this idea had shot into his mind all in an instant, though, unknown to himself, it had been growing for years, cherished by many a kind act to her father and by a simple gratitude on her part. He had spoken without feeling the absurdity of the proposal. He had never married, and he was unprepared to make any statement on such a theme; but now, having made it somehow, he would stand by it, in spite of any and all criticism. He had known Rosalie since her birth, her education was as good as a convent could secure, she was the granddaughter of a notable seigneur, and here she was, as fine a type of health, beauty and character as man could wish — and he was only fifty! Life was getting lonelier for him every day, and, after all, why should he leave distant relations and the Church his worldly goods? All this flashed through his mind as he waited for her answer. Now it seemed to him that he had meant to say this thing for many years. He had seen an awakening in her—he had suddenly been awakened himself.

"Monsieur, Monsieur," she said in a bewildered way, "do not amuse yourself at my expense."

"Would it be that, then?" he said, with a smile, behind which there was determination and self-will. "I want you to marry me; I do with all my heart. You shall have those ha'pence, and the kisses too, if so be you will take them—or not, as you will, Rosalie."

"Monsieur," she gasped, for something caught her in the throat, and the tears started to her eyes, "ask me to forget that you have ever said those words. Oh, Monsieur, it is not possible, it never could be possible! I am only the postmaster's daughter."

"You are my wife, if you will but say the word," he answered, "and I as proud a husband as the land holds!"

"You were always kind to me, Monsieur," she rejoined, her lips trembling; "won't you be so still?"

"I am too old?" he asked.

"Oh no, it is not that," she replied.

"You have as good manners as my mother had. You need not fear comparison with any lady in the land. Have I not known you all your life? I know the way you have come, and your birth is as good as mine."

"Ah, it is not that, Monsieur!"

"I give you my word that I do not come to you because no one else would have me," he said with a curious simplicity. "I never asked a woman to marry me—never! You are the first. There was talk once—but it was all false. I never meant to ask any one to marry me. But I have the wish now which I never had in my youth. I thought best of myself always; now, I think—I think better of you than—"

"Oh, Monsieur, I beg of you, no more! I cannot; oh, I cannot—"

"You—but no; I will not ask you, Mademoiselle. If you have some one else in your heart, or want some one else there, that is your affair, not mine—undoubtedly. I would have tried to make you happy; you would have had peace and comfort all your life; you could have trusted me—but there it is...." He felt all at once that he was unfair to her, that he had thrust upon her too hard a problem in too troubled an hour.

"I could trust you with my life, Monsieur Rossignol," she replied. "And I love you in a way that a man may be loved to no one's harm or sorrow: it is true that!" She raised her eyes to his simply, trustingly.

He looked at her steadily for a moment. "If you change your mind—"

She shook her head sadly.

"Good, then," he went on, for he thought it wise not to press her now, though he had no intention of taking her no as final. "I'll keep an eye on you. You'll need me some day soon; I can do things that the Cure can't, perhaps." His manner changed still more. "Now to business," he continued. "Your father has been talking about letters received and sent from the post-office. That is punishable. I am responsible for you both, and if it is reported, if the woman were to report it—you know the letter I mean—there would be trouble. You do not talk. Now I am going to ask the government to make you sole postmistress, with full responsibility. Then you must govern your father—he hasn't as much sense as you."

"Monsieur, we owe you so much! I am deeply grateful, and, whatever you do for us, you may rely on me to do my duty."

They could scarcely hear each other speak now, for the soldiers were coming nearer, and the fife-and-drum bands were screeching, 'Louis the King was a Soldier'.

"Then you will keep the government as your husband?" he asked, with forced humour, as he saw the Cure and the Notary approaching.

"It is less trouble, Seigneur," she answered, with a smile of relief.

M. Rossignol turned to the Cure and the Notary. "I have just offered Mademoiselle a husband she might rule in place of a government that rules her, and she has refused," he said in the Cure's ear, with a dry laugh.

"She's a sensible girl, is Rosalie," said the Cure, not apprehending.

The soldiers were now opposite the church, and riding at their head was the battalion Colonel, also member of the Legislature.

They all moved down, and Rosalie disappeared in the crowd. As the Seigneur and the Cure greeted the Colonel, the latter said:

"At luncheon I'll tell you one of the bravest things ever seen. Happened half-hour ago at the Red Ravine. Man who did it wore an eye-glass—said he was a tailor."

CHAPTER XXV
THE COLONEL TELLS HIS STORY

The Colonel had lunched very well indeed. He had done justice to every dish set before him; he had made a little speech, congratulating himself on having such a well-trained body of men to command, and felicitating Chaudiere from many points of view. He was in great good-humour with himself, and when the Notary asked him—it was at the Manor, with the soldiers resting on the grass without—about the tale of bravery he had promised them, he brought his fist down on the table with great intensity but little noise, and said:

"Chaudiere may well be proud of it. I shall refer to it in the Legislature on the question of roads and bridges—there ought to be a stone fence on that dangerous road by the Red Ravine—Have I your attention?"

He stood up, for he was an excitable and voluble Colonel, and he loved oration as a cat does milk. With a knife he drew a picture of the locale on the table cloth. "Here I was riding on my sorrel, all my noble fellows behind, the fife and drums going as at Louisburg—that day! Martial ardour united to manliness and local pride—follow me? Here we were, Red Ravine left, stump fences and waving fields of grain right. From military point of view, bad position—ravine, stump fence, brave soldiers in the middle, food for powder—catch it?—see?"

He emptied his glass, drew a long breath, and again began, the carving-knife cutting a rhetorical path before him. "I was engaged upon the military problem—demonstration in force, no scouts ahead, no rearguard, ravine on the right, stump fence on the left, red coats, fife-and-drum band, concealed enemy—follow me? Observant mind always sees problems everywhere—unresting military genius accustoms intelligence to all possible contingencies—'stand what I mean?"

The Seigneur took a pinch of snuff, and the Cure, whose mind was benevolent, listened with the gravest interest.

"At the juncture when, in my mind's eye, I saw my gallant fellows enfiladed with a terrible fire, caught in a trap, and I, despairing, spurring on to die at their head—have I your attention?—just at that moment there appeared between the ravine and the road ahead a man. He wore an eyeglass; he seemed an unconcerned spectator of our movements—so does the untrained, unthinking eye look out upon destiny! Not far away was a wagon, in it a man. Wagon bisecting our course from a cross-road—"

He drew a line on the table-cloth with the carvingknife, and the Notary said: "Yes, yes, the concession road."

"So, Messieurs. There were we, a battalion and a fife-and-drum band; there was the man with the eyeglass, the indifferent spectator, yet the engine of fate; there was the wagon, a mottled horse, and a man driving—catch it? The mottled horse took fright at our band, which at that instant strikes up 'The Chevalier Drew his Sabre'. He shies from the road with a leap, the man falls backwards into the wagon, and the reins drop. The horse dashes from the road into the open, and rushes on to the ravine. What good now to stop the fifes and drums-follow me? What can we, an armed force, bandoleered, knapsacked, sworded, rifled, impetuous, brave, what can we do before this tragedy? The man in the wagon senseless, the flying horse, the ravine, death! How futile the power of man—'stand what I mean?"

"Why didn't your battalion shoot the horse?" said the Seigneur drily, taking a pinch of snuff. "Monsieur," said the Colonel, "see the irony, the implacable irony of fate—we had only blank cartridge! But see you, here was this one despised man with an eye-glass, a tailor—takes nine tailors to make a man!—between the ravine and the galloping tragedy. His spirit arrayed itself like an army with banners, prepared to wrestle with death as Jacob wrestled with his shadow all the night 'sieur le Cure!"

The Cure bowed; the Notary shook back his oiled locks in excitement.

"Awoke a whole man—nine-ninths, as in Adam—in the obscure soul of the tailor, and, rushing forward, he seized the mottled horse by the bridle as he galloped upon the chasm: The horse dragged him on—dragged him on—on—on. We, an army, so to speak, stood and watched the Tailor and the Tragedy! All seemed lost, but, by the decree of fate—"

"The will of God," said the Cure softly.

"By the great decree, the man was able to stop the horse, not a half-dozen feet from the ravine. The horse and the insensible driver were spared death—death. So, Messieurs, does bravery come from unexpected places—see?"

The Seigneur, the Cure, and even the Notary clapped their hands, and murmured praises of the tailor-man. But the Colonel did not yet take his seat.

"But now, mark the sequel," he said. "As I galloped over, I saw the tailor look into the wagon, and turn away quickly. He waited by the horse till I came near, and then walked off without a word. I rode up, and tapped him with my sword upon the shoulder. 'A noble deed, my good man,' said I. 'I approve of your conduct, and I will remember it in the Legislature when I address the committee of the whole house on roads and bridges.' What do you think was his reply to my affable words? When I tapped him approvingly on the shoulder a second time, he screwed his eye-glass in his eye, and, with no emotion, though my own eyes were full of tears, he said, in a tone of affront, 'Look after the man there, constable,' and pointed to the wagon. Constable—mon Dieu! Gross manners even for a tailor!"

"I had not thought his manners bad," said the Cure, as the Colonel sat down, gulped a glass of brandy-and-water, and mopped his forehead.

"A most remarkable tailor," said the Seigneur, peering into his snuff-box.

"And the driver of the mottled horse?" asked the Notary.

"Knocked senseless. One of my captains soon restored him. He followed us into the village. He is a quack-doctor. I suppose he is now selling tinctures, pulling teeth, and driving away rheumatics. He gave me his card. I told him he should leave one on the tailor."

With a flourish he threw a professional card upon the table, before the Cure.

The Cure picked it up and read:

JOHN BROWN, B.A., M.D.,

Healer of Ailments that Defy the Ordinary Skill of Ordinary Medical Men. Rheumatism, Sciatica, Headache, Toothache, Asthma, Ague, Pleurisy, Gout, and all Chronic Diseases Yield Instantly to the Power of his Medicines.

Dr. Brown will publicly treat the most stubborn cases, laying himself open to the derision of mankind if he does not instantly give relief and benefit. His whole career has been a blessing to his fellows, and his journey now through this country, fresh from his studies in the Orient, is to introduce his remedies to a suffering world, for the conquest of malady, not for personal profit.

JOHN BROWN, B.A., M.D.,

Specialist in Chronic Diseases and General Practitioner.

CHAPTER XXVI
A SONG, A BOTTLE, AND A GHOST

All day John Brown, ex-clergyman and quack-doctor, harangued the people of Chaudiere from his gaily-painted wagon. He had the perfect gift of the charlatan, and he had discovered his metier. Inclined to the picturesque by nature, melodramatic and empirical, his earlier career had been the due fruit of habit and education. As a dabbler in mines he had been out of his element. He lacked the necessary reticence, and arsenic had not availed him, though it had tempted Billy Wantage to forgery; and because Billy hid himself behind the dismal opportunity of silence, had ruined the name of a dead man called Charley Steele. Since Charley's death John Brown had never seen Billy: he had left the town one woful day an hour after Billy had told him of the discovery Charley had made. From a far corner of the country he had read the story of Charley's death; of the futile trial of the river-drivers afterwards, ending in acquittal, and the subsequent discovery of the theft of the widows' and orphans' trust-moneys.

On this St. Jean Baptiste's day he was thinking of anything and everything else but Charley Steele. Nothing could have been a better advertisement for him than the perilous incident at the Red Ravine. Falling backwards when the horse suddenly bolted, his head had struck the medicine-chest, and he had lain insensible till brought back to consciousness by the good offices of the voluble Colonel. He had not, therefore, seen Charley. It was like him that his sense of gratitude to the unknown tailor should be presently lost in exploiting the interest he created in the parish. His piebald horse, his white "plug" hat, his gaily painted wagon, his flamboyant manner, and, above all, the marvellous tale of his escape from death, were more exciting to the people of Chaudiere than the militia, the dancing-bears, the shooting-galleries, or the boat-races. He could sing extremely well—had he not trained his own choir when he was a parson? had not Billy approved his comic songs?—and these comic songs, now sandwiched between his cures and his sales, created much laughter. He cured headaches, toothaches, rheumatism, and all sorts of local ailments "with despatch." He miraculously juggled away pains by what he called his Pain Paint, and he stopped a cough by a laugh and a dose of his Golden Pectoral. In the exuberance of trade, which steadily increased till sundown, he gave no thought to the tailor, to whom, however, he had sent by a messenger a two-dollar bill and two bottles of Pain Paint, with the lordly announcement that he would call in the evening and "present his compliments and his thanks." The messenger left the Pain Paint on the door-step of the tailor-shop, and the two dollars he promptly spent at the Trois Couronnes.

Rosalie Evanturel rescued the bottles from the doorstep and awaited Charley's return to his shop, that she might take them over to him, and so have an excuse to speak with him; for to-day her heart and mind were full of him. He had done a brave thing for the medicine-man, and had then fled from public gaze as a brave man should. There was no one to compare with him. Not even the Cure was his superior in ability, and certainly he was a greater man—though seemingly only a tailor—than M. Rossignol. M. Rossignol—she flushed. Who could have believed that the Seigneur would say those words to her this morning—to her, Rosalie Evanturel, who hadn't five hundred dollars to her name? That she should be asked to be Madame Rossignol! Confusion mingled with her simple pride, and she ran out into the street, to where her father sat listening to the medicine-man singing, in doubtful French:

"*I am a waterman bold,*

Oh, I'm a waterman bold:

But for my lass I have great fear,

Yes, in the isles I have great fear,

For she is young, and I am old,

And she is bien gentille!"

It was night now. The militia had departed, their Colonel roaring commands at them out of a little red drill-book; the older people had gone to their homes, but festive youth hovered round the booths and sideshows, the majority enjoying themselves at some expense in the medicine-man's encampment.

As Rosalie ran towards the crowd she turned a wistful glance to the tailor-shop. Not a sign of life there! She imagined M'sieu' to be at Vadrome Mountain, until, glancing round the crowd at the quack-doctor's wagon, she saw Jo Portugais gloomily watching the travelling tinker of human bodies. Evidently M'sieu' was not at Vadrome Mountain.

He was not far from her. At the side of the road, under a huge maple-tree with wide-spreading branches, Charley stood and watched John Brown performing behind the flaring oil-lights stuck on poles round his wagon, his hat now on, now off; now singing a comic song in English—-'I found Y' in de Honeysuckle Paitch;' now a French chanson—'En Revenant de St. Alban;' now treating a stiff neck or a bent back, or giving momentary help to the palsy of an old man, or again making a speech.

Charley was in touch again with the old life, but in a kind of fantasy only—a staring, high-coloured dream. This man—John Brown—had gone down before his old ironical questioning, had been, indirectly, the means of disgracing his name. A step forward to that wagon, a word uttered, a look, and he would have to face again the life he had put by for ever, would have to meet a hard problem and settle it—to what misery and tragedy, who might say? Under this tree he was M. Mallard, the infidel tailor, whose life was slowly entering into the life of this place called Chaudiere, slowly being acted upon by habit, which, automatically repeated, at length becomes character. Out in that red light, before that garish wagon, he would be Charley Steele, barrister, 'flaneur', and fop, who, according to the world, had misused a wife, misled her brother, robbed widows and orphans, squandered a fortune, become drunkard and wastrel, and at last had lost his life in a disorderly tavern at the Cote Dorion. This man before him had contributed to his disgrace; but once he had contributed to John Brown's disgrace; and to-day he had saved John Brown's life. They were even.

All the night before, all this morning, he had fought a fierce battle with his past—with a raging thirst. The old appetite had swept over him fiercely. All day he had moved in a fevered conflict, which had lifted him away from the small movements of everyday life into a region where only were himself and one strong foe, who tirelessly strove with him. In his old life he had never had a struggle of any sort. His emotions had been cloaked, his soul masked, there had been a film before his eyes, he had worn an armour of selfishness on a life which had no deep problems, because it had no deep feelings—a life never rising to the intellectual prowess for which it was fitted, save when under the stimulus of liquor.

From the moment he had waked from a long seven months' sleep in the hut on Vadrome Mountain, new deep feelings had come to him as he faced problems of life. Fighting had begun from that hour—a fighting which was putting his nature through bitter mortal exercises, yet, too, giving him a sense of being he had never known. He had now the sweetness of earning daily bread by the work of his hands; of giving to the poor, the needy, and the afflicted; of knowing for the first time in his life that he was not alone in the world. Out of the grey dawn of life a woman's voice had called to him; the look of her face had said to him: "Viens ici! Viens ici!"—"Come to me! Come to me!"

But with that call there was the answer of his soul, the desolating cry of the dispossessed Lear—"—never—never—never—never!"

He had not questioned himself concerning Rosalie—had dared not to do so. But now, as he stood under the great tree, within hand-touch of the old life, in imminent danger of being thrust back into it, the question of Rosalie came upon him with all the force of months of feeling behind it. Thus did he argue with himself:

"Do I love her? And if I love her, what is to be done? Marry her, with a wife living? Marry her while charged with a wretched crime? Would that be love? But suppose I never were discovered, and we might live here for ever, I as 'Monsieur Mallard,' in peace and quiet all the days of our life? Would that be love?... Could there be love with a vital secret, like, a cloud between, out of which, at any hour, might spring discovery? Could I build our life upon a silence which must be a lie? Would I not have to face the question, Does any one know cause or just impediment why this woman should not be married to this man? Tell Rosalie all, and let the law separate myself and Kathleen? That would mean Billy's ruin and imprisonment, and Kathleen's shame, and it might not bring Rosalir. She is a Catholic, and her Church would not listen to it. Would I have the right to bring trouble into her life? To wrong one woman should seem enough for one lifetime!"

At that instant Rosalie, who had been on the outskirts of the crowd, moved into his line of vision. The glare from the lights fell on her face as she stood by her father's chair, looking curiously at the quack-doctor who, having sold many bottles of his medicines, noy picked up a guitar and began singing an old dialect chanson of Saintonge:

"Voici, the day has come
When Rosette leaves her home!
With fear she walks in the sun,
For Raoul is ninety year,
And she not twenty-one.
La petit' Rosette,
She is not twenty-one.

"He takes her by the hand,
And to the church they go;
By parents 'twas well meant,
But is Rosette content?
'Tis gold and ninety year

She walks in the sun with fear,

La petit' Rosette,

Not twenty-one as yet!"

Charley's eyes, which had watched her these months past, noted the deepening colour of the face, the glow in the eyes, the glances of keen but agitated interest towards the singer. He could not translate her looks; and she, on her part, had she been compelled to do so, could only have set down a confusion of sensations.

In Rosette she saw herself, Rosalie Evanturel; in the man "de quatre-vingt-dix ans," who was to marry this Rosette of Saintonge, she saw M. Rossignol. Disconcerting pictures of a possible life with the Seigneur flitted before her mind. She beheld herself, young, fresh-cheeked, with life beating high and all the impulses of youth panting to use, sitting at the head of the seigneury table. She saw herself in the great pew at Mass, stiff with dignity, old in the way of manorial pride—all laughter dead in her, all spring-time joy overshadowed by the grave decorum of the Manor, all the imagination of her dreaming spirit chilled by the presence of age, however kindly and quaint and cheerful.

She shuddered, and dropped her eyes upon the ground, as, to the laughter and giggling of old and young gathered round the wagon, the medicine-man sang:

"He takes her by the hand,

And to her chamber fair—"

Then, suddenly turning, she vanished into the night, followed by the feeble inquiry of her father's eyes, the anxious look in Charley's.

Charley could not read her tale. He had, however, a hot impulse to follow and ask her if she would vanish from the scene if the medicine-man should sing of Rosette and a man of thirty, not ninety, years. The fight he had had all day with his craving for drink had made him feverish, and all his emotions—unregulated, under the command of his will only—were in high temperature. A reckless feeling seized him. He would go to Rosalie, look into her eyes, and tell her that he loved her, no matter what the penalty of fate. He had never loved a human being, and the sudden impulse to cry out in the new language was driving him to follow the girl whose spirit for ever called to him.

He made a step forward to follow her, but stopped short, recalled to caution and his danger by the voice of the medicine-man:

"I had a friend once—good fellow, bad fellow, cleverest chap I ever knew. Tremendous fop—ladies loved him—cheeks like roses—tongue like sulphuric acid. Beautiful to look at. Clothes like a fashion-plate—got any fashion-plates in Chaudiere? 'who's your tailor?'" he added, in the slang of the hour, with a loud laugh, then stopped suddenly and took off his hat. "I forgot," he added, with upturned eyes and a dramatic seriousness, "your tailor saved my life to-day-henceforth I am the friend of all tailors. Well, to continue. My friend that was—I call him my friend, though he ruined me and ruined others,—didn't mean to, but he did just the same,—he came to a bad end. But he was a great man while he lived. And what I'm coming to is this, the song he used to sing when, in youthful exuberance, we went on the war-path like our young friend over there"—he pointed to a young habitant farmer, who was trying hard to preserve equilibrium—"Brown's Golden Pectoral will cure that cough, my friend!" he added, as the young man, gloomily ashamed of the laughter of the crowd, hiccoughed and turned away to the tree under which Charley Steele stood. "Well," he went on, "I was going to say that my friend's name was Charley, and the song he used to sing when the roosters waked the morn was called 'Champagne Charlie.' He was called 'Champagne Charlie'—till he came to a bad end."

He twanged his guitar, cleared his throat, winked at Maximilian Cour the baker, and began:

"The way I gained my title's by a hobby which I've got

Of never letting others pay, however long the shot;

Whoever drinks at my expense is treated all the same;

Whoever calls himself my friend, I make him drink champagne.

Some epicures like Burgundy, Hock, Claret, and Moselle,

But Moet's vintage only satisfies this champagne swell.

What matter if I go to bed and head is muddled thick,

A bottle in the morning sets me right then very quick.

Champagne Charlie is my name;

Champagne Charlie is my name.

Who's the man with the heart so young,

Who's the man with the ginger tongue?

Champagne Charlie is his name!"

Under the tree, Charley Steele listened to this jaunty epitaph on his old self. At the first words of the coarse song there rushed on him the dreaded thirst. He felt his veins beating with desire, with anger, disgust, and shame; for there was John Brown, to the applause of the crowd, imitating his old manner, his voice, his very look. He started forward, but the drunken young habitant lurched sideways under the tree and collapsed upon the ground, a bottle of whiskey falling out of his pocket and rolling almost to his own feet.

"Champagne Charlie is my name,"

sang the medicine-man. All Charley's old life surged up in him as dyked water suddenly bursts bounds and spreads destruction. He had an uncontrollable impulse. As a starving animal snatches at the first food offered it, he stooped, with a rattle in his throat, seized the bottle, uncorked it, put it to his lips, and drank—drank—drank.

Then he turned and plunged away into the trees. The sound of the song followed him. It came to him, the last refrain, sung loudly to the laughter of the crowd, in imitation of his own voice as it used to be—it had been a different voice during this past year. He turned with headlong intention, and, as the last notes of the song and the applause that followed it, died away, threw back his head and sang out of the darkness:

"Champagne Charlie is my name—"

With a shrill laugh, like the half-mad cry of an outcast soul, he flung away farther into the trees.

There was a sudden silence. The crowd turned with half-apprehensive laughter to the trees. Upon John Brown the effect was startling. His face blanched, his eyes grew large with terror, his mouth opened in helpless agitation. Charley Steele was lying under the waters of the great river, his bones rotting there for a year, yet here was his voice coming out of the night, in response to his own grotesque imitation of the dead man. Seeing his agitation, women turned pale, men felt their flesh creep, imagination gave a thrilling coldness to the air. For a moment the silence was unbroken. Then John Brown stretched out his hand and said, in a hoarse whisper:

"It was his voice—Charley's voice, and he's been dead a year!"

Within half-an-hour, in utter collapse and fright, he was being driven to the next parish by two young habitants whom he paid to accompany him.

CHAPTER XXVII
OUT ON THE OLD TRAIL

There was one person in the crowd surrounding the medicine-man's wagon who had none of that superstitious thrill which had scattered the habitants into little awe-stricken groups, and then by twos and threes to their homes; none of that fear which had reduced the quack-doctor to such nervous collapse that he would not spend the night in the village. Jo Portugais had recognised the voice—that of Charley Steele the lawyer who had saved him from hanging years ago. It was little like the voice of M'sieu'! There was that in it which frightened him. He waited until he had seen the quackdoctor start for the next parish, then he went slowly down the street. There were people still about, so he walked on towards the river. When he returned, the street was empty. Keeping in the shadow of the trees, he went to Charley's house. There was a light in a window. He went to the back door and tried it. It was not locked, and, without knocking, he stepped inside the kitchen. Here was no light, and he passed into the hallway and on to a little room opening from the tailorshop. He knocked; then, not waiting for response, opened the door and entered.

Charley was standing before a mirror, holding a pair of scissors. He turned abruptly, and said forbiddingly: "I am at my toilet!"

Then, turning again to the mirror, with a shrug of the shoulders, he raised the shears to his beard. Before he could use them, Jo's hand was on his arm.

"Stop that, M'sieu'!" he said huskily.

Charley had drunk nearly a whole bottle of cheap whiskey within an hour. He was intoxicated, but, as had ever been the case with him, his brain was working clearly, his hand was steady; he was in that wide dream of clear-seeing and clear-knowing which, in old days, had given him glimpses of the real life from which, in the egotism of the non-intime, he had been shut out. Looking at Jo now, he was possessed by a composed intoxication like that in which he had moved during that last night at the Cote Dorion.

But now, with the baleful crust of egotism gone, with every nerve of life exposed, with conscience struggling to its feet from the torpor of thirty-odd vacant years, he was as two men in one, with different lives and different souls, yet as inseparable in their misery as those poor victims of Gallic tyranny, chained back to back and thrown into the Seine.

Jo's words, insistent and eager, suddenly roused in him some old memory, which stayed his hand.

"Why should I stop?" he asked quietly, and smiling that smile which had infuriated the river-drivers at the Cote Dorion.

"Are you going back, M'sieu?"

"Back where?" Charley's eyes were fixed on Jo with a penetrating intensity, heightened to a strange abstraction, as though he saw not Jo alone, but something great distances beyond.

Jo did not answer this question directly. "Some one came to-day—he is gone; some one may come to-morrow—and stay," he said meaningly.

Charley went over to the fire and sat down on a bench, opening and shutting the scissors mechanically. Jo was in the light, and Charley's eyes again studied him hard.

His memory was industriously feeling its way into the baffling distance.

"What if some one did come-and stay?" he urged quietly.

"You might be recognised without the beard."

"What difference would it make?" Charley's memory was creeping close to the hidden door. It was feeling-feeling for the latch.

"You know best, M'sieu'."

"But what do you know?" Charley's face now had a strained look, and he touched his lips with his tongue. "What John Brown knows, M'sieu'."

There flashed across Charley's mind the fatal newspaper he had read on the day he awakened to memory again in the but on Vadrome Mountain. He remembered that he had put it in the fire. But Jo might have read it before it was spread upon the bench-put it there of purpose for him to read. Yet what reason could Jo have for being silent, for hiding his secret?

There was silence for a space, in which Charley's eyes were like unmoving sparks of steel. He did not see Jo's face—it was in a mist—he was searching, searching, searching. All at once he felt the latch of the hidden door under his finger; he saw a court-room, a judge and jury, and hundreds of excited faces, himself standing in the midst. He saw twelve men file slowly into the room and take their seats-all save one, who stood still in his place and said: "Not guilty, your Honour!" He saw the prisoner leave the box and step down a free man. He saw himself coming out into the staring summer day. He watched the prisoner come to him and touch his arm, and say: "Thank you, M'sieu'. You have saved my life." He saw himself turn to this man:

He roused from his trance, he staggered to his feet, the shears rattled to the floor. Lurching forward, he caught Jo Portugais by the throat, and said, as he had said outside the court-room years ago:

"Get out of my sight. You're as guilty as hell!"

His grip tightened—tightened on Jo's throat. Jo did not move, though his face grew black. Then, suddenly, the hands relaxed, a bluish paleness swept over the face, and Charley fell sidewise to the floor before Jo could catch him.

All night, alone, the murderer struggled with death over the body of the lawyer who had saved his life.

CHAPTER XXVIII
THE SEIGNEUR GIVES A WARNING

Rosalie had watched a shut door for five days—a door from which, for months past, had come all the light and glow of her life. It framed a figure which had come to represent to her all that meant hope and soul and conscience-and love. The morning after St. Jean Baptiste's day she had awaited the opening door, but it had remained closed. Ensued watchful hours, and then from Jo Portugais she had learned that M'sieu' had been ill and near to death. She had been told the weird story of the medicine-man and the ghostly voice, and, without reason, she took the incident as a warning, and associated it with the man across the way. She was come of a superstitious race, and she herself had heard and seen things of which she never had been able to speak—the footsteps in the church the night she had screwed the little cross to the door again; the tiny round white light by the door of the church; the hood which had vanished into the unknown. One mystery fed another. It seemed to her as if some dreadful event were forward; and all day she kept her eyes fixed on the tailor's door.

Dead—if M'sieu' should die! If M'sieu' should die—it needed all her will to prevent herself from going over and taking things in her own hands, being his nurse, his handmaid, his slave. Duty—to the government, to her father? Her heart cried out that her duty lay where all her life was eddying to one centre. What would the world say? She was not concerned for that, save for him. What, then, would M'sieu' say? That gave her pause. The Seigneur's words the day before had driven her back upon a tide of emotions which carried her far out upon that sea where reason and life's conventions are derelicts, where Love sails with reckless courage down the shoreless main.

"If I could only be near him!" she kept saying to herself. "It is my right. I would give my life, my soul for his. I was with him before when his life was in danger. It was my hand that saved him. It was my love that tended him. It was my soul that kept his secret. It was my faith that spoke for him. It was my heart that ached for him. It is my heart that aches for him now as none other in all the world can. No one on earth could care as I care. Who could there be?" Something whispered in her ear, "Kathleen!" The name haunted her, as the little cross had done. Misery and anger possessed her, and she fought on with herself through dark hours.

Thus five days had gone, until at last a wagon was brought to the door of the tailor-shop, and M'sieu' came out, leaning on the arm of Jo Portugais. There were several people in the street at the time, and they kept whispering that M'sieu' had been at death's door. He was pale and haggard, with dark hollows under the eyes. Just as he got into the wagon the Cure came up. They shook hands. The Cure looked him earnestly in the face, his lips moved, but no one could have told what he said. As the wagon started, Charley looked across to the post-office. Rosalie was standing a little back from the door, but she stepped forward now. Their eyes met. Her heart beat faster, for there was a look in his eyes she had never seen before—a look of human helplessness, of deep anxiety. It was meant for her—for herself alone. She could not trust herself to go and speak to him. She felt that she must burst into tears. So, with a look of pity and pain, she watched the wagon go down the street.

Rat-tat-tat-tat-tat!—the Seigneur's gold-headed cane rattled on the front door of the tailor-shop. It was plain to be seen his business was urgent.

Madame Dauphin came hurrying from the postoffice, followed by Maximilian Cour and Filion Lacasse. "Ah, M'sieu', the tailor will not answer. There's no use knocking—not a bit, M'sieu' Rossignol," said Madame.

The Seigneur turned querulously upon the Notary's wife, yet with a glint of hard humour in his eye. He had no love for Madame Dauphin. He thought she took unfair advantages of M. Dauphin, whom also he did not love, but whose temperament did him credit.

"How should Madame know whether or no the gentleman will answer? Does Madame share the gentleman's confidence, perhaps?" he remarked.

Madame did not reply at once. She turned on the saddler and the baker. "I hope you'll learn a lesson," she cried triumphantly. "I've always said the tailor was quite the gentleman; and now you see how your betters call him. No, M'sieu', the gentleman will not answer," she added to the Seigneur.

"He is in bed yet, Madame?"

"His bed is empty there, M'sieu'," she said, impressively, and pointing.

"I suppose I should trust you in this matter; I suppose you should know. But, Dauphin—what does Dauphin say?"

The saddler laughed outright. Maximilian Cour suddenly blushed in sympathy with Madame Dauphin, who now saw the drift of the Seigneur's remarks, and was sensibly agitated, as the Seigneur had meant her to be. Had she not turned Dauphin's human sympathies into a crime? Had not the Notary supported the Seigneur in his friendly offices to Paulette Dubois; and had not Madame troubled her husband's life because of it? Madame bridled up now—with discretion, for it was not her cue to offend the Seigneur.

"All the village knows his bed's empty there, M'sieu'," she said, with tightening lips.

"I am subtracted from the total, then?" he asked drily.

"You have been away for the last five days—"

"Come, now, how did you know that?"

"Everybody knows it. You went away with the Colonel and the soldiers on St. Jean Baptiste's day. Since then M'sieu' the tailor has been ill. I should think Mrs. Flynn would have told you that, M'sieu'."

"H'm! Would you? Well, Mrs. Flynn has been away too—and you didn't know that! What is the matter with Monsieur Mallard?"

"Some kind of fever. On St. Jean Baptiste's day he was taken ill, and that animal Portugais took care of him all night—I wonder how M'sieu' can have the creature about! That St. Jean Baptiste's night was an awful night. Have you heard of what happened, M'sieu'? Ghost or no ghost—"

"Come, come, I want to know about the tailor, not of ghosts," impatiently interrupted the Seigneur. "Tiens! M'sieu', the tailor was ill for three days here, and he would let no one except the Cure and Jo Portugais near him. I went myself to clean up and make some broth, but that toad of a Portugais shut the door in my face. The Cure told us to go home and leave M'sieu' with Portugais. He must be very sick to have that black sheep about him—and no doctor either."

The saddler spoke up now. "I took him a bottle of good brandy and some buttermilk-pop and seed cake—I would give him a saddle if he had a horse—he got my thousand dollars for me! Well, he took them, but what do you think? He sent them right off to the shantyman, Gugon, who has a broken leg. Infidel or no, I'm on his side for sure. And God blesses a cheerful giver, I'm told."

It was the baker's chance, and he took it. "I played 'The Heart Bowed Down'-it is English-under his window, two nights ago, and he sent word for me to come and play it again in the kitchen. Ah, that is a good song, 'The Heart Bowed Down.'"

"You'd be a better baker if you fiddled less," said Madame Dauphin, annoyed at being dropped out of the conversation.

"The soul must be fed, Madame," rejoined the baker, with asperity.

"Where is the tailor now?" said the Seigneur shortly. "At Portugais's on Vadrome Mountain. They say he looked like a ghost when he went. Rosalie Evanturel saw him, but she has no tongue in her head this morning," added Madame.

The Seigneur moved away. "Good-bye to you—I am obliged to you, Madame. Good-bye, Lacasse. Come and fiddle to me some night, Cour."

He bowed to the obsequious three, and then bent his steps towards the post-office. They seemed about to follow him, but he stopped them with a look. The men raised their bonnets-rouges, the woman bowed low, and the Seigneur entered the post-office door.

From the shadows of the office Rosalie had watched the little group before the door of the tailor-shop. She saw the Seigneur coming across the street. Suddenly she flushed deeply, for there came to her mind the song the quack-doctor sang:

> "Voila, the day has come
>
> When Rosette leaves her home!
>
> With fear she walks in the sun,
>
> For Raoul is ninety year,
>
> And she not twenty-one."

As M. Rossignol's figure darkened the doorway, she pretended to be busy behind the wicket, and not to see him. He was not sure, but he thought it quite possible that she had seen him coming, and he put her embarrassment down to shyness. Naturally the poor child was not given the chance every day to receive an offer of marriage from a seigneur. He had made up his mind that she would be sure to accept him if he asked her a second time.

"Ah, Ma'm'selle Rosalie," he said gaily, "what have you to say that you should not come before a magistrate at once?"

"Nothing, if Monsieur Rossignol is to be the magistrate," she replied, with forced lightness.

"Good!" He looked at her quizzically through his gold-handled glass. "I can't frighten you, I see. Well, you must wait a little; you shall be sworn in postmistress in three days." His voice lowered, became more serious. "Tell me," he said, "do you know what is the matter with the gentleman across the way?" Turning, he looked across to the tailor-shop, as though he expected "the gentleman" to appear, and he did not see her turn pale. When his look fell on her again, she was self-controlled.

"I do not know, Monsieur."

"You have been opposite him here these months past—did you ever see anything not—not as it should be?"

"With him, Monsieur? Never."

"It is as though the infidel behaved like a good Catholic and a Christian?"

"There are good Catholics in Chaudiere who do not behave like Christians."

"What would you say, for instance, about his past?"

"What should I say about his past, Monsieur? What should I know?"

"You should know more than any one else in Chaudiere. The secrets of his breast might well be bared to you."

She started and crimsoned. Before her eyes there came a mist obscuring the Seigneur, and for an instant shutting out the world. The secrets of his breast—what did he mean? Did he know that on Monsieur's breast was the red scar which...

M. Rossignol's voice seemed coming from an infinite distance, and as it came, the mist slowly passed from her eyes.

"You will know, Mademoiselle Rosalie," he was saying, "that while I suggested that the secrets of his breast might well be bared to you, I meant that as an honest lady and faithful postmistress they were not. It was my awkward joke—a stupid gambolling by an old man who ought to know better."

She did not answer, and he continued:

"You know that you are trusted. Pray accept my apologies."

She was herself again. "Monsieur," she said quietly; "I know nothing of his past. I want to know nothing. It does not seem to me that it is my business. The world is free for a man to come and go in, if he keeps the law and does no ill—is it not? But, in any case, I know nothing. Since you have said so much, I shall say this, and betray no 'secrets of his breast'—that he has received no letter through this office since the day he first came from Vadrome Mountain."

The Seigneur smiled. "A wonderful tailor! How does he carry on business without writing letters?"

"There was a large stock of everything left by Louis Trudel, and not long ago a commercial traveller was here with everything."

"You think he has nothing to hide, then?"

"Have not we all something to hide—with or without shame?" she asked simply.

"You have more sense than any woman in Chaudiere, Mademoiselle."

She shook her head, yet she raised her eyes gratefully to him.

"I put faith in what you say," he continued. "Now listen. My brother, the Abbe, chaplain to the Archbishop, is coming here. He has heard of 'the infidel' of our parish. He is narrow and intolerant—the Abbe. He is going to stir up trouble against the tailor. We are a peaceful people here, and like to be left alone. We are going on very well as we are. So I wanted to talk to Monsieur to-day. I must make up my own mind how to act. The tailor-shop is the property of the Church. An infidel occupies it, so it is said; the Abbe does not like that. I believe there are other curious suspicions about Monsieur: that he is a robber, or incendiary, or something of the sort. The Abbe may take a stand, and the Cure's position will be difficult. What is more, my brother has friends here, fanatics like himself. He has been writing to them. They are men capable of doing unpleasant things—the Abbe certainly is. It is fair to warn the tailor. Shall I leave it to you? Do not frighten him. But there is no doubt he should be warned—fair play, fair play! I hear nothing but good of him from those whose opinions I value. But, you see, every man's history in this parish and in every parish of the province is known. This man, for us, has no history. The Cure even admits there are some grounds for calling him an infidel, but, as you know, he would keep the man here, not drive him out from among us. I have not told the Cure about the Abbe yet. I wished first to talk with you. The Abbe may come at any moment. I have been away, and only find his letters to-day."

"You wish me to tell Monsieur?" interrupted Rosalie, unable to hold silence any longer. More than once during the Seigneur's disclosure she had felt that she must cry out and fiercely repel the base insinuations against the man she loved.

"You would do it with discretion. You are friendly with him, are you not?—you talk with him now and then?"

She inclined her head. "Very well, Monsieur. I will go to Vadrome Mountain to-morrow," she said quietly. Anger, apprehension, indignation, possessed her, but she held herself firmly. The Seigneur was doing a friendly thing; and, in any case, she could have no quarrel with him. There was danger to the man she loved, however, and every faculty was alive.

"That's right. He shall have his chance to evade the Abbe if he wishes," answered M. Rossignol.

There was silence for a moment, in which she was scarcely conscious of his presence; then he leaned over the counter towards her, and spoke in a low voice.

"What I said the other day I meant. I do not change my mind—I am too old for that. Yet I'm young enough to know that you may change yours."

"I cannot change, Monsieur," she said tremblingly.

"But you will change. I knew your mother well, I know how anxious she was for your future. I told her once that I should keep an eye on you always. Her father was my father's good friend. I knew you when you were in the cradle—a little brown-haired babe. I watched you till you went to the convent. I saw you come back to take up the duties which your mother laid down, alas!—"

"Monsieur—!" she said choking, and with a troubled little gesture.

"You must let me speak, Rosalie. We got your father this post-office. It is a poor living, but it keeps a roof over your head. You have never failed us you have always fulfilled our hopes. But the best years of your life are going, and your education and your nature have not their chance. Oh, I've not watched you all these years for nothing. I never meant to ask you to marry me. It came to me, though, all at once, and I know that it has been in my mind all these years—far back in my mind. I don't ask you for my own sake alone. Your father may grow very ill—who can tell what may happen!"

"I should be postmistress still," she said sadly.

"As a young girl you could not have the responsibility here alone. And you should not waste your life it is a fine, full spirit; let the lean, the poor-spirited, go singly. You should be mated. You can't marry any of the young farmers of Chaudiere. 'Tis impossible. I can give you enough for any woman's needs—the world may be yours to see and use to your heart's content. I can give, too"—he drew himself up proudly—"the unused emotions of a lifetime." This struck him as a very fine and important thing to say.

"Ah, Monsieur, that is not enough," she responded.

"What more can you want?"

She looked up with a tearful smile. "I will tell you one day, Monsieur."

"What day?"

"I have not picked it out in the calendar."

"Fix the day, and I will wait till then. I will not open my mouth again till then."

"Michaelmas day, then, Monsieur," she answered mechanically and at haphazard, but with an urged gaiety, for a great depression was on her.

"Good. Till Michaelmas day, then!" He pulled his long nose, laughing silently.... "I leave the tailor in your hands. Give every man his chance, I say. The Abbe is a hard man, but our hearts are soft—eh, eh, very soft!" He raised his hat and turned to the door.

CHAPTER XXIX
THE WILD RIDE

There had been a fierce thunder-storm in the valley of the Chaudiere. It had come suddenly from the east, had shrieked over the village, levelling fences, carrying away small bridges, and ending in a pelting hail, which whitened the ground with pebbles of ice. It had swept up to Vadrome Mountain, and had marched furiously through the forest, carrying down hundreds of trees, drowning the roars of wild animals and the crying and fluttering of birds. One hour of ravage and rage, and then, spent and bodiless, the storm crept down the other side of the mountain and into the next parish, whither the affrighted quack-doctor had betaken himself. After, a perfect calm, a shining sun, and a sweet smell over all the land, which had thirstily drunk the battering showers.

In the house on Vadrome Mountain the tailor of Chaudiere had watched the storm with sympathetic interest. It was in accord with his own feelings. He had had a hard fight for months past, and had gone down in the storm of his emotions one night when a song called Champagne Charlie had had a weird and thrilling antiphonal. There had been a subsequent debacle for himself, and then a revelation concerning Jo Portugais. Ensued hours and days, wherein he had fought a desperate fight with the present—with himself and the reaction from his dangerous debauch.

The battle for his life had been fought for him by this gloomy woodsman who henceforth represented his past, was bound to him by a measureless gratitude, almost a sacrament—of the damned. Of himself he had played no conscious part in it till the worst was over. On the one side was the Cure, patient, gentle, friendly, never pushing forward the Faith which the good man dreamed should give him refuge and peace; on the other side was the murderer, who typified unrest, secretiveness, an awful isolation, and a remorse which had never been put into words or acts of restitution. For six days the tailor-shop and the life at Chaudiere had been things almost apart from his consciousness. Ever-recurring memories of Rosalie Evanturel were driven from his mind with a painful persistence. In the shadows where his nature dwelt now he would not allow her good innocence and truth to enter. His self-reproach was the more poignant because it was silent.

Watching the tempest-swept valley, the tortured forest, where wild life was in panic, there came upon him the old impulse to put his thoughts into words, "and so be rid of them," as he was wont to say in other days. Taking from his pocket some slips of paper, he laid them on the table before him. Three or four times he leaned over the paper to write, but the noise of the storm again and again drew his look to the window. The tempest ceased almost as suddenly as it had come, and, as the first sunlight broke through the flying clouds, he mechanically lifted a sheet of the paper and held it up to the light. It brought to his eyes the large water-mark, Kathleen!

A sombre look passed over his face, he shifted in his chair, then bent over the paper and began to write. Words flowed from his pen. The lines of his face relaxed, his eyes lightened; he was lost in a dream. He thought of the present, and he wrote:

> "Wave walls to seaward,
>
> Storm-clouds to leeward,
>
> Beaten and blown by the winds of the West;
>
> Sail we encumbered
>
> Past isles unnumbered,
>
> But never to greet the green island of Rest."

He thought of Father Loisel. He had seen the good man's lips tremble at some materialistic words he had once used in their many talks, and he wrote:

> "Lips that now tremble,
>
> Do you dissemble
>
> When you deny that the human is best? —
>
> Love, the evangel,
>
> Finds the Archangel?
>
> Is that a truth when this may be a jest?
>
> "Star-drifts that glimmer
>
> Dimmer and dimmer,
>
> What do ye know of my weal or my woe?
>
> Was I born under

The sun or the thunder?

What do I come from? and where do I go?

"Rest, shall it ever

Come? Is endeavour

But a vain twining and twisting of cords?

Is faith but treason;

Reason, unreason,

But a mechanical weaving of words?"

He thought of Louis Trudel, in his grave, and his own questioning: "Show me a sign from Heaven, tailorman!" and he wrote:

"What is the token,

Ever unbroken,

Swept down the spaces of querulous years,

Weeping or singing

That the Beginning

Of all things is with us, and sees us, and hears?"

He made an involuntary motion of his hand to his breast, where old Louis Trudel had set a sign. So long as he lived, it must be there to read: a shining smooth scar of excoriation, a sacred sign of the faith he had never been able to accept; of which he had never, indeed, been able to think, so distant had been his soul, until, against his will, his heart had answered to the revealing call in a woman's eyes. He felt her fingers touch his breast as they did that night the iron seared him; and out of this first intimacy of his soul he wrote:

"What is the token?

Bruised and broken,

Bend I my life to a blossoming rod?

Shall then the worst things

Come to the first things,

Finding the best of all, last of all, God?"

Like the cry of his "Aphrodite," written that last afternoon of the old life, this plaint ended with the same restless, unceasing question. But there was a difference. There was no longer the material, distant note of a pagan mind; there was the intimate, spiritual note of a mind finding a foothold on the submerged causeway of life and time.

As he folded up the paper to put it into his pocket, Jo Portugais entered the room. He threw in a corner the wet bag which had protected his shoulders from the rain, hung his hat on a peg of the chimney-piece, nodded to Charley, and put a kettle on the little fire.

"A big storm, M'sieu'," Jo said presently as he put some tea into a pot.

"I have never seen a great storm in a forest before," answered Charley, and came nearer to the window through which the bright sun streamed.

"It always does me good," said Jo. "Every bird and beast is awake and afraid and trying to hide, and the trees fall, and the roar of it like the roar of the chasse-galerie on the Kimash River."

"The Kimash River—where is it?"

Jo shrugged his shoulders. "Who knows!"

"Is it a legend, then?"

"It is a river."

"And the chasse-galerie?"

"That is true, M'sieu', no matter what any one thinks. I know; I have seen—I have seen with my own eyes." Jo was excited now.

"I am listening." He took a cup of tea from Portugais and drank eagerly.

"The Kimash River, M'sieu', that is the river in the air. On it is the chasse-galerie. You sell your soul to the devil; you ask him to help you; you deny God. You get into a canoe and call on the devil. You are lifted up, canoe and all, and you rush on down rapids, over falls, on the Kimash River in the air. The devil stands behind you and shouts, and you sing, 'V'la! l'bon vent! V'la l'joli vent!' On and on you go, faster and faster, and you forget the world, and you forget yourself, and the devil is with you in the air—in the chasse-galerie on the Kimash River."

"Jo," said Charley Steele, "do you honestly think there's a river like that?"

'M'sieu', I know it. I saw Ignace Latoile, who robbed a priest and got drunk on the communion wine—I saw him with the devil in the Black Canoe at the Saguenay. I could see Ignace; I could see the devil; I could see the Kimash River. I shall ride myself some day.

"Ride where?"

"What does it matter where?"

"Why should you ride?"

"Because you ride fast with the devil."

"What is the good of riding fast?"

"In the rush a man forget."

"What does he forget, my friend?"

There was a pause, in which a man with a load of crime upon his soul dwelt upon the words my friend, coming from the lips of one who knew the fulness of his iniquity. Then he answered:

"In the noise he forget that a voice is calling in his ear, 'You did It!' He forget what he see in his dreams. He forget the hand that touch him on the arm when he walk in the woods alone, or lie down to sleep at night, no one near. He forget that some one wait—wait—wait, till he has suffer long enough, or till, one day, he think he is happy again, and the Thing he did is far off like a dream—to drag him out to the death he did not die. He forget that he is alone—all alone in the world, for ever and ever and ever."

He suddenly sank upon the floor beside Charley, and a groan burst from his lips. "To have no friend—ah, it is so awful!" he said. "Never to see a face that look into yours, and know how bad are you, and doesn't mind. For five years I have live like that. I cannot let any one be my friend because I was that! They seem to know—everything, everybody—what I am. The little children when I pass them run away to hide. I have wake in the night and cry out in fear, it is so lonely. I have hear voices round me in the woods, and I run and run and run from them, and not leave them behind. Three times I go to the jails in Quebec to see the prisoners behind the bars, and watch the pains on their faces, to understand what I escape. Five times have I go to the courts to listen to murderers tried, and watch them when the Jury say Guilty! and the Judge send them to death—that I might know. Twice have I go to see murderers hung. Once I was helper to the hangman, that I might hear and know what the man said, what he felt. When the arms were bound, I felt the straps on my own; when the cap come down, I gasp for breath; when the bolt is shot, I feel the wrench and the choke, and shudder go through myself—feel the world jerk out in the dark. When the body is bundled in the pit, I see myself lie still under the quick-lime with the red mark round my throat."

Charley touched him on the shoulder. "Jo—poor Jo, my friend!" he said. Jo raised his eyes, red with an unnatural fire, deep with gratitude.

"As I sit at my dinner, with the sun shining and the woods green and glad, and all the world gay, I have see what happened all over again. I have see his strong hands; his bad face laugh at my words; I have see him raise his riding-whip and cut me across the head. I have see him stagger and fall from the blows I give him with the knife—the knife which never was found—why, I not know, for I throw it on the ground beside him! There, as I sit in the open day, a thousand times I have see him shiver and fall, staring, staring at me as if he see a dreadful thing. Then I stand up again and strike at him—at his ghost!—as I did that day in the woods. Again I see him lie in his blood, straight and white—so large, so handsome, so still! I have shed tears—but what are tears! Blind with tears I have call out for the devils of hell to take me with them. I have call on God to give me death. I have prayed, and I have cursed. Twice I have travelled to the grave where he lies. I have knelt there and have beg him to tell the truth to God, and say that he torture me till I kill him. I have beg him to forgive me and to haunt me no more with his bad face. But never—never—never—have I one quiet hour until you come, M'sieu'; nor any joy in my heart till I tell you the black truth—M'sieu'! M'sieu'!"

He buried his face between Charley's feet, and held them with his hands.

Charley laid a hand on the shaggy head as though it were that of a child. "Be still—be still, Jo," he said gently.

Since that night of St. Jean Baptiste's festival, no word of the past, of the time when Charley turned aside the revanche of justice from a man called Joseph Nadeau, had been spoken between them. Out of the delirium of his drunken trance had come Charley's recognition of the man he knew now as Jo Portugais. But the recognition had been sent again into the obscurity whence it came, and had not been mentioned since. To outward seeming they had gone on as before. As Charley saw the knotted brows, the staring eyes, the clinched hands, the figure of the woodsman rigid in its agony of remorse, he said to himself: "What right had I to save this man's life? To have paid for his crime would have been easier for him. I knew he was guilty. Perhaps it was my duty to see that every condition, to the last shade of the law, was satisfied, but was it justice to the poor devil himself? There he sits with a load on him that weighs him down every hour of his life. I called him back; I gave him life; but I gave him memory and remorse, and the ghosts that haunt him: the voice in his ear, the touch on his arm, the some one that is 'waiting—waiting—waiting!' That is what I did, and that is what the brother of the Cure did for me. He drew me back. He knew I was a drunkard, but he drew me back. I might have been a murderer like Portugais. The world says I was a thief, and a thief I am until I prove to the world I am innocent—and wreck three lives! How much of Jo's guilt is guilt? How much remorse should a man suffer to pay the debt of a life? If the law is an eye for an eye and a tooth for a tooth, how much hourly remorse and torture, such as Jo's, should balance the eye or the tooth or the life? I wonder, now!"

He leaned over, and, helping Jo to his feet, gently forced him down upon a bench near. "All right, Jo, my friend," he said. "I understand. We'll drink the gall together."

They sat and looked at each other in silence.

At length Charley leaned over and touched Jo on the shoulder.

"Why did you want to save yourself?" he said.

At that instant there was a knock at the door, and a voice said: "Monsieur!—Monsieur!"

Jo sprang to his feet with a sharp exclamation, then went heavily to the door and threw it open.

CHAPTER XXX
ROSALIE WARNS CHARLEY

Charley's eyes met Rosalie's with a look the girl had never seen in them before. It gave a glow to his haggard face.

Rosalie turned to Jo and greeted him with a friendlier manner than was her wont towards him. The nearer she was to Charley, the farther away from him, to her mind, was Portugais, and she became magnanimous.

Jo nodded' awkwardly and left the room. Looking after the departing figure, Rosalie said: "I know he has been good to you, but—but do you trust him, Monsieur?"

"Does not everybody in Chaudiere trust him?"

"There is one who does not, though perhaps that's of no consequence."

"Why do you not trust him?"

"I don't know. I never knew him do a bad thing; I never heard of a bad thing he has done; and—he has been good to you."

She paused, flushing as she felt the significance of her words, and continued: "Yet there is—I cannot tell what. I feel something. It is not reasonable to go upon one's feelings; but there it is, and so I do not trust him."

"It is the way he lives, here in these lonely woods—the mystery around him."

A change passed over her. With the first glow of meeting the object of her visit had receded, though since her last interview with the Seigneur she had not rested a moment, in her anxiety to warn him of his danger. "Oh, no," she said, lifting her eyes frankly to his: "oh, no, Monsieur! It is not that. There is mystery about you!" She felt her heart beating hard. It almost choked her, but she kept on bravely. "People say strange and bad things about you. No one knows"—she trembled under the painful inquiry of his eyes. Then she gained courage and went on, for she must make it clear she trusted him, that she took him at his word, before she told him of the peril before him — "No one knows where you came from... and it is nobody's business. Some people do not believe in you. But I believe in you — I should believe in you if every one doubted; for there is no feeling in me that says, 'He has done some wicked thing that stands-between us.' It isn't the same as with Portugais, you see — naturally, it could not be the same."

She seemed not to realise that she was telling more of her own heart than she had ever told. It was a revelation, having its origin in an honesty which impelled a pure outspokenness to himself. Reserve, of course, there had been elsewhere, for did not she hold a secret with him? Had she not hidden things, equivocated else where? Yet it had been at his wish, to protect the name of a dead man, for the repose of whose soul masses were now said, with expensive candles burning. For this she had no repentance; she was without logic where this man's good was at stake.

Charley had before him a problem, which he now knew he never could evade in the future. He could solve it by none of the old intellectual means, but by the use of new faculties, slowly emerging from the unexplored fastnesses of his nature.

"Why should you believe in me?" he asked, forcing himself to smile, yet acutely alive to the fact that a crisis was impending. "You, like all down there in Chaudiere, know nothing of my past, are not sure that I haven't been a hundred times worse than you think poor Jo there. I may have been anything. You may be harbouring a man the law is tracking down."

In all that befell Rosalie Evanturel thereafter, never could come such another great resolute moment. There was nothing to support her in the crisis but her own faith. It needed high courage to tell this man who had first given her dreams, then imagination, hope, and the beauty of doing for another's well-being rather than for her own — to tell this man that he was a suspected criminal. Would he hate her? Would his kindness turn to anger? Would he despise her for even having dared to name the suspicion which was bringing hither an austere Abbe and officers of the law?

"We are harbouring a man the law is tracking down," she said with an infinite appeal in her eyes.

He did not quite understand. He thought that perhaps she meant Jo, and he glanced towards the door; but she kept her eyes on him, and they told him that she meant himself. He chilled, as though ether were being poured through his veins.

Did the world know, then, that Charley Steele was alive? Was the law sending its officers to seize the embezzler, the ruffian who had robbed widow and orphan?

If it were so.... To go back to the world whence he came, with the injury he must do to others, and the punishment also that he must suffer, if he did not tell the truth about Billy! And Chaudiere, which, in spite of all, was beginning to have a real belief in him—where was his contempt for the world now!... And Rosalie, who trusted him—this new element rapidly grew dominant in his thoughts-to be the common criminal in her eyes!

His paleness gave way to a flush as like her own as could be.

"You mean me?" he asked quietly.

She had thought that his flush meant anger, and she was surprised at the quiet tone. She nodded assent. "For what crime?" he asked.

"For stealing."

His heart seemed to stand still. Then, it had come in spite of all it had come. Here was his resurrection, and the old life to face.

"What did I steal?" he asked with dull apathy. "The gold vessels from the Catholic Cathedral of Quebec, after—after trying to blow up Government House with gunpowder."

His despair passed. His face suddenly lighted. He smiled. It was so absurd. "Really!" he said. "When was the place blown up?"

"Two days before you came here last year—it was not blown up; an attempt was made."

"Ah, I did not know. Why was the attempt made to blow it up?"

"Some Frenchman's hatred of the English, they say."

"But I am not French."

"They do not know. You speak French as perfectly as English ah, Monsieur, Monsieur, I believe you are whatever you say." Pain and appeal rang from her lips.

"I am only an honest tailor," he answered gently. He ruled his face to calmness, for he read the agony in the girl's face, and troubled as he was, he wished to show her that he had no fear.

"It is for what you were they will arrest you," she said helplessly, and as though he needed to have all made clear to him. "Oh, Monsieur," she continued, in a broken voice, "it would shame me so to have you made a prisoner in Chaudiere—before all these silly people, who turn with the wind. I should not lift my head—but yes, I should lift my head!" she added hurriedly. "I should tell them all they lied—every one—the idiots! The Seigneur—"

"Well, what of the Seigneur-Rosalie?"

Her own name on his lips—the sound of it dimmed her eyes.

"Monsieur Rossignol does not know you. He neither believes nor disbelieves. He said to me that if you wanted consideration, to command him, for in Chaudiere he had heard nothing but good of you. If you stayed, he would see that you had justice—not persecution. I saw him two hours ago."

She said the last words shyly, for she was thinking why the Seigneur had spoken as he did—that he had taken her opinion of Monsieur as his guide, and she had not scrupled to impress him with her views. The Seigneur was in danger of becoming prejudiced by his sentiments.

A wave of feeling passed over Charley, a rushing wave of sympathy for this simple girl, who, out of a blind confidence, risked so much for him. Risk there certainly was, if she—if she cared for him. It was cruelty not to reassure her.

Touching his breast, he said gravely: "By this sign here, I am not guilty of the crime for which they come to seek me, Rosalie. Nor of any other crime for which the law might punish me—dear, noble friend."

He did so little to get such rich return. Her eyes leaped up to brighter degrees of light, her face shone with a joy it had never reflected before, her blood rushed to her finger-tips. She abruptly sat down in a chair and buried her face in her hands, trembling. Then, lifting her head slowly, after a moment she spoke in a tone that told him her faith, her gratitude—not for reassurance, but for confidence, which is as water in a thirsty land to a woman.

"Oh, Monsieur, I thank you, I thank you from the depth of my heart; and my heart is deep indeed, very, very deep—I cannot find what lies lowest in it! I thank you, because you trust me, because you make it so easy to—to be your friend; to say 'I know' when any one might doubt you. One has no right to speak for another till—till the other has given confidence, has said you may. Ah, Monsieur, I am so happy!"

In very abandonment of heart she clasped her hands and came a step nearer to him, but abruptly stopped still; for, realising her action, timidity and embarrassment rushed upon her.

Charley understood, and again his impulse was to say what was in his heart and dare all; but resolution possessed him, and he said quickly:

"Once, Rosalie, you saved me—from death perhaps. Once your hands helped my pain—here." He touched his breast. "Your words now, and what you do, they still help me—here... but in a different way. The trouble is in my heart, Rosalie. You are glad of my confidence? Well, I will give you more.... I cannot go back to my old life. To do so would injure others—some who have never injured me and some who have. That is why. That is why I do not wish to be taken to Quebec now on a false charge. That is all I can say. Is it enough?"

She was about to answer, but Jo Portugais entered, exclaiming. "M'sieu'," he cried, "men are coming with the Seigneur and Cure."

Charley nodded at Jo, then turned to Rosalie. "You need not be seen if you go out by the back way, Mademoiselle." He held aside the bear-skin curtain of the door that led into the next room.

There was a frightened look in her face. "Do not fear for me," he continued. "It will come right—somehow. You have done more for me than any one has ever done or ever will do. I will remember till the last moment of my life. Good-bye."

He laid a hand on her shoulder and gently pushed her from the room.

"God protect you! The Blessed Virgin speak for you! I will pray for you," she whispered.

CHAPTER XXXI
CHARLEY STANDS AT BAY

Charley turned quickly to the woodsman. "Listen," he said, and he told Jo how things stood.

"You will not hide, M'sieu'? There is time," Jo asked.

"I will not hide, Jo."

"What will you do?"

"I'll decide when they come."

There was silence for a moment, then the sound of voices on the hill-side.

Charley's soul rose up in revolt against the danger that faced him—not against personal peril, but the danger of being dragged back again into the life he had come from, with all that it involved—the futility of this charge against him! To be the victim of an error—to go to the bar of justice with the hand of injustice on his arm!

All at once the love of this new life welled up in him, as a spring of water overflows its bounds. A voice kept ringing in his ears, "I will pray for you." Subconsciously his mind kept saying, "Rosalie—Rosalie—Rosalie!" There was nothing now that he would not do to avert his being taken away upon this ridiculous charge. Mistaken identity? To prove that, he must at once prove himself—who he was, whence he came. Tell the Cure, and make it a point of honour for his secret to be kept? But once told, the new life would no longer stand by itself as the new life, cut off from all contact with the past. Its success, its possibility, must lie in its absolute separateness, with obscurity behind—as though he had come out of nothing into this very room, on that winter morning when memory returned.

It was clear that he must, somehow, evade the issue. He glanced at Jo, whose eyes, strained and painful, were fixed upon the door. Here was a man who suffered for his sake.... He took a step forward, as though with sudden resolve, but there came a knocking, and, pausing, he motioned Jo to open the door. Then, turning to a shelf, he took something from it hastily, and kept it in his hand.

Jo roused himself with an effort, and opened to the knocking.

Three people entered: the Seigneur, the Cure, and the Abbe Rossignol, an ascetic, severe man, with a face of intolerance and inflexibility. Two constables in plain clothes followed; one stolid, one alert, one English and one French, both with grim satisfaction in their faces—the successful exercise of his trade is pleasant to every craftsman. When they entered, Charley was standing with his back to the fireplace, his eye-glass adjusted, one hand stroking his beard, the other held behind his back.

The Cure came forward and shook hands in an eager friendly way.

"My dear Monsieur," said he, "I hope that you are better."

"I am quite well, thank you, Monsieur le Cure," answered Charley. "I shall get back to work on Monday, I hope."

"Yes, yes, that is good," responded the Cure, and seemed confused. He turned uneasily to the Seigneur. "You have come to see my friend Portugais," Charley remarked slowly, almost apologetically. "I will take my leave." He made a step forward. The two constables did the same, and would have laid their hands upon his shoulder but that the Seigneur said tartly:

"Stand off, Jack-in-boxes!"

The two stood aside, and looked covertly at the Seigneur, whose temper seemed unusually irascible. Charley's face showed no surprise, but he looked inquiringly at the Cure.

"If they wish to be measured for uniforms—or manners—I will see them at my shop," he said.

The Seigneur chuckled. Charley stepped again towards the door. The two constables stood before it. Again he turned inquiringly, this time towards the Cure. The Cure did not speak.

"It is you we wish to see, tailor," said the Abbe Rossignol.

Soft-tongued irony leaped to Charley's lips: "Have I, then, the honour of including Monsieur among my customers? I cannot recall Monsieur's figure. I think I should not have forgotten it."

It was now the old Charley Steele, with the new body, the new spirit, but with the old skilful mind, aggravatingly polite, non-intime—the intolerant face of this father of souls irritated him.

"I never forget a figure which has idiosyncrasy," he added, with a bland eye wandering over the priest's gaunt form. It was his old way to strike first and heal after—"a kick and a lick," as old Paddy Wier, whom he once saved from prison, said of him. It was like bygone years of another life to appear in defence when the law was tightening round a victim. The secret spring had been touched, the ancient machinery of his mind was working almost automatically.

The illusion was considerable, for the Seigneur had taken the only arm-chair in the room, a little apart, as it were, filling the place of judge. The priest-brother, cold and inveterate, was like the attorney for the crown. The Cure was the clerk of the court, who could only echo the decisions of the Judge. The constables were the machinery of the Law, and Jo Portugais was the unwilling witness, whose evidence would be the crux of the case. The prisoner—he himself was prisoner and prisoner's counsel.

A good struggle was forward.

He had enraged the Abbe as much as he had delighted the Abbe's brother; for nothing gave the Seigneur such pleasure as the discomfiture of the Abbe Rossignol, chaplain and ordinary to the Archbishop of Quebec. The genial, sympathetic nature of the Seigneur could not even be patient with the excessive piety of the churchman, who, in rigid righteousness, had thrashed him cruelly as a boy. At Charley's words upon the Abbe's figure, gaunt and precise as a swaddled ramrod, he pulled his nose with a grunt of satisfaction.

The Cure, the peace-maker, intervened. The tailor's meaning was sufficiently clear: if they had come to see him personally, then it was natural for him to wish to know the names and stations of his guests, and their business. The Seigneur was aware that the tailor did know, and he enjoyed the 'sang-froid' with which he was meeting the situation.

"Monsieur," said the Cure, in a mollifying voice, "I have ventured to bring the Seigneur of Chaudiere"—the Seigneur stood up and bowed gravely—"and his brother, the Abbe Rossignol, who would speak with you on private business"—he ignored the presence of the constables.

Charley bowed to the Seigneur and the Abbe, then turned inquiringly towards the two constables. "Friends of my brother the Abbe," said the Seigneur maliciously.

"Their names, Monsieur?" asked Charley.

"They have numbers," answered the Seigneur whimsically—to the Cure's pain, for levity seemed improper at such a time.

"Numbers of names are legally suspicious, numbers for names are suspiciously legal," rejoined Charley. "You have pierced the disguise of discourtesy," said the Seigneur, and, on the instant, he made up his mind that whatever the tailor might have been, he was deserving of respect.

"You have private business with me, Monsieur?" asked Charley of the Abbe.

The Abbe shook his head. "The business is not private, in one sense. These men have come to charge you with having broken into the cathedral at Quebec and stolen the gold vessels of the altar; also with having tried to blow up the Governor's residence."

One of the constables handed Charley the warrant. He looked at it with a curious smile. It was so natural, yet so unnatural, to be thus in touch with the habits of far-off times.

"On what information is this warrant issued?" he asked.

"That is for the law to show in due course," said the priest.

"Pardon me; it is for the law to show now. I have a right to know."

The constables shifted from one foot to the other, looked at each other meaningly, and instinctively felt their weapons.

"I believe," said the Seigneur evenly, "that—" The Abbe interrupted. "He can have information at his trial."

"Excuse me, but the warrant has my endorsement," said the Seigneur, "and, as the justice most concerned, I shall give proper information to the gentleman under suspicion." He waved a hand at the Abbe, as at a fractious child, and turned courteously to Charley.

"Monsieur," he said, "on the tenth of August last the cathedral at Quebec was broken into, and the gold altar-vessels were stolen. You are suspected. The same day an attempt was made to blow up the Governor's residence. You are suspected."

"On what ground, Monsieur?"

"You appeared in this vicinity three days afterwards with an injury to the head. Now, the incendiary received a severe blow on the head from a servant of the Governor. You see the connection, Monsieur?"

"Where is the servant of the Governor, Monsieur?"

"Dead, unfortunately. He told the story so often, to so much hospitality, that he lost his footing on Mountain Street steps—you remember Mountain Street steps possibly, Monsieur?—and cracked his head on the last stone."

There was silence for a moment. If the thing had not been so serious, Charley must have laughed outright. If he but disclosed his identity, how easy to dispose of this silly charge! He did not reply at once, but looked calmly at the Abbe. In the pause, the Seigneur added "I forgot to add that the man had a brown beard. You have a brown beard, Monsieur."

"I had not when I arrived here."

Jo Portugais spoke. "That is true, M'sieu'; and what is more, I know a newly shaved face when I see it, and M'sieu's was tanned with the sun. It is foolish, that!"

"This is not the place for evidence," said the Abbe sharply.

"Excuse me, Abbe," said his brother; "if Monsieur wishes to have a preliminary trial here, he may. He is in my seigneury; he is a tenant of the Church here—"

"It is a grave offence that an infidel, dropping down here from, who knows where—that an acknowledged infidel should be a tenant of the Church!"

"The devil is a tenant of the Almighty, if creation is the Almighty's," said Charley.

"Satan is a prisoner," snapped the Abbe.

"With large domains for exercise," retorted Charley, "and in successful opposition to the Church. If it is true that the man you charge is an infidel, how does that warrant suspicion?"

"Other thefts," answered the Abbe. "A sacred iron cross was stolen from the door of the church of Chaudiere. I have no doubt that the thief of the gold vessels of the cathedral was the thief of the iron cross."

"It is not true," sullenly broke in Jo Portugais.

"What proof have you?" said the Seigneur. Charley waved a deprecating hand towards Jo.

"I shall not call Portugais as evidence," he said.

"You are conducting your own case?" asked the Seigneur, with a grim smile.

"It is dangerous, I believe."

"I will take my chances," answered Charley. "Will you tell me what object the criminal could have in stealing the gold vessels from the cathedral?" he added, turning to the Abbe.

"They were gold!"

"And for taking the cross from the door of the church in Chaudiere?"

"It was sacred, and he was an infidel, and hated it."

"I do not see the logic of the argument. He stole the vessels because they were valuable, and the iron cross because he was an infidel! Now how do you know that the suspected criminal was an infidel, Monsieur?"

"It is well known."

"Has he ever said so?"

"He does not deny it."

"If you were charged with being an opium-eater, does it follow that you are one because you do not deny it? There was a Man who was said to blaspheme, to have all 'the crafts and assaults of the devil' — was it His duty to deny it? Suppose you were accused of being a highwayman, would you be less a highwayman if you denied it? Or would you be less guilty if you denied it?"

"That is beside the case," said the priest with acerbity.

"Faith, I think it is the case itself," said the Seigneur with a satisfied pull of his nose.

"But do you seriously suggest that only infidels rob churches?" Charley persisted.

"I am not here to be cross-examined," answered the Abbe harshly. "You are charged with robbing the cathedral and trying to blow up the Governor's residence. Arrest him!" he added, turning to the constables.

"Stand where you are, men," sharply threatened the Seigneur. "There are no lettres de cachet nowadays, Francois," he added tartly to his brother.

"If it is the exclusive temptation of an infidel to rob a church, has infidelity also an inherent penchant for arson? Is it a patent? Why did the infidel blow up the Governor's residence?" continued Charley.

"He did not blow it up, he only tried," interposed the Cure softly.

"I was not aware," said Charley. "Well, did the man who stole the patens from the altar—"

"They were chalices," again interrupted the Cure, with a faint smile.

"Ah, I was not aware!" again rejoined Charley. "I repeat, what reason had the person who stole the chalices to try to blow up the Governor's residence? Is it a sign of infidelity, or—"

"You can answer for that yourself," angrily interposed the Abbe. The strain was telling on his nerves.

"It is fair to give reasons for the suspicion," urged the Seigneur acidly.

"As I said before, Francois, this is not the fifteenth century."

"He hated the English government," said the Abbe. "I do not understand," responded Charley. "Am I then to suppose that the alleged criminal was a Frenchman as well as an infidel?"

There was silence, and Charley continued. "It is an unusual thing for a French Abbe to be so concerned for the safety of an English Protestant's life and housing... the Governor is a Protestant—eh? That is, indeed, a zeal almost Christian—or millennial."

The Abby turned to the Seigneur. "Are you going to interfere longer with the process of the law?"

"I think Monsieur has not quite finished his argument," said the Seigneur, with a twist of the mouth.

"If the man was a Frenchman, why do you suspect the tailor of Chaudiere?" asked Charley softly. "Of course I understand the reason behind all: you have heard that the tailor is an infidel; you have protested to the good Cure here, and the Cure is a man who has a sense of justice, and will not drive a poor man from his parish by Christian persecution— without cause. Since certain dates coincide and impulses urge, you suspect the tailor. Again, according to your mind, a man who steals holy vessels must needs be an infidel; therefore a tailor in Chaudiere, suspected of being an infidel, stole the holy chalices. It might seem a fair case for a grand jury of clericals. But it breaks down in certain places. Your criminal is a Frenchman; the tailor of Chaudiere is an Englishman."

The Abbe's face was contracted with stubborn annoyance, though he held his tongue from violence. "Do you deny that you are French?" he asked tartly.

"I could almost endure the suspicion because of the compliment to my command of your charming language."

"Prove that you are an Englishman. No one knows where you came from; no one knows what you are. You are a fair subject for suspicion, apart from the evidence shown," said the Abbe, trying now to be as polite as the tailor.

"This is a free country. So long as the law is obeyed, one can go where one wills without question, I take it."

"There is a law of vagrancy."

"I am a householder, a tenant of the Church, not a vagrant."

"Monsieur, you can have your choice of proving these things here or in Quebec," said the Abbe, with angry impatience again.

"I may not be compelled to prove anything. It is the privilege of the law to prove the crime against me."

"You are a very remarkable tailor," said the Abbe sarcastically.

"I have not had the honour of making you even a cassock, I think. Monsieur le Cure, I believe, approves of those I make for him. He has a good figure, however."

"You refuse to identify yourself?" asked the Abbe, with asperity.

"I am not aware that you possess any right to ask me to do so."

The Abbe's thin lips clipped-to like shears. He turned again towards the officers.

"It would relieve the situation," interposed the Seigneur, "if Monsieur could find it possible to grant the Abbe's demand."

Charley bowed to the Seigneur. "I do not know why I should be taken for a Frenchman or an infidel. I speak French well, I presume, but I spoke it from the cradle. I speak English with equally good accent," he added, with the glimmer of a smile; for there was a kind of exhilaration in the little contest, even with so much at stake. This miserable, silly charge had that behind it which might open up a grave, make its dead to walk, fright folk from their senses, and destroy their peace for ever. Yet he was cool and thinking clearly. He measured up the Abbe in his mind, analysed him, found the vulnerable spot in his nature, the avenue to the one place lighted by a lamp of humanity. He leaned a hand upon the ledge of the chimney where he stood, and said, in a low voice:

"Monsieur l'Abbe, it is sometimes the misfortune of just men to be terribly unjust. 'For conscience sake' is another name for prejudice—for those antipathies which, natural to us, are, at the same time, trap-doors, for our just intentions. You, Monsieur, have a radical antipathy to those men who are unable to see or to feel what you were privileged to see and feel from the time of your birth. You know that you are right. Do you think that those who do not see as you do are wicked because they were not given what you were given? If you are right, may they, poor folk! not be the victims of their blindness of heart—of the darkness born with them, or of the evils that overtake them? For conscience sake, you would crush out evil. To you an infidel—so called—is an evil-doer, a peril to the peace of God. You drive him out from among the faithful. You heard that a tailor of Chaudiere was an infidel. You did not prove him one, but you, for conscience sake, are trying to remove him, by fixing on him a crime of which he may, with slight show of reason, be suspected. But I ask you, would you have taken the same deep interest in setting the law upon this suspected man did you not believe him to be an infidel?"

He paused. The Abbe made no reply. The Cure was bending forward eagerly; the Seigneur sat with his hands over the top of his cane, his chin on his hands, never taking his eyes from him, save to glance once or twice at his brother. Jo Portugais was crouched on the bench, watching.

"I do not know what makes an infidel," Charley went on. "Is it an honest mind, a decent life, an austerity of living as great as that of any priest, a neighbourliness that gives and takes in fairness—"

"No, no, no," interposed the Cure eagerly. "So you have lived here, Monsieur; I can vouch for that. Charity and a good heart have gone with you always."

"Do you mean that a man is an infidel because he cannot say, as Louis Trudel said to me, 'Do you believe in God?' and replies, as I replied, 'God knows!' Is that infidelity? If God is God, He alone knows when the mind or the tongue can answer in the terms of that faith which you profess. He knows the secret desires of our hearts, and what we believe, and what we do not believe; He knows better than we ourselves know—if there is a God. Does a man conjure God, if he does not believe in God? 'God knows!' is not a statement of infidelity. With me it was a phrase—no more. You ask me to bare my inmost soul. I have not learned how to confess. You ask me to lay bare my past, to prove my identity. For conscience sake you ask that, and I for conscience sake say I will not, Monsieur. You, when you enter your priestly life, put all your past behind you. It is dead for ever: all its deeds and thoughts and desires, all its errors—sins. I have entered on a life here which is to me as much a new life as your priesthood is to you. Shall I not have the right to say, that may not be disinterred? Have I not the right to say, Hands off? For the past I am responsible, and for the past I will speak from the past; but for the deeds of the present I will speak only from the present. I am not a Frenchman; I did not steal the little cross from the church door here, nor the golden chalices in Quebec; nor did I seek to injure the Governor's residence. I have not been in Quebec for three years."

He ceased speaking, and fixed his eyes on the Abbe, who now met his look fairly.

"In the way of justice, there is nothing hidden that shall not be revealed, nor secret that shall not be made known," answered the Abbe. "Prove that you were not in Quebec on the day the robbery was committed." There was silence. The Abbe's pertinacity was too difficult. The Seigneur saw the grim look in Charley's face, and touched the Abbe on the arm. "Let us walk a little outside. Come, Cure" he added. "It is right that Monsieur should have a few minutes alone. It is a serious charge against him, and reflection will be good for us all."

He motioned the constables from the room. The Abby passed through the door into the open air, and the Cure and the Seigneur went arm in arm together, talking earnestly. The Cure turned in the doorway.

"Courage, Monsieur!" he said to Charley, and bowed himself out. Jo Portugais followed.

One officer took his place at the front door and the other at the back door, outside.

The Abby, by himself, took to walking backward and forward under the trees, buried in gloomy reflection. Jo Portugais caught his sleeve.

"Come with me for a moment, M'sieu'," he said. "It is important."

The Abby followed him.

CHAPTER XXXII
JO PORTUGAIS TELLS A STORY

Jo Portugais had fastened down a secret with clasps heavier than iron, and had long stood guard over it. But life is a wheel, and natures move in circles, passing the same points again and again, the points being distant or near to the sense as the courses of life have influenced the nature. Confession was an old principle, a light in the way, a rest-house for Jo and all his race, by inheritance, by disposition, and by practice. Again and again Jo had come round to the rest-house since one direful day, but had not, found his way therein. There were passwords to give at the door, there was the tale of the journey to tell to the door-keeper. And this tale he had not been ready to tell. But the man who knew of the terrible thing he had done, who had saved him from the consequences of that terrible thing, was in sore trouble, and this broke down the gloomy guard he had kept over his dread secret. He fought the matter out with himself, and, the battle ended, he touched the door-keeper on the arm, beckoned him to a lonely place in the trees, and knelt down before him.

"What is it you seek?" asked the door-keeper, whose face was set and forbidding.

"To find peace," answered the man; yet he was thinking more of another's peril than of his own soul. "What have I to do with the peace of your soul? Yonder is your shepherd and keeper," said the doorkeeper, pointing to where two men walked arm in arm under the trees.

"Shall the sinner not choose the keeper of his sins?" said the man huskily.

"Who has been the keeper all these years? Who has given you peace?"

"I have had no keeper; I have had no peace these many years."

"How many years?" The Abbe's voice was low and even, and showed no feeling, but his eyes were keenly inquiring and intent.

"Seven years."

"Is the sin that held you back from the comfort of the Church a great one?"

"The greatest, save one."

"What would be the greatest?"

"To curse God."

"The next?"

"To murder."

The other's whole manner changed on the instant. He was no longer the stern Churchman, the inveterate friend of Justice, the prejudiced priest, rigid in a pious convention, who could neither bend nor break. The sin of an infidel breaker of the law, that was one thing; the crime of a son of the Church, which a human soul came to relate in its agony, that was another. He had a crass sense of justice, but there was in him a deeper thing still: the revelation of the human soul, the responsibility of speaking to the heart which has dropped the folds of secrecy, exposing the skeleton of truth, grim and staring, to the eye of a secret earthly mentor.

"If it has been hidden all these years, why do you tell it now, my son?"

"It is the only way."

"Why was it hidden?"

"I have come to confess," answered the man bitterly. The priest looked at him anxiously. "You have spoken rightly, my son. I am not here to ask, but to receive."

"Forgive me, but it is my crime I would speak of now. I choose this moment that another should not suffer for what he did not do."

The priest thought of the man they had left in the little house, and the crime with which he was charged, and wondered what the sinner before him was going to say.

"Tell your story, my son, and God give your tongue the very spirit of truth, that nothing be forgotten and nothing excused."

There was a fleeting pause, in which the colour left the priest's face, and, as he opened the door of his mind—of the Church, secret and inviolate—he had a pain at his heart; for beneath his arrogant churchmanship there was a fanatical spirituality of a mediaeval kind. His sense of responsibility was painful and intense. The same pain possessed him always, were the sin that of a child or a Borgia.

As he listened to the broken tale, the forest around was vocal, the chipmunks scampered from tree to tree, the woodpecker's tap-tap, tap-tap, went on over their heads, the leaves rustled and gave forth their divine sweetness, as though man and nature were at peace, and there were no storms in sky above or soul beneath, or in the waters of life that are deeper than "the waters under the earth."

It was only a short time, but to the door-keeper and the wayfarer it seemed hours, for the human soul travels far and hard and long in moments of pain and revelation. The priest in his anxiety suffered as much as the man who did the wicked thing. When the man had finished, the priest said:

"Is this all?"

"It is the great sin of my life." He shuddered, and continued: "I have no love of life; I have no fear of death; but there is the man who saved me years ago, who got me freedom. He has had great sorrow and trouble, and I would live for his sake—because he has no friend."

"Who is the man?"

The other pointed to where the little house was hidden among the trees. The priest almost gasped his amazement, but waited.

Thereupon the woodsman told the whole truth concerning the tailor of Chaudiere.

"To save him, I have confessed my own sin. To you I might tell all in confession, and the truth about him would be buried for ever. I might not confess at all unless I confessed my own sin. You will save him, father?" he asked anxiously.

"I will save him," was the reply of the priest.

"I want to give myself to justice; but he has been ill, and he may be ill again, and he needs me." He told of the tailor's besetting weakness, of his struggles against it, of his fall a few days before, and the cause of it... told all to the man of silence.

"You wish to give yourself to justice?"

"I shall have no peace unless."

There was something martyr-like in the man's attitude. It appealed to some stern, martyr-like quality in the priest. If the man would win eternal peace so, then so be it. His grim piety approved. He spoke now with the authority of divine justice.

"For one year longer go on as you are, then give yourself to justice—one year from to-day, my son. Is it enough?"

"It is enough."

"Absolvo te!" said the priest.

CHAPTER XXXIII
THE EDGE OF LIFE

Meantime Charley was alone with his problem. The net of circumstances seemed to have coiled inextricably round him. Once, at a trial in court in other days, he had said in his ironical way: "One hasn't to fear the penalties of one's sins, but the damnable accident of discovery."

To try to escape now, or, with the assistance of Jo Portugais, when en route to Quebec in charge of the constables, and find refuge and seclusion elsewhere? There was nothing he might ask of Portugais which he would not do. To escape—and so acknowledge a guilt not his own! Well, what did it matter! Who mattered? He knew only too well. The Cure mattered—that good man who had never intruded his piety on him; who had been from the first a discreet friend, a gentleman,—a Christian gentleman, if there was such a sort of gentleman apart from all others. Who mattered? The Seigneur, whom he had never seen before, yet who had showed that day a brusque sympathy, a gruff belief in him? Who mattered?

Above all, Rosalie mattered. To escape, to go from Rosalie's presence by a dark way, as it were, like a thief in the night—was that possible? His escape would work upon her mind. She would first wonder, then doubt, and then believe at last that he was a common criminal. She was the one who mattered in that thought of escape escape to some other parish, to some other province, to some other country—to some other world!

To some other world? He looked at a little bottle he held in the palm of his hand.

A hand held aside the curtain of the door entering on the next room, and a girl's troubled face looked in, but he did not see.

Escape to some other world? And why not, after all? On the day his memory came back he had resisted the idea in this very room. As the fatalist he had resisted it then. Now how poor seemed the reasons for not having ended it all that day! If his appointed time had been come, the river would have ended him then—that had been his argument. Was that argument not belief in Somebody or Something which governed his going or staying? Was it not preordination? Was not fatalism, then, the cheapest sort of belief in an unchangeable Somebody or Something, representing purpose and law and will? Attribute to anything power, and there was God, whatever His qualities, personality, or being.

The little phial of laudanum was in his hand to loosen life into knowledge. Was it not his duty to eliminate himself, rather than be an unsolvable quantity in the problem of many lives? It was neither vulgar nor cowardly to pass quietly from forces making for ruin, and so avert ruin and secure happiness. To go while yet there was time, and smooth for ever the way for others by an eternal silence—that seemed well. Punishment thereafter, the Cure would say. But was it not worth while being punished, even should the Cure's fond belief in the noble fable be true, if one saved others here? Who—God or man—had the right to take from him the right to destroy himself, not for fear, not through despair, but for others' sake? Had he not the right to make restitution to Kathleen for having given her nothing but himself, whom she had learned to despise? If he were God, he would say, Do justice and fear not. And this was justice. Suppose he were in a battle, with all these things behind him, and put himself, with daring and great results, in some forlorn hope—to die; and he died, ostensibly a hero for his country, but, in his heart of hearts, to throw his life away to save some one he loved, not his country, which profited by his sacrifice— suppose that were the case, what would the world say?

"He saved others, himself he could not save"—flashed through his mind, possessed him. He could save others; but it was clear he could not save himself. It was so simple, so kind, and so decent. And he would be buried here in quiet, unconsecrated ground, a mystery, a tailor who, finding he could not mend the garment of life, cast it away, and took on himself the mantle of eternal obscurity. No reproaches would follow him; and he would not reproach himself, for Kathleen and Billy and another would be safe and free to live their lives.

Far, far better for Rosalie! She too would be saved—free from the peril of his presence. For where could happiness come to her from him? He might not love her; he might not marry her; and it were well to go now, while yet love was not a habit, but an awakening, a realisation of life. His death would settle this sad question for ever. To her he would be a softening memory as time went on.

The girl who had watched by the curtain stepped softly inside the room ... she divined his purpose. He was so intent he did not hear.

"I will do it," he said to himself. "It is better to go than to stay. I have never done a good thing for love of any human being. I will do one now."

He turned towards the window through which the sunlight streamed. Stepping forward into the sun, he uncorked the bottle.

There was a quick step behind him, and the girl's voice said clearly:

"If you go, I go also."

He turned swiftly, cold with amazement, the blood emptied from his heart.

Rosalie stood a little distance from him, her face pale, her hands held hard to her side.

"I understand all. I could not go outside, I stayed there"—she pointed to the other room—"and I know why you would die. You would die to save others."

"Rosalie!" he protested in a hoarse voice, and could say nothing more.

"You think that I will stay, if you go! No, no, no—I will not. You taught me how to live, and I will follow you now."

He saw the strange determination of her look. It startled him; he knew not what to say. "Your father, Rosalie—"

"My father will be cared for. But who will care for you in the place where you are going? You will have no friends there. You shall not go alone. You will need me—in the dark."

"It is good that I go," he said. "It would be wicked, it would be dreadful, for you to go."

"I go if you go," she urged. "I will lose my soul to be with you; you will want me—there!"

There was no mistaking her intention. Footsteps sounded outside. The others were coming back. To die here before her face? To bring her to death with him? He was sick with despair.

"Go into the next room quickly," he said. "No matter what comes, I will not—on my honour!"

She threw him a look of gratitude, and, as the bearskin curtain dropped behind her, he put the phial of laudanum in his pocket.

The door opened, and the Abbe Rossignol entered, followed by the Seigneur, the Cure, and Jo Portugais. Charley faced them calmly, and waited.

The Abbe's face was still cold and severe, but his voice was human as he said quickly: "Monsieur, I have decided to take you at your word. I am assured you are not the man who committed the crime. You probably have reasons for not establishing your identity."

Had Charley been a prisoner in the dock, he could not have had a moment of deeper amazement—even if after the jury had said Guilty, a piece of evidence had been handed in, proving innocence, averting the death sentence. A wave of excitement passed over him, leaving him cold and still. In the other room a girl put her hand to her mouth to stifle a cry of joy.

Charley bowed. "You made a mistake, Monsieur—pray do not apologise," he said.

CHAPTER XXXIV
IN AMBUSH

Weeks went by. Summer was done, autumn was upon the land. Harvest-home had gone, and the "fall" ploughing was forward. The smell of the burning stubble, of decaying plant and fibre, was mingling with the odours of the orchards and the balsams of the forest. The leafy hill-sides, far and near, were resplendent in scarlet and saffron and tawny red. Over the decline of the year flickered the ruined fires of energy.

It had been a prosperous summer in the valley. Harvests had been reaped such as the country had not known for years—and for years there had been great harvests. There had not been a death in the parish all summer, and births had occurred out of all usual proportion.

When Filion Lacasse commented thereon, and mentioned the fact that even the Notary's wife had had the gift of twins as the crowning fulness of the year, Maximilian Cour, who was essentially superstitious, tapped on the table three times, to prevent a turn in the luck.

The baker was too late, however, for the very next day the Notary was brought home with a nasty gunshot wound in his leg. He had been lured into duck-hunting on a lake twenty miles away, in the hills, and had been accidentally shot on an Indian reservation, called Four Mountains, where the Church sometimes held a mission and presented a primitive sort of passion-play. From there he had been brought home by his comrades, and the doctor from the next parish summoned. The Cure assisted the doctor at first, but the task was difficult to him. At the instant when the case was most critical the tailor of Chaudiere set his foot inside the Notary's door. A moment later he relieved the Cure and helped to probe for shot, and care for an ugly wound.

Charley had no knowledge of surgery, but his fingers were skilful, his eye was true, and he had intuition. The long operation over, the rural physician and surgeon washed his hands and then studied Charley with curious admiration.

"Thank you, Monsieur," he said, as he dried his hands on a towel. "I couldn't have done it without you. It's a pretty good job; and you share the credit."

Charley bowed. "It's a good thing not to halloo till you're out of the woods," he said. "Our friend there has a bad time before him—hein?"

"I take you. It is so." The man of knives and tinctures pulled his side-whiskers with smug satisfaction as he looked into a small mirror on the wall. "Do you chance to know if madame has any cordials or spirits?" he added, straightening his waistcoat and adjusting his cravat.

"It is likely," answered Charley, and moved away to the window looking upon the street.

The doctor turned in surprise. He was used to being waited on, and he had expected the tailor to follow the tradition.

"We might—eh?" he said suggestively. "It is usually the custom to provide refreshment, but the poor woman, madame, has been greatly occupied with her husband, and—"

"And the twins," Charley put in drily—"and a house full of work, and only one old crone in the kitchen to help. Still, I have no doubt she has thought of the cordials too. Women are the slaves of custom—ah, here they are, as I said, and—"

He stopped short, for in the doorway, with a tray, stood Rosalie Evanturel. The surgeon was so intent upon at once fortifying himself that he did not see the look which passed between Rosalie and the tailor.

Rosalie had been absent for two months. Her father had been taken seriously ill the day after the critical episode in the but at Vadrome Mountain, and she had gone with him to the hospital at Quebec, for an operation. The Abbe Rossignol had undertaken to see them safely to the hospital, and Jo Portugais, at his own request, was permitted to go in attendance upon M. Evanturel.

There had been a hasty leave-taking between Charley and Rosalie, but it was in the presence of others, and they had never spoken a word privately together since the day she had said to him that where he went she would go, in life or out of it.

"You have been gone two months," Charley said now, after their touch of hands and voiceless greeting. "Two months yesterday," she answered.

"At sundown," he replied, in an even voice.

"The Angelus was ringing," she answered calmly, though her heart was leaping and her hands were trembling. The doctor, instantly busy with the cordial, had not noticed what they said.

"Won't you join me?" he asked, offering a glass to Charley.

"Spirits do not suit me," answered Charley. "Matter of constitution," rejoined the doctor, and buttoned up his coat, preparing to depart. He came close to Charley. "Now, I don't want to put upon you, Monsieur," he said, "but this sick man is valuable in the parish—you take me? Well, it's a difficult, delicate case, and I'd be glad if I could rely on you for a few days. The Cure would do, but you are young, you have a sense of things— take me? Half the fees are yours if you'll keep a sharp eye on him—three times a day, and be with him at night a while. Fever is the thing I'm afraid of—temperature—this way, please!" He went to the window, and for a minute engaged Charley in whispered conversation. "You take me?" he said cheerily at last, as he turned again towards Rosalie.

"Quite, Monsieur," answered Charley, and drew away, for he caught the odour of the doctor's breath, and a cold perspiration broke out over him. He felt the old desire for drink sweeping through him. "I will do what I can," he said.

"Come, my dear," the doctor said to Rosalie. "We will go and see your father."

Charley's eyes had fastened on the bottles avidly. As Rosalie turned to bid him good-bye, he said to her, almost hoarsely: "Take the tray back to Madame Dauphin—please."

She flashed a glance of inquiry at him. She was puzzled by the fire in his eyes. With her soul in her face as she lifted the tray, out of the warm-beating life in her, she said in a low tone:

"It is good to live, isn't it?"

He nodded and smiled, and the trouble slowly passed from his eyes. The woman in her had conquered his enemy.

CHAPTER XXXV
THE COMING OF MAXIMILIAN
COUR AND ANOTHER

"It is good to live, isn't it?" In the autumn weather when the air drank like wine, it seemed so indeed, even to Charley, who worked all day in his shop, his door wide open to the sunlight, and sat up half the night with Narcisse Dauphin, sometimes even taking a turn at the cradle of the twins, while madame sat beside her husband's bed.

To Charley the answer to Rosalie's question lay in the fact that his eyes had never been so keen, his face so alive, or his step so buoyant as in this week of double duty. His mind was more hopeful than it had ever been since the day he awoke with memory restored in the silence of a mountain hut.

He had found the antidote to his great temptation, to the lurking, relentless habit which had almost killed him the night John Brown had sung Champagne Charlie from behind the flaring lights. From a determination to fight his own fight with no material aids, he had never once used the antidote sent him by the Cure's brother.

On St. Jean Baptiste's day his proud will had failed him; intellectual force, native power of mind, had broken like reeds under the weight of a cruel temptation. But now a new force had entered into him. As his fingers were about to reach for the spirit-bottle in the house of the Notary, and he had, for the first time in his life, made an appeal for help, a woman's voice had said, "It is good to live, isn't it?" and his hand was stayed. A woman's look had stilled the strife. Never before in his life had he relied on a moral or a spiritual impulse in him. What of these existed in him were in unseen quantities—for which there was neither multiple nor measure—had been primitive and hereditary, flowing in him like a feeble tincture diluted to inefficacy.

Rosalie had resolved him back to the original elements. The quiet days he had spent in Chaudiere, the self-sacrifice he had been compelled to make, the human sins, such as those of Jo Portugais and Louis Trudel, with which he had had to do, the simplicity of the life around him—the uncomplicated lie and the unvarnished truth, the obvious sorrow and the patent joy, the childish faith, and the rude wickedness so pardonable because so frankly brutal—had worked upon him. The elemental spirit of it all had so invaded his nature, breaking through the crust of old habit to the new man, that, when he fell before his temptation, and his body became saturated with liquor, the healthy natural being and the growing natural mind were overpowered by the coarse onslaught, and death had nearly followed.

It was his first appeal to a force outside himself, to an active principle unfamiliar to the voluntary working of his nature, and the answer had been immediate and adequate. Yet what was it? He did not ask; he had not got beyond the mere experience, and the old questioning habit was in abeyance. Each new and great emotion has its dominating moment, its supreme occasion, before taking its place in the modulated moral mechanism. He was touched with helplessness.

As he sat beside Narcisse Dauphin's bedside, one evening, the sick man on his way to recovery, there came to him the text of a sermon he had once heard John Brown preach: "Greater love hath no man than this, that a man lay down his life for his friend." He had been thinking of Rosalie and that day at Vadrome Mountain. She would not only have died with him, but she would have died for him, if need had been. What might he give in return for what she gave?

The Notary interrupted his thoughts. He had lain watching Charley for a long time, his brow drawn down with thought. At last he said:

"Monsieur, you have been good to me." Charley laid a hand on the sick man's arm.

"I don't see that. But if you won't talk, I'll believe you think so."

The Notary shook his head. "I've not been talking for an hour, I've no fever, and I want to say some things. When I've said them, I'll feel better— voila! I want to make the amende honorable. I once thought you were this and that—I won't say what I thought you. I said you interfered—giving advice to people, as you did to Filion Lacasse, and taking the bread out of my mouth. I said that!"

He paused, raised himself on his elbow, smoothed back his grizzled hair behind his ears, looked at himself in the mirror opposite with satisfaction, and added oracularly: "But how prone is the mind of man to judge amiss! You have put bread into my mouth—no, no, Monsieur, you shall hear me! As well as doing your own work, you have done my business since my accident as well as a lawyer could do it; and you've given every penny to my wife."

"As for the work I've done," answered Charley, "it was nothing—you notaries have easy times. You may take your turn with my shears and needle one day."

With a dash of patronage true to his nature, "You are wonderful for a tailor," the Notary rejoined. Charley laughed—seldom, if ever, had he laughed since coming to Chaudiere. It was, however, a curious fact that he took a real pleasure in the work he did with his hands. In making clothes for habitant farmers, and their sons and their sons' sons, and jackets for their wives and daughters, he had had the keenest pleasure of his life.

He had taken his earnings with pride, if not with exultation. He knew the Notary did not mean that he was wonderful as a tailor, but he answered to the suggestion.

"You liked that last coat I made for you, then," he said drily; "I believe you wore it when you were shot. It was the thing for your figure, man."

The Notary looked in the large mirror opposite with sad content. "Ah, it was a good figure, the first time I went to that hut at Four Mountains!"

"We can't always be young. You have a waist yet, and your chest-barrel gives form to a waistcoat. Tut, tut! Think of the twins in the way of vainglory and hypocrisy."

"'Twins' and 'hypocrisy'; there you have struck the nail on the head, tailor. There is the thing I'm going to tell you about."

After a cautious glance at the door and the window, Dauphin continued in quick, broken sentences: "It wasn't an accident at Four Mountains— not quite. It was Paulette Dubois—you know the woman that lives at the Seigneur's gate? Twelve years ago she was a handsome girl. I fell in love with her, but she left here. There were two other men. There was a timber-merchant,—and there was a lawyer after. The timber-merchant was married; the lawyer wasn't. She lived at first with the timber-merchant. He was killed—murdered in the woods."

"What was the timber-merchant's name?" interrupted Charley in an even voice.

"Turley—but that doesn't matter!" continued the Notary. "He was murdered, and then the lawyer came on the scene. He lived with her for a year. She had a child by him. One day he sent the child away to a safe place and told her he was going to turn over a new leaf—he was going to stand for Parliament, and she must go. She wouldn't go without the child. At last he said the child was dead; and showed her the certificate of death. Then she came back here, and for a while, alas! she disgraced the parish. But all at once she changed—she got a message that her child was alive. To her it was like being born again. It was at this time they were going to drive her from the parish. But the Seigneur and then the Cure spoke for her, and so did I—at last."

He paused and plaintively admired himself in the mirror. He was grateful that he had been clean-shaved that morning, and he was content to catch the citrine odour of the bergamot upon his hair.

New phases of the most interesting case Charley had ever defended spread out before him—the case which had given him his friend Jo Portugais, which had turned his own destiny. Yet he could not quite trace in it the vital association of this vain Notary now in the confessional mood.

"You behaved very well," said Charley tentatively.

"Ah, you say that, knowing so little! What will you say when you know all—ah! That I should take a stand also was important. Neither the Seigneur nor the Cure was married; I was. I have been long-suffering for a cause. My marital felicity has been bruised—bruised—but not broken."

"There are the twins," said Charley, with a half-closed eye.

"Could woman ask greater proof?" urged the Notary seriously, for the other's voice had been so well masked that he did not catch its satire. "But see my peril, and mark the ground of my interest in this poor wanton! Yet a woman—a woman-frail creatures, as we know, and to be pitied, not made more pitiable by the stronger sex.... But, see now! Why should I have perilled mine own conjugal peace, given ground for suspicion even—for I am unfortunate, unfortunate in the exterior with which Dame Nature has honoured me!" Again he looked in the mirror with sad complacency.

On these words his listener offered no comment, and he continued:

"For this reason I lifted my voice for the poor wanton. It was I who wrote the letter to her that her child was alive. I did it with high purpose—I foresaw that she would change her ways if she thought her child was living. Was I mistaken? No. I am an observer of human nature. Intellect conquered. 'Io triumphe'. The poor fly-away changed, led a new life. Ever since then she has tried to get the man—the lawyer—to tell her where her child is. He has not done so. He has said the child is dead—always. When she seemed to give up belief, then would come another letter to her, telling her the child was living—but not where. So she would keep on writing to the man, and sometimes she would go away searching—searching. To what end? Nothing! She had a letter some months ago, for she had got restless, and a young kinsman of the Seigneur had come to visit at the seigneury for a week, and took much notice of her. There was danger. Voila, another letter."

"From you?"

"Monsieur, of course! Will you keep a secret—on your sacred honour?"

"I can keep a secret without sacred honour."

"Ah, yes, of course! You have a secret of your own—pardon me, I am only saying what every one says. Well, this is the secret of the woman Paulette Dubois. My cousin, Robespierre Dauphin, a notary in Quebec, is the agent of the lawyer, the father of the child. He pities the poor woman. But he is bound in professional honour to the lawyer fellow, not to betray. When visiting Robespierre once I found out the truth-by accident.

"I told him what I intended. He gave permission to tell the woman her child was alive; and, if need be for her good, to affirm it over and over again—no more."

"And this?" said Charley, pointing to the injured leg, for he now associated the accident with the secret just disclosed.

"Ah, you apprehend! You have an avocat's mind—almost. It was at Four Mountains. Paulette is superstitious; so not long ago she went to live there alone with an old half-breed woman who has second-sight. Monsieur, it is a gift unmistakably. For as soon as the hag clapped eyes on me in the hut, she said: 'There is the man that wrote you the letters.' Well—what! Paulette Dubois came down on me like an avalanche—Monsieur, like an avalanche! She believed the old witch; and there was I lying with an unconvincing manner"—he sighed—"lying requires practice, alas! She saw I was lying, and in a rage snatched up my gun. It went off by accident, and brought me down. Did she relent? Not so. She helped to bind me up, and the last words she said to me were: 'You will suffer; you will have time to think. I am glad. You have kept me on the rack. I shall only be sorry if you die, for then I shall not be able to torture you till you tell me where my child is!' Monsieur, I lied to the last, lest she should come here and make a noise; but I'm not sure it wouldn't have been better to break faith with Robespierre, and tell the poor wanton where her child is. What would you do, Monsieur? I cannot ask the Cure or the Seigneur—I have reasons. But you have the head of a lawyer—almost—and you have no local feelings, no personal interest—eh?"

"I should tell the truth."

"Your reasons, Monsieur?"

"Because the lawyer is a scoundrel. Your betrayal of his secret is not a thousandth part so bad as one lie told to this woman, whose very life is her child. Is it a boy or a girl?"

"A boy."

"Good! What harm can be done? A left-handed boy is all right in the world. Your wife has twins—then think of the woman, the one ewe lamb of 'the poor wanton.' If you do not tell her, you will have her here making a noise, as you say. I wonder she has not been here on your door-step."

"I had a letter from her to-day. She is coming-ah, mon dieu!"

"When?"

There was a tap at the window. The Notary started. "Ah, Heaven, here she is!" he gasped, and drew over to the wall.

A voice came from outside. "Shall I play for you, Dauphin? It is as good as medicine."

The Notary recovered himself at once. His volatile nature sprang back to its pose. He could forget Paulette Dubois for the moment.

"It is Maximilian Cour in the garden," he said happily. Then he raised his voice. "Play on, baker; but something for convalescence—the return of spring, the sweet assonance of memory."

"A September air, and a gush of spring," said the baker, trying to crane his long neck through the window. "Ah, there you are, Dauphin! I shall give you a sleep to-night like a balmy eve." He nodded to the tailor. "M'sieu', you shall judge if sentiment be dead.

"I have racked my heart to play this time. I have called it, 'The Baffled Quest of Love'. I have taken the music of the song of Alsace, 'Le Jardin d'Amour', and I have made variations on it, keeping the last verse of the song in my mind. You know the song, M'sieu':

"'Quand je vais au jardin, Jardin d'amour,

Je crois entendu des pas,

Je veux fuir, et n'ose pas.

Voici la fin du jour...

Je crains et j'hesite,

Mon coeur bat plus vite

En ce sejour...

Quand je vais an jardin, jardin d'amour.'"

The baker sat down on a stool he had brought, and began to tune his fiddle. From inside came the voice of the Notary.

"Play 'The Woods are Green' first," he said. "Then the other."

The Notary possessed the one high-walled garden in the village, and though folk gathered outside and said that the baker was playing for the sick man, there was no one in the garden save the fiddler himself. Once or twice a lad appeared on the top of the wall, looking over, but vanished at once when he saw Charley's face at the window. Long ere the baker had finished, the song was caught up from outside, and before the last notes of the violin had died away, twenty voices were singing it in the street, and forty feet marched away with it into the dusk.

Darkness comes quickly in this land of brief twilight. Presently out of the soft shadowed stillness, broken by the note of a vagrant whippoorwill, crept out from Maximilian Cour's old violin the music of 'The Baffled Quest of Love'.

The baker was not a great musician, but he had a talent, a rare gift of pathos, and an imagination untrammelled by rigorous rules of harmony and construction. Whatever there was in his sentimental bosom he poured into this one achievement of his life. It brought tears to the eyes of Narcisse Dauphin. It opened a gate of the garden wall, and drew inside a girl's face, shining with feeling.

Maximilian Cour spoke for more than himself that night. His philandering spirit had, at middle age, begotten a desire to house itself in a quiet place, where the blinds could be drawn close, and the room of life made ready with all the furniture of love. So he had spoken to his violin, and it had answered as it had never done before. The soul of the lean baker touched the heart of a man whose life had been but a baffled quest, and the spirit of a girl whose love was her sun by day, her moon by night, and the starlight of her dreams.

From the shade of the window the man the girl loved watched her as she sank upon the ground and clasped her hands before her in abandonment to the music. He watched her when the baker, at last, overcome by his own feelings—and ashamed of them—got up and stole swiftly out of the garden. He watched her till he saw her drop her face in her hands; then, opening the door and stealing out, he came and laid a hand upon her shoulder, and she heard him say:

"Rosalie!"

CHAPTER XXXVI
BARRIERS SWEPT AWAY

Rosalie came to her feet, gasping with pleasure. She had been unhappy ever since she had returned from Quebec, for though she had sometimes been brought in contact with Charley in the Notary's house since the day of the operation, nothing had passed between them save the necessary commonplaces of a sick-room, given a little extra colour, perhaps, by the sense of responsibility which fell upon them both, and by that importance which hidden sentiment gives to every motion. The twins had been troublesome and ill, and Madame Dauphin had begged Rosalie to come in for a couple of hours every evening. Thus the tailor and the girl who, by every rule of wisdom, should have been kept as far apart as the poles, were played into each other's hands by human kindness and damnable propinquity. The man, manlike, felt no real danger, because nothing was said—after everything had been said for all time at the hut on Vadrome Mountain. He had not realised the true situation, because of late her voice, like his, had been even and her hand cool and steady. He had not noticed that her eyes were like hungry fires, eating up her face—eating away its roundness, and leaving a pathetic beauty behind.

It seemed to him that because there was silence—neither the written word nor the speaking look—that all was well. He was hugging the chain of denial to his bosom, as though to say, "This way is safety"; he was hiding his face from the beacon-lights of her eyes, which said: "This way is home."

Home? Pictures of home, of a home such as Maximilian Cour painted in his music, had passed before him now and then since that great day on Vadrome Mountain. A simple fireside, with frugal but comfortable fare; a few books; the study of the fields and woods; the daily humble task over which he could meditate as his hands worked mechanically; the happy face of a happy woman near—he had thought of home; and he had put it from him. No matter what the temptation, his must be, perhaps for ever, the bed and board unshared. He had had his chance in the old days, and he had thrown it away with insolent indifference, and an unpardonable contempt for the opinion of the world.

Now, with a blind fatuousness which had nothing to do with his old intellectual power, but was evidence of a primitive life of feeling, had vaguely imagined that because there were no clinging hands, or stolen looks, or any vow or promise, that all might go on as at present—upon the surface. With a curious absence of his old accuracy of observation he was treating the immediate past—his and Rosalie's past—as if it did not actually exist; as if only the other and farther past was a tragedy, and this nearer one a dream.

But the film fell from his eyes as Maximilian Cour played his 'Baffled Quest', with its quaint, searching pathos; and as he saw the figure of the girl alone in the shade of the great rose-bushes, past and present became one, and the whole man was lost in that one word "Rosalie!" which called her to her feet with outstretched hands.

The tears sprang to her eyes; her face upturned to his was a mute appeal, a speechless 'Viens ici'.

Past, present, future, duty, apprehension, consequences, suddenly fell away from Charley's mind like a garment slipping from the shoulders, and the new man, swept off his feet by the onrush of unused and ungoverned emotions, caught the girl to his arms with a desperate joy.

"Oh, do you care, then—for me?" wept the girl, and hid her face in his breast.

A voice came from inside the house: "Monsieur, Monsieur—ah, come, if you please, tailor!"

The girl drew back quickly, looked up at him for one instant with a triumphant happy daring, then, suddenly covered with confusion, turned, ran to the gate, opened it, passed swiftly out, and was swallowed up in the dusk.

CHAPTER XXXVII
THE CHALLENGE OF PAULETTE DUBOIS

"Monsieur, Monsieur!" came the voice from inside the house, querulously and anxiously. Charley entered the Notary's bedroom.

"Monsieur," said the Notary excitedly, "she is here—Paulette is here. My wife is asleep, thank God! but old Sophie has just told me that the woman asks to see me. Ah, Heaven above, what shall I do?"

"Will you leave it to me?"

"Yes, yes, Monsieur."

"You will do exactly as I say?"

"Ah, most sure."

"Very well. Keep still. I will see her first. Trust to me." He turned and left the room.

Charley found the woman in the Notary's office, which, while partly detached from the house, did duty as sitting-room and library. When Charley entered, the room was only lighted by two candles, and Paulette's face was hidden by a veil, but Charley observed the tremulousness of the figure and the nervous decision of manner. He had seen her before several times, and he had always noticed the air, half bravado, half shrinking, marking her walk and movements, as though two emotions were fighting in her. She was now dressed in black, save for one bright red ribbon round her throat, incongruous and garish.

When she saw Charley she started, for she had expected the servant with a message from the Notary—her own message had been peremptory.

"I wish to see the Notary," she said defiantly.

"He is not able to come to you."

"What of that?"

"Did you expect to go to his bedroom?"

"Why not?" She was abrupt to discourtesy.

"You are neither physician, nor relative."

"I have important business."

"I transact his business for him, Madame."

"You are a tailor."

"I learned that; I am learning to be a notary."

"My business is private."

"I transact his private business too—that which his wife cannot do. Would you prefer his wife to me? It must be either the one or the other."

The woman started towards the door in a rage. He stepped between. "You cannot see the Notary."

"I'll see his wife, then—"

"That would only put the fat in the fire. His wife would not listen to you. She is quick-tempered, and she fancies she has reasons for not liking you."

"She's a fool. I haven't been always particular, but as for Narcisse Dauphin—"

"He has been a good friend to you at some expense, the world says."

The woman struggled with herself. "The world lies!" she said at last.

"But he doesn't. The village was against you once. That was when the Notary, with the Seigneur, was for you—it has cost him something ever since, I'm told. You've never thanked him."

"He has tortured me for years, the oily, smirking, lying—"

"He has been your best friend," he interrupted. "Please sit down, and listen to me for a moment."

She hesitated, then did as he asked.

"He tells me that years ago he was in love with you. Hasn't he behaved better than some who said they loved you?"

The woman half started up, her eyes flashing, but met a deprecating motion of his hand and sat down again.

"He thought that if you knew your child lived, you would think better of life—and of yourself. He has his good points, the Notary."

"Why doesn't he tell me where my child is?"

"The Notary is in bed—you shot him! Don't you think it is doing you a good turn not to have you arrested?"

"It was an accident."

"Oh no, it wasn't! You couldn't make a jury believe that. And if you were in prison, how could you find your child? You see, you have treated the Notary very badly."

She was silent, and he added, slowly: "He had good reasons for not telling you. It wasn't his own secret, and he hadn't come by it in a strictly professional way. Your child was being well cared for, and he told you simply that it was alive—for your own sake. But he has changed his mind at last, and—"

The woman sprang from her seat. "He will tell me—he will tell me?"

"I will tell you."

"Monsieur—Monsieur—ah, my God, but you are kind! How should you know—what do you know?"

"I give you my word that by to-morrow evening you shall know where your child is."

For a moment she was bewildered and overcome, then a look of gratitude, of luminous hope, covered her face, softening the hardness of its contour, and she fell on her knees beside the table, dropped her head in her arms, and sobbed as if her heart would break.

"My little lamb, my little, little lamb-my own dearest!" she sobbed. "I shall have you again. I shall have you again—all my own!"

He stood and watched her meditatively. He was wondering why it was that grief like this had never touched him so before. His eyes were moist. Though he had been many things in his life, he had never been abashed; but a curious timidity possessed him now.

He leaned over and touched her shoulder with a kindly abruptness, a friendly awkwardness. "Cheer up," he said. "You shall have your child, if Dauphin can help you to it."

"If he ever tries to take him from me"—she sprang to her feet, her face in a fury—"I will—"

For an instant her overpowering passion possessed her, and she stood violent and wilful; then, under his fixed, exacting gaze, her rage ceased; she became still and grey and quiet.

"I shall know to-morrow evening, Monsieur? Where?" Her voice was weak and distant.

He thought for a time. "At my house-at nine o'clock," he answered at last.

"Monsieur," she said, in a choking voice, "if I get my child again, I will bless you to my dying day."

"No, no; it will be Dauphin you must bless," he said, and opened the door for her. As she disappeared into the dusk and silence he adjusted his eye-glass, and stared musingly after her, though there was nothing to see save the summer darkness, nothing to hear save the croak of the frogs in the village pond. He was thinking of the trial of Joseph Nadeau, and of a woman in the gallery, who laughed.

"Monsieur, Monsieur," called the voice of the Notary from the bedroom.

CHAPTER XXXVIII
THE CURE AND THE SEIGNEUR
VISIT THE TAILOR

It had been a perfect September day. The tailor of Chaudiere had been busier than usual, for winter was within hail, and careful habitants were renewing their simple wardrobes. The Seigneur and the Cure arrived together, each to order the making of a greatcoat of the Irish frieze which the Seigneur kept in quantity at the Manor. The Seigneur was in rare spirits. And not without reason; for this was Michaelmas eve, and tomorrow would be Michaelmas day, and there was a promise to be redeemed on Michaelmas day! He had high hopes of its redemption according to his own wishes; for he was a vain Seigneur, and he had had his way in all things all his life, as everybody knew. Importunity with discretion was his motto, and he often vowed to the Cure that there was no other motto for the modern world.

The Cure's visit to the tailor's shop on this particular day had unusual interest, for it concerned his dear ambition, the fondest aspiration of his life: to bring the infidel tailor (they could not but call a man an infidel whose soul was negative—the word agnostic had not then become usual) from the chains of captivity into the freedom of the Church. The Cure had ever clung to his fond hope; and it was due to his patient confidence that there were several parishioners who now carried Charley's name before the shrine of the blessed Virgin, and to the little calvaries by the road-side. The wife of Filion Lacasse never failed to pray for him every day. The thousand dollars gained by the saddler on the tailor's advice had made her life happier ever since, for Filion had become saving and prudent, and had even got her a "hired girl." There were at least a half-dozen other women, including Madame Dauphin, who did the same.

That he might listen again to the good priest on his holy hobby, inflamed with this passion of missionary zeal, the Seigneur, this morning, had thrown doubt upon the ultimate success of the Cure's efforts.

"My dear Cure" said the Seigneur, "it is true, I think, what the tailor suggested to my brother—on my soul, I wonder the Abbe gave in, for a more obstinate fellow I never knew!—that a man is born with the disbelieving maggot in his brain, or the butterfly of belief, or whatever it may be called. It's constitutional—may be criminal, but constitutional. It seems to me you would stand more chance with the Jew, Greek, or heretic, than our infidel. He thinks too much—for a tailor, or for nine tailors, or for one man."

He pulled his nose, as if he had said a very good thing indeed. They were walking slowly towards the village during this conversation, and the Cure, stopping short, brought his stick emphatically down in his palm several times, as he said:

"Ah, you will not see! You will not understand. With God all things are possible. Were it the devil himself in human form, I should work and pray and hope, as my duty is, though he should still remain the devil to the end. What am I? Nothing. But what the Church has done, the Church may do. Think of Paul and Augustine, and Constantine!"

"They were classic barbarians to whom religion was but an emotion. This man has a brain which must be satisfied."

"I must count him as a soul to be saved through that very intelligence, as well as through the goodness of his daily life, which, in its charity, shames us all. He gives all he earns to the sick and needy. He lives on fare as poor as the poorest of our people eat; he gives up his hours of sleep to nurse the sick. Dauphin might not have lived but for him. His heart is good, else these things were impossible. He could not act them."

"But that's just it, Cure. Doesn't he act them? Isn't it a whim? What more likely than that, tired of the flesh-pots of Egypt, he comes here to live in the desert—for a sensation? We don't know."

"We do know. The man has had sorrow and the man has had sin. Yes, believe me, there is none of us that suffers as this man has suffered. I have had many, many talks with him. Believe me, Maurice, I speak the truth. My heart bleeds for him. I think I know the thing that drove him here amongst us. It is a great temptation, which pursues him here—even here, where his life is so commendable. I have seen him fighting it. I have seen his torture, the piteous, ignoble yielding, and the struggle, with more than mortal energy, to be master of himself."

"It is—" the Seigneur said, then paused.

"No, no; do not ask me. He has not confessed to me, Maurice-naturally, nothing like that. But I know. I know and pity—ah, Maurice, I almost love.

You argue, and reason, but I know this, my friend, that something was left out of this man when he was made, and it is that thing that we must find, or he will die among us a ruined soul, and his gravestone will be the monument of our shame. If he can once trust the Church, if he can once say, 'Lord, into Thy hands I commend my spirit,' then his temptation will vanish, and I shall bring him in—I shall lead him home."

For an instant the Seigneur looked at him in amazement, for this was a Cure he had never known.

"Dear Cure, you are not your old self," he said gently.

"I am not myself—yes, that is it, Maurice. I am not the old humdrum Cure you knew. The whole world is my field now. I have sorrowed for sin, within the bounds of this little Chaudiere. Now I sorrow for unbelief. Through this man, through much thinking on him, I have come to feel the woe of all the world. I have come to hear the footsteps of the Master near. My friend, it is not a legend, not a belief now, it is a presence. I owe him much, Maurice. In bringing him home, I shall understand what it all means—the faith that we profess. I shall in truth feel that it is all real. You see how much I may yet owe to him—to this infidel tailor. I only hope I have not betrayed him," he added anxiously. "I would keep faith with him—ah, yes, indeed!"

"I only remember that you have said the man suffers. That is no betrayal."

They entered the village in silence. Presently, however, the sound of Maximilian Cour's violin, as they passed the bakery, set the Seigneur's tongue wagging again, and it wagged on till they came to the tailor's shop.

"Good-day to you, Monsieur," he said, as they entered.

"Have you a hot goose for me?"

"I have, but I will not press it on you," replied Charley.

"Should you so take my question—eh?"

"Should you so take my 'anser'?"

The pun was new to the Seigneur, and he turned to the Cure chuckling. "Think of that, Cure! He knows the classics." He laughed till the tears came into his eyes.

The next few moments Charley was busy measuring the two potentates for greatcoats. As it was his first work for them, it was necessary for the Cure to write down the Seigneur's measurements, as the tailor called them off, while the Seigneur did the same when the Cure was being measured. So intent were the three it might have been a conference of war. The Seigneur ventured a distant but self-conscious smile when the measurement of his waist was called, for he had by two inches the advantage of the Cure, though they were the same age, while he was one inch better in the chest. The Seigneur was proud of his figure, and, unheeding the passing of fashions, held to the knee-breeches and silk stockings long after they had disappeared from the province. To the Cure he had often said that the only time he ever felt heretical was when in the presence of the gaitered calves of a Protestant dean. He wore his sleeves tight and his stock high, as in the days when William the Sailor was king in England, and his long gold-topped Prince Regent cane was the very acme of dignity.

The measurement done, the three studied the fashion plates—mostly five years old—as Von Moltke and Bismarck might have studied the field of Gravelotte. The Seigneur's remarks were highly critical, till, with a few hasty strokes on brown paper, Charley sketched in his figure with a long overcoat in style much the same as his undercoat, stately and flowing and confined at the waist.

"Admirable, most admirable!" said the Seigneur. "The likeness is astonishing"—he admired the carriage of his own head in Charley's swift lines—"the garment in perfect taste. Form—there is nothing like form and proportion in life. It is almost a religion."

"My dear friend!" said the Cure, in amazement.

"I know when I am in the presence of an artist and his work. Louis Trudel had rule and measure, shears and a needle. Our friend here has eye and head, sense of form and creative gift. Ah, Cure, Cure, if I were twenty-five, with the assistance of Monsieur, I would show the bucks in Fabrique Street how to dress. What style is this called, Monsieur?" he suddenly asked, pointing to the drawing.

"Style a la Rossignol, Seigneur," said the tailor.

The Seigneur was flattered out of all reason. He looked across at the post-office, where he could see Rosalie dimly moving in the shade of the shop.

"Ah, if I had but ordered this coat sooner!" he said regretfully. He was thinking that to-morrow was Michaelmas day, when he was to ask Rosalie for her answer again, and he fancied himself appearing before her in the gentle cool of the evening, in this coat, lightly thrown back, disclosing his embroidered waistcoat, seals, and snowy linen. "Monsieur, I am highly complimented, believe me," he said. "Observe, Cure, that this coat is invented for me on the spot."

The Cure nodded appreciatively. "Wonderful! Wonderful! But do you not think," he added, a little wistfully—for, was he not a Frenchman, susceptible like all his race to the appearance of things?—"do you not think it might be too fashionable for me?"

"Not a whit—not a whit," replied the Seigneur generously. "Should not a Cure look distinguished—be dignified? Consider the length, the line, the eloquence of design! Ah, Monsieur, once again, you are an artist! The Cure shall wear it—indeed but he shall! Then I shall look like him, and perhaps get credit for some of his perfections."

"And the Cure?" said Charley.

"The Cure?—the Cure? Tiens, a little of my worldliness will do him good. There are no contrasts in him. He must wear the coat." He waved his walking-stick complacently, for he was thinking that the Cure's less perfect figure would set off his own well as they walked together. "May I have the honour to keep this as a souvenir?" he added, picking up the sketch.

"With pleasure," answered Charley. "You do not need it?"

"Not at all."

The Cure looked a little disappointed, and Charley, seeing, immediately sketched on brown paper the priestly figure in the new-created coat, a la Rossignol. On this drawing he was a little longer engaged, with the result that the Cure was reproduced with a singular fidelity—in face, figure, and expression a personality gentle yet important.

"On my soul, you shall not have it!" said the Seigneur. "But you shall have me, and I shall have you, lest we both grow vain by looking at ourselves." He thrust the sketch of himself into the Cure's hands, and carefully rolled up that of his friend.

The Cure was amazed at this gift of the tailor, and delighted with the picture of himself—his vanity was as that of a child, without guile or worldliness. He was better pleased, however, to have the drawing of his friend by him, that vanity might not be too companionable. He thanked Charley with a beaming face, and then the two friends bowed and moved towards the door. Suddenly the Cure stopped.

"My dear Maurice," said he, "we have forgotten the important thing."

"Think of that—we two old babblers!" said the Seigneur. He nodded for the Cure to begin. "Monsieur," said the Cure to Charley, "you maybe able to help us in a little difficulty. For a long time we have intended holding a great mission with a kind of religious drama like that performed at Ober-Ammergau, and called The Passion Play. You know of it, Monsieur?"

"Very well through reading, Monsieur."

"Next Easter we propose having a Passion Play in pious imitation of the famous drama. We will hold it at the Indian reservation of Four Mountains, thus quickening our own souls and giving a good object-lesson of the great History to the Indians."

The Cure paused rather anxiously, but Charley did not speak. His eyes were fixed inquiringly on the Cure, and he had a sudden suspicion that some devious means were forward to influence him. He dismissed the thought, however, for this Cure was simple as man ever was made, straightforward as the most heretical layman might demand.

The Cure, taking heart, again continued: "Now I possess an authentic description of the Ober-Ammergau drama, giving details of its presentation at different periods, and also a book of the play. But there is no one in the parish who reads German, and it occurred to the Seigneur and myself that, understanding French so well, by chance you may understand German also, and would, perhaps, translate the work for us."

"I read German easily and speak it fairly," Charley answered, relieved; "and you are welcome to my services."

The Cure's pale face flushed with pleasure. He took the little German book from his pocket, and handed it over.

"It is not so very long," he said; "and we shall all be grateful." Then an inspiration came to him; his eyes lighted.

"Monsieur," he said, "you will notice that there are no illustrations in the book. It is possible that you might be able to make us a few drawings—if we do not ask too much? It would aid greatly in the matter of costume, and you might use my library—I have a fair number of histories." The Cure was almost breathless, his heart thumped as he made the request. After a slight pause he added, hastily: "You are always doing for others. It is hardly kind to ask you; but we have some months to spare; there need be no haste." Charley hastened to relieve the Cure's anxiety. "Do not apologise," he said.

"I will do what I can when I can. But as for drawing, Monsieur, it will be but amateurish."

"Monsieur," interposed the Seigneur promptly, "if you're not an artist, I'm damned!"

"Maurice!" murmured the Cure reproachfully. "Can't help it, Cure. I've held it in for an hour. It had to come; so there it is exploded. I see no damage either, save to my own reputation. Monsieur," he added to Charley, "if I had gifts like yours, nothing would hold me. I should put on more airs than Beauty Steele."

It was fortunate that, at that instant, Charley's face was turned away, or the Seigneur would have seen it go white and startled. Charley did not dare turn his head for the moment. He could not speak. What did the Seigneur know of Beauty Steele?

To hide his momentary confusion, he went over to the drawer of a cupboard in the wall, and placed the book inside. It gave him time to recover himself. When he turned round again his face was calm, his manner composed.

"And who, may I ask, is Beauty Steele?" he said. "Faith I do not know," answered the Seigneur, taking a pinch of snuff. "It's years since I first read the phrase in a letter a scamp of a relative of mine wrote me from the West. He had met a man of the name, who had a reputation as a clever fop, a very handsome fellow. So I thought it a good phrase, and I've used it ever since on occasions. 'More airs than Beauty Steele.'—It has a sound; it's effective, I fancy, Monsieur?"

"Decidedly effective," answered Charley quietly. He picked up his shears. "You will excuse me," he said grimly, "but I must earn my living. I cannot live on my reputation."

The Seigneur and the Cure lifted their hats—to the tailor.

"Au revoir, Monsieur," they both said, and Charley bowed them out.

The two friends turned to each other a little way up the street. "Something will come of this, Cure," said the Seigneur. The Cure, whose face had a look of happiness, pressed his arm in reply.

Inside the tailor-shop, a voice kept saying, "More airs than Beauty Steele!"

CHAPTER XXXIX
THE SCARLET WOMAN

Since the evening in the garden when she had been drawn into Charley's arms, and then fled from them in joyful confusion, Rosalie had been in a dream. She had not closed her eyes all night, or, if she closed them, they still saw beautiful things flashing by, to be succeeded by other beautiful things. It was a roseate world. To her simple nature it was not so important to be loved as to love. Selfishness was as yet the minor part of her. She had been giving all her life—to her mother, as a child; to sisters at the convent who had been kind to her; to the poor and the sick of the parish; to her father, who was helpless without her; to the tailor across the way. In each case she had given more than she had got. A nature overflowing with impulsive affection, it must spend itself upon others. The maternal instinct was at the very core of her nature, and care for others was as much a habit as an instinct with her. She had love to give, and it must be given. It had been poured like the rain from heaven on the just and the unjust; on animals as on human beings, and in so far as her nature, in the first spring—the very April—of its powers, could do.

Till Charley had come to Chaudiere, it had all been the undisciplined ardour of a girl's nature. A change had begun in the moment when she had tearfully thrust the oil and flour in upon his excoriated breast. Later came real awakening, and a riotous outpouring of herself in sympathy, in observation, in a reckless kindness which must have done her harm but that her clear intelligence balanced her actions, and because secrecy in one thing helped to restrain her in all. Yet with all the fresh overflow of her spirit, which, assisted by her new position as postmistress, made her a conspicuous and popular figure in the parish, where officialdom had rare honour and little labour, she had prejudices almost unworthy of her, due though they were to radical antipathy. These prejudices, one against Jo Portugais and the other against Paulette Dubois, she had never been able entirely to overcome, though she had honestly tried. On the way to the hospital at Quebec, however, Jo had been so careful of her father, so respectful when speaking of M'sieu', so regardful of her own comfort, that her antagonism to him was lulled. But the strong prejudice against Paulette Dubois remained, casting a shadow on her bright spirit.

All this day she had moved about in a mellow dream, very busy, scarcely thinking. New feelings dominated her, and she was too primitive to analyse them and too occupied with them to realise acutely the life about her. Work was an abstraction, resting rather than tiring her.

Many times she had looked across at the tailor-shop, only seeing Charley once. She did not wish to speak with him now, nor to be near him yet; she wanted this day for herself only.

So it was that, soon after the Cure and the Seigneur had bade good-bye to Charley, she left the post-office and went quickly through the village to a spot by the river, where was a place called the Rest of the Flaxbeaters. It was an overhanging rock which made a kind of canopy over a sweet spring, where, in the days when their labours sounded through the valley, the flaxbeaters from the level below came to eat their meals and to rest.

This had always been a resort for her in the months when the flax-beaters did not use it. Since a child she had made the place her own. To this day it is called Rosalie's Dell; for are not her sorrows and joys still told by those who knew and loved her? and is not the parish still fragrant with her name? Has not her history become a living legend a thousand times told?

Leaving the village behind her, Rosalie passed down the high-road till she came to a path that led off through a grove of scattered pines. There would be yet a half-hour's sun and then a short twilight, and the river and the woods and the Rest of the Flax-beaters would be her own; and she could think of the wonderful thing come upon her. She had brought with her a book of English poems, and as she went through the grove she opened it, and in her pretty English repeated over and over to herself:

> "My heart is thine, and soul and body render
>
> Faith to thy faith; I give nor hold in thrall:
>
> Take all, dear love! thou art my life's defender;
>
> Speak to my soul! Take life and love; take all!"

She was lifted up by the abandonment of the verse, by the fulness of her own feelings, which had only needed a touch of beauty to give it exaltation. The touch had come.

She went on abstractedly to the place where she had trysted with her thoughts only, these many years, and, sitting down, watched the sun sink beyond the trees, the shades of evening fall. All that had happened since Charley came to the parish she went over in her mind. She remembered the day he had said this, the day he had said that; she brought back the night—it was etched upon her mind!—when he had said to her, "You have saved my life, Mademoiselle!" She recalled the time she put the little cross back on the church-door, the ghostly footsteps in the church, the light, the lost hood. A shudder ran through her now, for the mystery of that hood had never been cleared up. But the words on the page caught her eye again:

"*My heart is thine, and soul and body render*

Faith to thy faith..."

It swallowed up the moment's agitation. Never till this day, never till last night, had she dared to say to herself, He loves me. He seemed so far above her—she never had thought of him as a tailor!—that she had given and never dared hope to receive, had lived without anticipation lest there should come despair. Even that day at Vadrome Mountain she had not thought he meant love, when he had said to her that he would remember to the last. When he had said that he would die for love's sake, he had not meant her, but others—some one else whom he would save by his death. Kathleen, that name which had haunted her—ah, whoever Kathleen was, or whatever Kathleen had to do with him or his life, she had no reason to fear Kathleen now. She had no reason to fear any one; for had she not heard his words of love as he clasped her in his arms last night? Had she not fled from that enfolding, because her heart was so full in the hour of her triumph that she could not bear more, could not look longer into the eyes to which she had told her love before his was spoken?

In the midst of her thoughts she heard footsteps. She started up. Paulette Dubois suddenly appeared in the path below. She had taken the river-path down from Vadrome Mountain, where she had gone to see Jo Portugais, who had not yet returned from Quebec. Paulette's face was agitated, her manner nervous. For nights she had not slept, and her approaching meeting with the tailor had made her tremble all day. Excited as she was, there was a wild sort of beauty in her face, and her figure was lithe and supple. She dressed always a little garishly, but now there was only that band of colour round the throat, worn last night in the talk with Charley.

To both women this meeting was as a personal misfortune, a mutual affront. Each had a natural antipathy. To Rosalie the invasion of her beloved retreat was as hateful as though the woman had purposely intruded.

For a moment they confronted each other without speaking, then Rosalie's natural courtesy, her instinctive good-heartedness, overcame her irritation, and she said quietly:

"Good-evening, Madame."

"I am not Madame, and you know it," answered the woman harshly.

"I am sorry. Good-evening, Mademoiselle," rejoined Rosalie evenly.

"You wanted to insult me. You knew I wasn't Madame."

Rosalie shook her head. "How should I know? You have not always lived in Chaudiere, you have lived in Montreal, and people often call you Madame."

"You know better. You know that letters come to me from Montreal addressed Mademoiselle."

Rosalie turned as if to go. "I do not recall what letters pass through the post-office. I have a good memory for forgetting. Good-evening," she added, with an excess of courtesy. Paulette read the placid scorn in the girl's face; she did not see and would not understand that Rosalie did not scorn her for what she had ever done, but for something that she was.

"You think I am the dirt under your feet," she said, now white, now red, and mad with anger. "I'm not fit to speak with you—I'm a rag for the dust pile!"

"I have never thought so," answered Rosalie. "I have not liked you, but I am sorry for you, and I never thought those things."

"You lie!" was the rejoinder; and Rosalie, turning away quickly with trouble in her face, put her hands to her ears, and, hastening down the hillside, did not hear the words the woman called after her.

"To-morrow every one shall know you are a thief. Run, run, run! You can hear what I say, white-face! They shall know about the little cross to-morrow."

She followed Rosalie at a distance, her eyes blazing. As fate would have it, she met on the highroad the least scrupulous man in the parish, an inveterate gossip, the keeper of the general store, whose only opposition in business was the post-office shop. He was the centre of the village tittle-tattle, and worse. With malicious speed Paulette told him how she had seen Rosalie Evanturel nailing the little cross on the church door of a certain night. If he wanted proof of what she said, let him ask Jo Portugais.

Having spat out her revenge, she went on to the village, and through it to her house, where she prepared to visit the shop of the tailor. Her sense of retaliation satisfied, Rosalie passed from her mind; her child only occupied it. In another hour she would know where her child was—the tailor had promised that she should. Then perhaps she would be sorry for the accident to the Notary; for it was an accident, in spite of appearances.

It was dark when Paulette entered the door of the tailor's house. When she came out, a half-hour later, with elation in her carriage, and tears of joy running down her face, she did not look about her; she did not care whether or not any one saw her: she was possessed with only one thought—her child! She passed like a swift wind down the street, making for home and for her departure to the hiding-place of her child.

She had not seen a figure in the shadow of a tree near by as she came from the tailor's door. She had not heard a smothered cry behind her. She was not aware that in unspeakable agony another woman knocked softly at the door of the tailor's house, and, not waiting for an answer, opened it and entered. It was Rosalie Evanturel.

CHAPTER XL
AS IT WAS IN THE BEGINNING

The kitchen was empty, but light fell through the door of the shop opening upon the little hall between. Rosalie crossed the hall and stood in the doorway of the shop, a figure of concentrated indignation, despair, and shame. Leaning on his elbow Charley was bending over a book in the light of a candle on the bench be side him. He was reading aloud, translating into English the German text of the narrative the Cure had given him:

"And because of this divine interposition, consequent upon their
faithful prayers and their oblations, they did perform these holy
scenes from season to season, with solemn proof of piety and godly
living, so that it seemed the life of the Lord our Shepherd was ever
present with them, as though, indeed, Ober-Ammergau were Nazareth or
Jerusalem. And the hearts of all in the land did answer daily to
that sweet and lively faith, insomuch that even in times of war the
zeal of the people became an holy zeal, and their warfare noble; so
that they did accept both victory and defeat with equal humbleness.
Because there was no war in their hearts, but peace, and they did
fight to defend and not to acquire, they buried their foe with tears
and their own with singleness of heart and quiet joy, for that they
did rest from their labours. In this manner was the great tragedy
and glory of the world made to the people a present thing,
transforming them to the body of the Life that hath neither spot nor
blemish nor..."

Charley had not heard Rosalie enter, nor her footsteps in the hall. But now there ran through his reading a thread of something not of himself or of it. He had thrilled to the archaic but clear-hearted style of the old

German chronicler, and the warmth he felt had passed into his voice, so that it became louder.

As Rosalie listened to his reading, a hundred thoughts rushed through her mind. Paulette Dubois, the wanton woman, had just left his doorway secretly, yet there he was, instantly after, calmly reading a pious book! Her mind was in tumult. She could not reason, she could not rule her judgment. She only knew that the woman had come from this house, and hurried guiltily away into the dark. She only knew that the man the woman had left here was the man she loved—loved more than her life, for he embodied all her past; all her present—she knew that she could not live without him; all her future—for where he went she would go, whatever the fate.

Her judgment had been swept from its moorings. She had been carried on the wave of her heart's fever into this room, not daring to think this or that, not planning this or that, not accusing, not reproaching, not shaming herself and him by black suspicion, but blindly, madly demanding to see him, to look into his eyes, to hear his voice, to know him, whatever he was—man, lover, or devil. She was a child-woman—a child in her primitive feelings that threw aside all convention, because there was no wrong in her heart; a woman, because she was possessed by a jealousy which shamed and angered her, because its very existence put him on trial, condemned him. Her soul was the sport of emotions and passions stronger than herself, because the heritage, the instinct, of all the race of women, the eternal predisposition. At the moment her will was not sufficient to rule them to obedience. She was in the first subservience to that power which feeds the streams of human history.

As she now listened to Charley reading, a sudden revulsion of feeling came over her. Some note in his voice reassured her heart—if it needed reassuring. The quiet force of his presence stilled the tumult in her, so that her eyes could see without mist, her heart beat without agony; but every pulse in her was throbbing, every instinct was alive. Presently there rushed upon her the words that had rung in her ears and chimed in her heart at the Rest of the Flax-beaters:

> "Take all, dear love! thou art my life's defender;
>
> Speak to my soul! Take life and love; take all."

Feelings lying beneath the mad conflict of emotion which had sent her into this room in such unmaidenly fashion—feelings that were her deepest self-welled up. Her breath came hard and broken.

As Charley read on, a breathing seemed to answer his own. It became quicker than his own, it pierced the stillness, it filled the room with feeling, it came calling to him out of the silence. He swung round, and saw the girl in the doorway.

"Rosalie!" he cried, and sprang to his feet.

With a piteously pathetic cry, she flung herself on her knees beside the tailor's bench where he worked every day, and, burying her face in her arms as they rested on the bench, wept bitterly.

"Rosalie!" he said anxiously, leaning over her. "What is the matter? What has happened?"

She wept more bitterly still; she made a despairing gesture. His hand touched her hair; he dropped on a knee beside her.

"Oh, I am so ashamed, ashamed! I have been so wicked," she murmured.

"Rosalie, what has happened?" he urged gently. His own heart was beating hard, his own eyes were responding to hers. The new feelings alive in him, the forces his love had awakened, which, last night, had kept him sleepless, and had been upon him like a dream all day—they were at height in him now. He knew not how to command them.

"Rosalie, dearest, tell me all!" he persisted.

"I shall never—I have been—oh—you will never forgive me!" she said brokenly. "I knew it wasn't true, but I couldn't help it. I saw her—the woman—come from your house, and—"

"Hush! For God's sake, hush!" he broke in almost harshly. Then a better understanding came upon him, and it made him gentle with her.

"Ah, Rosalie, you did not think! But—but it was natural you should wish to see me...."

"But, as soon as I saw you, I knew that—that—" She broke down again and wept.

"I will tell you about her, Rosalie—" His fingers stroked her hair, and, bending over her, his face was near her hands.

"No, no, tell me nothing—oh, if you tell me!—"

"She came to hear from me what she ought to have heard from the Notary. She has had great trouble—the man—her child—and I have helped her, told her—" His face was so near now that his breath was on her hair. She suddenly raised her head and clasped his face in her hands.

"I knew—oh, I knew, I knew...!" she wept, and her eyes drank his.

"Rosalie, my life!" he cried, clasping her in his arms.

The love that was in him, new-born and but half understood, poured itself out in broken words like her own. For him there was no outside world; no past, no Kathleen, no Billy; no suspicion, or infidelity, or unfaith; no fear of disaster; no terrors of the future. Life was Now to him and to her: nothing brooded behind, nothing lay before. The candle spluttered and burnt low in the socket.

CHAPTER XLI
IT WAS MICHAELMAS DAY

Not a cloud in the sky, and, ruling all, a sweet sun, liberal in warmth and eager in brightness as its distance from the northern world decreased. As Mrs. Flynn entered the door of the post-office she sang out to Maximilian Cour, with a buoyant lilt: "Oh, isn't it the fun o' the world to be alive!"

The tailor over the way heard it, and lifted his head with a smile; Rosalie Evanturel, behind the postal wicket, heard it, and her face swam with colour. Rosalie busied herself with the letters and papers for a moment before she answered Mrs. Flynn's greeting, for there were ringing in her ears the words she herself had said a few days before: "It is good to live, isn't it?"

To-day it was so good to live that life seemed an endless being and a tireless happy doing—a gift of labour, an inspiring daytime, and a rejoicing sleep. Exaltation, a painful joy, and a wide embarrassing wonderment possessed her. She met Mrs. Flynn's face at the wicket with shining eyes and a timid smile.

"Ah, there y'are, darlin'!" said Mrs. Flynn. "And how's the dear father to-day?"

"He seems about the same, thank you."

"Ah, that's foine. Shure, if we could always be 'about the same,' we'd do. True for you, darlin', 'tis as you say. If ould Mary Flynn could be always ''bout the same,' the clods o' the valley would never cover her bones. But there 'tis—we're here to-day, and away tomorrow. Shure, though, I am not complainin'. Not I—not Mary Flynn. Teddy Flynn used to say to me, says he: 'Niver born to know distress! Happy as worms in a garden av cucumbers. Seventeen years in this country, Mary,' says he, 'an' nivir in the pinitintiary yet.' There y'are. Ah, the birds do be singin' to-day! 'Tis good! 'Tis good, darlin'! You'll not mind Mary Flynn callin' you darlin', though y'are postmistress, an' 'll be more than that—more than that wan day— or Mary Flynn's a fool. Aye, more than that y'll be, darlin', and y're eyes like purty brown topazzes and y're cheeks like roses-shure, is there anny lether for Mary Flynn, darlin'?" she hastily added as she saw the Seigneur standing in the doorway. He had evidently been listening.

"Ye didn't hear what y're ould fool of a cook was sayin'," she added to the Seigneur, as Rosalie shook her head and answered: "No letters, Madame—dear." Rosalie timidly added the dear, for there was something so great-hearted in Mrs. Flynn that she longed to clasp her round the neck, longed as she had never done in her life to lay her head upon some motherly breast and pour out her heart. But it was not to be now. Secrecy was her duty still.

"Can't ye speak to y're ould fool of a cook, sir?" Mrs. Flynn said again, as the Seigneur made way for her to leave the shop.

"How did you guess?" he said to her in a low voice, his sharp eyes peering into hers.

"By the looks in y're face these past weeks, and the look in hers," she whispered, and went on her way rejoicing.

"I'll wind thim both round me finger like a wisp o' straw," she said, going up the road with a light step, despite her weight, till she was stopped by the malicious grocer-man of the village, whose tongue had been wagging for hours upon an unwholesome theme.

Meanwhile, in the post-office, the Seigneur and Rosalie were face to face.

"It is Michaelmas day," he said. "May I speak with you, Mademoiselle?"

She looked at the clock. It was on the stroke of noon. The shop always closed from twelve till half-past twelve.

"Will you step into the parlour, Monsieur?" she said, and coming round the counter, locked the shop-door. She was trembling and confused, and entered the little parlour shyly. Yet her eyes met the Seigneur's bravely. "Your father, how is he?" he said, offering her a chair. The sunlight streaming in the window made a sort of pathway of light between them, while they were in the shade.

"He seems no worse, and to-day he is wheeling himself about."

"He is stronger, then—that's good. Is there any fear that he must go to the hospital again?"

She inclined her head. "The doctor says he may have to go any moment. It may be his one chance. The Cure is very kind, and says that, with your permission, his sister will keep the office here, if—if needed."

The Seigneur nodded briskly. "Of course, of course. But have you not thought that we might secure another postmistress?"

Her face clouded a little; her heart beat hard. She knew what was coming. She dreaded it, but it was better to have it over now.

"We could not live without it," she said helplessly.

"What we have saved is not enough. The little my mother had must pay for the visits to the hospital. I have kept it for that. You see, I need the place here."

"But you have thought, just the same. Do you not know the day?" he asked meaningly.

She was silent.

"I have come to ask you to marry me—this is Michaelmas day, Rosalie."

She did not speak. He had hopes from her silence. "If anything happened to your father, you could not live here alone—but a young girl! Your father may be in the hospital for a long time. You cannot afford that. If I were to offer you money, you would refuse. If you marry me, all that I have is yours to dispose of at your will: to make others happy, to take you now and then from this narrow place, to see what's going on in the world."

"I am happy here," she said falteringly.

"Chaudiere is the finest place in the world," he replied proudly, and as a matter of fact. "But, for the sake of knowledge, you should see what the rest of the world is. It helps you to understand Chaudiere better. I ask you to be my wife, Rosalie."

She shook her head sorrowfully.

"You said before, it was not because I am old, not because I am rich, not because I am Seigneur, not because I am I, that you refused me."

She smiled at him now. "That is true," she said.

"Then what reason can you have? None, none. 'Pon honour, I believe you are afraid of marriage because it's marriage. By my life, there's naught to dread. A little giving here and taking there, and it's easy. And when a woman is all that's good, to a man, it can be done without fear or trembling. Even the Cure would tell you that."

"Ah, I know, I know," she said, in a voice half painful, half joyous. "I know that it is so. But, oh, dear Monsieur, I cannot marry you—never—never."

He hung on bravely. "I want to make life easy and happy for you. I want the right to do so. When trouble comes upon you—"

"When it does I will turn to you—ah, yes, I would turn to you without fear, dear Monsieur," she said, and her heart ached within her, for a premonition of sorrow came upon her and filled her eyes, and made her heart like lead within her breast. "I know how true a gentleman you are," she added. "I could give you everything but that which is life to me, which is being, and soul, and the beginning and the end."

The weight of the revealing hour of her life, its wonder, its agony, its irrevocability, was upon her. It was giving new meanings to existence-primitive woman, child of nature as she was. All morning she had longed to go out into the woods and bury herself among the ferns and bracken, and laugh and weep for very excess of feeling, downright joy and vague woe possessing her at once. She looked the Seigneur in the eyes with consuming earnestness.

"Oh, it is not because I am young," she said, in a low voice, "for I am old—indeed, I am very old. It is because I cannot love you, and never can love you in the one great way; and I will not marry without love. My heart is fixed on that. When I marry, it will be when I love a man so much that I cannot live without him. If he is so poor that each meal is a miracle, it will make no difference. Oh, can't you see, can't you feel, what I mean, Monsieur—you who are so wise and learned, and know the world so well?"

"Wise and learned!" he said, a little roughly, for his voice was husky with emotion. "'Pon honour, I think I am a fool! A bewildered fool, that knows no more of woman than my cook knows Sanscrit. Faith, a hundred times less! For Mary Flynn's got an eye to see, and, without telling, she knew I had a mind set on you. But Mary Flynn thought more than that, for she has an idea that you've a mind set on some one, Rosalie. She thought it might be me."

"A woman is not so easily read as a man," she replied, half smiling, but with her eyes turned to the street. A few people were gathering in front of the house—she wondered why.

"There is some one else—that is it, Rosalie. There is some one else. You shall tell me who it is. You shall—"

He stopped short, for there was a loud knocking at the shop-door, and the voice of M. Evanturel calling: "Rosalie! Rosalie! Rosalie! Ah, come quickly—ah, my Rosalie!"

Without a look at the Seigneur, Rosalie rushed into the shop and opened the front door. Her father was deathly pale, and was trembling violently.

"Rosalie, my bird," he cried indignantly, "they're saying you stole the cross from the church door."

He was now wheeled inside the shop, and people gathered round, looking at him and Rosalie, some covertly, some as friends, some in a half-frightened way, as though strange things were about to happen.

"Shure, 'tis a lie, or me name's not Mary Flynn—the darlin'!" said the Seigneur's cook, with blazing face. "Who makes this charge?" roared an angry voice. No one had seen the Seigneur enter from the little room beside the shop, and at the sound of the sharp voice the people fell back, for he was as free with his stick as his tongue.

"I do," said the grocer, to whom Paulette Dubois had told her story.

"Ye shall be tarred and feathered before y'are a day older," said Mary Flynn.

Rosalie was very pale.

The Seigneur was struck by this and by the strangeness of her look.

"Clear the room," he said to Filion Lacasse, who was now a constable of the parish.

"Not yet!" said a voice at the doorway. "What is the trouble?" It was the Cure, who had already heard rumours of the scandal, and had come at once to Rosalie. M. Evanturel tried to speak, and could not. But Mary Flynn did, with a face like a piece of scarlet bunting. Having finished with a flourish, she could scarce keep her hands off the cowardly grocer.

The Cure turned to Rosalie. "It is absurd," he said. "Forgive me," he added to the Seigneur. "It is better that Rosalie should answer this charge. If she gives her word of honour, I will deny communion to whoever slanders her hereafter."

"She did it," said the grocer stubbornly. "She can't deny it."

"Answer, Rosalie," said the Cure firmly.

"Excuse me; I will answer," said a voice at the door. The tailor of Chaudiere made his way into the shop, through the fast-gathering crowd.

CHAPTER XLII
A TRIAL AND A VERDICT

"What right have you to answer for mademoiselle?" said the Seigneur, with a sudden rush of jealousy. Was not he alone the protector of Rosalie Evanturel? Yet here was mystery, and it was clear the tailor had something important to say. M. Rossignol offered the Cure a chair, seated himself on a small bench, and gently drew Rosalie down beside him.

"I will make this a court," said he. "Advance, grocer."

The grocer came forward smugly.

"On what information do you make this charge against mademoiselle?"

The grocer volubly related all that Paulette Dubois had said. As he told his tale the Cure's face was a study, for the night the cross was restored came back to him, and the events, so far as he knew them, were in keeping with the grocer's narrative. He looked at Rosalie anxiously. Monsieur Evanturel moaned, for he remembered he had heard Rosalie come in very late that night. Yet he fixed his eyes on her in dog-like faith.

"Mademoiselle will admit that this is true, I presume," said Charley.

Rosalie looked at him intently, as though to read his very heart. It was clear that he wished her to say yes; and what he wished was law.

"It is quite true," answered Rosalie calmly, and all fear passed from her.

"But she did not steal the cross," continued Charley, in a louder voice, that all might hear, for people were gathering fast.

"If she didn't steal it, why was she putting it back on the church door in the dark?" said the grocer. "Ah, hould y'r head, ould sand-in-the-sugar!" said Mrs. Flynn, her fingers aching to get into his hair. "Silence!" said the Seigneur severely, and looked inquiringly at Rosalie. Rosalie looked at Charley.

"It is not a question of why mademoiselle put the cross back," he said. "It is a question of who took the cross away, is it not? Suppose it was not a theft. Suppose that the person who took the relic thought to do a pious act—for your Church, Monsieur?"

"I do not see," the Cure answered helplessly. "It was a secret act, therefore suspicious at least."

"'Let your good gifts be in secret, and your Heavenly Father who seeth in secret will reward you openly,'" answered Charley. "That, I believe, is a principle you teach, Monsieur."

"At one time Monsieur the tailor was thought to have taken the cross," said the Seigneur suggestively. "Perhaps Monsieur was secretly doing good with it?" he added. It vexed him that there should be a secret between Rosalie and this man.

"It had to do with me, not I with it," he answered evenly. He must travel wide at first to convince their narrow brains. "Mademoiselle did a kind act when she nailed that cross on the church door again—to make a dead man rest easier in his grave."

A hush fell upon the crowd.

Rosalie looked at Charley in surprise; but she saw his meaning presently—that what she did for him must seem to have been done for the dead tailor only. Her heart beat hot with indignation, for she would, if she but might, cry her love gladly from the hill-tops of the world.

Alight began to break upon the Cure's mind. "Will Monsieur speak plainly?" he said.

"I did not see Louis Trudel take the cross, but I know that he did."

"Louis Trudel! Louis Trudel!" interposed the Seigneur anxiously. "What does this mean?"

"Monsieur speaks the truth," interposed Rosalie. The Cure recalled the death-bed of Louis Trudel, and the dying man's strange agitation. He also recalled old Margot's death, and her wish to confess some one else's wrong doing. He was convinced that Charley was speaking the truth.

"It is true," added Charley slowly; "but you may think none the worse of him when you know all. He took the cross for temporary use, and before he could replace it he died."

"How do you know what he meant, or did not mean?" said the Seigneur in perplexity. "Did he take you into his confidence?"

"The very closest," answered Charley grimly.

"Yet he looked upon you as an infidel, and said hard things of you on his death-bed," urged the Cure anxiously. He could not see the end of the tale, and he was troubled for both the dead man and the living.

"That was why he took me into his confidence. I will explain. I have not the honour to have the fulness of your Christian faith, Monsieur le Cure. I had asked him to show me a sign from heaven, and he showed it by the little iron cross."

"I can't make anything of that," said the Seigneur peevishly.

Rosalie sprang to her feet. "He will not tell the whole truth, Messieurs, but I will. With that little cross Louis Trudel would have killed Monsieur, had it not been for me."

A gasp of excitement went out from those who stood by.

"But for you, Rosalie?" asked the Cure.

"But for me. I saw Louis Trudel raise an iron against Monsieur that day in the shop. It made me nervous—I thought he was mad. So I watched. That night I saw a light in the tailor-shop late. I thought it strange. I went over and peeped through the cracks of the shutters. I saw old Louis at the fire with the little cross, red-hot. I knew he meant trouble. I ran into the house. Old Margot was beside herself with fear—she had seen also. I ran through the hall and saw old Louis upstairs with the burning cross. I followed. He went into Monsieur's room. When I got to the door"—she paused, trembling, for she saw Charley's reproving eyes upon her—"I saw him with the cross—with the cross raised over Monsieur."

"He meant to threaten me," interposed Charley quickly.

"We will have the truth!" said the Seigneur, in a husky voice.

"The cross came down on Monsieur's bare breast." The grocer laughed vindictively.

"Silence!" growled the Seigneur.

"Silence!" said Filion Lacasse, and dropped his hand on the grocer's shoulder. "I'll baste you with a stirrup-strap."

"The rest is well known," quickly interposed Charley. "The poor man was mad. He thought it a pious act to mark an infidel with the cross."

Every eye was fixed upon him. The Cure remembered Louis Trudel's last words: "Look—look—I gave—him—the sign—of...!" Old Margot's words also kept ringing in his ears. He turned to the Seigneur. "Monsieur," said he, "we have heard the truth. That act of Louis Trudel was cruel and murderous. May God forgive him! I will not say that mademoiselle did well in keeping silent—"

"God bless the darlin'!" cried Mrs. Flynn.

"—but I will say that she meant to do a kind act for a man's mortal memory—perhaps at the expense of his soul."

"For Monsieur to take his injury in silence, to keep it secret, was kind," said the Seigneur. "It is what our Cure here might call bearing his cross manfully."

"Seigneur," said the Cure reproachfully, "Seigneur, it is no subject for jest."

"Cure, our tailor here has treated it as a jest."

"Let him show his breast, if it's true," said the grocer, who, beneath his smirking, was a malignant soul.

The Cure turned on him sharply. Seldom had any one seen the Cure roused.

"Who are you, Ba'tiste Maxime, that your base curiosity should be satisfied—you, whose shameless tongue clattered, whose foolish soul rejoiced over the scandal? Must we all wear the facts of our lives—our joys, our sorrows, and our sins—for such eyes as yours to read? Bethink you of the evil things that you would hide—aye, every one here!" he added loudly. "Know, all of you, what goodness of heart towards a wicked man lay behind the secret these two have kept, that old Margot carried to her grave. When you go to your homes, pray for as much human kindness in you as a man of no Church or faith can show. For this child"—he turned to Rosalie-"honour her! Go now—go in peace!"

"One moment," said the Seigneur. "I fine Ba'tiste Maxime twenty dollars for defamation of character. The money to go for the poor."

"You hear that, ould sand-in-the-sugar!" said Mrs. Flynn. "Will you let me kiss ye, darlin'?" she added to Rosalie, and, waddling over, reached out her hands.

Rosalie's eyes were wet as she warmly kissed the old Irishwoman, and thereupon they entered into a friendship which was without end.

The Seigneur drove the crowd from the shop, and shut the door.

The Cure came to Charley. "Monsieur," said he, "I have no words. When I remember what agonies you suffered in those hours, how bravely you endured them—ah, Monsieur!" he added, with moist eyes, "I shall always feel that—that you are not far from the kingdom of God."

A silence fell upon them, for the Cure, the Seigneur, and Rosalie, as they looked at Charley, thought of the scar like a red cross on his breast.

It touched Charley with a kind of awe. He smiled painfully. "Shall I give you proof?" he said, making a motion to undo his waistcoat.

"Monsieur!" said the Seigneur reprovingly, and holding out his hand. "Monsieur! We are all gentlemen!"

CHAPTER XLIII
JO PORTUGAIS TELLS A STORY

Walking slowly, head bent, eyes unseeing, Charley was on his way to Vadrome Mountain, with the knowledge that Jo Portugais had returned.

The hunger for companionship was on him: to touch some mind that could understand the deep loneliness which had settled on him since that scene in the postoffice. It was the loneliness of a new and great separation. He had wakened to it to-day.

Once before, in the hut on Vadrome Mountain, he had wakened from a grave, had been born again. Last night had come still another birth, had come, as with Rosalie herself, knowledge, revelation, understanding. To Rosalie the new vision had come with a vague pain of heart, without shame, and with a wonderful happiness. Pain, shame, knowledge, and a happiness that passed suddenly into a despairing sorrow, had come to him.

In finding love he had found conscience, and in finding conscience he was on his way to another great discovery.

Looking to where Jo Portugais' house was set among the pines, Charley remembered the day—he saw the scene in his mind's eye—when Rosalie entered with the letter addressed "To the sick man at the house of Jo Portugais, at Vadrome Mountain," and he saw again her clear, unsoiled soul in the deep inquiring eyes.

"If you but knew"—he turned and looked down at the village below— "if you but knew!" he said, as though to all the world. "I have the sign from heaven—I know it now. To-day I wake to know what life means, and I see— Rosalie! I know now—but how? In taking all she had to give. What does she get in return? Nothing—nothing. Because I love her, because the whole world is nothing beside her, nor life, nor twenty lives, if I had them to give, I must say to her now: 'Rosalie, it was love that brought you to my arms, it is love that says, Thus far and no farther. Never again—never—never—never!' Yesterday I could have left her—died or vanished, without real hurt to her. She would have mourned and broken her heart and mended it again; and I should have been only a memory—of mystery, of tenderness. Then, one day she would have married, and no sting from my going would have remained. She would have had happiness, and I neither shame nor despair.... To-day it is all too late. We have drunk too deep-alas! too deep. She cannot marry another man, for ghosts will not lie for asking, and what is mine may not be another's. She cannot marry me, for what once was mine is mine still by ring and by book, and I should always be haunted by a torturing shadow. Kathleen has the right of way, not Rosalie. Ah, Rosalie, I dare not wrong you further. Yet to marry you, even as things are, if that might be! To live on here unrecognised? I am little like my old self, and year after year I should grow less and less like Charley Steele.... But, no, it is not possible!"

He stopped short in his thoughts, and his lips tightened in bitterness.

"God in heaven, what an impasse!" he said aloud.

There was a sudden crackling of twigs as a man rose up from a log by the wayside ahead of him. It was Jo Portugais, who had seen him coming, and had waited for him. He had heard Charley's words.

"Do you call me an impasse, M'sieu'?" Charley grasped Portugais' hand.

"What has happened, M'sieu'?" Jo asked anxiously. There was a brief silence, and then Charley told him of the events of the morning.

"You know of the mark-here?" he asked, touching his breast.

Jo nodded. "I saw, when you were ill."

"Yet you never asked!"

"I studied it out—I knew old Louis Trudel. Also, I saw ma'm'selle nail the cross to the church door. Two and two together in my mind did it. I didn't think Paulette Dubois would tell. I warned her."

"She quarrelled with mademoiselle. It was revenge.

"She might have been less vindictive. She had had good luck herself lately."

"What good luck had she, M'sieu'?"

Charley told Jo the story of the Notary, the woman, and the child.

Jo made no comment. They relapsed into silence. Arriving at the house, they entered. Jo lighted his pipe, and smoked steadily for a time without speaking. Buried in thought, Charley stood in the doorway looking down at the village. At last he turned.

"Where have you been these weeks past, Jo?"

"To Quebec first, M'sieu'."

Charley looked curiously at Jo, for there was meaning in his tone. "And where last?"

"To Montreal."

Charley's face became paler, his hands suddenly clinched, for he read the look in Jo's eyes. He knew that Jo had been looking at people and places once so familiar; that he had seen—Kathleen.

"Go on. Tell me all," he said heavily.

Portugais spoke in English. The foreign language seemed to make the truth less naked and staring to himself. He had a hard story to tell.

"It is not to say why I go to Montreal," he began. "But I go. I have my ears open; my eyes, she is not close. No one knows me—I am no account of. Every one is forgot the man, Joseph Nadeau, who was try for his life. Perhaps it is every one is forget the lawyer who save his neck—perhaps? So I stand by the streetside. I say to a man as I look up at sign-boards,' 'Where is that writing "M'sieu' Charles Steele," and all the res'?' 'He is dead long ago,' say the man to me. 'A good thing too, for he was the very devil.' 'I not understan',' I say. 'I tink that M'sieu' Steele is a dam smart man back time.' 'He was the smartes' man in the country, that Beauty Steele,' the man say. 'He bamboozle the jury hevery time. He cut up bad though.'"

Charley raised his hand with a nervous gesture of misery and impatience.

"'Where have you been,' that man say—'where have you been all these times not to know 'bout Charley Steele, hein?' 'In the backwoods,' I say. 'What bring you here now?' he ask. 'I have a case,' I say. 'What is it?' he ask. 'It is a case of a man who is punish for another man,' I say. 'That's the thing for Charley Steele,' he laugh. 'He was great man to root things out. Can't fool Charley Steele, we use to say here. But he die a bad death.' 'What was the matter with him?' I say. 'He drink too much, he spend too much, he run after a girl at Cote Dorion, and the river-drivers do for him one night. They say it was acciden', but is there any green on my eye? But he die trump— jus' like him. He have no fear of devil or man,' so the man say. 'But fear of God?' I ask. 'He was hinfidel,' he say. 'That was behin' all. He was crooked all roun'. He rob the widow and horphan?' 'I think he too smart for that,' I speak quick. 'I suppose it was the drink,' he say. 'He loose his grip.' 'He was a smart man, an' he would make you all sit up, if he come back,' I hanswer.

'If he come back!' The man laugh queer at that. 'If he comeback, there would be hell.' 'How is that?' I say. 'Look across the street,' he whisper. 'That was his wife.'"

Charley choked back a cry in his throat. Jo had no intention of cutting his story short. He had an end in view.

"I look across the street. There she is—' Ah, that is a fine woman to see! I have never seen but one more finer to look at—here in Chaudiere.' The man say: 'She marry first for money, and break her heart; now she marry for love. If Beauty Steele come back-eh! sacra! that would be a mess. But he is at the bottom of the St Lawrence—the courts say so, and the Church say so—and ghosts don't walk here.' 'But if that Beauty Steele come back alive, what would happen it?' I speak. 'His wife is marry, blockhead!' he say.

"'But the woman is his,' I hanswer. 'Do you think she would go back to a thief she never love from the man she love?' he speak back. 'She is not marry to the other man,' I say, 'if Beauty Steele is...' 'He is dead as a door,' he swear. 'You see that?' he go on, nodding down the street. 'Well, that is Billy.' 'Who is Billy?' I ask. 'The brother of her,' he say. 'Charley, he spoil Billy. Billy, he has not been the same since Charley's death-he is so ashame of Charley. When he get drunk he talk of nothing else. We all remember that Charley spoil him, and that make us sorry for him.' 'Excuse me,' I say. 'I think that Billy is a dam smart man. He is smart as Charley Steele.' 'Charley was the smartes' man in the country,' he say again. 'I've got his practice now, but this town will never be the same without him. Thief or no thief, I wish he is alive here. By the Lord, I'd get drunk with him!' He was all right, that man," Jo added finally.

Charley's agitation was hidden. His eyes were fixed on Jo intently. "That was Larry Rockwell. Go on," he said, in a hard metallic voice.

"I see—her, the next night again. It is in the white stone house on the hill. All the windows are open, an' I can hear her to sing. I not know that song. It begin, 'Oft in the stilly night'—like that."

Charley stiffened. It was the song Kathleen sang for him the night they became engaged.

"It is a good voice-that. I see her face, for there is a candle on the piano. I come close and closter to the house. There is big maple-trees—I am well hid. A man is beside her. He lean hover her an' put his hand on her shoulder. 'Sing it again, Kat'leen,' he say. 'I cannot to get enough.'"

"Stop!" said Charley, in a strained, harsh voice. "Not yet, M'sieu'," said Portugais. "It is good for you to hear what I say."

"'Come, Kat'leen!' the man say, an' he blow hout the candle. I hear them walk away, an' the door shut behin' them. Then I hear anudder voice—ah, that is a baby—very young baby!"

Charley quickly got to his feet. "Not another word!" he said.

"Yes, yes, but there is one word more, M'sieu'," said Jo, standing up and facing him firmly. "You must go back. You are not a thief. The woman is yours. You throw your life away. What is the man to you—or the man's brat of a child? It is all waiting for you. You mus' go back. You not steal the money, but that Billy—it is that Billy, I know. You can forgive your wife, and take her back, or you can say to both, Go! You can put heverything right and begin again."

Anger, wild words, seemed about to break from Charley's lips, but he conquered himself.

The old life had been brought back to him with painful acuteness and vividness. The streets of the town, the people in the street, Billy, the mean scoundrel, who could not leave him alone in the grave of obscurity, Kathleen—Fairing. The voice of the child—with her voice—was in his ears. A child! If he had had a child, perhaps——He stopped short in his thinking, his face all at once flooding with colour. For a moment he stood looking out of the window down towards the village. He could see the post-office like a toy house among toy houses. At last he turned to Jo.

"Never again while I live, speak of this to me: of the past, of going back, or of—of anything else," he said. "I cannot go back. I am dead and shamed. Let the dust of forgetfulness come and cover the past. I've begun life again here, and here I stay, and see it out. I shall work out the problem here." He dropped a hand on the other's shoulder. "Jo," said he, "we are both shipwrecks. Let us see how long we can float."

"M'sieu', is it worth it?" said Portugais, remembering his confession to the Abbe, and seeing the end of it all to himself.

"I don't know, Jo. Let us wait and see how Fate will play us."

"Or God, M'sieu'?"

"God or Fate—who knows"

CHAPTER XLIV
"WHO WAS KATHLEEN?"

The painful incidents of the morning weighed heavily upon Rosalie, and she was glad when Madame Dugal came to talk with her father, who was ailing and irritable, and when Mrs. Flynn drove her away with a kiss on either cheek, saying: "Don't come back, darlin', till there's roses in both cheeks, for y'r eyes are 'atin' up yer face!"

She had seen Charley take the path to Vadrome Mountain, and to the Rest of the Flax-beaters she betook herself, in the blind hope that, returning, he might pass that way. Under the influence of the fresh air and the quiet of the woods her spirits rose, her pulse beat faster, though a sense of foreboding and sorrow hovered round her. The two-miles walk to her beloved retreat seemed a matter of minutes only, so busy were her thoughts.

Her mind was one luxurious confusion, through which travelled a ghostly little sprite, who kept tumbling her thoughts about, sneering, smirking, whispering—"You dare not go to confession—dare not go to confession. You will never be the same again—never feel the same again—never think the same again; your dreams are done! You can only love. And what will this love do for you? What do you expect to happen—you dare not go to confession!"

Her reply had been the one iteration: "I love him—I love him—I love him. We shall be together all our lives, till we are old and grey. I shall watch him at his work, and listen to his voice. I shall read with him and walk with him, and I shall grow to think like him a little—in everything except religion. In everything except that. One day he will come to think like me—to believe in God."

In the dreamy happiness of these thoughts the colour came to her cheeks, the roses of light gathered in her eyes. In her tremulous ardour she scarcely realised how time passed, and her reverie deepened as the afternoon shadows grew and the sun made to its covert behind the hills. She was roused by a man's voice singing, just under the bluff where she sat. To her this voice represented the battle-call, the home-call, the life call of the universe. The song it sang was known to her. It was as old as Rizzio. It had come from old France with Mary, had been merged into English words and English music, and had voyaged to New France. There it had been sung by lovers in fair vales, on wide rivers, and in deep forests:

> *"What is not mine I may not hold,*
>
> *(Ah, hark the hunter's horn!),*
>
> *And what is thine may not be sold,*
>
> *(My love comes through the corn!);*
>
> *And none shall buy*
>
> *And none shall sell*
>
> *What Love works well?"*

In the walk back from Vadrome Mountain, a change — a fleeting change — had passed over Charley's mind and mood. The quiet of the woodland, the song of the birds, the tumbling brook, the smell of the rich earth, replenishing its strength from the gorgeous falling leaves, had soothed him. Thoughts of Rosalie took a new form. Her image possessed him, excluding the future, the perils that surrounded them. He had gone through so much within the past twenty-four hours that the capacity for suffering had almost exhausted itself, and in the reaction endearing thoughts of Rosalie had dominion over him. It was the reassertion of primitive man, the demands of the first element. The great problem was still in the background. The picture of Kathleen and the other man was pushed into the distance; thoughts of Billy and his infamy were thrust under foot — how futile to think of them! There was Rosalie to be thought of, the to-day and to-morrow of the new life.

Rosalie was of to-day. How strong and womanly she had been this morning, the girl whose life had been bounded by this Chaudiere, with a metropolitan convent and hospital as her only glimpses of the busy world. She would fit in anywhere — in the highest places, with her grace, and her nobleness of mind, arcadian, passionate and beautiful. There came upon him again the feeling of the evening before, when he saw her standing in his doorway, the night about them, jealous affection, undying love, in her eyes. It quickened his steps imperceptibly. He passed a stream, and glanced down into a dark pool involuntarily. It reflected himself clearly. He stopped short. "Is this you, Beauty Steele?" he said, and he caught his brown beard in his hand. "Beauty Steele had brains and no heart. You have heart, and your wits have gone wool-gathering. No matter!

What is not mine I may not hold,

(Ah, hark the hunter's horn!)'"

he sang, and came quickly along the stream where the flax-beaters worked in harvest-time, then up the hill, then—Rosalie.

She started to her feet. "I knew you would come—I knew you would!" she said.

"You have been waiting here for me?" he asked breathless, taking her hand.

"I felt you would come. I made you," she added smiling, and, eagerly answering the look in his eyes, threw her arms round his neck. In that moment's joy a fresh realisation of their fate came upon him with dire force, and a bitter protest went up from his heart, that he and she should be sacrificed.   .

Yet the impasse was there, and what could remove it—what clear the way?

He looked down at the girl whose head was buried in happy peace on his shoulder. She clung to him, as though in him was everlasting protection from the sprite that kept whispering: "You dare not go to confession—your dreams are done—you can only love." But she had no fear now.

As he looked down at her a swift change passed over him, and, almost for the first time since he was a little child, his eyes filled with tears. He hastily brushed them away, and drew her down on the seat beside him. He was wondering how he should tell her that they must not meet like this, that they must be apart. No matter what had happened, no matter what love there was, it was better that they should die—that he should die—than that they should meet like this. There was only one end to secret meetings, and discovery was inevitable. Then, with discovery, shame to her. For he must either marry her—how could he marry her?—or die. For him to die would but increase her misery.

The time had passed when it could be of any use. It passed that day in the hut on Vadrome Mountain when she said that if he died, she would die with him—"Where you are going you will be alone. There will be no one to care for you, no one but me." Last night it passed for ever. She had put her life into his hands; henceforth, there could never be a question of giving or taking, of withdrawing or advancing, for all was irrevocable, sealed with the great seal. Yet she must be saved. But how?

She suddenly looked up at him. "I can ask you anything I want now, can't I?" she said.

"Anything, Rosalie."

"You know that when I ask, it is because I want to know what you know, so that I may feel as you feel. You know that, don't you?"

"I know it when you tell me, wonderful Rosalie." What a revelation it was, this transmuting power, which could change mortal dross into the coin of immortal wealth!

"I want to ask you," she said, "who was Kathleen?" His blood seemed to go cold in his veins, and he sat without answering, shocked and dismayed. What could she know of Kathleen?

"Can't you tell me?" she asked anxiously yet fearfully. He looked so strange that she thought she had offended him. "Please don't mind telling me. I should understand everything—everything. Was it some one you loved—once?" It was hard for her to say it, but she said it bravely.

"No. I never loved any one in all the world, Rosalie—not till I loved you."

She gave a happy sigh. "Oh, it is wonderful!" she said. "It is wonderful and good! Did you—did you love me from the very first?"

"I think I did, though I didn't know it from the very first," he answered slowly. His heart beat hard, for he could not guess how she should know of Kathleen. It was absurdly impossible that she should know. "But many have loved you!" she said proudly. "They have not shown it," he answered grimly; then added quickly, and with aching anxiety: "When did you hear of—of Kathleen?"

"Oh, you are such a blind huntsman!" she laughed. "Don't you know where my little fox was hiding? Why, in the shop, when you held the note-paper up to the light, and looked startled, and bought all the paper we had that was water-marked Kathleen. Do you think that was clever of me? I don't."

"I think it was very clever," he said.

"Then she-Kathleen—doesn't really matter?" she asked eagerly. "Of course she can't, if you don't love her. But does she love you? Did she ever love you?" "Never in her life."

"So of course it doesn't matter," she rejoined. "Hush!" she added rapidly. "I see some one coming in the trees yonder. It may be some one for me. Father knows I come here sometimes. Go quickly and hide behind the rocks, please. I'll stay and see who it is. Please go—dearest."

He kissed her, and, keeping out of sight, got to a place of safety a few hundred feet away.

He saw the new-comer run to Rosalie, speak to her, saw Rosalie half turn in his own direction, then go hastily down the hillside with the messenger.

"It is her father!" he exclaimed, and followed at a distance. At the village he learned that M. Evanturel had had another seizure.

CHAPTER XLV
SIX MONTHS GO BY

Spring again—budding trees and flowing sap; the earth banks removed from the houses, and outside windows discarded; the ice tumbling and crunching in the river; the dormant farmer raising his head to the energy and delight of April.

The winter had been long and hard. Never had there been severer frost or deeper snow, and seldom had big game been so plentiful. In the snug warm stables the cattle munched and chewed the cud; the idle, long-haired horses grew as spirited in the keen air as in summer they were sluggish with hard work; and the farm-hands were abroad in the dark of the early mornings with lanterns, to feed the stock and take them out to water, singing cheerfully. All morning spread the clamour of the flail and the fanning-mill, the swish of the knife through the turnips and the beets, and the sound of the saw and the axe, as the youngest man of the family, muffled to the nose, sawed the wood into lengths or split the knots.

Night brought the cutting and stringing of apples, the shelling of the Indian corn, the making of rag carpets. On Saturday came the going to market with grain, or pork, or beef, or fowls frozen like stones; the gossip in the market-place. Then again sounded jingling sleigh-bells as, on the return road, the habitant made for home, a glass of white whiskey inside him, and black-eyed children in the doorway, swarming like bees at the mouth of a hive.

This particular winter in Chaudiere had been full of excitement and expectation. At Easter-time there was to be the great Passion Play, after the manner of that known as The Passion Play of Ober-Ammergau. Not one in a hundred habitants had ever heard of Ober-Ammergau, but they had all shared in picturesque processions of the Stations of the Cross to some calvaire; and many had taken part in dramatic scenes arranged from the life of Christ. Drama of a crude kind was deep in them; it showed in gesture, speech, and temperament.

In all the preparations Maximilian Cour was a conspicuous and useful official. Gifted with the dramatic temperament to a degree rare in so humble a man, he it was who really educated the people of Chaudiere in the details of the Passion Play to be produced by the good Catholics of the parish and the Indians of the reservation. He had gone to the Cure every day, and the Cure had talked with him, and then had sent him to the tailor, who had, during the past six months, withdrawn more and more from the life about him, practically living with shut door. No one ventured in unless on business, or were in need, or wished advice. These he never turned empty away.

Besides Portugais, Maximilian Cour was the one man received constantly by the tailor. With patience and insight Charley taught the baker, by drawings and careful explanations, the outlines of the representation, and the baker grew proud of the association, though Charley's face used to haunt him in his sleep. Excitable, eager, there was an elemental adaptability in the baker, as easily leading to Avernus as to Elysium. This appealed to Charley, realising, as he did, that Maximilian Cour was a reputable citizen by mere accident. The baker's life had run in a sentimental groove of religious duty; that same sentimentality would, in other circumstances, have forced him with equal ardour into the broad primrose path.

In the evening hours and on Sunday Charley had worked at his drawings for the scenery and costumes of the Play, and completed his translation of the German text, but there had been days when he could not put pen to paper. Life to him now was one aching emptiness—since that day at the Rest of the Flax-beaters Rosalie had been absent. On the very morning after their meeting by the river she had gone away with her father to the great hospital at Montreal—not Quebec this time, on the advice of the Seigneur— as the one chance of prolonging his life. There had come but one letter from her since that hour when he saw her in the Seigneur's coach with her father, moving away in the still autumn air, a piteous appeal in her eyes. The good-bye look she gave him then was with him day and night.

She had written him one letter, and he had written one in reply, and no more. Though he was wholly reckless for himself, for her he was prudent now—there was nothing else to do. To save her—if he could but save her from himself! If he might only put back the clock!

In his letter to her he had simply said that it were wiser not to write, since the acting postmistress, the Cure's sister, would note the exchange of letters, and this would arouse suspicion. He could not see what was best to do, what was right to do. To wait seemed the only thing, and his one letter ended with the words: Rosalie, my life is lived only in the thought of you. There is no hour but I think of you, no moment but you are with me. The greatest proof of love that man can give, I will give to you, in the hour fate wills—for us. But now, we must wait—we must wait, Rosalie. Do not write to me, but know that if I could go to you I would go; if I could say to you, Come, I would say it. If the giving of my life would save you any pain or sorrow, I would give it.

Sitting on his bench at work, it seemed to Charley that sometimes she was near him, and more than once he turned quickly round as though she were, in very truth, standing beside him. He thought of her continually, and often with an unbearable pain. He figured her in his mind as pale and distressed, and always her eyes had the piteous terror of that last look as she went away over the hills.

But the weeks had worn on, then the Seigneur, who had been to Montreal, came back with the news that Rosalie was looking as beautiful as a picture. "Grown a woman in beauty and in stature; comely—comely as a lady in a Watteau picture, my dear messieurs!" he had said to the Cure, standing in the tailor's shop.

Replying, the Cure had said: "She is in good hands, with good people, recommended to me by an abbe there; yet I am not wholly happy about her. When her trouble comes to her"—Charley's needle slipped and pierced his finger to the bone—"when her father goes, as he must, I fear, there will be no familiar face; she will hear no familiar voice."

"Faith, there you are wrong, my dear Cure" answered the Seigneur; "there'll be a face yonder she likes very well indeed, and a voice she's fond of too."

Charley's back was on them at that moment, of which he was glad, for his face was haggard with anxiety, and it seemed hours before the Cure said: "Whom do you mean, Maurice?" and hours before the Seigneur replied: "Mrs. Flynn, of course. I'm sending her tomorrow."

Mrs. Flynn had gone, and Charley had, in one sense, been made no happier by that, for it seemed to him that Rosalie would rather that strangers' eyes were on her than the inquisitively friendly eye of Mary Flynn.

Weeks had grown into months, and no news came—none save that which the Cure let fall, or was brought by the irresponsible Notary, who heard all gossip. Only the Cure's scant news were authentic, however, and

Charley never saw the good priest but he had a secret hope of hearing him say that Rosalie was coming back. Yet when she came back, what would, or could, he do? There was always the crime for which he or Billy must be punished. Concerning this crime his heart was growing harder—for Rosalie's sake. But there was Kathleen—and Rosalie was now in the city where she lived, and they might meet! There was one solution—if Kathleen should die! It sickened him that he could think of that with a sense of relief, almost of hope. If Kathleen should die, then he would be free to marry Rosalie—into what? He still could only marry her into the peril and menace of the law? Again, even if Kathleen did not stand in the way, neither the Cure nor any other priest would marry him to her without his antecedents being certified. A Protestant minister would, perhaps, but would Rosalie give up her faith? Following him without the blessing of the Church, she would trample under foot every dear tradition of her life, win the scorn of all of her religion, and destroy her own peace; for the faith of her fathers was as the breath of her nostrils. What cruelty to her!

But was it, after all, even true that he had but to call and she would come? In truth it well might be that she had learned to despise him; to feel how dastardly he had been to take her love, given in blind simplicity, bestowed like the song of the bird upon the listening fields—to take the plenteous fulness of her life, and give nothing in return save the empty hand, the hopeless hour, the secret sorrow.

Nothing could quench his misery. The physical part of him craved without ceasing for something to allay his distress. Again and again he fought his old enemy with desperate resolve. To fall again, to touch liquor once more, was to end all for ever. He fought on tenaciously and gloomily, with little of the pride of life, with nothing of the old stubborn self-will, but with a new-awakened sense. He had found conscience at last—and more.

The months went by and still M. Evanturel lingered on, and Rosalie did not come. The strain became too great at last. In the week preceding Easter, when all the parish was busy at Four Mountains, making costumes, rehearsing, building, putting up seats, cutting down trees, and erecting crosses and calvaries, Charley disclosed to Jo a new intention.

In the earlier part of the winter Jo and he had met two or three times a week, but now Jo had come to help him with his work in the shop— two silent, devoted companions. They understood each other, and in that understanding were life and death. For never did Jo forget that a year from the day he had confessed his sins he meant to give himself up to justice. This caused him no sleepless nights. He thought more of Charley than of himself, and every month now he went to confession, and every day he said his prayers. He was at his prayers when Charley went to tell him of his purpose. Charley had often seen Jo on his knees of late, and he had wondered, but not with the old pagan mind. "Jo," he said, "I am going away—to Montreal."

"To Montreal!" exclaimed Jo huskily. "You are going back—to stay?"

"Not that. I am going—to see—Rosalie Evanturel." Jo was troubled but not dumfounded. It had slowly crept into his mind that Charley loved the girl, though he had no real ground for suspicion. His will, however, had been so long the slave of the other man's that he had far-off reflections of his thoughts. He made no reply in words, but nodded his head.

"I want you to stay here, Jo. If I don't come back, and—and she does, stand by her, Jo. I can trust you." "You will come back, M'sieu'—but you will come back, then?" Jo asked heavily.

"If I can, Jo—if I can," he answered.

Long after he had gone, Jo wandered up and down among the trees on the river-road, up which Charley had disappeared with Jo's dogs and sled. He kept shaking his head mournfully.

CHAPTER XLVI
THE FORGOTTEN MAN

It was Easter morning, and the good sunrise of a perfect spring made radiant the high hill above the town. Rosy-fingered morn touched with magic colour the masts and scattered sails of the ships upon the great river, and spires and towers quivered with rainbow light. The city was waking cheerfully, though the only active life was in the pealing bells and on the deep flowing rivers. The streets were empty yet, save for an assiduous priest or the cart of a milkman. Here and there a window opened and a drowsy head was thrust into the eager air. These saw a bearded countryman with his team of six dogs and his little cart going slowly up the street. It was plain the man had come a long distance—from the mountains in the east or south, no doubt, where horses were few, and dogs, canoes, and oxen the means of transportation.

As the man moved slowly through the streets, his dogs still gallantly full of life after their hard journey, he did not stare about him after the manner of countrymen. His movements had intelligence and freedom. He was an unusual figure for a woodsman or river-man—he did not wear ear-rings or a waist-sash as did the river-men, and he did not turn in his toes like a woodsman. Yet he was plainly a man from the far mountains.

The man with the dogs did not heed the few curious looks turned his way, but held his head down as though walking in familiar places. Now and then he spoke to his dogs, and once he stopped before a newspaper office, which had a placard bearing these lines:

The Coming Passion Play In the Chaudiere Valley.

He looked at it mechanically, for, though he was concerned in the Passion Play and the Chaudiere Valley, it was an abstraction to him at this moment. His mind was absorbed by other things.

Though he looked neither to right nor to left, he was deeply affected by all round him.

At last he came to a certain street, where he and his dogs travelled more quickly. It opened into a square, where bells were booming in the steeple of a church. Shops and offices in the street were shut, but a saloon-door was open, and over the doorway was the legend: Jean Jolicoeur, Licensed to sell Wine, Beer, and other Spirituous and Fermented Liquors.

Nearly opposite was a lawyer's office, with a new-painted sign. It had once read, in plain black letters, Charles Steele, Barrister, etc.; now it read, in gold letters and many flourishes of the sign-painter's art, Rockwell and Tremblay, Barristers, Attorneys, etc.

Here the man looked up with trouble in his eyes. He could see dimly the desk and the window beside which he had sat for so many years, and on the wall a map of the city glowed with the incoming sun.

He moved on, passing the saloon with the open door. The landlord, in his shirt-sleeves, was standing in the doorway. He nodded, then came out to the edge of the board-walk.

"Come a long way, M'sieu'?" he asked.

"Four days' journey," answered the man gruffly through his beard, looking the landlord in the eyes. If this landlord, who in the past had seen him so often and so closely, did not recognise him, surely no one else would. It was, however, a curious recurrence of habit that, as he looked at the landlord, he instinctively felt for his eye-glass, which he had discarded when he left Chaudiere. For an instant there was an involuntary arrest of Jean Jolicoeur's look, as though memory had been roused, but this swiftly passed, and he said:

"Fine dogs, them! We never get that kind hereabouts now, M'sieu'. Ever been to the city before?"

"I've never been far from home before," answered the Forgotten Man.

"You'd better keep your eyes open, my friend, though you've got a sharp pair in your head—sharp as Beauty Steele's almost. There's rascals in the river-side drinking-places that don't let the left hand know what the right does."

"My dogs and I never trust anybody," said the Forgotten Man, as one of the dogs snarled at the landlord's touch. "So I can take care of myself, even if I haven't eyes as sharp as Beauty Steele's, whoever he is."

The landlord laughed. "Beauty's only skin-deep, they say. Charley Steele was a lawyer; his office was over there"—he pointed across the street. "He went wrong. He come here too often—that wasn't my fault. He had an eye like a hawk, and you couldn't read it. Now I can read your eye like a book. There's a bit of spring in 'em, M'sieu'. His eyes were hard winter-ice five feet deep and no fishing under—froze to the bed. He had a tongue like a cross-cut saw. He's at the bottom of the St. Lawrence, leaving a bad job behind him.

"Have a drink—hein?" He jerked a finger backwards to the saloon door. "It's Sunday, but stolen waters are sweet, sure!"

The Forgotten Man shook his head. "I don't drink, thank you."

"It'd do you good. You're dead beat. You've been travelling hard—eh?"

"I've come a long way, and travelled all night."

"Going on?"

"I am going back to-morrow."

"On business?"

Charley nodded—he glanced involuntarily at the sign across the street.

Jean Jolicoeur saw the look. "Lawyer's business, p'r'aps?"

"A lawyer's business—yes."

"Ah, if Charley Steele was here!"

"I have as good a lawyer as—"

The landlord laughed scornfully. "They're not made. He'd legislate the devil out of the Pit. Where are you going to stay, M'sieu'?"

"Somewhere cheap—along the river," answered the Forgotten Man.

Jolicoeur's good-natured face became serious. "I'll tell you a place—it's honest. It's the next street, a few hundred yards down, on the left. There's a wooden fish over the door. It's called The Black Bass—that hotel. Say I sent you. Good luck to you, countryman! Ah, la; la, there's the second bell—I must be getting to Mass!" With a nod he turned and went into the house.

The Forgotten Man passed slowly up the street, into the side street, and followed it till he came to The Black Bass, and turned into the small stable-yard. A stable-man was stirring. He at once put his dogs into a little pen set apart for them, saw them fed from the kitchen, and, betaking himself to a little room behind the bar of the hotel, ordered breakfast. The place was empty, save for the servant—the household were at Mass. He looked round the room abstractedly. He was thinking of a crippled man in a hospital, of a girl from a village in the Chaudiere Valley. He thought with a shiver of a white house on the hill. He thought of himself as he had never done before in his life. Passing along the street, he had realised that he had no moral claim upon anything or anybody within these precincts of his past life. The place was a tomb to him.

As he sat in the little back parlour of The Black Bass, eating his frugal breakfast of eggs and bread and milk, the meaning of it all slowly dawned upon him. Through his intellect he had known something of humanity, but he had never known men. He had thought of men in the mass, and despised them because of their multitudinous duplication, and their typical weaknesses; but he had never known one man or one woman from the subtler, surer divination of the heart. His intellect had made servants and lures of his emotions and his heart, for even his every case in court had been won by easy and selfish command of all those feelings in mankind which make possible personal understanding.

In this little back parlour it came to him with sudden force how, long ago, he had cut himself off from any claim upon his fellows—not only by his conduct, but by his merciless inhuman intelligence working upon the merciful human life about him. He never remembered to have had any real feeling till on that day with Kathleen—the day he died. The bitter complaint of a woman he had wronged cruelly, by having married her, had wrung from him his own first wail of life, in the one cry "Kathleen!"

As he sat eating his simple meal his pulses were beating painfully. Every nerve in his body seemed to pluck at the angry flesh. There flashed across his mind in sympathetic sensation a picture. It was the axe-factory on the river, before which he used to stand as a boy, and watch the men naked to the waist, with huge hairy arms and streaming faces, toiling in the red glare, the trip-hammers endlessly pounding upon the glowing metal. In old days it had suggested pictures of gods and demi-gods toiling in the workshops of the primeval world. So the whole machinery of being seemed to be toiling in the light of an awakened conscience, to the making of a man. It seemed to him that all his life was being crowded into these hours. His past was here— its posing, its folly, its pitiful uselessness, and its shame. Kathleen and Billy were here, with all the problems that involved them. Rosalie was here, with the great, the last problem.

"Nothing matters but that—but Rosalie," he said to himself as he turned to look out of the window at the wrangling dogs gnawing bones. "Here she is in the midst of all I once knew, and I know that I am no more a part of it than she is. She and Kathleen may have met face to face in these streets— who can tell! The world is large, but there's a sort of whipper-in of Fate, who drives the people wearing the same livery into one corner in the end. If they met"—he rose and walked hastily up and down—"what then? I have a feeling that Rosalie would recognise her as plainly as though the word Kathleen were stitched on her breast."

There was a clock on the wall. He looked at it. "It will not be safe to go out until evening. Then I can go to the hospital, and watch her coming out." He realised with satisfaction that many people coming from Mass must pass the inn. There was a chance of his seeing Rosalie, if she had gone to early Mass. This street lay in her way from the hospital. "One look—ah, one look!" For this one look he had come. For this, and to secure that which would save Rosalie from want always, if anything should happen to him. This too had been greatly on his mind. There was a way to give her what was his very own, which would rob no one and serve her well indeed.

Looking at his face in the mirror over the mantel, he said to himself

"I might have had ten thousand friends, yet I have a thousand enemies, who grin at the memory of the drunken fop down among the eels and the cat-fish. Every chance was with me then. I come back here, and—and Jolicoeur tells me the brutal truth. But if I had had ambition"—a wave of the feeling of the old life passed over him—"if I had had ambition as I was then, I should have been a monster. It was all so paltry that, in sheer disgust, I should have kicked every ladder down that helped me up. I should have sacrificed everything to myself."

He stopped short and stared, for, in the mirror, he saw a girl passing through the stable-yard towards the quarrelling dogs in the kennel. He clapped his hand to his mouth to stop a cry. It was Rosalie.

He did not turn round but looked at her in the mirror, as though it were the last look he might give on earth.

He could hear her voice speaking to the dogs: "Ah, my friends, ah, my dears! I know you every one. Jo Portugais is here. I know your bark, you, Harpy, and you, Lazybones, and you, Cloud and London! I know you every one. I heard you as I came from Mass, beauty dears. Ah, you know me, sweethearts? Ah, God bless you for coming! You have come to bring us home; you have come to fetch us home—father and me." The paws of one of the dogs was on her shoulder, and his nose was in her hair.

Charley heard her words, for the window was open, and he listened and watched now with an infinite relief in his look. Her face was half turned towards him. It was pale-very pale and sad. It was Rosalie as of old—thank

God, as of old!—but more beautiful in the touching sadness, the far-off longing, of her look.

"I must go and see your master," she said to the dogs. "Down—down, Lazybones!"

There was no time to lose—he must not meet her ere. He went into the outer hall hastily. The servant was passing through. "If any one asks for Jo Portugais," he said, "say that I'll be back to-morrow morning—I'm going across the river to-day."

"Certainly, M'sieu'," said the girl, and smiled because of the piece of silver he put in her hand.

As he heard the side door open he stepped through the front doorway into the street, and disappeared round a corner.

CHAPTER XLVII
ONE WAS TAKEN AND THE OTHER LEFT

Rosalie carried to the hospital that afternoon a lighter heart than she had known for many a day. The sight of Jo Portugais' dogs had roused her out of the apathy which had been growing on her in this patient but hopeless watching beside her father. She had always a smile and a cheerful word for the poor man. A settled sorrow hung upon her face, however, taking away its colour, but giving it a sweet gravity which made her slave more than one young doctor of the hospital, for whom, however, she showed no more than a friendly frankness, free from self-consciousness. For hours she would sit in reverie beside her sleeping father, her heart "over the water to Charley." As in a trance, she could see him sitting at his bench, bent over his work, now and again lifting up his head to look across to the post-office, where another hand than hers sorted letters now.

Day by day her father weakened and faded away. All that was possible to medical skill had been done. As the money left by her mother dwindled, she had no anxiety, for she knew that the life she so tenderly cherished would not outlast the gold which lengthened out the tenuous chain of being. This last illness of her father's had been the salvation of her mind, the saving of her health. Maybe it had been the saving of her soul; for at times a curious contempt of life came upon her—she who had loved it so eagerly and fully. There descended on her then the bitter conviction that never again would she see the man she loved. Then not even Mrs. Flynn could call back "the fun o' the world" to her step and her tongue and her eye. At first there had been a timid shrinking, but soon her father and herself were brighter and better for the old Irishwoman's presence, and she began to take comfort in Mrs. Flynn.

Mrs. Flynn gave hopefulness to whatever life she touched, and Rosalie, buoyant and hopeful enough by nature, responded to the living warmth and the religion of life in the Irishwoman's heart.

"'Tis worth the doin', ivery bit of it, darlin', the bither an' the swate, the hard an' the aisy, the rough an' the smooth, the good an' the bad," said Mrs.

Flynn to her this very Easter morning. "Even the avil is worth doin', if so be 'twas not mint, an' the good is in yer heart in the ind, an' ye do be turnip' to the Almoighty, repentin' an' glad to be aloive: provin' to Him 'twas worth while makin' the world an' you, to want, an' worry, an' work, an' play, an' pick the flowers, an' bleed o' the thorns, an' dhrink the sun, an' ate the dust, an' be lovin' all the way! Ah, that's it, darlin'," persisted Mrs. Flynn, "'tis lovin' all the way makes it aisier. There's manny kinds o' love. There's lad an' lass, there's maid an' man. An' that last is spring, an' all the birds singin', an' shtorms now an' thin, an' siparations, an' misthrust, an' God in hivin bein' that aisy wid ye for bein' fools an' children, an' bringin' ye thegither in the ind, if so be ye do be lovin' as man an' maid should love, wid all yer heart. Thin there's the love o' man an' wife. Shure, that's the love that lasts, if it shtarts right. Shure, it doesn't always shtart wid the sun shinin.' 'Will ye marry me?' says Teddy Flynn to me. 'I will,' says I. 'Then I'll come back from Canaday to futch ye,' says he, wid a tear in his eye.

"'For what's a man in ould Ireland that has a head for annything but puttaties! There's land free in Canaday, an' I'm goin' to make a home for ye, Mary,' says he, wavin' a piece of paper in the air. 'Are ye, thin?' says I. He goes away that night, an' the next mornin' I have a lether from him, sayin' he's shtartin' that day for Canaday. He hadn't the heart to tell me to me face. Fwaht do I do thin? I begs, borrers, an' stales, an' I reached that ship wan minnit before she sailed. There was no praste aboord, but we was married six weeks afther at Quebec. And thegither we lived wid ups an' downs—but no ups an' downs to the love of us for twenty years, blessed be God for all His mercies!"

Rosalie had listened with eyes that hungrily watched every expression, ears that weighed eagerly every inflection; for she was hearing the story of another's love, and it did not seem strange to her that a woman, old, red-faced, and fat, should be telling it.

Yet there were times when she wept till she was exhausted; when all her girlhood was drowned in the overflow of her eyes; when there was a sense of irrevocable loss upon her. Then it was, in her fear of soul and pitiful loneliness, that her lover—the man she would have died for—seemed to have deserted her. Then it was that a sudden hatred against him rose up in her—to be swept away as swiftly as it came by the memory of his broken tale of love, his passionate words: "I have never loved any one but you in all my life, Rosalie." And also, there was that letter from Chaudiere, which said that in the hour when the greatest proof of his love must be given he would give it. Reading the letter again, hatred, doubt, even sorrow, passed from her, and her imagination pictured the hour when, disguise and secrecy ended, he would step forward before all the world and say: "I take Rosalie Evanturel to be my wife." Despite the gusts of emotion that swayed her at times, in the deepest part of her being she trusted him completely.

When she reached the hospital this Sunday afternoon her step was quick, her smile bright—though she had not been to confession as was her duty on Easter day. The impulse towards it had been great, but her secret was not her own, and the passionate desire to give relief to her full heart was overborne by thought of the man. Her soul was her own, but this secret of their love was his as well as hers. She knew that she was the only just judge between.

Soon after she entered the ward, the chief surgeon said that all that could be done for her father had now been done, and that as M. Evanturel constantly asked to be taken back to Chaudiere (he never said to die, though they knew what was in his mind), he might now make the journey, partly by river, partly by land. It seemed to the delighted and excited Rosalie that Jo Portugais had been sent to her as a surprise, and that his team of dogs was to take her father back.

She sat by her father's bed this beautiful, wonderful Sunday afternoon, and talked cheerfully, and laughed a little, and told M. Evanturel of the dogs, and together they looked out of the window to the far-off hills, in their golden purple, beyond which, in the valley of the Chaudiere, was their little home. With her father's hand in hers the girl dreamed dreams again, and it seemed to her that she was the very Rosalie Evanturel of old, whose thoughts were bounded by a river and a hill, a post-office and a church, a catechism and a few score of books. Here in the crowded city she had come to be a woman who, bitterly shaken in soul, knew life's sufferings; who had, during the past few months, read with avidity history, poetry, romance, fiction, and the drama, English and French; for in every one she found something that said: "You have felt that." In these long months she had learned more than she had known or learned in all her previous life.

As she sat looking out into the eastern sky she became conscious of voices, and of a group of people who came slowly down the ward, sometimes speaking to the sick and crippled. It was not a general visitors' day, but one reserved for the few to come and say a kindly word to the suffering, to bring some flowers and distribute books. Rosalie had always been absent at this hour before, for she shrank from strangers; but to-day she had stayed on unthinking. It mattered nothing to her who came and went. Her heart was over the hills, and the only tie she had here was with this poor cripple whose hand she held. If she did not resent the visit of these kindly strangers, she resolutely held herself apart from the object of their visit with a sense of distance and cold dignity. If she had given Charley something of herself, she had in turn taken something from him, something unlike her old self, delicately non-intime. Knowledge of life had rationalised her emotions to a definite degree, had given her the pride of self-repression. She had had need of it in these surroundings, where her beauty drew not a little dangerous attention, which she had held at arm's-length—her great love for one man made her invulnerable.

Now, as the visitors came near, she did not turn towards them, but still sat, her chin on her hand, looking out across the hills, in resolute abstraction. She felt her father's fingers press hers, as if to draw her attention, for he, weak man, was ever ready to open his hand and heart to any friendly soul. She took no notice, but held his hand firmly, as though to say that she had no wish to see.

She was conscious now that they were beside her father's bed. She hoped that they would pass. But no, the feet stopped, there was whispering, and then she heard a voice say, "Rather rude!" then another, "Not wanted, that's plain!"—the first a woman's, the second a man's. Then another voice, clear and cold, and well modulated, said to her father: "They tell me you have been here a long time, and have had much pain. You will be glad to go, I am sure."

Something in the voice startled her. Some familiar sound or inflection struck upon her ear with a far-off note, some lost tone she knew. Of what, of whom, did this voice remind her? She turned round quickly and caught two cold blue eyes looking at her. The face was older than her own, handsome and still, and happy in a placid sort of way. Few gusts of passion or of pain had passed across that face. The figure was shapely to the newest fashion, the bonnet was perfect, the hand which held two books was prettily gloved. Polite charity was written in her manner and consecrated every motion. On the instant, Rosalie resented this fine epitome of convention, this dutiful charity-monger, herself the centre of an admiring quartet. She saw the whispering, she noted the well-bred disguise of interest, and she met the visitor's gaze with cold courtesy. The other read the look in her face, and a slightly pacifying smile gathered at her lips.

"We are glad to hear that your father is better. He has been ill a long time?"

Rosalie started again, for the voice perplexed her—rather, not the voice, but the inflection, the deliberation.

She bowed, and set her lips, but, chancing to glance at her father, she saw that he was troubled by her manner. Flashing a look of love at him, she adjusted the pillow under his head, and said to her questioner in a low voice: "He is better now, thank you."

Encouraged, the other rejoined: "May I leave one or two books for him to read—or for you to read to him?" Then added hastily, for she saw a curious look in Rosalie's eyes: "We can have mutual friends in books, though we cannot be friends with each other. Books are the go-betweens of humanity."

Rosalie's heart leapt, she flushed, then grew slightly pale, for it was not tone or inflection alone that disturbed her now, but words themselves. A voice from over the hills seemed to say these things to her. A haunting voice from over the hills had said them to her—these very words.

"Friends need no go-betweens," she said quietly, "and enemies should not use them."

She heard a voice say, "By Jove!" in a tone of surprise, as though it were wonderful the girl from Chaudiere should have her wits about her. So Rosalie interpreted it.

"Have you many friends here?" asked the cold voice, meant to be kindly and pacific. It was schooled to composure, because it gave advantage in life's intercourse, not from any inner urbanity.

"Some need many friends, some but a few. I come from a country where one only needs a few."

"Where is your country, I wonder?" said the cold echo of another voice.

Charley had passed out of Kathleen's life—he was dead to her, his memory scorned and buried. She loved the man to whom she supposed she was married; she was only too glad to let the dust of death and time cover every trace of Charley from her gaze; she would have rooted out every particle of association: yet his influence on her had been so great that she had unconsciously absorbed some of his idiosyncrasies—in the tone of his voice, in his manner of speaking. To-day she had even repeated phrases he had used.

"Beyond the hills," said Rosalie, turning away.

"Is it not strange?" said the voice. "That is the title of one of the books I have just brought—'Beyond the Hills'. It is by an English writer. This other book is French. May I leave them?"

Rosalie inclined her head. It would make her own position less dignified if she refused them. "Books are always welcome to my father," she said.

There was an instant's pause, as though the fashionable lady would offer her hand; but their eyes met, and they only bowed. The lady moved on with a smile, leaving a perfume of heliotrope behind her.

"Where is your country, I wonder?"—the voice of the lady rang in Rosalie's ears. As she sat at the window again, long after the visitors had disappeared, the words, "I wonder—I wonder—I wonder!" kept beating in her brain. It was absurd that this woman should remind her of the tailor of Chaudiere.

Suddenly she was roused by her father's voice. "This is beautiful—ah, but beautiful, Rosalie!"

She turned towards him. He was reading the book in his hand—'Beyond the Hills'. "Listen," he said, and he read, in English: "'Compensation is the other name for God. How often is it that those whom disease or accident has robbed of active life find greater inner rejoicing and a larger spiritual itinerary! It would seem that withdrawal from the ruder activities gives a clearer seeing. Also for these, so often, is granted a greater love, which comes of the consecration of other lives to theirs. And these too have their reward, for they are less encompassed by the vanities of the world, having the joy of self-sacrifice.'" He looked at Rosalie with an unnatural brightness in his eyes, and she smiled at him now and stroked his hand.

"It has been all compensation to me," he said, after a moment. "You have been a good daughter to me, Rosalie."

She shook her head and smiled. "Good fathers think they have good daughters," she answered, choking back a sob.

He closed the book and let it lie upon the coverlet. "I will sleep now," he said, and turned on his side. She arranged his pillow, and adjusted the bedclothes to his comfort.

"Good-night," he said, as, with a faint hand, he drew her head down and kissed her. "Good girl! Goodnight!"

She patted his hand. "It is not night yet, father."

He was already half asleep. "Good-night!" he said again, and fell into a deep sleep.

She sat down by the window, in her hand the book he had laid down. A hundred thoughts were busy in her brain—of her father; of the woman who had just left; of her lover over the hills. The woman's voice came to her again—a far-off mockery. She opened the book mechanically and turned over the pages. Presently her eyes were riveted to a page. On it was written the word Kathleen.

For a moment she sat transfixed. The word Kathleen and the haunting voice became one, and her mind ran back to the day when she had said to Charley: "Who is Kathleen?"

She sprang to her feet. What should she do? Follow the woman? Find out who and what she was? Go to the young surgeon who had accompanied them, ask him who she was, and so learn the clue to the mystery concerning her lover?

In the midst of her confusion she became sharply conscious of two things: the approach of Mrs. Flynn, and her father's heavy breathing. Dropping the book, she leaned over her father's bed and looked closely at him. Then she turned to the frightened and anxious Mrs. Flynn.

"Go for the priest," she said. "He is dying."

"I'll send some one. I'm stayin' here by you, darlin'," said the old woman, and hurried to the room of the young surgeon for a messenger.

As the sun went down, the cripple went out upon a long journey alone.

CHAPTER XLVIII
"WHERE THE TREE OF LIFE IS BLOOMING—"

As Charley walked the bank of the great river by the city where his old life lay dead, he struggled with the new life which—long or short—must henceforth belong to the village of the woman he loved.... But as he fought with himself in the long night-watch it was borne in upon him that though he had been shown the Promised Land, he might never find there a habitation and a home. The hymn he had mockingly sung the night he had been done to death at the Cote Dorion sang in his senses now, an ever-present mockery:

> *"On the other side of Jordan,*
>
> *In the sweet fields of Eden,*
>
> *Where the tree of life is blooming,*
>
> *There is rest for you.*
>
> *There is rest for the weary,*
>
> *There is rest for the weary,*
>
> *There is rest for the weary,*
>
> *There is rest for you."*

In the uttermost corner of his intelligence he felt with sure prescience that, however befalling, the end of all was not far off. In the exercise of new faculties, which had more to do with the soul than with reason, he now believed what he could not see, and recognised what was not proved. Labour of the hand, trouble, sorrow, and perplexity, charity and humanity, had cleared and simplified his life, had sweetened his intelligence, and taken the place of ambition. He saw life now through the lens of personal duty, which required that the thing nearest to one's hand should be done first.

But as foreboding pressed upon him there came the thought of what should come after—to Rosalie. His thoughts took a practical form—her good was uppermost in his mind. All Rosalie had to live on was her salary as postmistress, for it was in every one's knowledge that the little else she had was being sacrificed to her father's illness. Suppose, then, that through illness or accident she lost her position, what could she do? He might leave her what he had—but what had he? Enough to keep her for a year or two—no more. All his earnings had gone to the poor and the suffering of Chaudiere.

There was one way. It had suggested itself to him so often in Chaudiere, and had been one of the two reasons for bringing him here. There were his dead mother's pearls and one thousand dollars in notes behind a secret panel in the white house on the hill, in this very city where he was. The pearls were worth over ten thousand dollars—in all, there would be eleven thousand, enough to secure Rosalie from poverty. What should Kathleen do with his mother's pearls, even if they were found by her? What should she do with his money did she not loathe his memory? Had not all his debts been paid? These pearls and this money were all his own.

But to get them. To go now to the white house on the hill; to face that old life even for an hour, a knocking at the door of a haunted house—he shrank from the thought. He would have to enter the place like a thief in the night.

Yet for Rosalie he must take the risk—he must go.

CHAPTER XLIX
THE OPEN GATE

It was a still night, and the moon, delicately bright, gave forth that radiance which makes spiritual to the eye the coarsest thing. Inside the white house on the hill all was dark. Sleep had settled on it long before midnight, for, on the morrow, its master and mistress hoped to make a journey to the valley of the Chaudiere, where the Passion Play was being performed by habitants and Indians. The desire to see the play had become an infatuation in the minds of the two, eager for some interest to relieve the monotony of a happy life.

But as all slept, a figure in the dress of a habitant moved through the passages of the house stealthily, yet with an assurance unusual in the thief or housebreaker. In the darkest passages his step was sure, and his hand fastened on latch or door-knob with perfect precision. He came at last into a large hallway flooded by the moon, pale, watchful, his beard frosted by the light. In the stillness of his tread and the composed sorrow of his face he seemed like one long dead who "revisits the glimpses of the moon."

At last he entered a room the door of which stood wide open. In this room had been begotten, or had had exercise, whatever of him was worth approving in the days before he died. It was a place of books and statues and tapestry, and the dark oak was nobly smutched of Time. This sombre oaken wall had been handed down through four generations from the man's great-grandfather: the breath of generations had steeped it in human association.

Entering, he turned for an instant with clinched hands to look at another door across the hall. Behind that door were two people who despised his memory, who conspired to forget his very name. This house was the woman's, for he had given it to her the day he died. But that she could live there with all the old associations, with memories that, however bitter, however shaming, had a sort of sacredness, struck into his soul with a harrowing pain. There she was whom he had spared—himself; whose happiness had lain in his hands, and he had given it to her. Yet her very existence robbed himself of happiness, and made sorrowful a life dearer than his own.

Kathleen lay asleep in that room—he fancied he could hear her breathing; and, by the hospital on the hill, up beyond the point of pines, in a little cottage which he could see from the great window, lay Rosalie with sleepless eyes and wan cheeks, longing for morning and the stir of life to help her to forget.

For Rosalie he had come to this house once more. For her sake he was revisiting this torture-chamber, from which he knew he must go again, blanched and shaken, as a man goes from a tomb where his dead lie unforgiving.

He shut his teeth, went swiftly across the room, and beside a great carved oak table touched a hidden spring in the side of it. The spring snapped; the panel creaked a little and drew back. It seemed to him that the noise he made must be heard in every part of the house, so sensitive was his ear, so deep was the silence on which the sounds had broken. He turned round to the doorway to listen before he put his hand within the secret place.

There was no sound. He turned his attention to the table. Drawing forth two packets with a gasp of relief, he put them in his pocket, and, with extreme care, proceeded to close the panel. By rubbing the edges of the wood with grease from a candle on the table, he was able to readjust the panel in silence. But, as the spring came home, he became suddenly conscious of a presence in the room. A shiver passed through him. He turned round-softly, quickly. He was in the shadow and near great window-curtains, and his fingers instinctively clutched them as he saw a figure in white at the door of the room. Slowly, strangely deliberate, the figure moved further into the room.

Charley's breath stopped. He felt his face flush, and a strange weakness came on him. There before him stood Kathleen.

She was in her night-gown, and she stood still, as though listening; yet, as Charley looked closer, he realised that it was an unconscious, passive listening, and that she did not know he was there.

Her mind only was listening. She was asleep. Was it possible that his very presence in the house had touched some old note of memory, which, automatically responding, had carried her from her bed in this somnambulistic trance? That subtle telegraphy between our subconscious selves which we cannot reduce to a law, yet alarming us at times, announced to Kathleen's mind, independent of the waking senses, the presence once familiar to this house for so many years. In her sleep she had involuntarily responded to the call of Charley's approach.

Once, in the past, the night her uncle died, she had walked in her sleep, and the memory of this flashed upon Charley now. Silently he came closer to her. The moonlight shone on her face. He could see plainly she was asleep. His position was painful and perilous. If she waked, the shock to herself would be great; if she waked and saw him, what disaster might not occur!

Yet he had no agitation now, only clearness of mind and a curious sense of confusion that he should see her en dishabille—the old fastidious sense mingling with the feeling that she was now a stranger to him, and that, waking, she would fly embarrassed from his presence, as he was ready to fly from hers. He was about to steal to the door and escape before she waked, but she turned round, moved through the doorway, and glided down the hall. He followed silently.

She moved to the staircase, then slowly down it, and through a passage to a morning-room, where, opening a pair of French windows, she passed out onto the lawn. He followed, not more than a dozen paces behind her. His safety lay in getting outside, where he could easily hide among the bushes, should someone else appear and an alarm be raised.

She crossed the lawn swiftly, a white, ghostlike figure. In the middle of the lawn she stopped short once as if in doubt what to do—as a thought-reader pauses in his search for the mental scent again, ere he rushes upon the object of his search with the certainty of instinct.

Presently she moved on, going directly towards a gate that opened out on the cliff above the river. In Charley's day this gate had been often used, for it gave upon four steep wooden steps leading to a narrow shelf of rock below. From the edge of this cliff a rope-ladder dropped fifty feet to the river. For years he had used this rope-ladder to get down to his boat, and often, when they were first married, Kathleen used to come and watch him descend, and sometimes, just at the very first, would descend also. As he stole into the grounds this evening he had noticed, however, that the rope-ladder was gone, and that new steps were being built. He had also mechanically observed that the gate was open.

For an instant he watched her slowly moving towards the gate. At first he did not realise the situation. Suddenly her danger flashed upon him. Passing through the gateway, she must fall over the cliff.

Her life was in his hands.

He could rush forward swiftly and close the gate, then, raising an alarm, get away before he was seen; or—he could escape now.

What had he to do with her? A weird, painful suggestion crept into his brain: he was not responsible for her, and he was responsible for a woman up there by the hospital, whose home was the valley of the Chaudiere!

If Kathleen were gone, what barrier would there be between him and Rosalie? What had he to do with this strange disposition of events? Kathleen was never absent from her church twice on Sundays; she was devoted to work of all sorts for the church on week-days—where was her intervening personal Providence? If Providence permitted her to die?—well, she had had two years of happiness with the man she loved, at some expense to himself—was it not fair that Rosalie should have her share? Had he the right to call upon Rosalie for constant self-sacrifice, when, by shutting his eyes now, by being dead to Kathleen and her need, as he was dead to the world he once knew, the way would be clear to marry Rosalie?

Dead—he was dead to the world and to Kathleen! Should his ghost interpose between her and the death now within two-score feet of her? Who could know? It was grim, it was awful, but was it not a wild kind of justice? Who could blame? It was the old Charley Steele, the Charley Steele of the court-room, who argued back humanity and the inherent rightness of things.

But it was only a moment's pause. The thoughts flashed by like the lightning impressions of a dream, and a voice said in his ear, the voice of the new Charley with a conscience:

"Save her—save her!"

Even as he was conscious of another presence on the lawn, he rushed forward noiselessly. Stealing between Kathleen and the gate-she was within five feet of it he closed and locked it. Then, with a quick glance at her sleeping face-it was engraven on his memory ever after like a dead face in a coffin—he ran along the fence among the shrubbery. A man not fifty feet away called to him.

"Hush—she is asleep!" Charley whispered, and disappeared.

It was Fairing himself who saw this deed which saved Kathleen's life. Awaking, and not finding her, he had glanced towards the window, and had seen her on the lawn. He had rushed down to her, in time to see her saved by a strange bearded man in habitant dress. His one glance at the man's face, as it turned towards him, produced an extraordinary effect upon his mind, not soon to be dispelled—a haunting, ghostlike apparition, which kept reminding him of something or somebody, he could not tell what or whom. The whispering voice and the breathless words, "Hush—she is asleep!" repeated themselves over and over again in his brain, as, taking Kathleen's hand, he led her, unresisting, and still sleeping, back to her room. In agitated thankfulness he resolved not to speak of the event to Kathleen, or to any one else, lest it should come to her ears and frighten her.

He would, however, keep a sharp lookout for the man who had saved her life, and would reward him duly. The face of the bearded habitant came between him and his sleep.

Meanwhile this disturber of a woman's dreams and a man's sleep was hurrying to an inn in the town by the waterside, where he met another habitant with a team of dogs—Jo Portugais. Jo had not been able to bear the misery of suspense and anxiety, and had come seeking him. There was little speech between them.

"You have not been found out, M'sieu'?" was Jo's anxious question.

"No, no, but I have had a bad night, Jo. Get the dogs together."

A little later, as Charley made ready to go back to Chaudiere, Jo said:

"You look as if you'd had a black dream, M'sieu'." With the river rustling by, and the trees stirring in the first breath of dawn, Charley told Jo what had happened.

For a moment the murderer did not speak or stir, for a struggle was going on in his breast also; then he stooped quickly, caught his companion's hand, and kissed it.

"I could not have done it, M'sieu'," he said hoarsely. They parted, Jo to remain behind as they had agreed, to be near Rosalie if needed; Charley to return to the valley of the Chaudiere.

CHAPTER L
THE PASSION PLAY AT CHAUDIERE

For the first time in its history Chaudiere was becoming notable in the eyes of the outside world.

"We'll have more girth after this," said Filion Lacasse the saddler to the wife of the Notary, as, in front of the post-office, they stood watching a little cavalcade of habitants going up the road towards Four Mountains to rehearse the Passion Play.

"If Dauphin's advice had been taken long ago, we'd have had a hotel at Four Mountains, and the city folk would be coming here for the summer," said Madame Dauphin, with a superior air.

"Pish!" said a voice behind them. It was the Seigneur's groom, with a straw in his mouth. He had a gloomy mind.

"There isn't a house but has two or three boarders. I've got three," said Filion Lacasse. "They come tomorrow."

"We'll have ten at the Manor. But no good will come of it," said the groom.

"No good! Look at the infidel tailor!" said Madame Dauphin. "He translated all the writing. He drew all the dresses, and made a hundred pictures—there they are at the Cure's house."

"He should have played Judas," said the groom malevolently. "That'd be right for him."

"Perhaps you don't like the Passion Play," said Madame Dauphin disdainfully.

"We ain't through with it yet," said the death's-head groom.

"It is a pious and holy mission," said Madame Dauphin. "Even that Jo Portugais worked night and day till he went away to Montreal, and he always goes to Mass now. He's to take Pontius Pilate when he comes back. Then look at Virginie Morrissette, that put her brother's eyes out quarrelling—she's to play Mary Magdalene."

"I could fit the parts better," said the groom.

"Of course. You'd have played St. John," said the saddler—"or, maybe, Christus himself!"

"I'd have Paulette Dubois play Mary the sinner."

"Magdalene repented, and knelt at the foot of the cross. She was sorry and sinned no more," said the Notary's wife in querulous reprimand.

"Well, Paulette does all that," said the stolid, dark-visaged groom.

Filion Lacasse's ears pricked up. "How do you know—she hasn't come back?"

"Hasn't she, though! And with her child too—last night."

"Her child!" Madame Dauphin was scandalised and amazed.

The groom nodded. "And doesn't care who knows it. Seven years old, and as fine a child as ever was!"

"Narcisse—Narcisse!" called Madame Dauphin to her husband, who was coming up the street. She hastily repeated the groom's news to him.

The Notary stuck his hand between the buttons of his waistcoat. "Well, well, my dear Madame," he said consequentially, "it is quite true."

"What do you know about it—whose child is it?" she asked, with curdling scorn.

"'Sh-'sh!" said the Notary. Then, with an oratorical wave of his free hand: "The Church opens her arms to all—even to her who sinned much because she loved much, who, through woful years, searched the world for her child and found it not—hidden away, as it was, by the duplicity of sinful man"—and so on through tangled sentences, setting forth in broken terms Paulette Dubois's life.

"How do you know all about it?" asked the saddler. "I've known it for years," said the Notary grandly—stoutly too, for he would freely risk his wife's anger that the vain-glory of the moment might be enlarged.

"And you keep it even from madame!" said the saddler, with a smile too broad to be sarcastic. "Tiens! if I did that, my wife'd pick my eyes out with a bradawl."

"It was a professional secret," said the Notary, with a desperate resolve to hold his position.

"I'm going home, Dauphin—are you coming?" questioned his wife, with an air.

"You will remain, and hear what I've got to say. This Paulette Dubois— she should play Mary Magdalene, for—"

"Look—look, what's that?" said the saddler. He pointed to a wagon coming slowly up the road. In front of it a team of dogs drew a cart. It carried some thing covered with black. "It's a funeral! There's the coffin. It's on Jo Portugais' little cart," added Filion Lacasse.

"Ah, God be merciful, it's Rosalie Evanturel and Mrs. Flynn! And M'sieu' Evanturel in the coffin!" said Madame Dauphin, running to the door of the postoffice to call the Cure's sister.

"There'll be use enough for the baker's Dead March now," remarked M. Dauphin sadly, buttoning up his coat, taking off his hat, and going forward to greet Rosalie. As he did so, Charley appeared in the doorway of his shop.

"Look, Monsieur," said the Notary. "This is the way Rosalie Evanturel comes home with her father."

"I will go for the Cure" Charley answered, turning white. He leaned against the doorway for a moment to steady himself, then hurried up the street. He did not dare meet Rosalie, or go near her yet. For her sake it was better not.

"That tailor infidel has a heart. His eyes were leaking," said the Notary to Filion Lacasse, and went on to meet the mournful cavalcade.

CHAPTER LI
FACE TO FACE

"If I could only understand!"—this was Rosalie's constant cry in these weeks wherein she lay ill and prostrate after her father's burial. Once and once only had she met Charley alone, though she knew that he was keeping watch over her. She had first seen him the day her father was buried, standing apart from the people, his face sorrowful, his eyes heavy, his figure bowed.

The occasion of their meeting alone was the first night of her return, when the Notary and Charley had kept watch beside her father's body.

She had gone into the little hallway, and had looked into the room of death. The Notary was sound asleep in his arm-chair, but Charley sat silent and moveless, his eyes gazing straight before him. She murmured his name, and though it was only to herself, not even a whisper, he got up quickly and came to the hall, where she stood grief-stricken, yet with a smile of welcome, of forgiveness, of confidence. As she put out her hand to him, and his swallowed it, she could not but say to him—so contrary is the heart of woman, so does she demand a Yes by asserting a No, and hunger for the eternal assurance—she could not but say:

"You do not love me—now."

It was but a whisper, so faint and breathless that only the heart of love could hear it. There was no answer in words, for some one was stirring beyond Rosalie in the dark, and a great figure heaved through the kitchen doorway, but his hand crushed hers in his own; his heart said to her, "My love is an undying light; it will not change for time or tears"—the words they had read together in a little snuff-coloured book on the counter in the shop one summer day a year ago. The words flashed into his mind, and they were carried to hers. Her fingers pressed his, and then Charley said, over her shoulder, to the approaching Mrs. Flynn: "Do not let her come again, Madame. She should get some sleep," and he put her hand in Mrs. Flynn's. "Be good to her, as you know how, Mrs. Flynn," he added gently.

He had won the heart of Mrs. Flynn that moment, and it may be she had a conviction or an inspiration, for she said, in a softer voice than she was wont to use to any one save Rosalie:

"I'll do by her as you'd do by your own, sir," and tenderly drew Rosalie to her own room.

Such had been their first meeting after her return. Afterwards she was taken ill, and the torture of his heart drove him out into the night, to walk the road and creep round her house like a sentinel, Mrs. Flynn's words ringing in his ears to reproach him—"I'll do by her as you would do by your own, sir." Night after night it was the same, and Rosalie heard his footsteps and listened and was less sorrowful, because she knew that she was ever in his thoughts. But one day Mrs. Flynn came to him in his shop.

"She's wantin' a word with ye on business," she said, and gestured towards the little house across the way. "'Tis few words ye do be shpakin' to annybody, but if y' have kind words to shpake and good things to say, y' naidn't be bitin' yer tongue," she added in response to his nod, and left him.

Charley looked after her with a troubled face. On the instant it seemed to him that Mrs. Flynn knew all. But his second thought told him that it was only an instinct on her part that there was something between them—the beginning of love, maybe.

In another half-hour he was beside Rosalie's chair. "Perhaps you are angry," she said, as he came towards her where she sat in the great armchair. She did not give him time to answer, but hurried on. "I wanted to tell you that I have heard you every night outside, and that I have been glad, and sorry too—so sorry for us both."

"Rosalie! Rosalie" he said hoarsely, and dropped on a knee beside her chair, and took her hand and kissed it. He did not dare do more.

"I wanted to say to you," she said, dropping a hand on his shoulder, "that I do not blame you for anything—not for anything. Yet I want you to be sorry too. I want you to feel as sorry for me as I feel sorry for you."

"I am the worst man and you the best woman in the world."

She leaned over him with tears in her eyes. "Hush!" she said. "I want to help you—Charles. You are wise. You know ten thousand things more than I; but I know one thing you do not understand."

"You know and do whatever is good," he said brokenly.

"Oh, no, no, no! But I know one thing, because I have been taught, and because it was born with me. Perhaps much was habit with me in the past, but now I know that one thing is true. It is God."

She paused. "I have learned so much since—since then."

He looked up with a groan, and put a finger on her lips. "You are feeling bitterly sorry for me," she said. "But you must let me speak—that is all I ask. It is all love asks. I cannot bear that you should not share my thoughts. That is the thing that has hurt—hurt so all these months, these long hard months, when I could not see you, and did not know why I could not. Don't shake so, please! Hear me to the end, and we shall both be the better after. I felt it all so cruelly, because I did not—and I do not—understand. I rebelled, but not against you. I rebelled against myself, against what you called Fate. Fate is one's self, what one brings on one's self. But I had faith in you—always—always, even when I thought I hated you."

"Ah, hate me! Hate me! It is your loving that cuts me to the quick," he said. "You have the magnanimity of God."

Her eyes leapt up. "'Of God'—you believe in God!" she said eagerly. "God is God to you? He is the one thing that has come out of all this to me." She reached out her hand and took her Bible from a table. "Read that to yourself," she said, and, opening the Book, pointed to a passage. He read it:

> And they heard the voice of the Lord God walking in the garden in
> the cool of the day: and Adam and his wife hid themselves from the
> presence of the Lord God amongst the trees of the garden.
> And the Lord God called unto Adam, and said unto him, Where art
> thou?
> And he said, I heard Thy voice in the garden, and I was afraid,
> because I was naked; and I hid myself.
> And He said, Who told thee that thou wart naked? Hast thou eaten of
> the tree whereof I commanded thee that thou shouldest not eat?
> Closing the Book, Charley said: "I understand—I see."

"Will you say a prayer with me?" she urged. "It is all I ask. It is the only—the only thing I want to hurt you, because it may make you happier in the end. What keeps us apart, I do not know. But if you will say one prayer with me, I will keep on trusting, I will never complain, and I will wait—wait."

He kissed both her hands, but the look in his eyes was that of a man being broken on the wheel. She slipped to the floor, her rosary in her fingers. "Let us pray," she said simply, and in a voice as clear as a child's, but with the anguish of a woman's struggling heart behind.

He did not move. She looked at him, caught his hands in both of hers, and cried: "But you will not deny me this! Haven't I the right to ask it? Haven't I a right to ask of you a thousand times as much?"

"You have the right to ask all that is mine to give life, honour, my body in pieces inch by inch, the last that I can call my own. But, Rosalie, this is not mine to give! How can I pray, unless I believe!"

"You do—oh, you do believe in God," she cried passionately.

"Rosalie—my life," he urged, hoarse misery in his voice, "the only thing I have to give you is the bare soul of a truthful man—I am that now at least. You have made me so. If I deceived the whole world, if I was as the thief upon the cross, I should still be truthful to you. You open your heart to me— let me open mine to you, to see it as it is. Once my soul was like a watch, cased and carried in the pocket of life, uncertain, untrue, because it was a soul made, not born. I must look at the hands to know the time, and because it varied, because the working did not answer to the absolute, I said: 'The soul is a lie.' You—you have changed all that, Rosalie. My soul now is like a dial to the sun. But the clouds are there above, and I do not know what time it is in life. When the clouds break—if they ever break—and the sun shines, the dial will speak the truth, the whole truth, and nothing but the truth—"

He paused, confused, for he had repeated the words of a witness taking the oath in court.

"'So help me God!'" she finished the oath for him. Then, with a sudden change of manner, she came to her feet with a spring. She did not quite understand. She was, however, dimly conscious of the power she had over his chivalrous mind: the power of the weak over the strong—the tyranny of the defended over the defender. She was a woman tortured beyond bearing; and she was fighting for her very life, mad with anguish as she struggled.

"I do not understand you," she cried, with flashing eyes. "One minute you say you do not believe in anything, and the next you say, 'So help me God!'"

"Ah, no, you said that, Rosalie," he interposed gently.

"You said I was as magnanimous as God. You were laughing at me then, mocking me, whose only fault is that I loved and trusted you. In the wickedness of your heart you robbed me of happiness, you—"

"Don't—don't! Rosalie! Rosalie!" he exclaimed in shrinking protest.

That she had spoken to him as her deepest heart abhorred only increased her agitated denunciation. "Yes, yes, in your mad selfishness, you did not care for the poor girl who forgot all, lost all, and now—" She stopped short at the sight of his white, awe stricken face. His eye-glass seemed like a frost of death over an eye that looked upon some shocking scene of woe. Yet he appeared not to see, for his fingers fumbled on his waistcoat for the monocle—fumbled—vaguely, helplessly. It was the realisation of a soul cast into the outer darkness. Her abrupt silence came upon him like the last engulfing wave to a drowning man—the final assurance of the end, in which there is quiet and the deadly smother.

"Now—I know-the truth!" he said, in a curious even tone, different from any she had ever heard from him. It was the old Charley Steele who spoke, the Charley Steele in whom the intellect was supreme once more. The judicial spirit, the inveterate intelligence which put justice before all, was alive in him, almost rejoicing in its regained governance. The new Charley was as dead as the old had been of late, and this clarifying moment left the grim impression behind that the old law was not obsolete. He felt that in the abandonment of her indignation she had mercilessly told the truth; and the irreducible quality of mind in him which in the old days made for justice, approved. There was a new element now, however—that conscience which never possessed him fully until the day he saw Rosalie go travelling over the hills with her crippled father. That picture of the girl against the twilight, her figure silhouetted in the clear air, had come to him in sleeping and waking dreams, the type and sign of an everlasting melancholy. As he looked at her blindly now, he saw, not herself, but that melancholy figure. Out of the distance his own voice said again:

"Now—I know-the truth!"

She had struck with a violence she did not intend, which, she knew, must rend her own heart in the future, which put in the dice-box the last hopes she had. But she could not have helped it—she could not have stayed the words, though a suspended sword were to fall with the saying. It was the cry of tradition and religion, and every home-bred, convent-nurtured habit, the instinct of heredity, the wail of woman, for whom destiny, or man, or nature, has arranged the disproportionate share of life's penalties. It was the impotent rebellion against the first curse, that man in his punishment should earn his bread by the sweat of his brow—which he might do with joy—while the woman must work out her ordained sentence "in sorrow all the days of her life."

In her bitter words was the inherent revolt of the race of woman. But now she suddenly felt that she had flung him an infinite distance from her; that she had struck at the thing she most cherished—his belief that she loved him; that even if she had told the truth—and she felt she had not—it was not the truth she wished him most to feel.

For an instant she stood looking at him, shocked and confounded, then her changeless love rushed back on her, the maternal and protective spirit welled up, and with a passionate cry she threw herself in the chair again in very weakness, with outstretched hands, saying:

"Forgive me—oh, forgive me! I did not mean it—oh, forgive your Rosalie!"

Stooping over her, he answered:

"It is good for me to know the whole truth. What hurts you may give me will pass—for life must end, and my life cannot be long enough to pay the price of the hurts I have given you. I could bear a thousand—one for every hour—if they could bring back the light to your eye, the joy to your heart. Could prayer, do you think, make me sorrier than I am? I have hurt what I would have spared from hurt at the cost of my life—and all the lives in all the world!" he added fiercely.

"Forgive me—oh, forgive your Rosalie!" she pleaded. "I did not know what I was saying—I was mad."

"It was all so sane and true," he said, like one who, on the brink of death, finds a satisfaction in speaking the perfect truth. "I am glad to hear the truth—I have been such a liar."

She looked up startled, her tears blinding her. "You have not deceived me?" she asked bitterly. "Oh, you have not deceived me—you have loved me, have you not?" It was that which mattered, that only. Moveless and eager, she looked—looked at him, waiting, as it were, for sentence.

"I never lied to you, Rosalie—never!" he answered, and he touched her hand.

She gave a moan of relief at his words. "Oh, then, oh, then... " she said, in a low voice, and the tears in her eyes dried away.

"I meant that until I knew you, I kept deceiving myself and others all my life—"

"But without knowing it?" she said eagerly.

"Perhaps, without quite knowing it."

"Until you knew me?" she asked, in quick, quivering tones.

"Till I knew you," he answered.

"Then I have done you good—not ill?" she asked, with painful breathlessness.

"The only good there may be in me is you, and you only," he said, and he choked something rising in his throat, seeing the greatness of her heart, her dear desire to have entered into his life to his own good. He would have said that there was no good in him at all, but that he wished to comfort her.

A little cry of joy broke from her lips. "Oh, that—that!" she cried, with happy tears. "Won't you kiss me now?" she added softly.

He clasped her in his arms, and though his eyes were dry, his heart wept tears of blood.

CHAPTER LII
THE COMING OF BILLY

Chaudiere had made—and lost—a reputation. The Passion Play in the valley had become known to a whole country—to the Cure's and the Seigneur's unavailing regret. They had meant to revive the great story for their own people and the Indians—a homely, beautiful object-lesson, in an Eden—like innocence and quiet and repose; but behold the world had invaded them! The vanity of the Notary had undone them. He had written to the great papers of the province, telling of the advent of the play, and pilgrimages had been organised, and excursions had been made to the spot, where a simple people had achieved a crude but noble picture of the life and death of the Hero of Christendom. The Cure viewed with consternation the invasion of their quiet. It was no longer his own Chaudiere; and when, on a Sunday, his dear people were jostled from the church to make room for strangers, his gentle eloquence seemed to forsake him, he spoke haltingly, and his intoning of the Mass lacked the old soothing simplicity.

"Ah, my dear Seigneur!" he said, on the Sunday before the playing was to end, "we have overshot the mark."

The Seigneur nodded and turned his head away. "There is an English play which says, 'I have shot mine arrow o'er the house and hurt my brother.' That's it—that's it! We began with religion, and we end with greed, and pride, and notoriety."

"What do we want of fame! The price is too high, Maurice. Fame is not good for the hearts and minds of simple folk."

"It will soon be over."

"I dread a sordid reaction."

The Seigneur stood thinking for a moment. "I have an idea," he said at last. "Let us have these last days to ourselves. The mission ends next Saturday at five o'clock. We will announce that all strangers must leave the valley by Wednesday night. Then, during those last three days, while yet the influence of the play is on them, you can lead your own people back to the old quiet feelings."

"My dear Maurice—it is worthy of you! It is the way. We will announce it to-day. And see now.... For those three days we will change the principals; lest those who have taken the parts so long have lost the pious awe which should be upon them. We will put new people in their places. I will announce it at vespers presently. I have in my mind who should play the Christ, and St. John, and St. Peter—the men are not hard to find; but for Mary the Mother and Mary Magdalene—"

The eyes of the two men suddenly met, a look of understanding passed between them.

"Will she do it?" said the Seigneur.

The Cure nodded. "Paulette Dubois has heard the word, 'Go and sin no more'; she will obey."

Walking through the village as they talked, the Cure shrank back painfully several times, for voices of strangers, singing festive songs, rolled out upon the road. "Who can they be?" he said distressfully.

Without a word the Seigneur went to the door of the inn whence the sounds proceeded, and, without knocking, entered. A moment afterwards the voices stopped, but broke out again, quieted, then once more broke out, and presently the Seigneur issued from the door, white with anger, three strangers behind him. All were intoxicated.

One was violent. It was Billy Wantage, whom the years had not improved. He had arrived that day with two companions—an excursion of curiosity as an excuse for a "spree."

"What's the matter with you, old stick-in-the-mud?" he shouted. "Mass is over, isn't it? Can't we have a little guzzle between prayers?"

By this time a crowd had gathered, among them Filion Lacasse. At a motion from the Seigneur, and a whisper that went round quickly, a dozen habitants swiftly sprang on the three men, pinioned their arms, and carrying them bodily to the pump by the tavern, held them under it, one by one, till each was soaked and sober. Then their horses and wagon were brought, and they were given five minutes to leave the village.

With a devilish look in his eye, and drenched and furious, Billy was disposed to resist the command, but the faces around him were determined, and, muttering curses, the three drove away towards the next parish.

CHAPTER LIII
THE SEIGNEUR AND THE CURE
HAVE A SUSPICION

Presently the Seigneur and the Cure stood before the door of the tailor-shop. The Cure was about to knock, when the Seigneur laid a hand upon his arm.

"There is no use; he has been gone several days," he said.

"Gone—gone!" said the Cure.

"I came to see him yesterday, and not finding him, I asked at the post-office." M. Rossignol's voice lowered. "He told Mrs. Flynn he was going into the hills, so Rosalie says."

The Cure's face fell. "He went away also just before the play began. I almost fear that—that we get no nearer. His mind prompts him to do good and not evil, and yet—and yet.... I have dreamed a good dream, Maurice, but I sometimes fear I have dreamed in vain."

"Wait-wait!"

M. Loisel looked towards the post-office musingly. "I have thought sometimes that what man's prayers may not accomplish a woman's love might do. If—but, alas, what do we know of his past! Nothing. What do we know of his future? Nothing. What do we know of the human heart? Nothing—nothing!"

The Seigneur was astounded. The Cure's meaning was plain. "What do you mean?" he asked, almost gruffly.

"She—Rosalie—has changed—changed." In his heart he dwelt sorrowfully upon the fact that she had not been to confession to him for many, many months.

"Since her father's death—since her illness?"

"Since she went to Montreal seven months ago. Even while she was so ill these past weeks, she never asked for me; and when I came... Ah, if it is that her heart has gone out to the man, and his does not respond!"

"A good thing, too!" said the other gloomily. "We don't know where he came from, and we do know that he is a pagan."

"Yet there she sits now, hour after hour, day after day—so changed."

"She has lost her father," urged M. Rossignol anxiously.

"I know the grief of children—this is not such a grief. There is something more. But I cannot ask. If she were a sinner—but she is without fault. Have we not watched her grow up here, mirthful, brave, pure-souled—"

"Fitted for any station," interposed the Seigneur huskily. Presently he laid a hand upon the Cure's arm. "Shall I ask her again?" he said, breathing hard. "Do you think she has found out her mistake?"

The Cure was so taken aback that at first he could not speak. When he realised, however, he could scarce suppress a smile at the other's simple vanity. But he mastered himself, and said: "It is not that, Maurice. It is not you."

"How did you know I had asked her?" asked his friend querulously.

"You have just told me."

M. Rossignol felt a kind of reproval in the Cure's tone. It made him a little nervous. "I'm an old fool, but she needed some one," he protested. "At least I am a gentleman, and she would not be thrown away."

"Dear Maurice!" said the Cure, and linked his arm in the other's. "In all respects save one, it would have been to her advantage. But youth is the only comrade for youth. All else is evasion of life's laws."

The Seigneur pressed his arm. "I thought you less worldly-wise than myself; I find you more," he said.

"Not worldly-wise. Life is deeper than the world or worldly wisdom. Come, we will both go and see Rosalie."

M. Rossignol suddenly stopped at the post-office door, and half turned towards the tailor-shop. "He is young. Suppose that he drew her love his way, but gave her nothing in return, and—"

"If it were so"—the Cure paused, and his face darkened—"if it were so, he should leave her forever; and so my dream would end."

"And Rosalie?"

"Rosalie would forget. To remember, youth must see and touch and be near, else it wears itself out in excess of feeling. Youth feels more deeply than age, but it must bear daily witness."

"Upon my honour, Cure, you shall write your little philosophies for the world," said M. Rossignol, and then knocked at the door.

"I will go in alone, Maurice," the Cure urged. "Good-you are right," answered the other. "I will go write the proclamation denying strangers the valley after Wednesday. I will enforce it, too," he added, with vigour, and, turning, walked up the street, as Mrs. Flynn admitted the Cure to the post-office.

A half-hour later M. Loisel again appeared at the post-office door, a pale, beautiful face at his shoulder.

He had not been brave enough to say what was on his mind. But as he bade her good-bye, he plucked up needful courage.

"Forgive me, Rosalie," he said, "but I have sometimes thought that you have more griefs than one. I have thought"—he paused, then went on bravely—"that there might be—there might be unwelcomed love, or love deceived."

A mist came before her eyes, but she quietly and firmly answered: "I have never been deceived in love, Monsieur Loisel."

"There, there!" he hurriedly and gently rejoined. "Do not be hurt, my child. I only want to help you." A moment afterwards he was gone.

As the door closed behind him, she drew herself proudly up.

"I have never been deceived," she said aloud. "I love him—love him—love him."

CHAPTER LIV
M. ROSSIGNOL SLIPS THE LEASH

It was the last day of the Passion Play, and the great dramatic mission was drawing to a close. The confidence of the Cure and the Seigneur was restored. The prohibition against strangers had had its effect, and for three whole days the valley had been at rest again. Apparently there was not a stranger within its borders, save the Seigneur's brother, the Abbe Rossignol, who had come to see the moving spectacle.

The Abbe, on his arrival, had made inquiries concerning the tailor of Chaudiere and Jo Portugais, as persistently about the one as the other. Their secrets had been kept inviolate by him.

It was disconcerting to hear the tales people told of the tailor's charity and wisdom. It was all dangerous, for what was, accidentally, no evil in this particular instance, might be the greatest disaster in another case. Principle was at stake. He heard in stern silence the Cure's happy statement that Jo Portugais had returned to the bosom of the Church, and attended Mass regularly.

"So it may be, my dear Abbe," said M. Loisel, "that the friendship between him and our 'infidel' has been the means of helping Portugais. I hope their friendship will go on unbroken for years and years."

"I have no idea that it will," said the Abbe grimly. "That rope of friendship may snap untimely."

"Upon my soul, you croak like a raven!" testily broke in M. Rossignol, who was present. "I didn't know there was so much in common between you and my surly-jowled groom. He gets his pleasure out of croaking. 'Wait, wait, you'll see—you'll see! Death, death, death—every man must die! The devil has you by the hair—death—death—death!' Bah! I'm heartily sick of croakers. I suppose, like my grunting groom, you'll say about the Passion Play, 'No good will come of it—wait—wait—wait!' Bah!"

"It may not be an unmixed good," answered the ascetic.

"Well, and is there any such thing on earth as an unmixed good? The play yesterday was worth a thousand sermons. It was meant to serve Holy Church, and it will serve it. Was there ever anything more real—and touching—than Paulette Dubois as Mary Magdalene yesterday?"

"I do not approve of such reality. For that woman to play the part is to destroy the impersonality of the scene."

"You would demand that the Christus should be a good man, and the St. John blameless—why shouldn't the Magdalene be a repentant woman?"

"It might impress the people more, if the best woman in your parish were to play the part. The fall of virtue, the ruin of innocence, would be vividly brought home. It does good to make the innocent feel the terror and shame of sin. That is the price the good pay for the fall of man—sorrow and shame for those who sin." The Seigneur, rising quickly from the table, and kicking his chair back, said angrily: "Damn your theories!" Then, seeing the frozen look on his brother's face, continued, more excitedly: "Yes, damn, damn, damn your theories! You always took the crass view. I beg your pardon, Cure—I beg your pardon."

He then went to the window, threw it open, and called to his groom.

"Hi, there, coffin-face," he said, "bring round the horses—the quietest one in the stable for my brother—you hear? He can't ride," he added maliciously.

This was his fiercest stroke, for the Abbe's secret vanity was the belief that he looked well on a horse, and rode handsomely.

CHAPTER LV
ROSALIE PLAYS A PART

From a tree upon a little hill rang out a bell—a deep-toned bell, bought by the parish years before for the missions held at this very spot. Every day it rang for an instant at the beginning of each of the five acts. It also tolled slowly when the curtain rose upon the scene of the Crucifixion. In this act no one spoke save the abased Magdalene, who knelt at the foot of the cross, and on whose hair red drops fell when the Roman soldier pierced the side of the figure on the cross. This had been the Cure's idea. The Magdalene should speak for mankind, for the continuing world. She should speak for the broken and contrite heart in all ages, should be the first-fruits of the sacrifice, a flower of the desert earth, bedewed by the blood of the Prince of Peace.

So, in the long nights of the late winter and early spring, the Cure had thought and thought upon what the woman should say from the foot of the cross. At last he put into her mouth that which told the whole story of redemption and deliverance, so far as his heart could conceive it—the prayer for all sorts and conditions of men and the general thanksgiving of humanity.

During the last three days Paulette Dubois had taken the part of Mary Magdalene. As Jo Portugais had confessed to the Abbe that notable day in the woods at Vadrome Mountain, so she had confessed to the Cure after so many years of agony—and the one confession fitted into the other: Jo had once loved her, she had treated him vilely, then a man had wronged her, and Jo had avenged her—this was the tale in brief. She it was who laughed in the gallery of the court-room the day that Joseph Nadeau was acquitted.

It had pained and shocked the Cure more than any he had ever heard, but he urged for her no penalty as Portugais had set for himself with the austere approval of the Abbe. Paulette's presence as the Magdalene had had a deep effect upon the people, so that she shared with Mary the Mother the painfully real interest of the vast audience.

Five times had the bell rung out in the perfect spring air, upon which the balm of the forest and the refreshment of the ardent sun were poured. The quick anger of M. Rossignol had passed away long before the Cure, the Abbe, and himself had reached the lake and the great plateau. Between the acts the two brothers walked up and down together, at peace once more, and there was a suspicious moisture in the Seigneur's eyes. The demeanour of the people had been so humble and rapt that the place and the plateau and the valley seemed alone in creation with the lofty drama of the ages.

The Cure's eyes shone when he saw on a little knoll in the trees, apart from the worshippers and spectators, Charley and Jo Portugais. His cup of content was now full. He had felt convinced that if the tailor had but been within these bounds during the past three days, a work were begun which should end only at the altar of their parish church. To-day the play became to him the engine of God for the saving of a man's soul. Not long before the last great tableau was to appear he went to his own little tent near the hut where the actors prepared to go upon the stage. As he entered, some one came quickly forward from the shadow of the trees and touched him on the arm.

"Rosalie!" he cried in amazement, for she wore the costume of Mary Magdalene.

"It is I, not Paulette, who will appear," she said, a deep light in her eyes.

"You, Rosalie?" he asked dumfounded. "You are distrait. Trouble and sorrow have put this in your mind. You must not do it."

"Yes, I am going there," she said, pointing towards the great stage. "Paulette has given me these to wear"—she touched the robe—"and I only ask your blessing now. Oh, believe, believe me, I can speak for those who are innocent and those who are guilty; for those who pray and those who cannot pray; for those who confess and those who dare not! I can speak the words out of my heart with gladness and agony, Monsieur," she urged, in a voice vibrating with feeling.

A luminous look came into the Cure's face. A thought leapt up in his heart. Who could tell!—this pure girl, speaking for the whole sinful, unbelieving, and believing world, might be the one last conquering argument to the man.

He could not read the agony of spirit which had driven Rosalie to this— to confess through the words of Mary Magdalene her own woe, to say it out to all the world, and to receive, as did Paulette Dubois, every day after the curtain came down, absolution and blessing. She longed for the old remembered peace.

The Cure could not read the struggle between her love for a man and the ineradicable habit of her soul; but he raised his hand, made the sacred gesture over leer, and said: "Go, my child, and God be with you."

He could not see her for tears as she hurried away to where Paulette Dubois awaited her—the two at peace now. At the hands of the lately despised and injurious woman Rosalie was made ready to play the part in the last act, none knowing save the few who appeared in the final tableau, and they at the last moment only.

The bell began to toll.

A thousand people fell upon their knees, and with fascinated yet abashed and awe-struck eyes saw the great tableau of Christendom: the three crosses against the evening sky, the Figure in the centre, the Roman populace, the trembling Jews, the pathetic groups of disciples. A cloud passed across the sky, the illusion grew, and hearts quivered in piteous sympathy. There was no music now—not a sound save the sob of some overwrought woman. The woe of an oppressed world absorbed them. Even the stolid Indians, as Roman soldiers, shrank awe-stricken from the sacred tragedy. Now the eyes of all were upon the central Figure, then they shifted for a moment to John the Beloved, standing with the Mother.

"Pauvre Mere! Pauvre Christ!" said a weeping woman aloud.

A Roman soldier raised a spear and pierced the side of the Hero of the World. Blood flowed, and hundreds gasped. Then there was silence—a strange hush as of a prelude to some great event.

"It is finished. Father, into Thy hands I commend my spirit," said the Figure.

The hush was broken by such a sound as one hears in a forest when a wind quivers over the earth, flutters the leaves, and then sinks away— neither having come nor gone, but only lived and died.

Again there was silence, and then all eyes were fixed upon the figure at the foot of the cross-Mary the Magdalene.

Day after day they had seen this figure rise, come forward a step, and speak the epilogue to this moving miracle-drama. For the last three days Paulette Dubois had turned a sorrowful face upon them, and with one hand upraised had spoken the prayer, the prophecy, the thanksgiving, the appeal of humanity and the ages. They looked to see the same figure now, and waited. But as the Magdalene turned, there was a great stir in the multitude, for the face bent upon them was that of Rosalie Evanturel. Awe and wonder moved the people.

Apart from the crowd, under a clump of trees, knelt a woodsman from Vadrome Mountain, and the tailor of Chaudiere stood beside him.

When Charley, touched by the heavy scene, saw the figure of the Magdalene rise, he felt a curious thrill of fascination. When she turned, and he saw the face of Rosalie, the blood rushed to his face; then his heart seemed to stand still. Pain and shame travelled to the farthest recesses of his nature. Jo Portugais rose to his feet with a startled exclamation.

Rosalie began to speak. "This is the day of which the hours shall never cease—in it there shall be no night. He whom ye have crucified hath saved you from the wrath to come. He hath saved others, Himself He would not save. Even for such as I, who have secretly opened, who have secretly entered, the doors of sin—"

With a gasp of horror and a mad desire to take her away from the sight of this gaping, fascinated crowd, Charley made to rush forward, but Jo Portugais held him back.

"Be still. You will ruin her, M'sieu'!" said Jo.

"—even for such as I am," the beautiful voice went on, "hath He died. And in the ages to come, women such as I, and all women who sorrow, and all men who err and are deceived, and all the helpless world, will know that this was the Friend of the human soul." Not a gesture, not a movement, only that slight, pathetic figure, with pale, agonised face, and eyes that looked—looked—looked beyond them, over their heads to the darkening east, the clouded light of evening behind her. Her voice rang out now valiant and clear, now searching and piteous, yet reaching to where the farthermost person knelt, and was lost upon the lake and in the spreading trees.

"What ye have done may never be undone; what He hath said shall never be unsaid. His is the Word which shall unite all languages, when ye that are Romans shall be no more Romans, and ye that are Jews shall still be Jews, reproached and alone. No longer shall men faint in the glare—the shadow of the Cross shall screen them. No more shall woman bear her black sorrows, alone; the Light of the World shall cheer her."

As she spoke, the cloud drew back from the sunset, and the saffron glow behind lighted the cross, and shone upon her hair, casting her face in a gracious shadow. Her voice rose higher. "I, the Magdalene, am the first-fruits of this sacrifice: from the foot of the cross I come. I have sinned more than all. I have shamed all women. But I have confessed my sin, and He is faithful and just to forgive us our sins and to cleanse us from all unrighteousness."

Her voice now became lower, but clear and even, pathetically exulting:

"O world, forgive, as He hath forgiven you! Fall, dark curtain, and hide this pain, and rise again upon forgiven sin and a redeemed people!"

She stood still, with her eyes upraised, and the curtain came slowly down.

For a long time no one in all the gathered multitude stirred. Far over under the trees a man sat upon the ground, his head upon his arms, and his arms upon his knees, in a misery unmeasurable. Beside him stood a woodsman, who knew of no word to say that might comfort him.

A girl, in the garb of the Magdalene, entered the tent of the Cure, and, speaking no word, knelt and received absolution of her sins.

CHAPTER LVI
MRS. FLYNN SPEAKS

CHARLEY left Jo Portugais behind, and went home alone. He watched at a window till he saw Rosalie return. As she passed quickly down the street with Mrs. Flynn to her own door, he observed that her face was happier than he had seen it for many a day. Her step was lighter, there was a freedom in her air, a sense of confidence in her carriage.

She bore herself as one who had done a thing which relaxed a painful tension. There was a curious glow in her eyes and face, and this became deeper as, showing himself at the door, she saw him, smiled, and stood still. He came across the street and took her hand.

"You have been away," she said softly. "For a few days," he answered.

"Far?"

"At Vadrome Mountain."

"You have missed these last days of the Passion Play," she said, a shadow in her eyes.

"I was present to-day," he answered.

She turned away her head quickly, for the look in his eyes told her more than any words could have done, and Mrs. Flynn said:

"'Tis a day for everlastin' mimory, sir. For the part she played this day, the darlin', only such as she could play! 'Tis the innocent takin' the shame o' the guilty, and the tears do be comin' to me eyes. 'Tis not ould Widdy Flynn's eyes alone that's wet this day, but hearts do be weepin' for the love o' God."

Rosalie suddenly opened the door, and, without another look at Charley, entered the house.

"'Tis one in a million!" said Mrs. Flynn, in a confidential tone, for she had a fixed idea that Rosalie loved Charley and that he loved her, and that the only thing that stood in the way of their marriage was religion. From the first Charley had conquered Mrs. Flynn. That he was a tailor was a pity and a shame, but love was love, and the man had a head on him and a heart in him; and love was love! So Mrs. Flynn said:

"'Tis one that a man that's a man should do annything for, was it havin' the heart cut out uv him, or givin' the last drop uv his blood. Shure, for such as her, murder, or false witness, or givin' up the last wish or thought a man hugged to his boosom, would be as aisy as aisy."

Charley laughed to himself, her purpose was so obvious, but his heart went out to her, for she was a friend, and, whatever came to him, Rosalie would not be alone.

"I believe every word of yours," he said, shaking her hand, "and we'll see, you and I, that no man marries her who isn't ready to do what you say."

"Would you do it yourself—if it was you?" she asked, flushing for her boldness.

"I would," he answered.

"Then do it," she said, and fled inside the house and shut the door.

"Mrs. Flynn—good Mrs. Flynn!" he said, and went back sadly to his house, and shut himself up with his thoughts. When night drew on he went to bed, but he could not sleep. He got up after a time, and taking pen and paper, wrote for a long time. Having finished, he took what he had written, and placing it with the two packets-of money and pearls—which he had brought from his old home, he addressed it to the Cure, and going to the safe in the wall of the shop, placed them inside and locked the door.

Then he went to bed, and slept soundly—the deep sleep of the just.

CHAPTER LVII
A BURNING FIERY FURNACE

Every man within the limits of the parish was in his bed, save one. He was a stranger who, once before, had visited Chaudiere for one brief day, when he had been saved from death at the Red Ravine, and had fled the village that night because, as he thought, he had heard the voice of his old friend's ghost in the trees. Since that time he had travelled in many parishes, healing where he could, entertaining where he might, earning money as the charlatan. He was now on his way back through the parishes to Montreal, and his route lay through Chaudiere. He had hoped to reach Chaudiere before nightfall—he remembered with fear the incident from which he had fled many months before; but his horse had broken its leg on a corduroy bridge, a few miles out from the parish in the hills, and darkness came upon him before he could hide his wagon in the woods and proceed afoot to Chaudiere. He had shot his horse, and rolled it into the swift torrent beneath the bridge.

Travelling the lonely road, he drank freely from the whiskey-horn he carried, to keep his spirits up, so that by the time he came to the outskirts of Chaudiere he was in a state of intoxication, and reeled impudently along with the "Dutch courage" the liquor had given him. Arrived at the first cluster of houses in the place, he paused uncertain. Should he knock here or go on to the tavern? He shivered at thought of the tavern, for it was near it he had heard Charley Steele's voice calling to him out of the trees. If he knocked here, would the people admit him in his present state?—he had sense enough to know that he was very drunk. As he shook his head in owlish gravity, he saw the church on the hill not far away. He chuckled to himself. The carpet in the chancel and the hassocks at the altar would make a good bed. No fear of Charley's ghost coming inside the church— it wouldn't be that kind of a ghost. As he travelled the intervening space, shrugging his shoulders, staggering serenely, he told himself in confidence that he would leave the church at dawn, go to the tavern, purchase a horse as soon as might be, and get back to his wagon.

The church door was unlocked, and he entered and made his way to the chancel, found surplices in the vestry and put a hassock inside one for a pillow. Then he sat down and drew the loose rug of the chancel-floor over him, and took another drink from the whiskey horn. Lighting his pipe, he smoked for a while, but grew drowsy, and his pipe fell into his lap. With eyes nearly shut he struck another match, made to light his pipe again, but threw the match away, still burning. As he did so the pipe dropped again from his mouth, and he fell back on the hassock-pillow he had made.

The lighted match fell on a surplice which had dropped from his arms as he came from the vestry, and set it afire. In five minutes the whole chancel was burning, and the sleeping man waked in the midst of smoke and flame. He staggered to his feet with a terror-stricken cry, stumbled down the aisle, through the front door, and out into the night. Reaching the road, he turned his face again to the hill where his wagon lay hid. If he could reach that, he would be safe; nobody would suspect him. He clutched the whiskey-horn tight and broke into a run. As he passed beyond the village his excited imagination heard Charley Steele's ghost calling after him. He ran harder. The voice kept calling from Chaudiere.

Not Charley's voice, but the voices of many people in Chaudiere were calling. Some wakeful person had seen the glare in the church windows and had given the alarm, and now there rang through the streets the call-"Fire! Fire! Fire!"

Charley and Jo were among the last to wake, for both had slept soundly, but Jo was roused by a handful of gravel thrown at his window and a warning cry, and a few moments later he and Charley were in the street with a hurrying crowd. Over all the village was a red glare, lighting up the sky, burnishing the trees. The church was a mass of flames.

Charley was as pale as the rest of the crowd; for he thought of the Cure, he thought of this people to whom their church meant more than home and vastly more than friend and fortune. His heart was with them all: not because it was their church that was burning, but because it was something dear to them.

Reaching the hill, he saw the Cure coming from the vestry of the burning church, bearing some vessels of the altar. Depositing them in the arms of his weeping sister, he turned again towards the door. People clung to him, and would not let him go.

"See, it is all inflames," they cried. "Your cassock is singed. You shall not go."

At that moment Charley and Portugais came up. A hurried question to the Cure from Charley, a key handed over, a nod from Jo, and before the

Cure could prevent them the two men had rushed through the smoke and flame into the vestry, Portugais holding Charley's hand.

The crowd outside waited in a terrible anxiety. The timbers of the chancel portion of the building seemed about to fall, and still the two men did not appear. The people called; the Cure clinched his hands at his side— he was too fearful even to pray.

But now the two men appeared, loaded with the few treasures of the church. They were scorched and singed, and the beards of both were burned, but, stumbling and exhausted, they brought their loads to the eager arms of the waiting habitants.

Then from the other end of the church came a cry: "The little cross—the little iron cross!" Then another cry: "Rosalie Evanturel! Rosalie Evanturel!" Some one came running to the Cure.

"Rosalie Evanturel has gone inside for the little cross on the pillar. She is in the flames; the door has fallen in. She can't get out again."

With a hoarse cry, Charley darted back inside the vestry door. A cry of horror went up.

It was only a minute and a half, but it seemed like years, and then a man in flames appeared in the fiery porch—and not alone. He carried a girl in his arms. He wavered even at the threshold with the timbers swaying overhead, but, with a last effort, he plunged forward through the furnace, and was caught by eager hands on the margin of endurable heat. The two were smothered in quilts brought from the Cure's house, and carried swiftly to the cool safety of the grass and trees beyond. The woman had fainted in the flame of the church; the man dropped insensible as they caught her from his arms.

As they tore away Charley's coat muffling his face, and opened his shirt, they stared in awe. The cross which Rosalie had torn from the pillar, Charley had thrust into his bosom, and there it now lay on the red scar made by itself in the hands of Louis Trudel.

M. Loisel waved the people back. He raised Charley's head. The Abbe Rossignol, who had just arrived with the Seigneur, lifted the cross from the insensible man's breast.

He started when he saw the scar. Then he remembered the tale he had heard. He turned away gravely to his brother. "Was it the cross or the woman he went for?" he asked.

"Great God—do you ask!" the Seigneur said indignantly. "And he deserves her," he muttered under his breath.

Charley opened his eyes. "Is she safe?" he asked, starting up.

"Unscathed, my son," the Cure said.

Was this tailor-man not his son? Had he not thirsted for his soul as a hart for the water-brooks?

"I am very sorry for you, Monsieur," said Charley.

"It is God's will," was the reply, in a choking voice. "It will be years before we have another church—many, many years."

The roof gave way with a crash, and the spire shot down into the flaming debris.

The people groaned.

"It will cost sixty thousand dollars to build it up again," said Filion Lacasse.

"We have three thousand dollars from the Passion Play," said the Notary. "That could go towards it."

"We have another two thousand in the bank," said Maximilian Cour.

"But it will take years," said the saddler disconsolately.

Charley looked at the Cure, mournful and broken but calm. He saw the Seigneur, gloomy and silent, standing apart. He saw the people in scattered groups, looking more homeless than if they had no homes. Some groups were silent; others discussed angrily the question, who was the incendiary—that it had been set on fire seemed certain.

"I said no good would come of the play-acting," said the Seigneur's groom, and was flung into the ditch by Filion Lacasse.

Presently Charley staggered to his feet, purpose in his face. These people, from the Cure and Seigneur to the most ignorant habitant, were hopeless and inert. The pride of their lives was gone.

"Gather the people together," he said to the Notary and Filion Lacasse. Then he turned to the Cure and the Seigneur.

"With your permission, messieurs," he said, "I will do a harder thing than I have ever done. I will speak to them all."

Wondering, M. Loisel added his voice to the Notary's, and the word went round. Slowly they all made their way to a spot the Cure indicated.

Charley stood on the embankment above the road, the notables of the parish round him.

Rosalie had been taken to the Cure's house. In that wild moment in the church when she had fallen insensible in Charley's arms, a new feeling had sprung up in her. She loved him in every fibre, but she had a strange instinct, a prescience, that she was lying on his breast for the last time. She had wound her arms round his neck, and, as his lips closed on hers, she had cried: "We shall die together—together."

As she lay in the Cure's house, she thought only of that moment.

"What are they cheering for?" she asked, as a great noise came to her through the window.

"Run and see," said the Cure's sister to Mrs. Flynn, and the fat woman hurried away.

Rosalie raised herself so that she could look out of the window. "I can see him," she cried.

"See whom?" asked the Cure's sister.

"Monsieur," she answered, with a changed voice. "He is speaking. They are cheering him."

Ten minutes later, the Cure and the Notary entered the room. M. Loisel came forward to Rosalie, and took her hands in his.

"You should not have done it," he said.

"I wanted to do something," she replied. "To get the cross for you seemed the only payment I could make for all your goodness to me."

"It nearly cost you your life—and the life of another," he said, shaking his head reproachfully.

Cheering came again from the burning church. "Why do they cheer?" she asked.

"Why do they cheer? Because the man we have feared, Monsieur Mallard—"

"I never feared him," said Rosalie, scarcely above her breath.

"Because he has taught them the way to a new church again—and at once, at once, my child."

"A remarkable man!" said Narcisse Dauphin. "There never was such a speech. Never in any courtroom was there such an appeal."

"What did he do?" asked Mademoiselle Loisel, her hand in Rosalie's.

"Everything," answered the Cure. "There he stood in his tattered clothes, the beard burnt to his chin, his hands scorched, his eyes bloodshot, and he spoke—"

"'With the tongues of men and of angels,'" said M. Dauphin enthusiastically.

The Cure frowned and continued: "'You look on yonder burning walls,' he said, 'and wonder when they will rise again on this hill made sacred by the burial of your beloved, by the christening of your children, the marriages which have given you happy homes, and the sacraments which are to you the laws of your lives. You give one-twentieth of your income yearly towards your church—then give one-fortieth of all you possess today, and your church will be begun in a month. Before a year goes round you will come again to this venerable spot and enter another church here. Your vows, your memories, and your hopes will be purged by fire. All that you possess will be consecrated by your free-will offerings.'—Ah, if I could but remember what came afterwards! It was all eloquence, and generous and noble thought."

"He spoke of you," said the Notary—"he spoke the truth; and the people cheered. He said that the man outside the walls could sometimes tell the besieged the way relief would come. Never again shall I hear such a speech."

"What are they going to do?" asked Rosalie, and withdrew her trembling hand from that of Madame Dugal.

"This very day, at my office, they will bring their offerings, and we will begin at once," answered M. Dauphin. "There is no man in Chaudiere but will take the stocking from the hole, the bag from the chest, the credit from the bank, the grain from the barn for the market, or make the note of hand to contribute one-fortieth of all he is worth for the rebuilding of the church."

"Notes of hand are not money," said the Cure's sister, the practical sense ever uppermost.

"They shall all be money—hard cash," said the Notary. "The Seigneur is going to open a sort of bank, and take up the notes of hand, and give bank-bills in return. To-day I go with his steward to Quebec to get the money."

"What does the Abbe Rossignol say?" said the Cure's sister.

"Our church and parish are our own," interposed the Cure proudly. "We do our duty and fear no abbe."

"Voila!" said M. Dauphin, "he never can keep hands off. I saw him go to Jo Portugais a little while ago. 'Remember!' he said—I can't make out what he was after. We have enough to remember to-day, for sure."

"Good may come of it, perhaps," said M. Loisel, looking sadly out upon the ruins of his church.

"See, 'tis the sunrise!" said Mrs. Flynn's voice from the corner, her face towards the eastern window.

CHAPTER LVIII
WITH HIS BACK TO THE WALL

In four days ten thousand dollars in notes and gold had been brought to the office of the Notary by the faithful people of Chaudiere. All day in turn M. Loisel and M. Rossignol sat in the office and received that which represented one-fortieth of the value of each man's goods, estate, and wealth—the fortieth value of a woodsawyer's cottage, or a widow's garden. They did it impartially for all, as the Cure and three of the best-to-do habitants had done for the Seigneur, whose four thousand dollars had been paid in first of all.

Charley had been confined to his room for three days, because of his injuries and a feverish cold he had caught, and the habitants did not disturb his quiet. But Mrs. Flynn took him broth made by Rosalie's hands, and Rosalie fought with her desire to go to him and nurse him. She was not, however, the Rosalie of the old impulse and impetuous resolve—the arrow had gone too deep; she waited till she could see his face again and look into his eyes. Not apathy, but a sense of the inevitable was upon her, and pale and fragile, but with a calm spirit, she waited for she knew not what.

She felt that the day of fate was closing down. She must hold herself ready for the hour when he would need her most. At first, when the conviction had come to her that the end of all was near, she had revolted. She had had impulse to go to him at all hazards, to say to him: "Come away— anywhere, anywhere!" But that had given place to the deeper thing in her, and something of Charley's spirit of stoic waiting had come upon her.

She watched the people going to the Notary's office with their tributes and free-will offerings, and they seemed like people in a play—these days she lived no life which was theirs. It was a dream, unimportant and temporary. She was feeling what was behind all life, and permanent. It could not last, but there it was; and she could not return to the transitory till this cloud of fate was lifted. She was much too young to suffer so, but the young ever suffer most.

On the fourth day she saw Charley. He came from his shop and went to the Notary's office. At first she was startled, for he was clean-shaven—

the fire had burned his beard to the skin. She saw a different man, far removed from this life about them both—individual, singular. He was pale, and his eye-glass, with the cleanshaven face, gave an impression of refined separateness. She did not know that the same look was in both their faces. She watched him till he entered the Notary's shop, then she was called away to her duties.

Charley had come to give his one-fortieth with the rest. When he entered the Notary's office, the Seigneur and M. Dauphin stood up to greet him. They congratulated him on his recovery, while feeling also that the change in his personal appearance somehow affected their relations. A crowd gathered round the door of the shop. When Charley made his offering, with a statement of his goods and income, the Seigneur and Notary did not know what to do. They were disposed to decline it, for since Monsieur was no Catholic, it was not his duty to help. At this moment of delicate anxiety M. Loisel entered. With a swift bright flush to his cheek he saw the difficulty, and at once accepted freely.

"God bless you," he said, as he took the money, and Charley left. "It shall build the doorway of my church."

Later in the day the Cure sent for Charley. There were grave matters to consider, and his counsel was greatly needed. They had all come to depend on the soundness of his judgment. It had never gone astray in Chaudiere, they said. They owed to him this extraordinary scheme, which would be an example to all modern Christianity. They told him so. He said nothing in reply.

In an hour he had planned for them a scheme for the consideration of contractors; had drawn, with the help of M. Loisel, an architect's rough plan of the new church, and, his old professional instincts keenly alive, had lucidly suggested the terms and safeguards of the contracts.

Then came the question of the money contributed. The day before, M. Dauphin and the Seigneur's steward had arrived in safety from Quebec with twenty thousand dollars in bank-bills. These M. Rossignol had exchanged for the notes of hand of such of the habitants as had not ready cash to give. All of this twenty thousand dollars had been paid over. They had now thirty thousand dollars in cash, besides three thousand which the Cure had at his house, the proceeds of the Passion Play. It was proposed to send this large sum to the bank in Quebec in another two days, when the whole contributions should be complete.

As to the safety of the money, the timid M. Dauphin did not care to take responsibility. Strangers were still arriving, ignorant of the fact that the Passion Play had ceased, and some of them must be aware that this large sum of money was in the parish—no doubt also knew that it was in his house. It was therefore better, he urged, that M. Rossignol or the Cure should take charge of it. M. Loisel urged that secrecy as to the resting-place of the money was important. It was better that it should be deposited in the most unlikely place, and with some unofficial person who might not be supposed to have it in charge.

"I have it!" said the Seigneur. "The money shall be placed in old Louis Trudel's safe in the wall of the tailor-shop."

It was so arranged, after Charley's protests of unwillingness, and counter-appeals from the others. That evening at sundown thirty-three thousand dollars was deposited in the safe in the old stone wall of the tailorshop, and the lock was sealed with the parish seal.

But the Notary's wife had wormed the secret from her husband, and she found it hard to keep. She told it to Maximilian Cour, and he kept it. She told it to her cousin, the wife of Filion Lacasse, and she did not keep it. Before twenty-four hours went round, a dozen people knew it.

The evening of the second day, another two thousand dollars was added to the treasure, and the lock was again sealed—with the utmost secrecy. Charley and Jo Portugais, the infidel and the murderer, were thus the sentries to the peace of a parish, the bankers of its gifts, the security for the future of the church of Chaudiere. Their weapons of defence were two old pistols belonging to the Seigneur.

"Money is the master of the unexpected," the Seigneur had said as he handed them over. He chuckled for hours afterwards as he thought of his epigram. That night, as he turned over in bed for the third time, as was his custom before going to sleep, another epigram came to him—"Money is the only fox hunted night and day." He kept repeating it over and over again with vain pride.

The truth of M. Rossignol's aphorisms had been demonstrated several days before. On his return from Quebec with the twenty thousand dollars of the Seigneur's money, M. Dauphin had dwelt with great pride on the discretion and energy he and the steward had shown; had told dramatically of the skill which had enabled them to make a journey of such importance so secretly and safely; had covered himself with blushes for his own coolness and intrepidity. Fortune had, however, favoured his reputation and his intrepidity, for he had been pursued from the hour he and his companion left Quebec. A taste for the picturesque had impelled him to arrange for two relays of horses, and this fact saved him and the twenty thousand dollars he carried. Two hours after he had left Quebec, four determined men had got upon his trail, and had only been prevented from overtaking him by the freshness of the horses which his dramatic foresight had provided.

The leader of these four pursuers was Billy Wantage, who had come to know of the curious action of the Seigneur of Chaudiere from an intimate friend, a clerk in the bank. Billy's fortunes were now in a bad way, and, in desperate straits for money, he had planned this bold attempt at the highwayman's art with two gamblers, to whom he owed money, and a certain notorious horse-trader of whom he had made a companion of late. Having escaped punishment for a crime once before, through Charley's supposed death, the immunity nerved him to this later and more dangerous enterprise. The four rode as hard as their horses would permit, but M. Dauphin and his companion kept always an hour or more ahead, and, from the high hills overlooking the village, Billy and his friends saw the two enter it safely in the light of evening.

His three friends urged Billy to turn back, since they were out of provisions and had no shelter. It was unwise to go to a tavern or a farmer's house, where they must certainly be suspected. Billy, however, determined to make an effort to find the banking-place of the money, and refused to turn back without a trial. He therefore proposed that they should separate, going different directions, secure accommodation for the night, rest the following day, and meet the next night at a point indicated. This was agreed upon, and they separated.

When the four met again, Billy had nothing to communicate, as he had been taken ill during the night before, and had been unable to go secretly into Chaudiere village. They separated once more. When they met the next night Billy was accompanied by an old confederate. As he was entering Chaudiere the previous evening, he had met John Brown, with his painted wagon and a new mottled horse. John Brown had news of importance to give; for, in the stable-yard of the village tavern, he had heard one habitant confide to another that the money for the new church was kept in the safe of the tailor-shop. John Brown was as ready to share in Billy's second enterprise as he had been to incite him to his first crime.

So it was that as the Seigneur made his epigram and gloated over it, the five men, with horses at a convenient distance, armed to the teeth, broke stealthily into Charley's house.

They entered silently through the kitchen window, and made their way into the little hall. Two stood guard at the foot of the stairs, and three crept into the shop.

This night Jo Portugais was sleeping up-stairs, while Charley lay upon the bench in the tailor-shop. Charley heard the door open, heard unfamiliar steps, seized his pistol, and, springing up, with his back to the safe, called out loudly to Jo. As he dimly saw men rush at him, he fired. The bullet reached its mark, and one man fell dead. At that moment a dark-lantern was turned full on Charley, and a pistol was fired pointblank at him.

As he fell, shot through the breast, the man who had fired dropped the lantern with a shriek of terror. He had seen the ghost of his brother-in-law-Charley Steele.

With a quaking cry of warning to the others, Billy bolted from the house, followed by his companions, two of whom were struggling with Jo Portugais on the stairway. These now also broke and ran.

Jo rushed into the shop, and saw, as he thought, Charley lying dead—saw the robber dead upon the floor. His master and friend gone, the conviction seized him that his own time had come. He would give himself to justice now—but to God's justice, not to man's. The robbers were four to one, and he would avenge his master's death and give his own life to do it! It was all the thought of a second. He rushed out after the robbers, shouting as he ran, to awake the villagers. He heard the marauders ahead of him, and, fleet of foot, rushed on. Reaching them as they mounted, he fired, and brought down his man—a shivering quack-doctor, who, like his leader, had seen a sight in the tailor-shop that struck terror to his soul. Two of the others then fired at Jo, who had caught a horse by the head. He fell without a sound, and lay upon his face—he did not hear the hoofs of the escaping horses nor any other sound. He had fallen without a pang beside the quackdoctor, whose medicines would never again quicken a pulse in his own body or any other.

Behind, in the village, frightened people flocked about the tailor-shop. Within, Mrs. Flynn and the Notary crudely but tenderly bound up the dreadful wound in Charley's side, while Rosalie pillowed his head on her bosom.

With a strange quietness Rosalie gave orders to the Notary and Mrs. Flynn. There was a light in her eyes—an unnatural light—of strength and presence of mind. Her hand was steady, and as gently as a mother with a child she wiped the moist forehead, and poured a little brandy between the set teeth.

"Stand back—give him air," she said, in a voice of authority to those who crowded round.

People fell back in awe, for, amid tears and excitement and fear, this girl had a strange convincing calm. By the time Charley's wound was stopped, messengers were on the way to the Cure and the Seigneur. By Rosalie's instructions the dead body of the robber was removed, Charley's bed up-stairs was prepared for him, a fire was lighted, and twenty hands were ready to do accurately her will. Now and again she felt his pulse, and she watched his face intently. In her bitter sorrow her heart had a sort of thankfulness, for his head was on her breast, he was in her arms. It had been given her once more to come first to his rescue, and with one wild cry, unheard by any one, to call out his beloved name.

The world of Chaudiere, roused by the shooting, had then burst in upon them; but that one moment had been hers, no matter what came after. She had no illusions—she knew that the end was near: the end of all for him and for them both.

The Cure entered and hurried forward. There was the seal of the parish intact on the door of the safe, but at what cost!

"He has given his life for the church," he said, then commanded all to leave, save those needed to carry the wounded man up-stairs.

Still it was Rosalie that directed the removal. She held his hand; she saw that he was carefully laid down; she raised his head to a proper height; she moistened his lips and fanned him. Meanwhile the Cure fell upon his knees, and the noise of talk and whispering ceased in the house.

But presently there was loud murmuring and shuffling of feet outside again, and Rosalie left the room hurriedly and went below to stop it. She met the men who were bringing the body of Jo Portugais into the shop.

Up-stairs the Cure's voice prayed: "Of Thy mercy, O Lord, hear our prayer. Grant that he be brought into Thy Church ere his last hour come. Forgive, O Lord—"

Charley stirred and opened his eyes. He saw the Cure bowed in prayer; he heard the trembling voice. He touched the white head with his hand.

CHAPTER LIX
IN WHICH CHARLEY MEETS A STRANGER

The Cure came to his feet with a joyful cry. "Monsieur—my son," he said, bending over him.

"Is it all over?" Charley asked calmly, almost cheerfully. Death now was the only solution of life's problems, and he welcomed it from the void.

The Cure went to the door and locked it. The deepest desire of his life must here be uttered, his great aspiration be realised.

"My son," he said, as he came softly to the bedside again, "you have given to us all you had—your charity, your wisdom, your skill. You have "—it was hard, but the man's wound was mortal, and it must be said "you have consecrated our new church with your blood. You have given all to us; we will give all to you—"

There was a soft knocking at the door. He went and opened it a very little. "He is conscious, Rosalie," he whispered. "Wait—wait—one moment."

Then came the Seigneur's voice saying that Jo was gone, and that all the robbers had escaped, save the two disposed of by Charley and Jo.

The Cure turned to the bed once more. "What did he say about Jo?" Charley asked.

"He is dead, my son, and the quack-doctor also. The others have escaped."

Charley turned his face away. "Au revoir, Jo," he said into the great distance.

Then there was silence for a moment, while outside the door a girl prayed, with an old woman's arm around her.

The Cure leaned over Charley again. "Shall not the sacraments of the Church comfort you in your last hours?" he said. "It is the way, the truth, and the life. It is the Voice that says: 'Peace' to the vexed mind. Human intellect is vanity; only the soul survives. Will you not hear the Voice? Will you not give us who love and honour you the right to make you ours for ever? Will you not come to the bosom of that Church for which you have given all?"

"Tell them so," Charley said, and he motioned towards the window, under which the people were gathered.

With a glad exclamation the Cure hastened to the window, and, in a voice of sorrowful exultation, spoke to the people below.

Charley reckoned swiftly with his fate. What was there now to do? If his wound was not mortal, what tragedy might now come! For Billy's hand— the hand of Kathleen's brother—had brought him low. If the robbers and murderers were captured, he must be dragged into the old life, and to what an issue—all the old problems carried into more terrible conditions. And Rosalie—in his half-consciousness he had felt her near him; he felt her near him now. Rosalie—in any case, what could there be for her? Nothing. He had heard the Cure whisper her name at the door. She was outside-praying for him. He stretched out a hand as though he saw her, and his lips framed her name. In his weakness and fading life he had no anguish in the thought of her. Life and Love were growing distant though he loved her as few love and live. She would be removed from want by him—there were the pearls and the money in the safe with the money of the Church; there was the letter to the Cure, his last testament, leaving all to her. He, sleeping, would fear no foe; she, awake in the living world, would hold him in dear remembrance. Death were the better thing for all. Then Kathleen in her happiness would be at peace; and even Billy might go unmolested, for, who was there to recognise Billy, now that Portugais was dead?

He heard the Cure's voice at the window—"Oh, my dear people, God has given him to us at last. I go now to prepare him for his long journey, to—"

Charley realised and shuddered. Receive the sacraments of the Church? Be made ready by the priest for his going hence—end all the soul's interrogations, with the solving of his own mortal problems? Say "I believe," confess his sins, and, receiving absolution, lie down in peace.

He suddenly raised himself on his elbow, flinging his body over. The bandage of his wound was displaced, and blood gushed out upon the white clothes of the bed. "Rosalie!" he gasped. "Rosalie, my love! God keep..."

As he sank back he heard the priest's anguished voice above him, calling for help. He smiled.

"Rosalie—" he whispered. The priest ran and unlocked the door, and Rosalie entered, followed by the Seigneur and Mrs. Flynn.

"Quick! Quick!" said the priest. "The bandage slipped."

The bandage slipped—or was it slipped? Who knows!

Blind with agony, and as in a direful dream, Rosalie made her way to the bed. The sight of his ensanguined body roused her, and, murmuring his name—continually murmuring his name—she assisted Mrs. Flynn to bind up the wound again. Standing where she stood when she had stayed Louis Trudel's arm long ago, with an infinite tenderness she touched the scar-the scar of the cross—on his breast. Terrible as was her grief, her heart had its comfort in the thought—who could rob her of that for ever?—that he would die a martyr. It did not matter now who knew the story of her love. It could not do him harm. She was ready to proclaim it to all the world. And those who watched knew that they were in the presence of a great human love.

The priest made ready to receive the unconscious man into the Church. Had Charley not said, "Tell them so?" Was it not now his duty to say the sacred offices over a son of the Church in his last bitter hour? So it was done while he lay unconscious.

For hours he lay still, and then the fevered blood, poisoned by the bullet which had brought him down, made him delirious, gave him hallucinations—open-eyed illusions. All the time Rosalie knelt at the foot of the bed, her piteous tearless eyes for ever fixed on his face.

Towards evening, with an unnatural strength, he sat up in bed.

"See," he whispered, "that woman in the corner there. She has come to take me, but I will not go." Fantasy after fantasy possessed him-fantasy, strangely mixed with facts of his own past. Now it was Kathleen, now Billy, now Jo Portugais, now John Brown, now Suzon Charlemagne at the Cote Dorion, again Jo Portugais. In strange, touching sentences he spoke to them, as though they were present before him. At length he stopped abruptly, and gazed straight before him—over the head of Rosalie into the distance.

"See," he said, pointing, "who is that? Who? I can't see his face—it is covered. So tall-so white! He is opening his arms to me. He is coming—closer—closer. Who is it?"

"It is Death, my son," said the priest in his ear, with a pitying gentleness.

The Cure's voice seemed to calm the agitated sense, to bring it back to the outer precincts of understanding. There was an awe-struck silence as the dying man fumbled, fumbled, over his breast, found his eye-glass, and, with a last feeble effort, raised it to his eye, shining now with an unearthly fire. The old interrogation of the soul, the elemental habit outlived all else in him. The idiosyncrasy of the mind automatically expressed itself.

"I beg—your—pardon," he whispered to the imagined figure, and the light died out of his eyes, "have I—ever—been—introduced—to you?"

"At the hour of your birth, my son," said the priest, as a sobbing cry came from the foot of the bed.

But Charley did not hear. His ears were for ever closed to the voices of life and time.

CHAPTER LX
THE HAND AT THE DOOR

The eve of the day of the memorable funeral two belated visitors to the Passion Play arrived in the village, unknowing that it had ended, and of the tragedy which had set a whole valley mourning; unconscious that they shared in the bitter fortunes of the tailor-man, of whom men and women spoke with tears. Affected by the gloom of the place, the two visitors at once prepared for their return journey, but the manner of the tailorman's death arrested their sympathies, touched the humanity in them. The woman was much impressed.

They asked to see the body of the man. They were taken to the door of the tailor-shop, while their horses were being brought round. Within the house itself they were met by an old Irishwoman, who, in response to their wish "to see the brave man's body," showed them into a room where a man lay dead with a bullet through his heart. It was the body of Jo Portugais, whose master and friend lay in another room across the hallway. The lady turned back in disappointment—the dead man was little like a hero.

The Irishwoman had meant to deceive her, for at this moment a girl who loved the tailor was kneeling beside his body, and, if possible, Mrs. Flynn would have no curious eyes look upon that scene.

When the visitors came into the hall again, the man said: "There was another; Kathleen—a woodsman." But standing by the nearly closed door, behind which lay the dead tailor of Chaudiere—they could see the holy candles flickering within—Kathleen whispered "We've seen the tailor—that's enough. It's only the woodsman there. I prefer not, Tom."

With his fingers at the latch, the man hesitated, even as Mrs. Flynn stepped apprehensively forward; then, shrugging a shoulder, he responded to Kathleen's hand on his arm. They went down the stairs together, and out to their carriage.

As they drove away, Kathleen said: "It's strange that men who do such fine things should look so commonplace."

"The other one might have been more uncommon," he replied.

"I wonder!" she said, with a sigh of relief, as they passed the bounds of the village. Then she caught herself flushing, for she suddenly realised that the exclamation was one so often on the lips of a dead, disgraced man whose name she once had borne.

If the door of the little room upstairs had opened to the fingers of the man beside her, the tailor of Chaudiere, though dead, would have been dearly avenged.

CHAPTER LXI
THE CURE SPEAKS

The Cure stood with his back to the ruins of the church, at his feet two newly made graves, and all round, with wistful faces, crowds of reverent habitants. A benignant sorrow made his voice in perfect temper with the pensive striving of this latest day of spring. At the close of his address he said:

"I owe you much, my people. I owe him more, for it was given him, who knew not God, to teach us how to know Him better. For his past, it is not given you to know. It is hidden in the bosom of the Church. Sinner he once was, criminal never, as one can testify who knows all"—he turned to the Abbe Rossignol, who stood beside him, grave and compassionate—"and his sins were forgiven him. He is the one sheaf which you and I may carry home rejoicing from the pagan world of unbelief. What he had in life he gave to us, and in death he leaves to our church all that he has not left to a woman he loved—to Rosalie Evanturel."

There was a gasping murmur among the people, but they stilled again, and strained to hear.

"He leaves her a little fortune, and to us all else he had. Let us pray for his soul, and let us comfort her who, loving deeply, reaped no harvest of love.

"The law may never reach his ruthless murderers, for there is none to recognise their faces; and were they ten times punished, how should it avail us now! Let us always remember that, in his grave, our friend bears on his breast the little iron cross we held so dear. That is all we could give—our dearest treasure. I pray God that, scarring his breast in life, it may heal all his woes in death, and be a saving image on his bosom in the Presence at the last."

He raised his hands in benediction.

EPILOGUE

Never again was there a Passion Play in the Chaudiere Valley. Spring-times and harvests and long winters came and went, and a blessing seemed to be upon the valley, for men prospered, and no untoward things befel the people. So it was for twenty years, wherein there had been going and coming in quiet. Some had gone upon short mortal journeys and had come back, some upon long immortal voyages, and had never returned. Of the last were the Seigneur and a woman once a Magdalene; but in a house beside a beautiful church, with a noble doorway, lived the Cure, M. Loisel, aged and serene. There never was a day, come rain or shine, in which he was not visited by a beautiful woman, whose life was one with the people of the valley.

There was no sorrow in the parish which the lady did not share, with the help of an old Irishwoman called Mrs. Flynn. Was there sickness in the parish, her hand smoothed the pillow and soothed the pain. Was there trouble anywhere, her face brought light to the door way. Did any suffer ill-repute, her word helped to restore the ruined name. They did not know that she forgave so much in all the world, because she thought she had so much in herself to forgive.

She was ever called "Madame Rosalie," and she cherished the name, and gave commands that when her grave came to be made near to a certain other grave, Madame Rosalie should be carved upon the stone. Cheerfulness and serenity were ever with her, undisturbed by wish to probe the mystery of the life which had once absorbed her own. She never sought to know whence the man came; it was sufficient to know whither he had gone, and that he had been hers for a brief dream of life. It was better to have lived the one short thrilling hour with all its pain, than never to have known what she knew or felt what she had felt. The mystery deepened her romance, and she was even glad that the ruffians who slew him were never brought to justice. To her mind they were but part of the mystic machinery of fate.

For her the years had given many compensations, and so she told the Cure, one midsummer day, when she brought to visit him the orphaned son of Paulette Dubois, graduated from his college in France and making ready to go to the far East.

"I have had more than I deserve—a thousand times," she said.

The Cure smiled, and laid a gentle hand upon her own. "It is right for you to think so," he said, "but after a long life, I am ready to say that, one way or another, we earn all the real happiness we have. I mean the real happiness—the moments, my child. I once had a moment full of happiness."

"May I ask?" she said.

"When my heart first went out to him"—he turned his face towards the churchyard.

"He was a great man," she said proudly.

The Cure looked at her benignly: she was a woman, and she had loved the man. He had, however, come to a stage of life where greatness alone seemed of little moment. He forbore to answer her, but he pressed her hand.